The Widow's Weeds

Book Three in the *Widows* Series

By

Allie Cresswell

Also in the *Widows* Series

The Hoarder's Widow

Suddenly-widowed Maisie sets out to clear her late husband's collection. The hoard is endless, stacked into every room in the house, teetering in piles along the landing and forming a scree up the stairs.

As Maisie disassembles his stash, she is forced to confront the issues that drove her husband to squirrel away other people's trash; after all, she knows virtually nothing about his life before they met. Finally, in the last bastion of his accumulation, she discovers the key to his hoarding and understands— much too late—the man she married.

Then, with empty rooms in a house that is too big for her, she must ask herself: what next?

The Widow's Mite

Minnie Price married late in life. Now she is widowed. And starving. No one suspects this respectable churchgoer can barely keep body and soul together. Why would they, while she resides in the magnificent home she shared with Peter? Her friends and neighbours are oblivious to her plight and her adult stepchildren have their own reasons to make things worse rather than better. But she is thrown a lifeline when an associate of her late husband arrives with news of an investment about which her stepchildren know nothing.

Can she release the funds before she finds herself homeless and destitute?

This book is

dedicated to

all the Vanessas,

everywhere.

A poor old Widow in her weeds
Sowed her garden with wildflower seeds.

Walter de la Mare

Chapter One – Viola

The last day of Viola's twenty-five-year marriage to Graham began like many other days.

A slight movement beside her in the bed told her it was morning, but she didn't open her eyes. She waited, feigning sleep. She heard Graham stretch and yawn and gather himself to get up. The mattress dipped, his side of the duvet was thrown over her and he was on his feet. Then the shower room door closed. Only then did she open her eyes enough to see it was barely light. Through the slice of vision she allowed herself, she saw the chest of drawers in the corner, still shadowed with gloom. Her pots of cream on its surface were amorphous shapes in varying shades of dull. The thin curtains were grey film. Outside, in the bluish dawn, a blackbird sang.

From the shower room came a gush from the cistern and then a frantic knock and rattle as the ancient plumbing protested at the shower being switched on. Still, she did not move her head. Instead, she practised the art perfected over the years of abandoning her body to inhabit her mind, withdrawing to that secret chamber where no one could intrude. In her mind's eye she viewed the room: the chair with his dirty laundry balled up on its seat; beneath the chair lay the weights he had insisted he wanted, but never used; the trouser press with his suit trousers hanging in its toothless jaws and his jacket over the attached hanger; the executive luggage packed for his conference. Beyond the room she visualised the rest of the cottage: low beams, a rickety staircase, the kitchen with her herb pots on the windowsill and the slumbering spaniel in his bed by the range. The house—an old, low house, whitewashed, small-windowed, climber encrusted—was folded into a narrow valley cut into the plain by a determined stream. The valley's slopes were crazily terraced and full of plants that didn't belong to that northern clime but the gorge had its own microclimate so they were protected from the winds that swept the bucolic grasslands above. Those pastures were grazed by cows that steamed eerily in the cool dawn, like meteorites freshly dropped to earth. She soared over it all, her mind at liberty even as her body lay like a corpse in the bed.

Perhaps she had dozed off again. The next thing she was aware of was the click of a cup on the glass top of her bedside table, and then the rattle of curtain rings along the pole.

'Good morning,' he said, without looking at her. He scrutinised himself in the long mirror, straightening his tie, peering into his eyes to make sure there was no crusty residue at the corners, checking his teeth for shreds of breakfast cereal. Then the mattress creaked as he perched next to her. 'Off to the conference. Best to make an early start.' He spoke in a low voice, although there was no one else he might wake now.

She struggled to a sitting position and reached for her tea, feigning more bleariness than she felt to avoid meeting his eye. 'Yes,' she said, 'thank you.' The tea was weak, the way he liked it, but if twenty-five years of marriage had not taught him that she liked it stronger, nothing would now. 'How long will it take you?'

This was the kind of question he liked. He waggled his head from side to side, weighing the options, considering contraflows, diversions, clever ways he had devised over the years to by-pass bottlenecks. 'If I avoid the road works between junctions 21 and 29,' he speculated, 'and all other things being equal, I might make it by eleven. The opening speeches begin at two, so I'll have chance to check in to my hotel.'

'And your presentation?'

'Not until tomorrow. Today, I'm chairing a meeting at four, and there's a Q and A before dinner.'

'And you'll be back——?' This was a loaded question. It would have been safer not to utter it but Viola's tongue had a habit of acting of its own volition.

Sure enough, Graham pounced. 'Why? What does it matter? Do you have plans?'

The little pebble of anxiety in Viola's solar plexus—a constant companion, but one she endured as one does a limp or a tendency to deafness—gave an unpleasant churn. She mastered it by shrugging and taking a long drink of tea. 'I just wondered … so I can have dinner ready if you need it,' she said unctuously.

His eyes narrowed but he let it go. 'Thursday, late,' he said. 'I *probably* will have eaten. The conference ends Wednesday lunchtime, but, while I'm down there, I might as well drop in to …' She stopped listening as he enumerated business visits he had planned, projects he wanted to look over, important male colleagues he hoped to touch base with. They formed part of a world that Graham deliberately kept her out of, using acronyms and abbreviated references designed to bamboozle her. As if she were interested.

'Don't worry about calling,' she said. 'I know how busy you'll be, and I'll be fine.'

'I'll call if I want to,' he said bullishly. 'What are your plans?'

This was a trick question. She pretended to consider. 'If the soil's warm enough, I'll probably get the potatoes in the ground. They've all chitted now. I may even plant the parsnips out …' Here was Viola's world, the world she kept as separate from Graham as his was from her. She rambled for a few moments, paying him back for his litany just before.

He cut across her itinerary. 'You won't go out?' It was hard to tell if it was a question or an instruction.

Some devil in her made her say, 'I don't *think* so. Unless I go to the library. I've ordered a book that may come in.'

'What kind of book?'

'A gardening book.' She placed her mug on the bedside table. 'Don't make yourself late Graham.'

He remained on the edge of the bed. 'You know I like to think of you here, while I'm away,' he said. He reached out and took her hand. This was a discussion they'd had many times. He wished to picture her just as he had left her. She in the bed, the bed in the room, the room in the house, the house in its curious gash of valley. He wanted her to remain in stasis, like a doll in a dolls' house—petrified, just as the children might have left her. Reinforcing this notion was the fact that sometimes, when he returned, he was angry she was not in the exact place he had left her—and that the lawn had been mown, fresh firewood brought in, that she was wearing a different dress. He wanted to think time here in their valley stopped the moment he departed.

Perhaps it did. When he was away, the cottage and the garden and the oceans of green grass that surrounded them, seemed to her enchanted, apart from time, sheltered and inviolable.

'I know you do,' Viola replied, with a little surge of defiance. 'But I'm not a prisoner, am I?'

Graham's hand tightened on hers until she winced. Then he released it. 'Of course you're not.'

A few moments later, the wetness of his kiss still on her cheek, she heard the thud of the old door, the growl of his car engine and the crunch of tyres on the gravel as he drove down the track. She smiled. Sammy, the spaniel, nosed his way into the room and leapt on to the bed. It was not allowed, but when Graham was away the rules were different.

Later, although it was still relatively early and cool—the sun was not yet over the ridge behind the house—the house doors and all the windows were open to the air. The effect was antiseptic, a fresh, cold dousing. The house was already clean, but if there had been dust and cobwebs, they would have been swept away in the cleansing draught. All trace of Graham was gone. He too had been swept away. His shoes were in the closet, his breakfast dishes washed and dried and returned to the cupboards. His newspaper stack was put out for recycling. His dirty clothes, his towel, and even the bedsheets that smelled of him, were already washed and pegged on the line. And because the line was in a part of the garden the sun had not yet reached, it was as though the sheets—and he—had been relegated to shadow.

The slope across the little stream was bright though, bathed in sunshine. Her garden rampaged in its hard-dug terraces, rank upon rank to the top of the rise—geranium and geum, columbine, dianthus, all their buds emerging from nests of leaves, with shy promise of the summer to come. In between, clumps of miniature narcissi and tulips were as high as hippies on sun and dew. She moved along snipping off dead heads and fading flowers, winkling out weeds, murmuring to herself, or to them, 'You can be divided. You need more space; that fleabane will have to move. Oh! Here are the calendula, showing themselves at last.' Sammy walked behind her, snuffling here and there, touching the back of her leg with his nose when she stood still for too long. It was their routine. The grounds had to be inspected, jobs for the day identified. This must be cut back, that tied up, a space made here for a newly rooted cutting, seeds harvested, water and mulch applied. He scouted for vermin, for scents he did not recognise, for fox spoor or—better—the unmistakable smell of rabbit that made him giddy with excitement although he probably did not know why. He always watched her, appeared to read her signs and seemed to absorb her contentment into himself.

Viola worked all day in the garden, bending, snipping, digging, nurturing. At noon she stopped to eat a sandwich, seated on a tree stump. Sammy got the crusts. Higher up in the curious valley the trees were alive with birds and the stream giggled between stony banks. Later, she would walk Sammy that way, through the gate into the tangled woodland that belonged to a landowner who never came to manage his timber, clear undergrowth or husband the earth. Over the years she had made a pathway, beating back brambles, pushing aside fallen branches, placing a flat stone mid-stream so that she could cross. It was her passageway to further enchantment and the anticipation it held infected her as rabbits did Sammy.

Somewhere high, high overhead a skylark flung himself across the sky, his joyous trill a hymn to the beauty of the day. She looked up, squinting into the blue. He was too high to make out but her heart soared—as his did—above the slate roof of the cottage, the just-budded leaves of the trees, the odd groin of land that separated fields from more fields, gouged over the years by the work of water. She could picture it all beneath her like a picture in a story book, a childish vision of country living—the scene too pastoral, the cottage too pretty, the gardens too neat, the pastures too lush, the cows cleaner than real cows ever were.

It couldn't be real, but it *was,* and for those precious days, it was all hers.

The skylark floated to earth and so did she, gently, coming back to herself on her handy stump, the last quarter of sandwich still in her hand.

The sun was at its zenith now and the cottage basked in brilliant light, a flash of white washing dazzling the eye. Here, on the house side of the valley, the garden was laid out like an intricate carpet: borders, pergolas and a matrix of vegetable beds on a background of luxuriant green lawn.

Slowly, slowly, the sun fell beyond the far ridge and the terraces of flowers lost their brightness. The windows of the cottage shone like amber mirrors in the late afternoon light. Viola put away her gardening tools and went indoors.

There were three messages on the answering machine, all from Graham, his ire mounting with each one, all variations on a theme: Where was she? Why didn't she answer the phone? What the hell was going on?

Viola consulted her watch. It was six-thirty. Presumably the Q and A Graham had mentioned would now be in full swing. She called his number and was pleased that the call went straight to voicemail.

'I've just come in,' she said, affecting a spurious breathlessness. 'I've been in the garden all day. All the potatoes and parsnips are in, and there are the loveliest fritillaries blooming in the shady border. I'm going to take Sammy out now. I want to see if the wild primroses are still in bloom. Enjoy the dinner, Graham, and I hope your presentation goes well tomorrow. Good night.'

She replaced the handset and surveyed the room. It was benign, orderly, safe. The fire was laid ready—it would be needed later, when clear night skies would leach warmth from the earth. Her laundry was folded and airing above the range; the whole house smelled of clean cotton and countryside. She fed Sammy, closed the windows and took a bath before sitting at her solitary table to eat tuna salad. Then she put on a warm jacket and stout shoes, whistled to Sammy and walked up the narrowing path into the woods.

Viola's valley was in shadow, the sun having slipped below its craggy escarpment, but as she walked up the narrowing gorge she could see the tops of the trees beyond still illuminated by that lingering, rosy light. It was late April, and the trees were just coming into leaf. The greenish haze around every branch and twig was almost luminous. Everywhere, she could hear the busy chatter of birds building nests and calling for mates.

At the very top corner of their property was a wooden gate, kept closed by a piece of old twine that hooked over the gatepost. She let herself through and Sammy scampered ahead into the unkempt woodland. The glossy leaves of bluebells carpeted the forest floor but were not yet in flower. White umbels of wild garlic lined each side of the tumbling stream, the smell pungent beneath the canopy of trees. She used her steppingstone to cross the burbling water. Her feet followed the old path almost of their own volition—it was so familiar to her—wending along the left-hand bank of the watercourse, between boulders and over fallen branches. Here and there she stopped to snip off a bramble vine that threatened to snake across it; she always carried secateurs in the back pocket of her jeans. As she climbed, the dusk that wallowed on the valley floor got left behind, the air felt lighter and so did Viola's spirit.

Somewhere up the groin of land, deep in the undergrowth, she could hear Sammy dashing here and there, darting between the trees, nosing into brakes of elder and willow. Occasionally he would flush a pheasant. It chattered as it flapped away. There were deer in the woods too, and badgers, but Sammy knew enough to stay away from them.

At a point familiar to her but invisible to anyone else, she turned from the stream and began to climb up the steep, needle-soft slope of a fir plantation.

The route switch-backed left and right, zigzagging between tree trunks. The birds' songs were strangely muted here, the atmosphere hushed and enchanted, a million miles away from her homely little cottage—not to mention Graham who, at that moment, might as well have been on another planet.

Eventually she emerged from the trees and met a fence that held the plantation back from a wide prairie of grass. It stretched away to the horizon where the setting sun turned the green to ochre. Here were the cows she had imagined that morning, cropping the turf, their sides sleek and fat, their shadows elongated by the slanting light. Viola made her way along the fence, again, pursuing a familiar route, shading her eyes with her hand. At some point Sammy emerged from the woods, one ear inside out, his tongue lolling, as if to check on her whereabouts before disappearing again into the forest in a flash of liver and white.

Viola's heart beat hard, partly from the climb and partly in anticipation of what was to come.

The fence ended in a right angle, but just there the barbed wire had been replaced with smooth and Viola stepped between the two strands with a practised stride. She was on a grassy bridle track that separated the spruce wood from a much older, deciduous forest. To the right the path curved and fell away so she could not see more than ten yards or so along it. To the left it terminated in a five-barred gate that gave access to the field. Here she paused, leaning on the gate as the sun at last slipped out of sight. An eerie, ultraviolet haze spread across the wide spread of grazing land. The cows faded to shadows, dark smudges on the dimness. A little breeze sprang up and riffled the feathery layers of Viola's hair. She gave an involuntary shiver, and zipped her coat to her throat.

Sammy appeared at her feet, throwing himself down into the cool, grey grass, his sides heaving, his breath throwing whips of vapour into the suddenly-chill air.

They waited together.

Presently she heard the soft susurration of footsteps through the grass of the bridleway, smelled the strong aromas of old tweed and pipe tobacco and coal tar soap and felt the press of a large, warm body against her back. His hands took hold of the top rung of the gate, either side of hers and slid inwards until they covered hers.

'Your hands are cold,' he said, chafing them a little.

She turned her head and took the kiss he offered.

By the time Viola returned to her cottage the moon was high, throwing milky light over the old house, her slumbering garden, the gelid slide of the stream between its banks. There was no wind and the air in the little valley had a petrified quality she had not been conscious of in the woods, higher up the slope, or at the old stone house where she had spent the past few hours. Indeed, that house had been warm—though dusty, disorganised and impossibly doggy—and it had been a struggle to disentangle herself from its comforts to return home. She loitered in the moonlit garden for a few moments, wondering about covering her newly-planted seedlings with protective fleece. Would there be a frost? No, she decided. She turned her mind—and her steps—to the pristine cleanliness of her house, the fire laid ready, the cup of hot chocolate and the slice of cake she had promised herself for supper—although it was past midnight. She tended to sleep little whilst Graham was away. Spending those hours without him in sleep seemed such a waste. Sammy plodded contentedly behind her, his mad caper through the woods and a period of socialising with a motley pack of assorted rescue dogs having exorcised his vim. It was not until Viola put her key into the lock and pushed open the old, stiff door into the porch that his ears pricked up. He made a warning noise in his throat—not a growl, more of a query—but Viola was busy unlacing her boots and did not pick up on it.

She put her boots by the door and hung her coat on one of the hooks, then she opened the inner door that would take her into the lounge. The lamp she had left burning on a low table was off, and there was a smell in the room she could not identify at first. She reached out a hand for the light switch. Sammy pressed against the back of her legs.

Then it came, a swingeing blow to her out-stretched arm. She felt the bone break like a stick. She took a breath but before she could scream a fist connected with her jaw, snapping her head violently to one side and throwing her whole body backwards onto the half-open door. She almost fell over Sammy. He let out a snarl but there was as much fear in it as rage. Nevertheless, he launched out from behind a staggering Viola. He too was punched aside, his body landing with a sickening smack against the wall. Viola struggled to retain her feet but the pain and white noise in her head and the agony of her arm sucked away all her reason. She could taste blood in her mouth. The assailant turned his attention back to her. A swift kick to her knee sent her feet from under her and she slid the rest of the way to the floor, her body on its side on the wide, polished boards of the lounge floor, her legs over the threshold of the porch. Another kick, to her bottom, fired an arrow of pain up her spine that met the one in her neck in an explosion of agony that bloomed like an exotic flower. There was a pause. In the darkness, she could hear breathing, heavy and stertorous. Sammy whimpered but lay still. Viola steeled herself for what would follow because—surely?—this would not be the end of it. It seemed her assailant too was asking himself how—whether—to continue. She felt his indecision. Then he stepped over her, into the porch. He slammed the inner door once, twice, dealing hammer-blows to her thighs as they impeded the door. The pain was excruciating.

She must have lost consciousness. The warm wetness of Sammy's tongue on her face brought her back round, his anxious whimpers penetrating the agony that swarmed in every cell. She was still wedged against the inner door, crushed, broken, and very cold. The front door was open to the night. The chill poured into the house, crawling over her with icy fingers. The moon had set, the darkness as invasive and malevolent as the cold. I must move, close the door. My arm is broken. I suppose I'll have to call an ambulance.

She moved the fingers of one hand experimentally but the merest quiver sent firebolts of reciprocal pain through every fibre. The floor beneath her felt oddly gritty. This fact rang a bell of vague curiosity in a far ventricle of her befuddled brain. It couldn't be dirt. She had swept and mopped the floor earlier that day. She moaned. Her lips were crusted, her jaw out of line. She tried to lick her lips but it hurt too much. Sammy must have been reassured, though. He laid himself against her and put his head next to hers. She wished she could close the door. She was cold. So cold.

She came round as she was being rolled onto a stretcher. A plastic mask pressed down on her face—the pressure from the elastic on her wounded face was terrible—and some impediment was in her mouth. Oxygen. They must be giving her oxygen. Her mouth was so dry and sore, she could not swallow or lick her lips. What she wanted was water but when she tried to speak, it was impossible. She heard the distant crackle of conversation over a two-way radio and was conscious of people around her working deftly as they murmured reassurance.

Someone—a woman—said, 'So what happened here? Who called it in?'

Another voice—one she recognised—said, 'I did. I'm Douglas Canterbury. I'm a neighbour. Her husband called me. He said she wasn't answering the phone and he was worried about her. He's away on business. I came right down and found … this. Will she be alright?' If he received an answer it was lost to Viola. She tried to process what he'd said but putting thoughts together in any coherent way was so difficult, they were like pieces of smashed porcelain that would never fit right again. She regarded the smithereens hopelessly. *Graham* had …? And why *Douglas*, of all people? Unless … but she gave up on it. It was too difficult. She concentrated on what she *could* make sense of: the aroma of Douglas's pipe, the fusty smell of him—very strange here in her house, like two separate worlds colliding. How had Graham even known his number? Did he suspect …?

Someone said, 'Sharp scratch,' and she felt a needle going into her arm. Why did they always say that? It wasn't a *scratch*. Scratches were what you got from brambles and blackthorns. It was a *prick* and this one was damned sharp … but then a flood of warmth crept up her arm and the pain that wracked her body began to ebb.

Douglas said, 'What do you make of the state of the house? I mean … what kind of a burglar—?'

'We don't know that it *was* a burglary,' said another voice—a man's voice this time. 'That will have to be established.'

'Just vandalism then, do you think?'

Douglas must have put the stem of his pipe in his mouth. She could hear the click of it between his teeth.

With a momentous effort she opened her eyes. One eye co-operated. The other felt sealed shut. Douglas loomed over her, into her field of vision. He was creased with concern, his hair still tousled from sleep. She could see, beneath his waxed jacket, the crinkled lapel of his paisley pyjamas. His eyes tried to speak the words that he could not utter here, now, where people might overhear.

'Don't worry,' he said. 'I'll look after Sammy until … until …' he left the end of his sentence hanging.

'I doubt she can hear you,' said one of the paramedics. 'She's had enough morphine to knock out a horse.'

She was hoisted into the air. The pain—still present in spite of the morphine—clamoured in protest but at a strange distance, as though it had been locked in a far room. This pleased Viola—she liked things to be neatly compartmentalised, especially unpleasant things. Just before she was carried from the house she swivelled her eye to take in the lounge. It must have been early morning. Everything—in the dawn light—was rendered in amethyst hues and bloomed as though dusted with pale lilac-coloured snow. It drifted against the fireplace and coated all the upholstery. It hovered in a miasma in the air of the room and she could see it forming a fine coating on the epaulettes of the paramedics. The mechanism of her brain clicked and whirred, trying but failing to make sense of it. Then something shifted—a brief jolt of connection—and she knew what it was; she had seen it before. Flour, icing sugar, bicarbonate of soda and cream of tartar, all the contents of her baking cupboard. She knew that in the kitchen the surfaces would be larded with condiments, a garish gloop of ketchup and mustard and mayonnaise broadcast across the room like a modern art installation. She wanted to stay, to clean up. How could she leave things like this? Panic rose even as her heart sank, but just that small, physical confluence caused her pain, and what little acuity had briefly glimmered, now dulled to opacity.

The hospital ward was insufferably hot. Viola's bed was in an angle of picture windows that faced east and south, pouring light relentlessly onto her for most of the day. She felt like a macabre exhibit at a ghoul show; her bruises were garish, morphing from aubergine to gooseberry. The swelling of her broken eye socket, cheekbone and jaw was grotesque. She could barely eat or speak through her wired jaw. Her arm was plastered, both the radius and the ulna had been shattered. Her fractured femurs—also in casts—meant that she was marooned, utterly immobilised, on the bed. She was catheterised and connected via tubes to various drips. She wondered how many kilos of bolts, nuts and metal rods were keeping her bones in place.

For the first few days—how many?—she was barely conscious. Time was lost in an analgesic haze. Her wired-up jaw and bruised vertebra meant she could barely nod or shake her head when a policewoman came to take her statement. Viola implied that her memory was dim. She had got home from a walk with the dog and then she had been attacked. No, she couldn't remember what time it had been. No, she didn't see a face.

Graham came, sat at her bedside and held her hand. She allowed it to lie limp and unresisting in his, not returning the pressure he sometimes applied. Although conscious, she feigned catalepsy during these visits, shrinking back into the fortified chamber she had constructed where no one could intrude and where no violence could touch her. From there, she could avoid seeing and speaking to him. She did not have to meet his eye. She did not know what she would find there. You never *did* know, with Graham. He asked her nothing about the attack, her injuries, what *exactly* had happened—why would he?—and offered little in the way of comfort or sympathy. Instead, he told her—in pedantic detail—about his conference; the protracted speeches at the dinner, which had dragged on until almost eleven. He'd had to walk from the conference centre to his hotel; no taxi could be found. It must have been a good forty minutes' walk, he said. He had felt no qualms about leaving his car in the carpark; there was CCTV, after all. He had called her from his room and been worried that there had been no answer *at that late hour*. He went over and over it, rehearsing his version of events, speaking them into his carefully constructed reality while she lay beneath the white sheet with her eyes closed, wishing he would go away.

On the next visit he said, 'I suppose the police have been to see you? They've been all over the house although I've told them that, as far as I can see, nothing was stolen.'

She gave a slight nod.

'What did you tell them?' he asked, speciously benign.

She gave a little cough to clear her throat. It felt thick and dry. 'Nothing,' she got out.

'Nothing at all?'

She swivelled her bloodshot eye towards him. 'I told them I couldn't remember.'

She did not tell him that the policewoman had brought with her a file of notes, transcripts of previous interviews following other "accidental" injuries—a hand crushed in a car door, a concussion following a fall downstairs, a laceration caused by broken glass, hypothermia as a result of spending a night inadvertently locked in a shed.

'It could be,' the young woman had said, 'that all these injuries were genuinely the result of accidents, although, to be frank, that would make you extraordinarily unlucky.' She had fixed Viola with a questioning look. 'Is there anything you want to tell me?'

Viola had closed her eyes. 'There's nothing I want to tell you.'

The policewoman had sighed. 'I wonder if you know,' she observed, 'how much time and effort and expense the force puts into these cases. The forensics alone … If this *isn't* a matter involving an outside agent, all that could be dispensed with. Do you see? If it's what we might call a domestic matter—'

'I'm tired,' Viola had said. 'I'd like to rest now.'

Graham was speaking again. 'I just can't *imagine* where you were, Viola. Walking the dog? In the woods, in the dark, *for all that time …?*'

Viola swept a thick, coated tongue over her dry lips. 'I was walking the dog, in the woods, in the dark,' she said, but her sarcasm came out clogged and ineffectual. 'I'm thirsty. There's water in the jug.'

Graham picked up the tumbler and poured water into it before placing it to her lips. She sipped. He pressed the edge of the glass to her bruised mouth and tipped it up too far, pouring water into her mouth until she gagged and coughed, which was agony. She couldn't turn her face away and so she closed her mouth and tilted her chin, mustering what defiance she could. The water spilled down and soaked her hospital gown. She narrowed both eyes, pouring all her scorn into them.

'What are you doing?' a deep, quiet but authoritative voice said.

Graham sprang from where he had been leaning over Viola. It hurt Viola to smile but she allowed herself a small one, nevertheless. She did not often see Graham discomposed.

An enormous, ebony-skinned young man stood at the foot of her bed. He was both tall and wide, with thick, muscular arms and a thoroughly intimidating mien. His eyes looked fiercely at Graham but when he turned them to Viola their fire evaporated and they grew benign. He threw her a wide, white smile.

'I'm Eric,' he said. 'I'm a member of the physiotherapy team here.' His smooth brow creased when he saw the state of her gown and bedsheets. 'You need a change,' he said, reaching out to draw the curtain round Viola's bed, shutting Graham out with a twitch of his arm. 'I'll fetch a nurse.'

She heard Graham say, 'I'll see you tomorrow, Viola,' and Eric's stiff, severe reply, 'Let me walk you out.'

Gradually, Viola's pain-relief medication was reduced and everything—the ward, her injuries and her personal situation—came into sharper focus. It was harder to retreat behind her impregnable wall of denial. Her catheter was removed, but the discomfort of that was only replaced by the awkwardness and indignity of the bed pan. Eric came every day and showed her how she could alter her position in the bed and hoist her hips up using the metal sides of the bed and a bar that was anchored to the ceiling above her. It was hard, with only one arm, and the relatively small amount of exertion—for so little gain—left her exhausted. Her sense of being trapped—in every way—was acute. She missed the numbing effect of the drugs, their physical and emotional dulling, the hazy morphing of one day into another. This new clarity of everything was stark and thorny. The searing sunlight bothered her—but here was no escape from it. Equally barbed was her memory of the attack—much clearer than she had implied to the policewoman—and a sense that this time, things had gone too far. This tiger could not *again* be put back into its cage. She tried to ease her mind by thinking of her garden. She wondered if anyone was watering it. She wanted to go home, but going home meant going back to Graham, and she wasn't sure she could face that yet.

The three other women in the ward were elderly. Viola took a casual interest in them but only as a means of distracting herself from the melee of thoughts that chased themselves around her mind. One of the women called piteously for aid from the moment she awoke until her son and daughter-in-law arrived at visiting time, when she zipped closed her mouth and would utter no syllable until they departed at the ringing of the bell an hour later. They were scarcely out of the doors before her pathetic cries resumed. The second patient would speak only German, feigning not to understand the nurses when they spoke to her although she called out the answers to a daytime quiz show in faultless English. The third lady was afflicted by sporadic paroxysms of weeping. She burrowed into her covers; her thin shoulders shaken with sobs. When the lights were dimmed however, the three women became surprisingly garrulous, exchanging their life-stories under the cover of darkness. The weeping woman admitted to giving birth to an illegitimate child when she had been in her teens. A married but childless cousin had brought the boy up as her own. The German-speaking lady claimed to have known Goering. The lady who spent the day pleading for help expressed confidence that her father would soon come to take her home, and the others forbore to suggest that, as she herself was in her nineties, this was improbable.

Viola lay propped on her pillows and tried to distance herself from their daytime antics and their nocturnal whisperings. She refused to meet any eye and certainly ignored any attempt to engage her in conversation. Characteristically a spiky, acerbic woman, she refused to allow the unnatural intimacy of the hospital ward to break down the barriers she had habitually erected. Metaphorically, she burrowed into herself, just as the weeping woman opposite hid herself beneath her covers, equally distraught. She tried to recapture the woolly-headedness that had anaesthetised her body and mind but it would not come. While she lay in apparent somnolence, her mind was a swarm of clamouring thoughts, panic and dread—quite as painful to her as her bodily injuries. What would she do? What *could* she do? The nagging of her dilemma was as incessant as the pleas of the woman in the bed across the room—both went on and on—and as incomprehensible as the German the other patient expectorated at the bewildered nurses. It was like being lost in a maze—of neatly mown paths between serried hedges of clipped yew, arbours with perennials, a fountain and an old stone seat at its centre. She wandered its pathways in her imagination, finding impediments at every turn.

Her son came to visit her. Brian was a bright boy, with his father's burly frame but his mother's gimlet intelligence. She had not wanted to send him to boarding school, but then again she *had* wanted to remove him from the sometimes-toxic atmosphere of home, so when Graham had insisted on it she had not put up more than a token resistance. Thankfully, Brian had thrived there, enjoying the sporting opportunities and quickly assimilating the nice manners and clipped accents of the other boys. Most of them had been born with many advantages, but intelligence was not one of them and Brian had risen to the top in most of his subjects. He had been accepted at a prestigious university where a top-flight stock broking firm had already offered him a position when his degree was done. He was resourceful, self-reliant and ambitious. His future was assured and Viola was glad of it. She did not want him mired in his parents' situation.

With Brian she did attempt some communication, rasping out answers to his questions, trying to assuage his distress at the state of her but unable to agree to his assertion that now, *surely,* things had gone too far.

'What can I do?' she croaked.

'You haven't even accused him,' Brian said.

'I don't know that it *was* him.'

'You *do,*' he replied darkly. 'Come on, Mum, we *both* do.'

'He was at a conference,' she managed. 'At a dinner. There will have been dozens of witnesses.'

'You know what those affairs are like,' Brian sneered. 'Alcohol-soaked. Who will be able to put their hand on their heart and say for sure that he was there for the whole time?'

'There was CCTV in the carpark. His car will have been there all night.'

'*His* car will … Oh! I know, he'll have all the angles covered. You won't be able to *prove* anything and, in the end, it will be your word against his.'

'Exactly.'

Brian sat back in the plastic chair and helped himself to the chocolates he had brought. 'You should just cut your losses. A clean break. The house will be worth a mint. I know there's no mortgage.'

'I'd want to stay in the house,' Viola put in quickly. It was about the only thing she *did* know.

Brian's matter-of-fact response to this intensely personal, painful and unpleasant situation surprised her. He shook his head. 'I think that will be a no-go. You won't be able to afford to buy him out. I don't think the rest of your joint assets will balance out the value of the property. Shall I speak to him about it?'

Viola baulked at this idea. 'Oh no, Brian. I can't let you get involved. I don't want you taking sides.' She wanted to change the subject. 'Have you been home? Have you seen Sammy?'

'No. I spoke to that neighbour though. Lord Canterbury? It was him who called me, actually.'

This was news to Viola. 'What? *Douglas* called you? Not your *father*?'

'No. I found out from His Lordship. I didn't know you and Dad were so friendly with him—hobnobbing with the great and the good. Anyway, he sends you his best wishes and he says Sammy's doing fine. Funny bloke, isn't he? I always thought he was a bit of a recluse. He wondered about coming to see you but I told him you probably wouldn't want him to.'

'You were right,' said Viola. 'I'm worried about the garden. If you do speak to him again, could you ask him to …'

He eyed his mother with a lop-sided grin. 'He's landed gentry, Mum. He has acres of land, who knows how many tenant farms … he won't have time to go and hoe your raised beds.'

'I suppose not,' she said.

The days dragged on and on, the passing time punctuated by the clatter of the tea trolley and the dispensing of medications. Visitors came and went, bringing flowers that wilted almost immediately, and confectionery that the patients did not want but which were devoured by the visitors themselves, the nursing staff and the porters. The German-speaking lady was taken away; she had got a place at a nursing home. The condition of the weeping woman deteriorated suddenly and she received farewell visits from a number of relatives. Viola wondered if one of them was the son she had been forced to abandon. One night the entire ward was kept awake by the deep-chested rattle of the woman's death-throes and in the morning the curtains around her bed were closed.

The auxiliary nurse who helped Viola with her ablutions said that soon she would be able to have her hair washed. There was a little salon with a back-wash in the basement where hairdressers came in on a voluntary basis. They'd just need to be sure that the bruising in Viola's vertebrae had improved sufficiently. Viola had never been so glad about anything in her entire life. Her hair—mousey brown and fine—felt like a bird's nest. Eric helped her get out of bed and into a wheelchair. With one arm in plaster, she couldn't easily operate the chair herself. Her legs—thick and stiff in their casts—didn't feel as though they belonged to her. He wheeled her into the dayroom where an enormous television blared inanity but where at least there was a selection of *Gardeners' World* magazines.

It was while she was in the dayroom—she had managed, by dint of awkward swivelling and going round in several circles, to reach the television and pull the plug on the damned thing—that a woman called Gwen came to see her.

Gwen was a smartly-dressed woman in her mid-fifties, with pepper-and-salt hair, cut short.

She held out a large hand. 'Hello dear. I'm Gwen Barker. Can we have a chat?'

Viola looked up from an interesting article about the propagation of citrus trees. 'Who are you?'

'I'm Gwen Barker,' Gwen repeated, pulling one of the chairs round so that she could sit at a tangent to Viola. 'You look as though you've been in the wars.'

Viola raised a cynical eyebrow. 'Do you think so?'

'Yes, you poor lamb,' Gwen said, ignoring Viola's attitude. 'But nothing I haven't seen before. In fact, I've seen much worse.'

'Oh? Well, I must say, *that's* a comfort.'

'Indeed. It pays to look on the bright side, doesn't it? I'm a cup-half-full person myself. You?'

Viola suppressed the desire to look about her and declare that she had no cup at all. Instead, she said, 'Is there something I can help you with?'

'That's ever so kind of you,' said Gwen, lifting a capacious handbag onto her lap and rummaging about in it. She brought out a sheaf of leaflets. 'I work as part of a team of volunteers, here at the hospital and also at a location in town. We help women who are the victims of domestic abuse.'

Viola stared hard at her magazine article. 'Oh, yes?'

'Indeed. Tell me dear, is that something you've had experience of?'

Viola hesitated. It would be easy to put on a show of being appalled, insulted. Instinctively she glanced at the clock. It was a quarter to three. In fifteen minutes, Graham could arrive for the visiting hour.

'There's no need to be afraid,' said Gwen, seeming to read Viola's mind. 'If your hubby comes, I can string him some tale. He won't need to know what we've been discussing. *Are* you afraid of your husband?'

Something in Viola, some steely receptacle that she had been in the habit of keeping tightly shut, opened a chink. She could not tell what horrors it might contain. A fat tear oozed from her eye and fell with a splat on the glossy page of the magazine. 'Why would you think that?' she asked in a voice that she had intended to be sneering but that came out as a squeak.

Gwen leaned a little closer. Her knee pressed against the arm of Viola's wheelchair. 'A number of reasons, my dear. One of the hospital staff here has voiced a concern. And then there's a police file. We work closely with the domestic abuse team at the constabulary. And then last of all, we had a call from, let's say, a well-wisher. He was very anxious that someone should come and speak to you.'

'Was it … Brian?' Viola faltered.

'Brian would be …?'

'My son.'

'I see. Well, I couldn't say. He didn't leave a name. But *someone* is very worried about you. Someone cares about you, very much.'

Viola found that her hand had been taken. The single tear on the page was joined by others. The effort of holding them back exerted all kinds of pressure on Viola's wounded facial muscles as well as on her pride, which would not normally have allowed her to show emotion publicly. She snatched at one of the leaflets that Gwen held in her other hand. 'I'll read one of these, if you like.'

'Certainly. Help yourself.' Gwen fanned them out as though about to do a conjuring trick with them. 'There is legal advice here—some firms do work *pro bono* in these cases, you know—and information about financial support. Erm … let's see … oh yes, counselling, claiming benefits—'

'I'm not saying they're relevant to me,' Viola interrupted. 'The thing is, you see, I can be such a shrew. I wind him up. I'd try the patience of a saint and Graham … he … I give as good as I get, sometimes. I'm my own worst enemy …' she trailed off, surprised and appalled that she had confessed so much. Where had *that* come from? But then she realised these were exactly the accusations Graham levelled at her. When things got what he called "out of hand," it was always Viola's fault.

'Oh, me too,' said Gwen, not at all perturbed by Viola's confession. 'My ex and I used to argy-bargy all the time but you know, that's still no excuse for …' She lifted her other hand and touched Viola's ravaged face and then her own eye where the faint trace of a white scar could be seen beneath the bristly brow.

Viola met Gwen's eyes for the first time. 'Were *you* …?'

'Oh yes. But that's a *long* time ago. Since then, I've built a new life for myself, made friends. You see, there *is* life beyond—'

'The grave?'

Gwen laughed. 'Well, *I* happen to think so, yes, but I'm not wearing my evangelistic hat today. Beyond abuse, I was going to say.' She looked up at the clock. It was a minute to three. She gathered her belongings together and stood up, careful to return the chair to its original position against the wall. 'May I come and see you again?' she asked.

Viola nodded and closed the magazine, concealing the leaflets.

Graham did not visit Viola that day, and although she tried to concentrate on the *Gardeners' World* magazines, she found her eyes straying again and again to the leaflets Gwen had left with her.

She and Graham had experienced these "episodes" before and got over them. His violence did not surface often, but in a way that made it the more menacing—she never knew when it might rear its head. It had helped her to think of Graham and his temper as two separate things, to believe that he was as much a victim of his inner demon as she was, that he was helpless to withstand its precipitate, overwhelming force. But this latest incident—the forethought that had gone into its execution—gave the lie to that idea. She imagined him slyly limiting his alcohol intake at the dinner, slipping away when all the other delegates were too drunk to notice his disappearance. He must already have arranged a hire car for the drive home, or perhaps a car from the pool that his company kept in readiness. His motivation for all that premeditation could only have been the coldly deliberate intention to inflict harm, and then to cover his tracks. Of course, she knew in her heart that Graham had cause for jealousy. Her affair with Douglas would have been reason enough for his anger, had he known about it. He had made no reference to *that*, implying only her protracted absence that evening as the spur for his ire, and yet his meticulous planning suggested that this had not been a spontaneous act. He must suspect ... was that why he had telephoned Douglas—presumably from his car as he hared back to his hotel—as a warning? To incriminate him? Or had it been simply coincidence, his attempt to ensure that Viola did not die whilst casting himself in the role of concerned, solidly-alibied spouse? It was a mystery, another tortuous loop in the perverted pit of Graham's brain that Viola had no desire to plumb.

Hidden in the leaves of her magazine, the leaflets informed Viola of the aid available to what they described as "survivors" of domestic abuse. There were refuges, counselling, legal aid, restraining orders. If she pressed charges she could have Graham charged and possibly even imprisoned. She did not think she wanted to follow that route. One hand toyed with her stiff, grime-coated hair. She had the undeniable sense that a line had been crossed, leaving her marooned in a strange country.

She looked up to see Douglas approaching across the day room. He was a thick-set man, tall but tending to stoop. He wore clothes that had been expensive when bought but that now showed sign of age and wear. His trousers had not been washed or pressed for some time and their houndstooth design did not go well with the checked jacket. His shirt was creased. But he had shaved—his chin looked raw—and he had made some attempt to smooth his coarse, brindled hair. He was handsome, in that way people who are careless of their appearance manage. He clutched a box of chocolates in his large hands. He looked impossibly out of place, and she knew what it had cost him to come—he who in general eschewed public places and crowds of people. Like Viola herself he had constructed a mott-and-bailey around his life. Within it were his dogs, his books, his rack of pipes and his long-suffering housekeeper, Mrs Gibbs who, other than herself, was the only female who had been allowed to cross the threshold of his stately old pile in twenty years.

Douglas smiled when he saw her and accelerated his steps to arrive at her side. He placed the chocolates without comment on a table.

'Your son said not to come,' he said, creasing himself into the chair Gwen had occupied earlier, 'but I decided that I would.'

'I look a mess,' said Viola, patting her hair hopelessly.

'No wonder, after what happened,' said Douglas. 'It's a miracle you're alive. How are you doing?'

'Alright, I think. I'm having physio and occupational therapy. It's a matter of waiting for the fractures to heal.'

'Poor old thing,' he said. He peered through the glazed partition into the ward. 'Why have they put you in with all the old biddies?'

Viola shrugged. 'It was the only bed they had, apparently.'

Douglas frowned. 'Don't you have private health insurance? You ought to be at the Bupa place.'

'Graham has private health insurance. I don't.'

Douglas glowered at Graham's name. 'So he'd get all the bells and whistles then, if he were in your shoes? You really ought to report him, Viola. I know the Chief Constable. I could make sure the whole thing was handled sensitively—for *you*, that is. I can't promise that Graham would get kid glove treatment.'

Viola said, 'I don't know for sure that it was Graham.' But she knew that was a lie. 'The police can't prove it,' she amended. 'Did you call a women's refuge place, Douglas?'

'Someone had to,' he said darkly. 'I take it he won't be visiting. I shouldn't like to have to pretend to be nice to him.'

Viola shrugged. 'What did he say, when he telephoned you that night?'

'Oh, an Oscar-winning performance. So sorry to trouble me. I was the only neighbour whose number he could find. He was in Birmingham. I think he said that two or three times. Would I very much mind going down to your place because he was sure something was wrong.'

'So he didn't hint that you and I might have been together?'

Douglas shook his head and leaned closer to say, 'Do you think he knows?'

Viola considered. 'I don't know. *Something* made him plan this. But, to be truthful, at this point I'm beginning not to care *what* Graham knows. I'm ...' she hesitated, reluctant to speak the words. Once out, they would be hard to swallow back down. 'I'm thinking of asking him for a divorce.'

Douglas rocked backwards, pressing himself into his chair. His eyes slid away from hers. 'Oh,' he said.

Neither of them spoke for a moment. Viola tried to read his sudden reticence.

'I was wondering,' she began, 'whether, when things have blown over …'

His hand reached out almost as though it was independent from the rest of him, defying the inclination of Douglas and the remainder of his body. His fingers found hers and gave her hand a pleading little pat. 'Well, old thing,' he muttered, still not meeting her eyes, 'I don't know about that. I mean, my place—you've said it yourself—hardly homely. I'm so used to my own bachelor ways. And as much as one deplores the whole thing—the title and so on—it does make one rather vulnerable to scandal.'

Viola bit back the retort that *by then*, there would be no scandal—she would be a decently divorced woman—but she would not demean herself by begging. Gently, she disengaged her hand from his. 'I see,' she said, swallowing down the clog of disappointment that obstructed her throat. She let out a long, shuddering sigh. 'Of course. I just thought I'd mention it.' It took all her steely determination to keep the tears at bay. She blinked and pretended to remove a lash from her eye.

Douglas sat uncomfortably on the grey plastic chair and stared hard at a stain on the knee of his trousers. His hand remained where she had abandoned it, resting uncomfortably on the arm of her wheelchair.

Later, on the ward, when the lights had been dimmed and the squeak of the nurses' shoes on the polished floor had receded, Viola wept into her pillow. She did not weep for Douglas, for Graham or even for herself. She did not weep for the wreckage of her marriage, which she had tried—at such cost— to keep alive but which she had to acknowledge was now beyond resuscitation. She wept for her garden, the poor unwatered seedlings in the greenhouse, the tender perennials that would fall prey to pests and inveigling weeds, the unpruned roses and unmown lawns. She mourned the blooms she would not see, the produce she would not harvest, the obliteration of her life's work by spiteful nettle and vicious thorn.

Chapter Two - Maisie
Six years later

It is a Friday afternoon in early June. The renovations at Maisie Wilde's house, *Old Farm Hall,* are well underway, a long-overdue revamp of electrics and plumbing, carpentry and décor. Rather than having the thing tackled piecemeal—as most people would do—Maisie is having the whole thing done in one herculean, amalgamated flurry of knockings-out and prisings-up, brick dust and rubble.

She has waited long enough.

Old Farm Hall is a large property standing in substantial grounds, its situation at one time relatively rural but nowadays encroached upon by the industrial, commercial and residential expansion of the town. Living in it alone would have been hard to justify, and after her husband's death Maisie had considered selling up. But a sense that its potential—like her own—has never been properly realised, and that there is a need for larger properties where people can live in co-operative community, has stayed her hand. She has been left surprisingly well-provided for financially by a generous pension, a life-insurance policy, a death-in-service benefit and a substantial, previously unknown-of deposit in a savings account. This, and her natural, inbuilt desire to nurture has brought her vision for her home into sharp relief. She struggled to explain it to her children, but they—she is the first to admit it—lack imagination. They are all grown and live independently. Whatever she does with *Old Farm Hall* cannot materially impinge on them and so, in the end, they have let her have her way.

So now, the house is hidden behind a palisade of scaffolding and tented by plastic as the rooftiles are removed, old purlins replaced, insulation and new felt installed. Her house swarms with workmen brandishing tools to wrench out the ancient timber windows, disconnect antediluvian bathroom suites, smooth out crumbling plaster and replace archaic wiring. The garage at the side of the house has been demolished and already a splendid new extension is chest-high; it will house a utility room, loo, shower and a storeroom below and a bedroom suite for Maisie above, with a fancy bathroom and a dressing area. A skip on the drive contains the remnants of Maisie's old kitchen units, the recalcitrant solid-fuel cooking range and the Baby Belling two-ring hob that was brought in "as a temporary measure" some thirty years before. Everything in the house will be sanded and varnished, smoothed and painted, oiled and upgraded, but its original features—fire-surrounds and panelling, cornices and ceiling roses—will remain intact.

Maisie and her friend and housemate Minnie Price have decamped for the duration to Minnie's old house on the Crescent, yielding up the entire field of operations to their project manager, Trevor Vine. Trevor is what Maisie and Minnie think of as "a safe pair of hands"—a homely, no-nonsense bloke with vast experience of building work. Nothing seems to faze or surprise him. He is capable and stoic, and handy enough in all the trades to have won the respect of brickies, chippies, pipeys and sparks. He doesn't say much. What he does say is spoken staccato-style, sentences boiled down to their essential nouns and verbs. Mainly he only wags his large, grizzled head sagely as they list their requirements: walk-in showers, draught-free windows and, today, an appeal for plentiful plug-sockets.

He extracts a stubby pencil from the fold of his ear and brings a crumpled envelope from the pocket of his boiler suit. 'What kind?' he enquires. 'White? Black? Chrome? Antique brass?'

'What's the difference in the cost?' Minnie asks although in fact the cost has nothing to do with her. Maisie will be paying for everything.

Maisie places a friendly but faintly admonishing hand on Minnie's arm. 'What would be right for the era of the house?'

Trevor sucks his teeth. The house is Edwardian, at one time a farm, and then adopted by a local businessman as a gentleman's residence. 'Brass,' he opines. 'Double stepped.'

'That's what we'll have then,' says Maisie. 'Anything else?'

'All these showers.' Trevor points to the plans that have been pinned to the kitchen wall. Each of the four bedrooms will have an *ensuite* bathroom and the two attic rooms will share another. Then there are the ones in the extension. 'Need a big tank.'

'Yes indeed,' says Maisie with carefree relish. At one time, when her husband was alive, this kind of issue would have proved insuperable, an impediment that would stymie progress for weeks, months, even years. Now it is hardly an obstacle at all, the smallest possible bump in the road that she can step over with ease and elegance. 'Yes please, Trevor, a lovely big tank with lashings of hot water available 24/7.'

Beside her, she feels Minnie stiffen. Maisie addresses her next comment to her friend. 'The solar panel will give us free hot water every day that the sun shines,' she says. 'So, really, the bigger the better, don't you think?'

Maisie likes to consult Minnie on most matters. *Old Farm Hall* will be Minnie's home for the foreseeable future and so it only seems fair that she should have some say. Some of the carpets and furniture from Minnie's former home will be coming to *Old Farm Hall* in due course, now that her step-children's plans to appropriate every stick have been blocked. Maisie has managed to convince Minnie that this is a more than adequate contribution to their shared living arrangements going forward.

Now that the business of the day has been dealt with, Maisie and Minnie tour the house to inspect the works, stepping carefully over gaps in the floorboards, squeezing past ladders and stooping to avoid the spaghetti of wires that dangle from various holes in the ceilings. Minnie's room, which is at the back of the house, already has the stud walls of its new shower room in place.

'I can easily turn my bed the other way,' she says. 'It will fit nicely in the alcove, don't you think?'

'I do,' says Maisie, 'but I still wonder if the front room wouldn't suit you better, the one that used to be mine. It's much larger and sunnier.'

'Oh no,' Minnie objects. 'All that sunlight will fade the fabric.' Minnie is a seamstress. She makes bridal and evening wear and also runs an alteration service for the local dry-cleaner. Up until very recently these occupations were her sole source of income, and scarcely kept the wolf from the door.

Maisie touches her friend's arm. 'You will be able to sew in the old housekeeper's parlour, Minnie. That way you won't miss out on all the fun.'

Maisie has no absolute idea what the "fun" might be, or who might generate it, but she has a firm conviction that, before long, her house will be peopled by more occupants, people who, like Minnie—and Maisie herself—need company and companionship, a little respite from life's troubles, a haven to call home.

As they go through the house they collect the workmen's mugs to refill for morning tea. They will have to be washed in the old scullery sink, the only one that remains in the house. There too is a kettle and milk, sugar and several packets of biscuits—the workmen seem to consume all these in prodigious quantities. Minnie applies herself to this task while Maisie goes out of the back door to begin work in the garden. There are early peas to pick, as well as the last of the strawberries. The onion bed needs weeding. She ought to deadhead the geums and stake up the delphiniums. Later, when the sun slips behind the trees, she will water the tomatoes in the greenhouse. She will happily occupy herself in this—her happy place—for the rest of the day, deaf to the cacophony of shouts and hammering from the men and the blare of their radios. Only a sudden hush from the building behind will tell her the day has ended, the men are gone.

Before Maisie has even found the shallow basket she likes to use to collect her garden produce, Minnie steps out of the shadow of the terrace with two mugs of tea. They take them to a stone seat in the parterre to sip companionably.

'You'll be off to the citadel, after this?' Maisie asks.

Minnie nods. Recently, she has transferred her religious allegiance from St Stephen's—a rather stuffy, high Anglican church—to the Salvation Army, where she works with the homeless two or three days a week. 'We had a donation of men's clothes last week. I didn't finish going through them all.

Lots are perfectly good but there were some broken zips and torn linings I want to deal with. You're sure you don't mind my taking the car?'

Maisie shakes her head. 'I'll have no need of it. There's plenty here to keep me busy. Gloria said she might drop round. You know what she's like. A whiff of testosterone and she can't help herself.' Maisie looks at the house, where three shirtless men are working on the roof and another gang is busy installing new windows. She sighs. 'I wish Viola was here. The lawn needs cutting and she's so much better with the mower than I am. I can't get the thing to start.'

'She's very capable,' says Minnie, but, to Maisie, the compliment smacks of insincerity. Minnie and Viola are not natural friends although, in recent weeks they have been getting on slightly better. Minnie is soft, under-confident and indecisive—sometimes, to be truthful, feeble and downright dim—whilst Viola is prickly and no sufferer of fools; she can be derisive and cruel and *has* been so to Minnie. Viola has gone on an extended visit to her son in London. In some ways this isn't an unwelcome development since her recent recourse to alcohol has been worse than ever, marring several social occasions that would have been enjoyable if not for Viola's Chardonnay-soured ill-humour. They would not see her again until the twenty-first, in Oxford, for the wedding.

Viola's sudden decision to stay with her son surprised Maisie. One moment they had all been talking excitedly about the wedding, the next Viola had taken herself off, and just a few days later had come the news that she had gone to London. Although of course very proud of Brian, Viola has never seemed especially close to him, and Maisie understands that Brian has a new partner on the scene. Maisie cannot imagine that the arrival of Viola, for a stay of some duration, will add much polish to the shine of new love. But what does she know?

Their quiet tea-break is interrupted by the arrival of Gloria. She tip-taps around the house in high-heeled sandals wholly unsuitable for a building site, yoo-hooing gaily to the lads, who have finished their tea and returned to work.

'Hi Jacko,' she flutes to a man carrying roof slates along a platform of the scaffolding. He is broad-chested, hirsute and less than half her age. 'Coo-ee Stefan!' she cries to another workman, who wears a bulging toolbelt slung low across his hips. 'Ooo! Look at you with all your tackle on display!' She holds a carrier bag aloft and waggles it provocatively, setting her 40G-cups into reciprocal motion. 'I've brought you all choccy treats for breaktime. Come and get it boys!'

Maisie rushes across the parterre. 'Gloria,' she says firmly, 'they've just had their break. I need them to get on with their work. You'll have to leave those snacks indoors for later.'

Gloria's face falls momentarily but she quickly recovers her good humour and follows Maisie to the stone seat. Minnie moves up to make room. 'It's just as enjoyable to watch the show from here isn't it?' Gloria says, using her hand to make a visor and ogle the men on the roof. 'Is that why you're sitting here?'

'Not at all,' says Minnie primly. 'We like to look at the garden.'

'Oh yes,' Gloria says, glancing at the herbaceous borders. 'Very nice. I had a forlorn hope that Gwen would be here. It isn't her day at the shop and she isn't at home. I suppose I should have known better.' Dragging her eyes from the roofers she says, 'Gwen spends all her waking hours with Val these days, not to mention her sleeping hours I shouldn't wonder. What do you think of that little liaison?'

Gwen, not a widow but a longstanding divorcée, is the self-appointed leader of the widows' clique but has recently been distracted by a romantic attachment to Val, who runs the urban farm and animal shelter located on fields behind *Old Farm Hall*. Gwen's sexuality was no surprise to any of her friends, but up until a month or so ago it had remained in the closet along with Gwen's tweedy trews and stout lace-up brogues. Maisie considers Val an obliging neighbour but not exactly a friend; she resisted Maisie's early overtures of friendship. It sometimes seems as though Gwen is succeeding where Maisie failed, gradually coaxing Val into their group. But, as Gloria implies, more often it looks like Val is stealing their friend away. Gwen has missed two of their whist evenings and a weekly luncheon, "otherwise engaged" with Val.

'I don't think anything about it,' Minnie replies to Gloria's question. 'It's none of my business.'

'I think it's sweet,' says Maisie. 'I haven't known Gwen as long as the rest of you, but I don't think I've ever seen her happier.'

Gloria sighs. 'I'm sure Amy feels that Gwen has abandoned her.'

Amy, the elder stateswoman of the group, has limited mobility and relies on Gwen for all kinds of day-to-day aid, but their friendship goes back a long way. Without Gwen for company, Amy will indeed be bereft. Maisie frowns. 'The rest of us will just have to make sure Amy is always catered for. I hope to call on her this afternoon.'

Maisie suppresses a sigh. She had planned to spend the entire day in the garden and it will be a sacrifice to give that up, but she can't bear to think of Amy being lonely. 'We could go together, Minnie, when you get back from the citadel. What do you think?'

'Oh well,' says Minnie. 'Whatever you like.'

Gloria heaves another heavy sigh. 'Maybe I'm just envious. We're all great friends and so on, but if *I* had the chance of love, I'd drop you lot in a heartbeat.'

'I don't think Gwen has "dropped" us exactly,' Maisie says. 'She just has other fish to fry.'

Minnie stands. 'I must be going. I'm due at the citadel at ten.' She turns to Maisie. 'I'll be back about three. We can go to Amy's on the way back to the Crescent.'

Maisie looks towards the garden. 'That's fine. I can pick her some lettuce and harvest some tomatoes from the greenhouse. Some of them are just about ripe. I suppose there's a tin of something we can open to have with salad, for our supper?'

Minnie, who is minutely up to date with their entire inventory of groceries, nods. 'Yes. Tuna, ham, corned beef. And plenty of eggs.'

'You two,' Gloria scoffs. 'Such an example of perfect domesticity.'

'You're welcome to join us,' Maisie offers, rising and collecting the mugs. 'But now I really must get on. Those peas won't pick themselves.'

'I'll put those in the scullery for you,' says Gloria, taking the cups. 'I have to put my choccy goodies indoors anyway. I'll let you know about tonight, if that's alright. You never know, I might get lucky. On the other hand, a salad would be good for me, I suppose. My wedding outfit is a tad on the tight side.' She fluffs her blonded hair and adjusts the neckline of her blouse—already low enough in all conscience—before heading indoors.

Maisie locates her garden trug and makes her way to the vegetable garden. The day is bright with summer sun, warm but for a brisk breeze, and she is glad of her light cardigan. She picks a basket of peas and then moves on to the strawberry beds. Not many remain. Some plants are already throwing out suckers. They will need potting up for next year. She removes her gardening gloves and runs a hand through her hair.

Gloria's earlier reference to her wedding outfit reminded Maisie of her own *ensemble*. She has it organised apart from a handbag—she is yet to find one in just the right shade of apricot. Several, bought on-line, have had to be returned, their colour too coral, too shrimp or too cantaloupe to match the gauzy apricot of her dress. She supposes she will have to take a trip into town. There are two or three boutiques she hasn't tried yet that might have something.

The arrival of Gwen and Val disturbs her train of thought. They emerge through the gate at the back of the garden that leads to the scrubby fields of the urban farm, confirming Gloria's earlier suspicions. Gwen, in deference to the weather, wears a pair of light chinos and a short-sleeved gingham shirt. She also wears an air of supreme personal gratification. Val sports her usual farm dungarees and muck-encrusted wellingtons, but has left off her ubiquitous bobble-hat. She looks quite different without it. She has fine, flyaway hair in a rather stunning shade of white-blonde. It is nicely arranged, free of straw, its feathers lifting in the little breeze, and softens the bony contours of Val's face, distracting from the thread-veins that lace her cheeks and nose from years spent outdoors.

Maisie greets them both, stretching her back and laying aside her bowl. 'Hello you two,' she says. 'Gloria was here earlier. You've missed her, though.'

'Oh that's a pity,' says Gwen, but somewhat automatically.

Val says nothing. She doesn't meet Maisie's eye, but her lowered lids have more of coyness about them than shyness. With half a pace sideways, her shoulder touches Gwen's arm. Maisie finds the gesture very touching.

'I'm afraid I can't offer you much in the way of refreshment,' she says.

'Oh! We haven't come to be entertained,' Gwen assures her. 'We wanted to have a word about your daughter's wedding.'

'Oh yes?'

'Two matters, really. Firstly, Val here, she's not quite sure … I mean, she wonders … because, you know, she wasn't there when you so kindly extended your invitation—'

'Of course you're included Val,' says Maisie, adding, 'if you'd *like* to come.' Val has always been such a crusty, taciturn creature that Maisie half-doubts it. The farm is her *milieu*—she is a woman of wind and animal waste and wheelbarrows—but then, looking at Val now, she realises someone new is emerging from that dusty chrysalis. Even so, the leap from urban farm to Oxford College seems an ambitious one. What on earth, for example, will she wear? Maisie has only once, to her recollection, seen Val in anything other than farm clothes.

Val's expression suggests she shares all of Maisie's reservations, but Gwen is oblivious.

'That's just what *I* said,' Gwen cries, turning to Val and wrapping, briefly, a reassuring arm around her shoulders. 'But that brings us to our second difficulty. Val isn't sure the farm trust will allow the time off.'

'They never have before,' Val mutters.

'You've never *asked* before,' Gwen puts in. 'I should think that after so many years' loyal service you're due a holiday.'

'And it's only a long weekend,' says Maisie. 'Surely they can get someone to cover?'

Gwen shifts from foot to foot. 'As to that, we wondered—Val and I—about taking a few days afterwards. *Together*, you know. Just the two of us. The Cotswolds are so lovely—'

'I think that's a splendid idea,' Maisie says, perhaps a little too brightly. There had been talk, earlier in the year, of the women taking a group holiday. Not the little coach-tours they usually booked but a proper holiday, possibly even abroad. But if Gwen is going away with Val, it seems unlikely that her commitments at the charity shop and the animal shelter, not to mention the Scouts and various church committees, will permit a further leave of absence, even if the farm trust does grant Val a holiday. Like Gloria, and probably Amy, Maisie feels rather abandoned.

Gwen steps closer to Maisie and lowers her voice to a confidential tone. 'The thing is,' she says, 'Val isn't *far* off retirement age but she's by no means ready to be pensioned off. For a start, that charming chalet is her home. She doesn't want to vacate it. And then, like me, she likes to be useful. Her work amongst those poor animals is her *life.*'

'You're worried,' Maisie interprets, 'that if the trust brings in a *temporary* replacement they may decide to make it *permanent.*'

'And I've got nowhere else,' Val laments.

Gwen squares her shoulders. 'Not that *any* of us would *ever* see you homeless, dear,' she declares. 'I for one—'

'I'm sure you're worrying unnecessarily,' says Maisie quickly, before Gwen commits herself—and the others—too far. 'You're an employee and you have rights. They can hardly refuse you a holiday when you've hardly taken a single day in thirty years! I can ask my son, if you like. He's a paralegal.'

Gwen's thoughts have clearly travelled the same trajectory. 'That's just what we hoped!' She turns to Val. 'I'm sure Maisie's son will back me up. They can't refuse you. I'm so sure of it that I suggest we go straight into town. I want you to try on that dress-and-jacket that came into the shop on Monday.

I put it in the stockroom *immediately* to make sure no one else bought it. I'm sure it's your size, and the colour's *so* pretty.' She turns to Maisie. 'It's a *beautiful* shade of peach. Don't you think Val will look amazing in it?'

Maisie swallows. Peach is perilously close to apricot. Vying with the rush of anxiety that the outfit in the charity shop might be similar—oh God! might even be *identical*—to the designer ensemble Maisie has splashed an eye-watering amount of cash on, is the vision Gwen has conjured of Val in smart clothes. It really is an anomaly, a circle she can hardly square. Instinctively, she looks at Val, whose doubtful eye says she shares the difficulty.

'You really mustn't go to any trouble and certainly to no expense,' Maisie says. 'My daughter's idea is that the wedding will be informal. To be honest, she wouldn't have bothered at all, but the Foreign Office insisted and her fiancé's mother felt the same. That dress you wore to the party in May was lovely, Val—'

'Oh, I think we can do better than that,' Gwen says. 'We wouldn't want to let the side down, would we Val? And the most wonderful thing of all is that it will look perfect against my trouser suit. It's a lovely shade of coral.'

They turn and move off together, through the orchard and back to the garden gate. They are still in Maisie's line of sight when Gwen takes hold of Val's hand.

Maisie carries the bowl of fruit to a shady arbour at the side of the vegetable garden where there is a rickety old wooden bench. She sits gingerly and eats the strawberries one by one, their warm sweetness delicious in her mouth, and gazes across the garden at her house.

The roofers labour beneath the plastic sheeting that covers the whole structure. The heat within its canopy must be suffocating. She sees Trevor Vine mount the stepladders to the top-most platform and survey the progress. He speaks a word or two to the foreman, pointing out some issue with the chimney. Beneath him the gang of glaziers lifts one of the new bedroom windows into position. The plan is to replicate the original sash casements of the property, with clear glazed panels below and square muntins above; but unlike the original windows these will not be draughty or rattle in the wind. The internal shutters have been removed and carried away for expert restoration by a carpenter. Maisie and Minnie have chosen fabrics for blinds and curtains—each room will have its own, tasteful colour theme and style but all will reflect the building's original era. Luckily Minnie's house is of a similar period and had been furnished to suit, so the various pieces that are to come from there will fit in seamlessly.

Maisie allows herself a moment to envision the completed whole, not a new occupation for her. Throughout her marriage, while the house languished beneath Clifford's piecemeal approach to repair and restoration, her vision for it had been almost the only thing sustaining her. It was a vision they had shared but one he had signally failed to bring about—by indecision, by ineptitude, by parsimony and by procrastination. She doesn't blame him. Once she understood the root cause of all Clifford's peculiarities she had forgiven him completely. But she would labour no longer under its restrictions. She has the money, the ideas and the purpose. And what clearer proof does she need of how securely she is on the right track than Val's hints just now? Another single person, a little older in years, potentially in need of a home. A home that she—Maisie—can offer. And here it is, metamorphosing before her eyes, as she herself has been metamorphosed by Gwen and the rest of her friends.

How grateful she had been for them in the first raw gash of her widowhood. How comforting it had been to be taken in amongst them and accepted, borne along as though by a raft of strong arms as she assimilated the loss as well as the unsuspected gains occasioned by Clifford's death. If she is honest she is *still* assimilating both. Of course she misses Clifford and she is sad that he died but her bereavement is such a complex cocktail of sweet and sour. There is no gainsaying that Clifford's death brought about a great deal of good for herself—a vast opening of unsuspectedly deep financial reserves, yes, but also of opportunity—a blossoming of a bouquet of flowers of which she is the principal bloom. Guilt, sadness and pleasure course through her in such dizzying tides and contraflows that her widowhood sometimes energises and sometimes enervates her; she is as likely to laugh as to cry.

Conflicted emotions keep her awake at night. Grief is a many-faceted thing, and none of its faces are what she had anticipated.

Amy's little bungalow is located within a sequestered corner of a large housing estate, in a cul-de-sac with little traffic except for the mobility scooters used by the residents. The dwellings cluster around a communal green maintained by the council but which Viola recently augmented by planters filled with colourful annuals, and baskets hanging low enough for the residents to water them from the safety of their wheelchairs and zimmers. Today is another warm day, and all the inhabitants have their French doors propped wide open to admit any breeze, while snowy net curtains do their best to shade the rooms within.

Minnie and Maisie find Amy indoors, watching the final few serves in a particularly exciting tennis semi-final. Amy is thin, frail, with white hair and deeply lined skin, but it would be a mistake to assume her agedness extends to her intelligence. Her shrewd eyes are fixed on the screen and every ounce of her considerable intellect is focussed on the game. Minnie and Maisie mouth greetings as they pass Amy's orthopaedic armchair and make their way into the tiny kitchen to gather the makings of tea. Dolly the poodle leaps onto the sofa and settles herself against a cushion on a square of blanket kept there just for her. Amy is happy for her friends to make themselves at home but she insists on the observation of certain standards, and Dolly knows her place. By now, Maisie too knows which china Amy likes to use in the afternoons and where the napkins and cake forks are kept. Meanwhile, Minnie goes through to Amy's bedroom to decant a bag of mending and ironing she had taken away with her on her last visit. Maisie waits for the kettle to boil so she can warm the pot—Amy claims to know when this has been neglected—listening to the thonk, thonk, thonk of the tennis ball as it ricochets off the competitors' racquets. There is a thunderous round of applause as match point is won. Then Amy turns off the television.

'There's a lemon drizzle in the tin,' she calls through.

'Yes, I've found it.' Maisie glances over at where it sits, neatly placed on a doily atop a fluted, gold-rimmed Royal Doulton plate. 'Is it one of Gwen's?'

'No. One of the ladies at the bridge club gave it to me. I haven't seen Gwen for a few days. Have you?'

'Yes,' says Maisie, carrying in the tray. 'This morning, in fact.'

'She was with Val, I suppose?'

Maisie nods. She has no wish to be drawn into a discussion about Gwen and Val. On the other hand, a hint now might save Amy disappointment later. 'Val is worried she may not get cover for the farm while she's at the wedding and … afterwards. They plan a short holiday in the Cotswolds.'

Amy sniffs. '*Do* they? Well, it is a lovely part of the country.'

'That's what Gwen said. Val hasn't been away for years and years. But she's anxious about asking the trust for time off, so it may come to nothing.'

'Even so …' Amy sips absent-mindedly at the tea Maisie has passed to her. 'Ah well,' she says presently, 'I suppose it was always on the cards.'

'Do you feel a bit jealous? Gloria says she does,' Maisie offers. 'But we really oughtn't to. Gwen gives and gives and gives. Which of us hasn't benefitted from her generous heart? Now, it's time for her to take a little for herself.'

'But do you really think Val will provide?' Amy queries. 'I don't know. I've hardly exchanged two words with the woman. And that's it, really. She's so quiet and self-effacing. Look at that party you had. She'd been in the gazebo an hour before anyone noticed her! Gwen's so outgoing, such a sociable creature, with an enormous circle of friends. How on earth will Val fit in? My worry is—and I can see it happening already—that Val will take Gwen away from everything. Far from *giving*, she'll end up taking away.'

Maisie considers. Gwen's *raison d'être* is helping people; it's what she does. Maisie had never thought of Val as someone in need of rescue. On the other hand, it must have been incredibly lonely, year after year, with only the animals in her care for company. Guilt gnaws at Maisie. She should have done more, been a better neighbour. But now, in their newly fledged relationship, it is Gwen who is delightedly taking the lead, and Val who seems bemused—astonished even—to have been so singled out. No, Val has no agenda, no scheme afoot to separate Gwen from her friends and, in spite of what Amy says, they do have things in common. 'I think Gwen sees them as kindred spirits in terms of their commitment to their causes. Val has her animals and Gwen has—'

'Her lame ducks?' Amy finishes, with a dry laugh. 'I suppose we'll just have to hope she doesn't swap one for the other. Now then, let's try that cake.'

Maisie is relieved the conversation seems to be over. Amy's lounge is cluttered, full of porcelain ornaments, antimacassars, lace doilies and stuffed toys that fix their eyes on you with importunate appeal. Numerous bowls of *potpourri* emit stiflingly floral aromas. While they talk, Maisie feels an increasing sense of befuddlement and breathlessness. It is insufferably hot. She gulps her tea down.

Minnie comes in with a dress on a hanger. 'Is this the frock that needs to go to the cleaner's? I can take it if you like, Amy.'

Amy looks up. 'Oh yes. I thought I'd wear it for your daughter's wedding.' She turns to Maisie. 'Will it do?'

Maisie peers over her teacup, and her sense of disorientation increases. The dress—a delicate crêpe, Empire line with a pleated skirt and pretty lace trim at the neck—is light salmon pink, not apricot but not far off. She thinks she might cry, but quells her dismay sufficiently to croak out, 'Very suitable. Lovely in fact. Shall you wear a hat?'

'Oh no.' Amy shakes her head. 'I can't abide hats. Shall you?'

Maisie, unable to speak, makes a vague movement over her head to imply she plans headgear of some description.

'Maisie is being very tight-lipped about her wedding outfit,' says Minnie, helping herself to tea. 'Even I haven't seen it.'

'A fascinator, I bet,' says Amy, who tries to divine everyone's secrets. 'Not that you'll need it with a certain gentleman of our acquaintance. He's *already* fascinated.' Her eyes—blue, and very bright—twinkle naughtily. A spinster, Amy takes a lively interest in the love lives of others and is a voracious consumer of bodice-rippers.

'Oh *Amy,*' Maisie protests, her voice unnaturally shrill. Amy has been predicting romance between Maisie and Oliver Harrington from the first moment they'd met. Maisie flushes hot all over with awkwardness and irritation. There really is nothing between herself and Oliver—is there? And also, a fascinator is *exactly* what she plans to wear for the wedding. She leaps up. 'Goodness! It's so *hot* in here.' She hurries to the open French door where a whiffle of breeze cools her skin. In an effort to restore herself to some kind of equilibrium she focusses on the neat square of green, the bright array of flowers in the tubs, a blackbird drinking at the birdbath.

Behind her, Amy tells Minnie about the bridge club, much depleted with the absence of both Gwen and Viola.

'And I had to drive myself, with Gwen "otherwise engaged",' says Amy with a trace of bitterness. 'I don't mind too much while the evenings are so light, but come the autumn I'll just have to give it up if no one will drive me. My eyes aren't good enough to drive in the dark. *And* I had to play with June Possett. She *will* bid out of turn.'

'Things will have resolved by then,' Minnie assures her, stroking Dolly. 'Viola will be back from her son's, even if Gwen decides—'

'She's already decided,' Amy puts in. 'And, you know Viola's rarely sober enough to play these days.' She sighs and dabs her mouth with her napkin. 'Such a shame if I have to give it up. I'm sure bridge is one of the few things keeping my atrophied old brain going.'

'There's nothing atrophied about your brain, Amy,' says Maisie, coming back into the room, her good humour restored. 'And, as for Gwen, I've never seen her happier, have you?' It is the remark she'd made earlier, to Gloria. In the end, isn't happiness that all that matters?

Maisie pours herself another cup of tea, emptying the pot.

'I'll make more,' offers Minnie. 'We must keep our fluid levels up.'

While Minnie is in the kitchen, Amy remarks, 'It did seem a very sudden decision of Viola's, to go off and see her son.' She picks up her phone and jabs at the screen. 'She isn't answering my texts,' she says. 'I suppose she is alright. I mean, if there'd been an accident, we would have heard? People who drink, you know, they do tend to damage themselves.'

'I'm sure she's fine,' Maisie assures her. 'Gwen said it was a sudden impulse.' But Amy's surprise at Viola's spur-of-the-moment departure is exactly what Maisie herself feels. Lately, Viola had been spending more time in *Old Farm Hall*'s garden, often arriving bleary with the previous night's excesses but seeming to find some solace amongst the vegetables and perennials. Her impromptu trip down south, especially now, with the garden is at its loveliest, does seem odd.

While the others discuss some alterations Amy wants done to her dress—the hemline raised, the waist reduced—Maisie drinks more tea and lets her mind wander. The peas ought to be podded and blanched and put in the freezer. Will there be time, when I get home? How similar, will Val's peach dress be to my own outfit? And now Amy's also proposing to wear a comparable colour, ought I to rethink my whole *ensemble*? Why can't I just *say*, 'Oh, please choose something else, or we'll look like we're in uniform!'? I *am* the mother-of-the-bride, after all. Surely they'd understand. Oh God!

She comes back to herself to find both Minnie and Amy regarding her.

'Are you alright, Maisie?' Amy asks. 'Only, if it isn't convenient—'

'Convenient?' Maisie turns to Minnie. 'I'm sorry, you've lost me.'

Minnie explains. 'I suggested Amy come back with us to the Crescent and share our evening meal. Only salad, I know, but it's nice to have company, isn't it? That's alright, isn't it? I don't mind driving her back.'

'Of course it's alright,' Maisie assures them. 'Gloria said she might come too, so we'll be quite a party.'

'My garden does get a very pleasant breeze from the sea,' says Minnie, and Maisie thinks it is the only positive thing she has ever heard Minnie say about the enormous house she shared with her late husband. 'I think we'll all be cooler there. Maisie, I'm quite worried about you. I think you've had too much sun today.'

Chapter Three - Viola

Viola's stay in hospital was protracted, lasting through the remainder of April and into May. She was moved to a cottage hospital and then, for a mercifully brief spell, to a nursing home, where even the sight—let alone the smell—of the variously flaccid, frail and forgetful residents galvanised her into a determined dash for recovery. Eric the hospital physiotherapist was replaced by Nancy, a butch, no-nonsense ex-army medic more used to dealing with wounded service men than middle-aged women. Viola and Nancy developed an acerbic, mutually abrasive relationship that did Viola the power of good. They parried expletives and cutting disparagements as Viola tortured her shattered body on the gymnasium equipment, determined not to weaken under Nancy's coldly autocratic eye.

Graham took Viola's application for divorce characteristically. At first with boyish, almost disarming confusion: this was not *really* what she wanted, was it? Oh Viola, really! Of all the silly things to have done. And then with attempted remorse: yes, he could see she was serious, and what else could he expect? He had behaved atrociously. He didn't deserve her, but she must believe him, things would be different from now on. When he saw his pleas and self-recrimination could not move her, he became threatening: fine, if she was determined to ruin both their lives, he wouldn't stand in her way. But she'd find she had far more to lose then he had. She didn't imagine he'd sell the house, did she? And as for their savings, *what* savings did she mean exactly? Finally, he took recourse to his old ways, cornering her in her room and coming at her with a clenched fist. Only Nancy, arriving for their physiotherapy session, saved Viola from further attack.

A restraining order was filed. The reception staff were told on no account to admit any visitors to Viola's room except her son, her solicitor and her forensic accountant.

Nancy added some self-defence techniques into Viola's rehabilitation. They practised setting firm verbal boundaries and maintaining a nonconfrontational stance, as well as hand-strikes, eye-jabbing and the effectiveness of a knee to the groin.

'A key, or a stiletto, can be an effective weapon,' Nancy said.

'I can't see you in stilettos,' Viola retorted. 'You're more of a Doc Martin girl, aren't you?'

'A steel toecap has its advantages,' Nancy said.

In July Viola was discharged and, with Brian's help, became the tenant of a ground floor flat in Southquay. Southquay was at some little remove along the coast from Millport, the county town, and a good few miles from the house in the narrow valley. They had chosen Southquay to reduce the likelihood of Viola bumping into Graham. Millport was where Graham went to the gym and played golf and, they speculated, would tend to do his shopping now he had to shift for himself. It had a mainline railway station and although Graham did not often travel by train, it was not unheard of. The terms of the financial settlement were still not finalised and Viola had no desire to be anywhere that he might come across her—especially as she knew her forensic accountant was trawling through every detail of Graham's tax affairs, investments and even his business expenses.

Southquay was a genteel, sleepy seaside town typified by Victorian architecture, wide boulevards and several parks. It was much favoured by retired couples because of its leisure facilities—it boasted two golf courses, several bowling greens and a small theatre—and also because of its plethora of residential, care and nursing homes. The town had wide, flat pavements and a smooth promenade along which mobility scooters could glide with ease. Bungalows sat alongside large, bay-windowed Victorian mansions, many of which had been converted to flats. The properties along the seafront were surrounded by broad expanses of severely manicured lawns and bordered by the kinds of shrubs that do well in a salty breeze: ceanothus, rhododendron, cistus and escallonia.

After a day of wrangling Scandinavian flat-pack furniture, Viola and Brian strolled along the seafront in search of a fish and chip supper. She threaded her arm through his and hardly used the walking stick, the only aid she now allowed herself. It was a fine evening. The sea winked shards of silver gilt in the rays of the slanting sun. Dogs ran deliriously across the exposed sands.

'Do you think you'll have Sammy back now?' Brian asked. He had ensured that dogs were permitted in the flat. 'I think you should, you know. It will do you good to get out every day and,' he indicated the beach, 'he'll love this, won't he?'

As far as Viola knew, Graham had made no attempt to reclaim Sammy and she supposed the dog was still living with Douglas, from whom she had not heard in weeks. 'I don't know,' she said. 'I may have to get some sort of job, and I don't approve of leaving dogs home alone all day.'

Privately, she thought about the flat. It had a minute patch of grey shingle beyond its patio doors that seemed to be in perpetual shadow; only weeds and a very determined buddleia bush had made any attempt to survive in its unpromising gravel. As an outdoor space it was hardly suitable for a dog. The flat itself was square and boxy, unrelieved by any even faintly architectural flourish, painted in off-white with a grey, utilitarian carpet. She would not complain. How could she, when her finances were as yet so up in the air? It had been brilliant of Brian to take the time and trouble to find it for her and to negotiate the lease, even though he had only just graduated and started work with the investment bank. But her heart had sunk to her boots when she saw it for the first time—so dull, so bland, so small—such a far cry from the low-beamed house and the glorious garden she had left behind.

'I suppose,' she said, 'there really is no chance I could have the house?'

'None at all,' Brian said matter-of-factly. 'It's on the market and you'll get half its value.'

'And the furniture?'

She felt him suppress a quiver of irritation. 'We've spent all day getting that Ikea stuff assembled,' he said. 'You haven't got room for any of your old pieces and in any case, I don't think they would look right in the flat.'

'Not there, no,' she conceded. 'But once the house is sold I can look to buy somewhere, I suppose. The flat is only temporary.'

Brian made no immediate reply.

They found a fish and chip shop and ate their supper sitting on one of the benches on the promenade, fending off seagulls.

Presently Viola said, 'Has your father mentioned where he will live, once the house is sold?' She didn't like interrogating Brian. So far, he had done such a good job of remaining nominally neutral between his parents in spite of being much more on her side than on Graham's. He approved of the divorce but that didn't mean he wanted to sever ties with his father altogether. And she didn't want him to.

'No,' he said, screwing up the paper wrapping and throwing it into a bin. He licked his fingers. 'But don't worry, I won't let him *think* of settling here. Even if he knew you were here—which he doesn't—this isn't the kind of place that will appeal to him. Too far from the motorway for one thing. It wouldn't surprise me if he moved down country, to be nearer to head office.'

'If he did, I could move back to the village, at least,' mused Viola.

'Why would you do that? It isn't as though you had any friends there.'

Viola thought about Douglas. 'No,' she said, 'you're right.'

Later, back in the flat, Viola could hear the murmur of next door's television through the wall as she made up a bed for Brian on the new *Vretstorp* bed-settee. She had not bought a television. Her *Kallax* bookshelves were empty, waiting to be filled, but she had a radio. She was to have an old laptop computer of Brian's but broadband had not yet been connected to the flat. She speculated briefly about the neighbours. There were six flats in the block, three on the ground floor and three above. None of the residents had come to say hello as she and Brian had manhandled the boxes inside, and when they returned from their evening walk all the curtains and blinds were closed. The only positive thing she could think of was that one of the upper neighbours had some tomato plants and a bird feeder on their little balcony. That said something, didn't it?

Brian came in from the bathroom. 'The shower's actually quite good. Good pressure I mean. I'm sure you'll be able to get that mould off the grout with some bleach.'

'Yes. Will one pillow be enough? If not, you can have mine. We only bought two, which was a bit short-sighted of us, wasn't it?'

'One's fine. I can supplement it with one of those garish cushions you insisted on.'

Viola picked it up. Was it garish? It had a large, floral motif. It matched the curtains and the *Klockbuske* rug. Why she had bought a rug she did not know. If was not as though there was a hearth to lay it in front of, and no Sammy to lie on it. 'I liked the colours,' she said, tucking it under the pillow.

'I've been thinking,' said Brian, so casually that Viola instinctively knew he was about to introduce a topic that had been on his mind a long time.

'Oh yes?'

'When the house is sold, and if it turns out that you're pretty settled here, I could invest the money for you. You'd have an income from it, of course, but with the amount you're likely to get, I could make some significant investments and you'd see a considerable return.'

Viola perched on the bony arm of the *Ektorp* armchair. 'I'll think about it, Brian,' she said.

The next day, after waving Brian off, she stood in her cramped little flat and looked about her hopelessly at the chunky, budget furniture. There were only a few pieces, yet it crowded the room and left her breathless. The remains of breakfast were clustered on the minuscule kitchen table. A couple of bowls, two mugs and a milk jug—so few things and yet too many for its small surface. Diminutive as it was, it was too big for the kitchen. She could not open the fridge unless she moved one of the chairs. But that would be alright. She only needed one chair, after all.

The previous day, in Ikea, she had experienced a kind of euphoria, choosing things in bright, primary colours, gaily adding crockery and bedding and lamps and innumerable tea-lights into their two trolleys. She and Brian laughed at the unpronounceable names and she had felt at the beginning of a new and exciting road. But now, alone in the insipid surroundings of the flat, the colours seemed artificial, the fun evaporated, the optimism drenched in a sudden and grim reality. The ugly view of other flats across the block-paved carpark—she could just make them out through the mottled glass of the windows—did nothing to ameliorate a sudden sense of overwhelming despair.

What have I given up, for *this?*

Sternly, she shook herself from this slough of despond. She stripped the bedding from the quilt Brian had used and opened the washing machine to bundle it in, but a thick rime of blackish mould on the rubber gasket made her recoil with disgust.

She dumped the bedding on the kitchen floor and rummaged in a drawer, brought out a pad of paper and a pen and wrote the word *bleach* in a firm hand.

By August Viola had done the best possible with the unpromising little flat. It was clean. The windows gleamed, polished inside and out. The washing machine and—when she had come to closely examine them, the fridge and the oven—had needed a thorough scrub with proprietary products requiring rubber gloves and plentiful ventilation. She had washed down all the paintwork in the flat and gouged out the mouldy grout of the shower, replacing it with new, in arctic white. The activity was therapeutic. It was good to be busy, to fill a day that would otherwise be empty—and daunting in its emptiness—with purposeful bustle. She fell into the unyielding seat of the *Ektorp* every evening feeling shattered, her body aching but, in some way she couldn't define, better. It was as though not just the flat but something else, something inside her, was being scoured.

She wasn't lonely. She was used to spending time on her own, inhabiting a private space that could not, unlike her body, be violated. She had become accustomed to feeding it with information from books and the stimulation of radio programs, and exercising it with sudoku puzzles and crosswords. Within it she had become self-sufficient, but she dwelt in it now with a vague discontent almost bordering on resentment. Narrow as her life had been before it had not been *this* narrow. There, she'd had her house and garden: that little idyll amongst the grassy pastures, the tumbling rill, her riotous borders and regimented raised beds. How she missed them! Her dog, and the wide wanderings they'd had through the trees of the plantation and further afield. How often, now, did she reach down a hand to the space near her feet where Sammy would have been, finding only empty air? Of course when Graham was at home she had always been on edge but in truth he had not been at home much in the scheme of things, and for the majority of time she had been her own mistress in her own domain. Now she was reduced to what felt little more than a cell, sterile and inhospitable in spite of the artificial brightness of the cushions and the brash colours of the crockery.

She thought a lot about her marriage to Graham, how and why it had gone so wrong. What she could have done to keep it from the disastrous trajectory it had taken. What about it all—if anything—was her fault? She did not deceive herself about her own failings: she'd had an affair. It had taken guile and subterfuge to carry on with Douglas behind Graham's back. She had frequently lied to her husband about her whereabouts even while knowing full well what discovery would mean. Perhaps, in the end, he *had* found her out. Perhaps her own faithlessness had thrown his volatile temper into overdrive. In which case, who had she to blame for her present situation other than herself?

On the other hand she did not minimise the fact that she had been a victim—a survivor, she knew, was the proper term—of an abusive relationship. How could she have stayed after what he had subjected her to? Good God, she had almost died! In spite of the limited confines of her constricted little life she had to admit it felt good to wake each morning without that churn of anxiety in her guts, to do things as she wanted to without the ever-present fear of some malicious reprisal. She would not relish an encounter with him but she was no longer *afraid* of him. She had escaped. Even so, at night she double locked the doors and checked the window catches.

These thoughts kept her company as she scrubbed and polished every corner and surface of the flat. At times her soul—like her hands—felt raw, abrased by the ceaseless circle of recrimination and excuse. Sometimes her drive to clean felt like an obsession. Did the hinges of the doors really need a burnish with Brasso? Would it matter if the skirting board behind the fridge was a bit dusty? Was this whole preoccupation with cleanliness simply a displacement activity to put off … what? Actually *beginning* her new life? But each day when she felt it possess her, she was as helpless as the sponges and cloths in her bucket, destined to be seized and doused in detergent and squeezed into the furthermost recesses of the built-in wardrobe in quest of any tiny wisp or infinitesimal trace of grime that must be eradicated before anything new could start.

Negotiations between the lawyers dragged on. Viola's solicitor advised her to demand spousal maintenance and, going forward, a share of Graham's pension, since she hadn't one of her own. Graham, in his turn, claimed half the value of the diamond ring Viola had inherited from her mother, and insisted that she reimburse him for the Rolex he bought her for their twenty-fifth anniversary—or return it to him. Since Graham himself was in possession of both these items—she rarely wore jewellery of any kind and certainly had not been wearing any on the night she had been beaten to a pulp—Viola's solicitor said Graham must produce both items forthwith. The watch, certainly, was a gift and beyond the scope of the negotiations. The ring might be contentious but would have to be valued. And so things proceeded, like a game of tennis, Viola's future a ball batted this way and that, its final resting place as yet unresolved.

The weather that summer was poor. Usually a squally wind and dull, brown seas meant the promenade was empty of all but the hardiest people. A handful of day-trippers in thick anoraks sat close together on the wrought iron benches and drank coffee from thermos flasks they had brought with them, struggling to keep their packets of sandwiches from becoming airborne or being snatched by the ever-present gulls. Viola made a point of a brisk walk every day, whatever the weather, along the sea front or around one of the municipal parks where the breeze was less sharp. Doing so required the summoning of a certain quantity of courage. The more she scarified the interior of the flat, the more deeply sequestered she felt within it—protected, almost like an embryo burrowing into the lining of a womb. The ritual of stepping out of her door and crossing the quadrangle of carpark became an effort of will. By nature a resilient woman with no time for what she would have described as sentimental clap-trap, she pulled on her shower-proof jacket, seized her walking stick and sallied forth.

The public gardens, like the promenade, were deserted. Viola lamented the bruised, battered annuals that hung limply from hanging baskets, the tousled perennials that lay defeated over the ornamental borders. A council employee toured the paths collecting litter or attempting to stake the broken stems of delphinium and hollyhock. One day he caught Viola collecting seeds from a particularly attractive, pale pink aquilegia.

She leapt back onto the path guiltily. 'I don't even know why I want these,' she said breathlessly. 'I haven't a garden now.'

'They'll do alright in a pot,' he said. 'I can probably find you one or two, if you like.'

He took her along the neatly edged paths to where a small wrought iron gate in a beech hedge gave access to a utilitarian area of compost heaps and tool sheds used by the park-keepers. He disappeared into one of the sheds for a few moments while Viola looked around and inhaled the familiar, evocative scents of fermenting grass cuttings and leaf mould. She found they conjured such a powerful wave of nostalgia that tears sprang into her eyes and she had to rummage in her coat pocket for a tissue. Just inside the door of the shed she saw a neat arrangement of spades and forks, hoes, rakes and a set of long-armed loppers. Her hands itched to take hold of them. In a moment of utter madness she considered grabbing one of the tools and making off with it. These two sensations—the emotional and the physical manifestations of what she had lost and what she most of all wanted, right now, to *do*—were the strongest she had experienced since the pain that had wracked her body in the hospital. She had a sudden, vivid image in her mind's eye of her garden: the terraces rank with weeds, the plants choked and dying, the vegetables in the raised beds all gone to seed and wasted. Gripped by a sense of urgency, almost of panic, she turned and hurried away through the gate and along the path to the exit before the man emerged from the shed.

When nearly home she slowed her pace and looked around at the three blocks that made a horseshoe around the square of parking. The windows of her neighbours looked down on her, blank and unseeing. The upper flats had small balconies. Some even had little bistro tables and a couple of all-weather chairs, but she never saw anyone sitting out, even in those lucky west-facing flats that caught the evening sun. A property management company sent a team of gardeners round once a month to mow the narrow strip of lawn that ran along the back of the blocks and to trim the thick, prickly pyracantha hedges. Here and there rosebay willowherb and ragwort succeeded in sprouting between the pavers and some of the ground floor patios, like hers, were home to a straggly buddleia, but apart from those the place was sterile and dingy. The tomato plants on her neighbour's veranda had keeled over and the birds had given up on the feeder because it was never replenished. She could hardly criticise. She had felt disinclined to do anything with her own little patch of ground. The flowers of catsear—a pernicious weed she would normally have rooted out without a thought—added courageous but oddly tender spots of colour to the otherwise drab square of ground and she found she could not bear to do away with them.

Later that afternoon she took the handful of papery aquilegia seed-heads purloined from the park and crushed them between her palms, then sprinkled the tiny black seeds over the grey, doubtful gravel.

Of her neighbours she saw little but she found herself mildly curious about them. It turned out the flat above her was empty. The one next door seemed to be inhabited by a single man who went out to work early each day and did not return until late. Once, on a rare dry and warm day, she saw a clothes maiden on his patio festooned with pants and socks. On bin day his wheelie was overflowing with pizza boxes and take away containers.

The flat on the far end of the block was owned by an older man. Viola saw him shuffle off—she presumed—to the shops most days, returning home a few hours later with his purchases, but these seemed very few for the number of hours he was away. She speculated he spent time at a drop-in centre or the library, whiling away the long, lonely hours. At weekends he had visitors, likely a son and daughter-in-law and their two children. The youngsters brought scooters and spent the time endlessly circling the carpark. Viola wondered why the whole family didn't go out to the seafront where there was a skatepark that would be much more fun for the kids, where the old man could get some fresh air and where they could buy ice cream or tea and buns in one of the innumerable cafés.

She decided the flat above the old man's must be a holiday let. Different people came and went, arriving usually on Saturday with suitcases and boxes of groceries. They went off every day to visit—she supposed—museums and stately homes. Between holiday-makers, a van bearing the name *Dot's Domestic Services* pulled into the carpark and disgorged two very young women equipped with buckets and mops and bales of clean bedding. They were in the flat barely an hour before they re-emerged and perched on a low brick wall awaiting collection, smoking cigarettes and staring at their phones.

That left only one flat in the block of six, the upper middle one, whose occupant had tried and failed to grow tomatoes and feed the birds. The entrance to all the upstairs flats was on the far end of the building so Viola could not see who came and went. It seemed to her the curtains were rarely opened. Sometimes there was a small red car parked in the far corner of the carpark, close to the door, but Viola would have had to step through her patio doors and press herself into the thick, prickly hedge beyond it to see its owner. She refused to demean herself that far, but she was curious.

She spent a lot of time at her patio doors, staring out into the square, watching the sparrows in the pyracantha hedge. Hard green berries had formed. Come winter those would make good sustenance for the birds if the maintenance team did not remove them. Her flat was quiet but not silent. The fridge hummed and occasionally shuddered. The clock she had bought in Ikea had a tick so loud she had removed it from the bedroom after only two nights. Sometimes she could hear the creak of someone moving upstairs, presumably along the upper corridor. She learned to recognise the thud of the outer door as her neighbour arrived home, the jingle of his key, the click of his catch as his door sealed him in for the night. Once or twice she contemplated opening her own door at just that moment. She could take a bag of rubbish to the bin … but told herself she did not care enough to mount such a performance. The old man at the end did not use the shared entrance at all. He came and went through his patio door, squeezing himself round the end of the hedge. It was quicker, she supposed, but awkward. How did he not snag his shopping bags and his shapeless navy anorak on the thorns?

August became September, and then October. The trees in the park began to shed their leaves. The park keeper raked them up into piles and then loaded them into a trailer that he towed behind a little tractor. If the man saw her he made no sign of it. One day she found the perennials all along the border had been cut back, the soil mulched with bark chippings, the big square of summer bedding plants all removed and replaced with winter pansies and primroses. There was no sign of the park keeper after that. She supposed he had moved on to winter work: drain-clearing, grit-spreading, pot-hole repair.

November passed and December came and still Viola's financial settlement and divorce seemed no nearer.

'Dad's gone away for Christmas,' Brian told her on the phone. 'He's taken extended leave and gone off to Thailand.'

'Good heavens,' Viola said, 'really?' The Graham she knew would never have done such a thing. 'Spending the money before I can get my hands on it,' she muttered sourly. But then, 'I suppose he still *has* his job. He hasn't been sacked?' In the end she had decided not to press charges for the common assault that Nancy had prevented, although Nancy—pumped up from having deftly wrestled Graham into a head-lock—had been very keen she should. But Viola knew that things had a habit of getting out and it wasn't impossible that Graham's bosses had got wind of the incident.

'Oh no,' Brian assured her. 'In fact I think things have been going rather well for him. He brought in a big new client or something and was told to take extra holiday as a reward. I think they even paid for his flights.'

'Nice for him,' Viola murmured.

'We'll have a good time, Mum.' Brian had booked them into a country house hotel for Christmas. 'Open fires, carol singers, mulled wine, clay pigeon shooting ...'

'It sounds like heaven.' Viola cast an eye over the flat. She had not bothered with any decorations. What was the point? But she had treated herself to a poinsettia. Ordinarily she didn't particularly care for houseplants, but this one had been moping in a crate outside the supermarket, lashed by rain, presented in a perfectly hideous pot larded with Christmas sparkles. She had not been able to walk past it. It sat now on a low table, not too near the radiator, lovingly dosed with just the right amount of water and a proprietary fertiliser. Lots of its bracts had fallen off but she could see new ones ready to unfurl. She hoped it would survive her absence.

'You should get your train tickets in the post any day. I booked them yesterday. And I'll collect you at Cheltenham Spa as we agreed. Have you had any more thoughts about those investments? It's always best to get in on the ground floor, you know. I could bring the paperwork with me and talk you through it at the hotel. Oh! And I'll bring that laptop I promised you as well.'

'How can I decide anything before I know what I'm going to get?' she asked. 'And I really do think I'll want to move from here. It's been fine, you know, as a temporary thing, but I'd like to think that one day I'll have a garden again.'

She could tell she had displeased him. He had been mentioning the potential investment with careful casualness but at regular intervals for the past few weeks. She was beginning to wonder if it mattered more to him than just the judicious investment of her divorce settlement; if he himself had something to gain. Of course she didn't care. Where would she have been without his financial support for the past few months?

'You've been *so* good Brian. I must owe you thousands of pounds, one way or another.'

Brian sighed. 'I'm earning plenty here. As you say, we can sort everything out once you have your money. If this opportunity goes by, there'll be others. I'll see you on the twenty-third.'

This conversation took place on the twenty-first of December, the shortest day. Viola's flat—never very light—was gloomier even than usual and she kept the lamps lit all day. Rain lashed her windows and it seemed the low bruise of cloud would descend even further and press itself against the glass. Nevertheless, Viola would not be deterred in her determination to go out. She zipped up her coat and pulled a waterproof hat over her hair, donning sturdy boots in the tiny vestibule before setting out.

Her walk was a quick sprint through the rain to the supermarket where she picked over the lacklustre, imported fruit and vegetables, grumbling all the while. Why was nothing grown locally? Why did everything lack flavour? In the end she chose a cauliflower and some cheese that at least was British and was on her way to the checkout when she saw a box of assorted wonky carrots and forked parsnips, some old potatoes and a crabby onion or two, all passing themselves off as a "winter casserole mix." She grabbed the box, loath to see it go to waste. Although it would be awkward to carry home, she would rescue what she could from it and make soup.

Somewhere in the shop a choir of schoolchildren warbled out a discordant rendition of *In the Bleak Midwinter*. A child had been stationed in every aisle, armed with a collecting bucket. It was impossible to avoid them and Viola struggled with her box, her basket and her shopping bag to scrabble a few coins from her purse.

Waiting in the checkout queue she saw a woman she thought she recognised. Tall and thick-set, with iron grey hair cut very short, wearing a mannish anorak and with a capacious shopping bag over her arm. Her trolley was being unloaded by a young woman, hardly more than a teenager. Her daughter perhaps? The girl had a curtain of dirty brown hair that shielded her face, and wore a disreputable-looking coat over holey leggings. Viola shifted her basket to the other arm and shuffled forward. Where had she seen that woman before? Then it came to her, and as it did the woman turned and saw Viola. The woman's face lit up immediately—clearly, she had an excellent memory for faces.

'Oh! Hello,' she hooted across the two or three checkouts that separated them. 'How lovely to see you! How are you? Viola, isn't it?'

'Yes,' Viola said, but frowning. Two or three heads had turned and she felt oddly exposed. 'I'm fine, thank you.' She began a fruitless and wholly unnecessary search in her shopping bag for her money, which was in fact, in her pocket, not wanting to engage with the woman without quite knowing why.

After Viola had paid for her shopping the woman—Gwen, she recalled now—was waiting for her. The younger woman hovered a few paces away, scrolling her phone with a hand that was wrapped in crepe bandage. Viola could see her face now. She had a bruise on her cheek and steristrips on one side of her mouth. Her eyes were puffy from crying.

Gwen took a step closer to Viola and said in a low voice, 'Yes, poor thing. I've just been to collect her from the Accident and Emergency department of Southquay General. We're going to look after her for a while. But how are you doing? I must say you look better than when I last saw you.'

'I was half-dead *then*,' Viola returned, 'so I would hope for some small improvement on *that*.'

'Naturally,' said Gwen, unmoved by Viola's rancour.

Impulsively, Viola said, 'I left my husband.'

'Oh, well done my dear,' said Gwen, laying a hand briefly on Viola's arm. '*So brave of you. And all on your own, without any support.'

'My son has supported me,' Viola put in quickly. 'He's been marvellous as a matter of fact.'

'Of course. Splendid. And you're living …?'

'Here in Southquay, temporarily. Things seem to take an age to sort out.'

'Oh they *do,*' gushed Gwen.

Mercifully, the choral entertainment came to an end but the respite was a brief one; the shop's in-house audio blared out the opening bars of *Merry Christmas Everyone*. People who had paid for their shopping jostled each other to escape.

'Oh, what a racket,' said Viola crossly. 'We're in the way. I must be going.'

She shifted the box of vegetables to her other arm. She was almost sorry she had bought them. They must weigh three or four pounds, far more than she could eat.

'Oh, so must we,' said Gwen, 'but I'm so glad to have seen you. Why don't you let me give you a lift home? Where did you say you were living?'

Through the huge plate glass of the supermarket window, Viola could see the carpark was a lake, its further reaches invisible in a thick miasma of fine rain. Already the floodlights around the carpark had come on although it was barely three o'clock. 'I don't want to trouble you,' she said. 'You've got …' She nodded at the waif who was now slumped against the window. She was pale to the point of being translucent.

'Oh my goodness, Shakira, are you alright?' Gwen was instantly at the girl's side, wrapping a strong arm around her. 'You poor dear,' Gwen crooned. She waved an arm at their trolley. 'Would you mind, Viola dear?' Then she began to steer her charge towards the doors.

Viola plonked her own shopping on top of the trolley, noting distractedly the packet of sugary cereal, the jar of chocolate spread, the white loaf, bags of crisps, bottle of banana milk, pizza and cans of fizzy pop it contained—nothing fresh, nothing green, nothing healthy or nourishing—and hurried after them. Before she knew it she had stowed all the shopping into the back of a red hatchback and had been bundled into the back seat while Shakira lolled almost insensible in the front.

Gwen, driving them a tortuous route through the rain-lashed streets said, 'I've got to go the long way round. The road along the promenade is flooded. Did you know? They've been threatening to improve the drains along there for years. Perhaps now they'll get round to it.'

Viola ought not to have been surprised—but somehow was—when Gwen turned into the parking area of her own block of flats. She killed the engine and turned in her seat to say, 'The charity I work for—I think I told you about it when we last met—keeps one of these flats for women like Shakira. A temporary refuge. We keep its existence under wraps. Some of the men our clients are escaping from can be very devious and determined, but this place is right off the radar and we like to keep it that way. I know I can rely on your discretion. If you don't mind, I'll take Shakira up and get her settled. She's been in a hospital cubical all night and before that … well, perhaps I don't have to elucidate. She's shattered, poor thing, but nothing a good night's sleep and a hot meal won't cure. Then I'll run you home.'

'But I *am* home,' said Viola, pointing to her own flat.

'No! How extraordinary! Well, in that case, perhaps I can trespass on your goodwill to give me a hand.'

They manhandled a semi-comatose Shakira through the door at the far end of the block and up the stairs. Gwen extracted a key from a key safe adjacent to the door of the middle flat and they went in. Like Viola's, it was bare and functional, but reasonably clean, and equipped with everything a woman who had left home with nothing but the clothes she stood up in could need. There was a saggy settee, an armchair and a small television in the lounge. The bedroom had a bed, all made up with clean sheets, and a wardrobe. The kitchen had a kettle and a toaster as well as the basic appliances. Gwen and Viola removed Shakira's coat and grubby trainers, then tucked her in to bed where she turned over and fell instantly into a deep sleep.

'I'll bring up the shopping,' Viola whispered as they tip-toed out of the room. 'And later, when I've made it, I'll bring her some soup.'

'That's very good of you my dear,' said Gwen. 'I really can't stay. I have the Scouts' Christmas party at six and I haven't made a single sandwich or a square of flapjack yet.'

'It's no trouble,' said Viola, surprising herself, because ordinarily she was the last person to get involved in someone else's drama.

'Shakira's mother is coming tomorrow from … somewhere. After that, we'll see. Quite often clients only stay here a night or two before we can move them in with a relative or friend. What surprises us is that, so often, nobody has the least idea what's been going on. Shakira's mother, for instance, was adamant the young man who's been beating the living daylights out of her daughter couldn't possibly be the culprit because, and I quote, "he works in a bank".'

'I can easily believe it,' murmured Viola.

'Of course *you* can,' said Gwen. 'But what I really mean is, once it's out in the open, very few clients are utterly without aid. Shakira's mother will take her off our hands, I'm sure. But before that, probably this evening, one of our volunteers will come and make sure the poor little thing is alright, so you won't be lumbered with her. You mustn't feel at all obliged. Oh Viola, I'm *so* glad I bumped into you.'

Gwen did really look almost overcome with pleasure, as though the two women had been long-standing friends who had inexplicably lost touch.

'Now I know where you are, I'll call, shall I? I'd love to know how you're getting on. Didn't I tell you there was life *after* …' She left the last word of her sentence unspoken. Abuse, Viola supposed that she meant. So why didn't she say it? What was the use of pretending?

Viola spoke the word. 'Abuse. Yes. There is life afterwards.'

But later, at home, as the vegetables bubbled in the pan, she wondered if she could really claim she had found it. Life.

When she returned to the upstairs flat with the soup and some sandwiches, Viola found an Asian woman in the process of unpacking a holdall.

'Are you Shakira's mother?' she enquired.

'Oh no. I'm Uma, one of the volunteers. You're the lady who lives downstairs? Gwen told me you might come.' She nodded towards the tray. 'Shakira's still asleep, I'm afraid, but we can leave her a note to tell her to pop the soup into the microwave when she's ready.'

'I should have cling-filmed the sandwiches,' said Viola.

'There's probably some in one the drawers. I'll look in a moment,' said Uma. She brought a packet of serviceable Marks and Spencer's underwear, a sweatshirt that looked practically new and a pair of tracksuit bottoms from her bag, followed by some sanitary pads, travel-sized toiletries and a new toothbrush. 'People donate these,' she explained. 'The women run away with literally nothing. A change of clothes and some personal requisites can make all the difference in the first twenty-four hours.'

Viola went into the kitchen and placed the soup on the counter. Uma was right, there was clingfilm in the drawer and she wrapped some around the sandwiches. The other groceries Shakira herself had chosen lay neatly corralled on a little breakfast bar. A torn envelope displayed Gwen's mobile number in large, clear writing.

Uma had closed the curtains more tightly, shutting out the miserable night, and switched on a couple of table lamps that bathed the flat in a warmer and more welcoming light. Now that Viola looked properly, she could see the flat was not in fact as bland as she had at first thought. Here and there were mementoes of previous refugees. One had left a rather accomplished pencil sketch of Southquay pier propped up on a shelf. The settee had an intricate crocheted blanket folded on one arm. Someone else had left a greeting card—the view showing an optimistic sunrise over water—saying simply *Look forward. Dawn is coming.* It was unsigned. Viola supposed the tomato plants and the bird feeder had been someone else's way of offering comfort. Such small signs, insignificant in themselves, but conveying so much. She picked up the blanket and felt its softness against her cheek, imagining the hands that made it; scarred perhaps, or misshapen, trembling and afraid and yet tender enough, with sufficient compassion still remaining to make these million stitches to benefit some other poor soul. Viola found herself unusually moved by the notion. Her eyes filled with tears.

She realised Uma was standing in the doorway, looking on. She, too, was glassy-eyed.

'Were *you* ...' Viola got out.

Uma nodded. 'Oh yes. Many years ago now.'

Viola croaked, 'Me too.'

Uma's sari rustled as she took the four or five strides across the room. She reached out and folded Viola into her arms. Viola was surprised to find how easy it was to be encompassed by such strength and comfort and ... she struggled to identify it ... such *understanding*. She neither sobbed nor trembled, but lay her head on Uma's shoulder, breathing in scents of spice

and jasmine and Persil, as tears poured in an unstoppable torrent from her
eyes.

Chapter Four – Maisie

'Will you come out to dinner with me?'

Oliver Harrington's words catch Maisie by surprise. She is in the front garden of *Old Farm Hall*, tying up a rambling rose to a rather dilapidated old arbour over which she has allowed it to scramble for the past year or so. The arbour had been brought home by Clifford years ago, after one of his visits to a house clearance sale. It was decrepit *then*, but of course Clifford promised to fix it up. 'A few well-placed screws, a bracing piece or two and a good coat of creosote and it'll be good as new,' he'd said, but like so many of his bargain buys, it remained untouched. The arbour has called Clifford so powerfully to her mind that the sudden appearance of Oliver on the drive unnerves her, like being hooked from a dream—or a nightmare—by the cold drench of a jug of water. The two men could not be more different. Clifford had been shy, socially ill-at-ease, curmudgeonly and brusque. Oliver is suave and affable, supremely at home in any social situation, and he is good-looking—something even Maisie couldn't have claimed for Clifford. At the moment, Oliver's dark, wavy hair is glossy with moisture—he must be fresh from the shower—and swept back by designer sunglasses pushed up onto his head. His skin is tanned from the summer's exceptionally hot, dry weather even though as manager of the near-by pub he spends little time outdoors. He wears a short-sleeved shirt, well-pressed, and light chinos. Clifford habitually wore a boiler suit or other workwear, much patched and often daubed with paint.

Maisie lifts her arm to wipe sweat from her forehead, her ball of gardening twine clutched in her gloved hand.

'Gosh, you startled me, Oliver.'

Behind her, men swarm over the house, banging and sawing. Two or three portable stereos blare out different radio stations. Oliver waves his hand in that direction. 'Not surprising,' he says. 'How are the works progressing?'

Oliver has shown a keen interest in the renovations to Maisie's house, taking the time and trouble to listen to the litany of Clifford's attempts at restorative carpentry, plumbing and decoration. He is careful never to place blame for the spectacular lack of progress that prevailed over twenty-odd years. He seems to understand Maisie's vision for the place, and has made one or two excellent suggestions for improvements to her scheme. It was his idea, for instance, that she moves from her usual bedroom and take over the new suite above what used to be the garage. 'It will still be your house,' he had said. 'It's only right you should have the nicest room, and a little privacy might be good from time to time. You deserve a place to retreat to.' Now she thinks about it, it was also Oliver's suggestion they have a downstairs walk-in shower. 'You won't want people trooping through the house in their muddy gardening gear,' he had said, 'and in the *very* distant future an accessible bathroom might be a god-send.' She feels he is "on board" in a way that is reassuring, but also excites her curiosity. After all, what is it to him?

'Oh well, you know,' she says. 'It's hard to see the wood for the trees, sometimes.'

'Is it? In what way?' He takes the half dozen steps across the strip of lawn and perches on the seat of the arbour, ignoring its coating of lichen, which will surely stain his trousers, and the ominous creak it makes as he places his weight on it.

This is the trouble with Oliver. He is sometimes a bit intense, taking even the most casual comment too seriously. Oliver's overtures to her are not unpleasing but they are a bit awkward. She likes him, of course. Who wouldn't? He is gallant, amiable and good-humoured, but he is also something of a force of nature; it is difficult to resist his superior strength of character and he tends to impose his will with a heady cocktail of stubborn chivalry. Also, he is a Harrington, and the Harringtons are a family with whom Maisie has a complicated and not altogether comfortable history. A further complication is that she finds she cannot think of Oliver without thinking also of James Armstrong; the one conjures the other as though they were connected by a piece of elastic. James has all Oliver's charm without any of his bullishness. He is understated whilst Oliver is all brashness and bravado. Once—in a moment of madness—James had kissed her and she responded passionately until they both leapt apart, stunned and awkward at what had happened. James is not free. Of the entire cohort of friends, he is the only one with a spouse still in existence. But his wife, Elspeth, is ill, confined to a home with early onset dementia. Some days, he says, she does not even recognise him. But the fact remains she is his wife and Maisie is not ready to trample on that sacred bond.

Oliver continues to regard her, patting the doubtful wooden slats of the seat next to him. His smile is both confidentially inviting and laced with a kind of imperative that must be obeyed.

She sighs and takes the place he indicates. 'It's all happening at once,' she says. 'There isn't a single room that doesn't have its floorboards up, or its windows out, or isn't being spattered with plaster.'

'But that's a good thing, isn't it? Real progress on every front?'

'Oh yes, but then there are the constant decisions that have to be made. Where will the plug sockets go? Should the light switches be one-way or two-way? What tiles do I want for this *ensuite*? Do I want the same in every *ensuite*? Or different? Then there's the kitchen. I do want a range cooker; it's what I'm used to, and I expect to be catering on a fairly large scale. But then there are the economics of it. An Aga has to be on all the time. Well that's not very cost effective, is it? And if the summers are going to be hot, like this …' She trails off, unsure where this has come from. She has plucked niggles from the back of her mind and presented them to him as though they are major preoccupations. Of course, these things do have to be decided and Trevor refers issues to her several times a day, but they are hardly *problems*.

Oliver steeples his hands and considers. 'The Aga thing doesn't need to be a conundrum. I think you can get an Aga Companion. It looks like an Aga, and it sits alongside as though the two are one and the same, but it works on gas or electric like any regular cooker, so in the summer you can switch the main one off and just use that. Look, I've got the day off. Why don't I follow you back to the Crescent so you can get changed, and then we'll head off to that big outlet village on the bypass? They've got everything there: kitchens, appliances, tiles. There'll be leaflets and what-have-you, and people you can ask. And then, I'll take you out to dinner. What do you say?'

What *can* she say? Or rather, she asks herself as she stows away her gardening tools and pops indoors to tell Trevor she will be out for the rest of the day—why didn't I say, when Oliver had first enquired about the project, 'Fine. Everything is going splendidly, thank you.'? And how can I blame Oliver when he has simply offered a solution to an issue I told him I had?

But the idea of spending the day with Oliver sets off a fizz of something in her stomach. She can't identify it. It is delightful to have the attention of a man like Oliver, and she knows she will enjoy herself. But she is conscious of an undercurrent in his intentions. She has known since her garden party that he has an agenda and she is not sure she shares it.

Back at the Crescent she makes a brief explanation to Minnie, who is working on some zips and hems sent by the dry cleaners.

'I suppose you wouldn't like to come?' she asks.

But Minnie indicates her work. 'Not today.'

Maisie takes a quick shower and is grateful for her accommodating hair, which falls easily into style with only a quick whizz of the hairdryer and a hurried comb-through with her fingers. She pulls on some cool linen trousers and a loose *broderie Anglaise* top, then thrusts her feet into a pair of comfortable sandals. When she gets to the turn in the stair, Oliver is waiting in the hall below, his hand on the newel post as he gazes up at her. He does not speak, but his eyes pour torrents of words into the mote-dancing air, and as she descends the last flight, he lifts his hand to take hers. It is impossible not to understand him, and yet Maisie endeavours to do so with an artificial, 'Thank you, kind sir,' and a silly attempt at a curtsey, as though they were actors in a Regency romance.

Oliver bends to whisper, 'Ready, then?' into her ear. He lets go of her hand and skips past her to open the front door, lifting her handbag from a bureau as he passes.

'I should check I've got my—' Maisie begins.

'No need, it's all in there. I had a quick peek. Purse, phone, keys, tissues. All present and correct. And I put your sunglasses in there too. They were on the counter in the kitchen and I thought you'd probably need them.'

His gallantry, which sweeps her out of the door and ushers her into the car, his deft handling of the seatbelt, the thrill of being in an open-topped classic sports car with a handsome man, are all marred by a sense of disquiet.

He looked in her handbag?

Perhaps it is an old-fashioned notion but Maisie has the idea that to look in a woman's handbag—and especially for a man to do so—is taboo. What else did she have in there? Tampons, just in case. And that tiny, folded bit of paper with her PIN, in case she ever forgets it. And it troubles her that he knows her so well as to identify exactly the items she habitually takes everywhere.

As they drive down the Crescent and turn left, away from the town and onto the bypass, as the onslaught of breeze and countryside smells assault her, as her hair is whipped around her face and the engine under the bonnet snarls, Maisie finds herself sitting rigidly in her seat, grasping her bag with both hands.

Oliver drives competently, overtaking lorries and double-declutching to tackle the steep inclines, putting the classic car through its paces. Neither of them speaks; the roar of the engine and the buffeting of air would have made it difficult. Oliver's eyes are inscrutable behind the lenses of his sunglasses and, almost resentfully, Maisie reaches into her bag to put her own sunglasses on, noticing the small smile playing round the corner of Oliver's mouth.

Presently, as they wait at some traffic lights, he turns his head towards her. 'Is everything alright?'

Maisie nods, but adds, 'I don't think you should look in a lady's handbag, Oliver.'

His expression is unreadable. Only the slight lift of his sunglasses indicates the raising of his eyebrows—but whether he is surprised, offended or amused, she cannot tell. Then the lights change and he turns his attention back to the road with a shrug. 'Ok.'

His reaction wrong-foots her. She feels prim and ungrateful. After all, he had only wanted to make sure she had everything she needed. He had been looking after her, and who could complain about that?

Maisie cannot deny enjoying the day. Once they are in the kitchen showroom, the matter of the handbag is forgotten as they tour the various displays, discussing the pros and cons not only of the different models of cookers on offer—and the wide range of accessories—but also the configuration of cupboards, the optimum distance between fridge and sink, and the suitability of different kinds of cookware. Maisie is to have everything new; her old crockery and utensils, serving dishes and saucepans have all been recycled or sent to charity shops. They had not been new when she had got them, often being scavenged from car boot sales by Clifford or bought as job lots from auctions. Not that there is anything wrong with second-hand goods, but this renovation is about new beginnings and Maisie means to begin afresh in every way.

Oliver is the epitome of patience as Maisie picks up items to examine them, questions the sales assistants and collects leaflets to show Minnie later. She is offered—and accepts—a free kitchen design, making an appointment for a salesman to call the following week to measure up and advise. Maisie gives her name and address and later, when the assistant refers to Oliver as 'Mr Wilde,' she can reply with a laugh that is nearly free of discomfiture and almost without a blush, 'Oh! This isn't my husband. This is just a friend.'

Oliver laughs at the assistant's error too, but his jokey, 'I should be so lucky,' rings a vaguely perplexing note.

The afternoon wears on as they visit bathroom showrooms and tile warehouses also situated on the site, as well as—at Oliver's insistence—

clothing and shoe stores. He hovers at a distance as she fingers the fabric of summer dresses and looks at swimwear. An emerald-green two-piece tempts her, but she eventually rejects it, saying, 'It isn't as though I have a holiday planned.' She tries on and buys some sandals though, and it is almost five o'clock before they emerge from the last shop, loaded down with boutique carrier bags, plus samples and brochures. Oliver places everything in the little boot of the car before they drive off again, back on the bypass but not in the direction of Millport.

'Where are we going?' Maisie enquires.

But Oliver throws her an enigmatic smile and says, 'Are you warm enough? There's a blanket in the back if you need it.'

The day is still warm and Maisie shakes her head. 'Later, perhaps, on our way home,' she says.

'I might not take you home,' says Oliver, mischievously, like a man testing the ice before he stands on it. 'I might whisk you away to my secret castle and lock you in.'

She smiles, joining in the game. 'I think you'll find there'll be a search party,' she says. 'You won't be able to keep me prisoner for long.' James Armstrong comes, unbidden, to her mind, but she replaces him with Gareth, her soldier-son, and even poor Dominic, her other son, who hasn't a heroic bone in his body and yet, she feels, would battle dragons to rescue her. Then she laughs at herself; her daughter Frances is more indomitable, determined and combative than either of the boys.

'Oh, you mean the cardiganed crusaders?' Oliver scoffs, and Maisie feels a stab of resentment that he should refer to her friends so scathingly. 'I don't see Miss Snow scaling the walls of my keep very easily,' he goes on. 'I suppose Gloria might overpower the sentries with her perfume.'

'Oliver!' cries Maisie. 'That's going too far.'

'Oh,' he says, 'you know I'm only in jest. A worthier group of women couldn't be found. Now then, I hope you're hungry. I know I am.'

Their destination is Bellborough, a town some distance away. The place is of historical note, with cobbled streets and ancient, timbered buildings whose upper floors lean together conspiratorially. Tourists still roam the pavements even though most of the shops are closed. In the market square the stall holders stow their unsold wares into vans.

Oliver negotiates the maze of narrow streets with ease and miraculously finds a parking space beneath the castle walls.

'Is this where I'm to be imprisoned?' Maisie asks, as he helps her from the car. The place is all-but ruined, with a roofless keep and various tumbles of stone indicating former structures, long since collapsed.

Oliver seems to consider, implying the idea has come fresh from her, and was not his own suggestion half an hour before. 'If you like. Although there are probably more comfortable lodgings, if you *want* to stay.' He looks up and down the street, as though there is a serious possibility they might decide to book in somewhere for the night, as though Maisie, in her enquiry, has indicated she is open to the idea, if he is. He points to a hanging sign halfway down the street. 'That place, the Orb and Sceptre, is supposed to be pretty good. It's an old coaching inn, but run now by a chain. Very high-end. Very discreet.'

'Discreet?!' Maisie throws out, half-appalled at the direction the conversation is taking them. Does he mean it's a no-questions-asked knocking shop? A place where business executives might take their secretaries? Nothing could disgust her more.

He beetles an eyebrow. 'I mean,' he says patiently, 'that their management of the place is discreet. You wouldn't know it's part of a chain. They work hard to maintain the individual character of each place they own. A bit like James does with his pubs. Each one is unique.'

Maisie wishes Oliver had not mentioned James. His name invokes his image, creating a comparison that is unfair to Oliver and unworthy of Maisie herself. 'And is that where we're going?' she says, too brightly, feeling caught out. Oliver's ability to throw her off balance really is unnerving. Her state of mind now is so different from earlier, while they were looking around the shops. Then they had been easy and chummy. Now there is an undercurrent Maisie can't fathom.

'No,' he says, tucking her arm into the crook of his elbow. It is a trait of his, this taking of her arm. On the face of it, it's a gentlemanly gesture, indicating his readiness to give aid, to lead, that she can lean on him if she needs to. It is more formal than the taking of a hand and less intimate—less possessive?—than the wrapping of an arm around her shoulder. Even so, she feels it is something of a presumption. She doesn't need his aid, although it goes without saying that she expects him to lead, as otherwise she has no clue of their destination. She ponders this as she finds herself trotting by his side, almost helplessly borne along the *olde worlde* streets of the town. She tells herself it is merely a gesture of friendship; that if Gloria, say, were to take her arm, there would be no ambiguity in the gesture at all. So why does it feel different with Oliver?

Her answer comes just a few moments later. They walk along the street for some few yards and then turn sharply into an alley. The entrance is low and Oliver has to duck his head. They are forced to walk close together as he does not relinquish her arm so she can go before or after him. And then he slips his arm around her. 'Watch that wall,' he warns, pulling her away from its uneven brick, and closer into his side. 'It's rough. It will graze your arm.'

Their progress is further impeded by a man pushing a bicycle towards them. Abruptly, Oliver presses her against the wall—its roughness notwithstanding—shielding her with his bulk as man and bike go by. Oliver's body is firm and warm, and she can smell washing powder and cologne. With her face against his chest she feels his quick, ragged breathing. His hands, one on her shoulder, the other in the small of her back, are warm, and Maisie is conscious, in spite of herself, of an answering flutter in her belly.

Even after the man disappears through the mouth of the alleyway, still they stand, locked in an embrace that is awkward but also intense.

'Maisie …' Oliver's voice is low. His hips move against her, perhaps accidentally, to reposition his feet, which are either side of hers, but perhaps—and which Maisie, at the moment, feels more likely—exerting a deliberately sexual pressure.

Her voice will not come. She swallows, trying to free her throat of whatever impediment prevents it. Her own arms hang limp at her sides. If I want this, I need only raise my arms, place a hand on his back and exert the smallest pressure of encouragement. Do I want it? That *he* does is now beyond doubt.

… or almost beyond doubt, for in the space of her indecision he releases her and, in a voice that is level and ordinary, says, 'I think you'll like it here. The food is excellent, very authentic. It's run by an Italian couple. Their *arancini* is the best I've ever tasted.'

Maisie flounders in Oliver's wake as he marches towards the end of the passageway and thanks her lucky stars she didn't make any gesture which, it now seems, would have been inappropriate.

The alley opens into a charming courtyard, with tables set out between tubs of flowers beneath a vine-smothered pergola. By now it is dusk and, in any case, this sequestered little yard would hardly get much sun. Lights, hidden amongst the foliage, twinkle prettily and there are candles on the tables. From somewhere there comes the sound of running water and, emanating from within the small restaurant, are strains of violin music and the mouth-watering aromas of garlic and dough. There are already diners at the tables and Maisie, discomfited from the oddness of their clinch in the alleyway, entertains a sudden doubt that, with the town so busy, they will get a table. The awkwardness of wandering the town with Oliver in search of dinner would be intolerable. He would be embarrassed by his lack of forethought— and she realises, she is ravenously hungry.

'I made a booking,' says Oliver, as if reading her thoughts. 'Just in case you were free.' He looks at his watch. 'And we're right on time.'

Later, as she lies in her bed in the house in the Crescent, Maisie can't sleep. The Crescent is a quiet, very exclusive road and Minnie's house backs on to the golf course, beyond which is the sea. Often at her own house, Maisie listens to the roar of distant traffic and makes-believe it is the rumble of surf pounding onto shingle. It is a knack she has—some would call it a gift—of making the best out of every situation. It has served her well over the years. There have been times when her life was unspeakably bleak. But a determined, cup-half-full attitude has seen her over many a crevasse, ironing what to others might have been insurmountable difficulties into navigable terrain. One of those helpful strategies is an ability to look at things from other people's point of view. Thus she became Clifford's acolyte, seeing potential and possibility where he saw it, but then allowing herself to be bamboozled—as he was—by the number of solutions to every problem which had hampered him in just choosing one and getting on with it. As a result the frustration of her situation had been lessened, and the acrimonious arguments they might have had over the stalemate had been averted. She had chosen to be as ardently sure as he was that, somehow, things in their malfunctioning home would one day come right. And, in the end, she was justified, although what Clifford would make of this end-game is a decidedly moot point.

Maisie thinks over her evening with Oliver. Other than the awkwardness in the little alleyway, the time had passed swiftly and pleasantly. They had spoken of … she casts her mind back … the renovations, the food—he had been right about the *arancini*—and the suddenness of Viola's decision to stay with her son. Oddly, Oliver has told her nothing of himself. She supposes that, like most men, he is reluctant to open up, to speak of his feelings, but if he wishes to take their friendship to another level—and, on the ambiguous evidence she has, that is a big 'if'—she thinks it is peculiar he has not shared with her something of his past, something of the 'real' Oliver Harrington.

She guesses him to be about her own age, which is forty-seven. Lots of men have been married and divorced once or even twice by that time but there is no indication Oliver has ever been married or had a significant romantic relationship. He certainly never mentions an ex. She knows he spent time in the merchant navy. Perhaps that was not conducive to long-term relationships, although some men manage it. The only other thing she knows about Oliver for certain is that of his two sisters, one—Elspeth—is married to James Armstrong but is now in a home suffering from dementia. The other sister, Louisa—to whom Oliver was particularly attached—died tragically young, a long way from home. She had needed help but Oliver's father had refused it. As a result, Oliver and his father are estranged. Maisie surmises old Mr Harrington was a domineering presence in the family home. His wife had also suffered mental illness and been shut up in an institution by the time Oliver was ten years of age. Maisie imagines family life could not have been happy for Oliver but she doubts any of these things are sufficient explanation for why Oliver himself has apparently avoided marriage or any significant personal relationship. There are signs he is re-evaluating his single status but the signs are muddled, and Maisie does not trust herself to read them correctly. Once or twice—in the hallway, for example, and again in the alley—she had been almost sure he was on the cusp of a declaration or a gesture from which there would be no going back, but each time he seemed to back off. Perhaps he has been waiting for some encouragement?

She turns over in the bed, pushing the sheets down. The window is open and a small breeze riffles the curtain but the room is hot, she is hot with a prickling heat that is almost an itch. Of course, she must not assume Oliver has a serious relationship on his mind. If he has an agenda at all it might not be anything other than a friendly sexual liaison. Friends with benefits, she thinks it is called. Not to judge anyone, but he has misunderstood me entirely if he thinks I would be party to anything like that.

I haven't been widowed twelve months yet. Perhaps it's too soon to consider a new relationship. On the other hand, those few months of widowhood have seen exponential change in me, in terms of my situation, my outlook and, yes, probably in my appearance. Before, with Clifford, there wasn't the time or the money … and frankly, I had no motivation to dress well, to have my hair done or to wear even the small touches of makeup that I do now. These things make me happy. Perhaps it's that happiness that Oliver likes.

On balance, she *is* happy, notwithstanding her widowhood. It is just strange that the scales should be so evenly weighted. Her well of loss has been amply filled. Accepting that fact, though, threatens to pull the plug on it. It can't be right, can it?

Sick of tossing and turning, and in an attempt to get away from the inferno of heat that seems intent on melting her bones, she gets out of the bed and opens the curtains in order to admit more breeze. The moon has set and Minnie's garden is in darkness. On the far horizon Maisie thinks she can see the first, dim paling of dawn.

She finds her mind dragged back to the topic of Oliver. The real question is, do I like *him?* Well of course I do. Who wouldn't? And naturally it is flattering to be singled out by a man like Oliver. It would be easy to be swept off her feet by him; he is a man seemingly so certain of himself that it would be hard to mount a credible opposition and she is not sure right now that she wants to. She indulges herself in a fantasy, imagining that, on their way home along the almost deserted bypass, in an area of dense forest, he had pulled the car into one of several parking and picnic areas that give access to forest trails and mountain-biking routes. It would have been almost impenetrably dark and, of course, there would have been no other cars. The scent of the pine forest would be intense, the stars visible in the circle of velvet sky above the secluded little glade. What if he had reached across to her? What if he had kissed her? She allows herself to imagine it; the softness of his lips on hers, then, perhaps, his tongue in her mouth. She thinks of his hands—large hands, he has, always clean and nicely manicured—undoing the buttons of her *broderie Anglaise* blouse and touching her breasts. The heat that had assailed her in the bed now scorches her again. In the darkness, she is blushing. She stands with her hands on the window ledge, consumed by heat but also shivering in her thin nightdress as she permits the reel of her daydream to unspool in the private gloom of her room. Skipping over the impracticalities—the tiny interior of the car, the bulk of Oliver's six-foot frame, the impediments of gear stick and hand brake, the sheer impossibility of shedding clothes unless one had the suppleness of a yogi—she imagines their two bodies, naked. She chooses to believe him a very skilled and generous lover. She allows her hand to lift the hem of her nightdress.

Afterwards, she does not upbraid herself. A confidential chat with Gloria a few weeks earlier had enlightened and exonerated her. Gloria called it "a widow's easement," and had a drawer full of luridly coloured appliances for its achievement. Maisie lies in the bed, satiated and cool, feeling that now sleep will come, only vaguely troubled by the remembrance that, at the peak of her expiation, it was not Oliver Harrington's face she had seen in her mind's eye. It was James Armstrong's.

A few days later, the ladies gather at one of their favourite cafés, located within a large garden centre. The café is in a pleasant, glazed atrium with windows on three sides. Today, another glorious day, bi-fold doors are wide open to admit what small amount of breeze is available, and ceiling blinds provide shade. As always, the place is busy, mainly with older couples and groups of females much like their own. The hubbub of conversation melds with the clatter of cutlery on plates and, in the background, the shriek of the coffee machine as it dispenses drinks.

Minnie, along with Amy in her wheelchair, are deployed to save a table while Gwen and the others queue for food and beverages.

Minnie moves some abandoned crockery to a kitchen trolley and manoeuvres an adjacent table so there will be room for them all. 'There,' she says, wiping at a spill on the table with a spare napkin. 'They must be short-staffed today. You don't usually see things left on the tables, do you?'

'No,' says Amy, unbuttoning her cardigan, 'and it isn't even the school holidays yet. I notice we are favoured with Gwen's company today.'

'Oh, don't be like that, Amy,' scolds Minnie. 'Let's just enjoy the outing. Do you want to take that cardigan off? Shall I help you? You mustn't overheat.'

'Oh no,' Amy says. 'I'll be alright. There's actually quite a refreshing breeze just here.' In spite of her words, Amy continues to fiddle with her cardigan. At last she says, 'But no Val? I expected her to become a regular member of the group now she and Gwen are—'

'She's kept ever so busy at the farm,' says Minnie quickly. 'She isn't a lady of leisure, like us.'

Amy objects. 'You're hardly a lady of leisure. You're still doing your sewing, aren't you, when you're not at the citadel?'

'The citadel isn't work,' says Minnie. 'I enjoy it. And I like to feel useful.'

Amy makes a moue. 'It's a long time since I was of use to anyone,' she laments.

'It's no use feeling sorry for yourself,' says Minnie. 'If you're missing Gwen's company perhaps you'd consider becoming one of our befrienders. You'd only need to talk to people. You could do that, couldn't you? Very often, the people who come to the citadel are just lonely. Of course they need a meal and a shower. Sometimes they need medical advice. But often as not they just want someone to talk to.'

'I couldn't talk to them about God. Isn't that the idea? You wait until they're at the end of their tethers and then you introduce religion as the panacea to all their troubles?'

'Oh no,' says Minnie. 'I never knew you were such a cynic! We try to *demonstrate* God's love but we never preach about it.'

'Mmm,' Amy quirks a doubtful eyebrow. 'Aren't homeless people all drunks or drug addicts or suffering from mental illnesses? I'm sure they all smell. You know I can't abide that. I'll happily make a donation, if it will help.'

'Oh yes.' Minnie sighs. 'Of course. We always need funds.'

The others arrive burdened with trays.

'The soup today was carrot and coriander,' says Gwen to Amy, 'so I dithered over that because I know you like it. But in the end I got you a panini instead. Did I do right?'

'You did. It's too hot for soup,' says Amy, adding, in a tone of martyrdom, 'But anything will do for me.'

'I got soup,' says Gloria, sliding her bowl on to the table, sloshing some over the edge. 'I'm trying to cut down on carbs or I'll never fit into the suit I've bought for Maisie's wedding.'

Maisie slams her tray down. It holds her own lunch as well as Minnie's, a pot of tea for them both and all the accompanying paraphernalia that goes with it. The teapot, near the edge of the tray, had been burning her thumb while the woman behind the counter painstakingly counted out cucumber slices. Then, for some reason, Maisie's contactless payment failed and she'd had to fiddle in her purse to find her PIN. The delay held up the queue, making Maisie uncomfortable.

'It isn't *my* wedding,' she objects, more sharply than intended. She shuffles things around on the table to make room and with a bump accidentally spills yet more of Gloria's soup.

'Careful, Maisie!' Gloria leaps to her feet in an overly dramatic gesture—there is no danger of her being scalded.

Minnie implements the napkin again and Maisie says, 'Sorry,' but crossly.

They settle to their food. Amy laboriously decants all the filling from her panini, pushing the bread to one side.

'You might as well have had the salad,' Gwen remarks. 'I wish you'd been more specific about what you wanted, Amy.'

'I'm not fussy,' Amy says. 'I told you—anything will do for me.'

'But it's so wasteful,' Minnie chimes in. 'And the panini was at least a pound more than a salad would have been.'

Amy glares at Minnie. 'It's my pound, isn't it? Now, if you don't mind, I'll eat my lunch.'

Maisie toys with her food. She's chosen quiche. It looks pallid and unappetising. The atmosphere around the table is tainted and her thumb is throbbing from where it was pressed against the scalding teapot.

Gwen says, 'You're out of sorts, Maisie dear. Is anything wrong?'

'No! Nothing at all!' The forced brightness fools no one; not even herself.

'Trouble in paradise, I expect,' says Amy, under her breath.

Gloria is all ears. 'What do you mean?'

'Yes, what *do* you mean, Amy?' Maisie echoes the remark through a clenched jaw.

Amy blinks, a specious attempt at innocence. 'Oh! Nothing. Only … a little bird told me you were out on a hot date the other night.'

'A little bird …?' Maisie glowers at Minnie.

'I didn't say anything about a date, hot or otherwise,' Minnie declares, but with a blush. Then stammers, 'It … it wasn't a secret, was it?'

'Clearly not,' Maisie fumes, pushing her plate to one side. Her appetite is completely gone.

'Who was the lucky man?' Gloria's glutinously mascaraed eyes are agog.

'Oliver took me to look at some range cookers. Really! Talk about making a mountain out of a molehill!'

'The lady doth protest too much, methinks,' mutters Amy.

Gloria sniggers. 'Do tell *all*, Maisie. I want every juicy detail.'

Maisie is conscious of an angry panic that has been mounting in her since the fuss at the servery, but she attempts to laugh it off. 'Nothing happened,' she assures them. 'We looked at kitchens. Also tiles and flooring. I have all the brochures and some samples, if you don't believe me.'

'And then he drove you all the way to Bellborough for a romantic dinner in an Italian restaurant,' Amy crows.

Minnie blushes to the roots of her hair. 'I didn't say it was romantic,' she falters. Her eyes ooze apologetic dismay at Maisie.

'Oh, but I bet it was,' coos Gloria.

Maisie presses her lips into a narrow line. How could Minnie gossip behind my back? And why can't I laugh the whole thing off. Gwen's right, I'm *not* myself today. Tears press against her eyes.

'Oh stop it, all of you,' says Gwen. 'Can't you see you're upsetting her? I'm sure there's nothing to tell.'

'Whereas *you* have plenty to tell,' Gloria puts in, turning abruptly from Maisie and fixing a gooey eye on Gwen instead. 'If anyone has a romantic story, it's you. Tell us the lurid details.'

Amy shudders. 'Oh no, please *don't.*'

Gwen dabs her mouth with a napkin and then folds it carefully into a square. 'Oh dear,' she says to no one in particular. 'It looks like this heat is getting to us all. My appetite is quite spoilt.'

They sit in silence for a time, avoiding one another's eyes. Gloria, frustrated on both fronts, retrieves a compact and repairs her lipstick. Gwen feigns interest in a family with a small baby at another table.

Minnie reaches for the teapot and asks in a small voice, 'More tea, Maisie?'

Maisie shakes her head. She has suppressed the tears but is still struggling to contain emotion that threatens to spill over at any minute—a senseless fury almost amounting to rage, and over such a silly thing.

After a few moments Gwen drags her eyes from the baby and says, 'What colour is your suit, Gloria? Is it the cerise one you showed me in the catalogue?'

'No. They didn't have it in my size so in the end I went for Rose Quartz. It's linen, so it will crease to buggery, but it has such an elegant jacket and I have a hat that—'

The magma of Maisie's irritation suddenly erupts. 'Oh! For the love of God!' She pushes her chair back and stands abruptly. Her hands grip the table but her body is trembling so violently that the crockery chimes. With visible effort, she masters herself sufficiently to say, 'Excuse me. I think … I just need to …' but no further explanation will come. She grabs her bag and rushes from the restaurant.

The others look after her in concern.

'She's been out of sorts for days,' Minnie discloses. 'In a daydream half the time, and then all snappy. It isn't like her at all.'

'No, it isn't,' Gwen says. 'Do you think one of us should go after her?'

'It could be sexual frustration,' Gloria offers in a tone that manages to be both straightforward and salacious.

'Or a broken heart,' Amy adds. 'I wonder if she … you know … and then he turned her down.'

They all consider the likelihood of this.

'I think she's just got a lot on her plate at the moment,' opines Gwen at last. 'All the work on the house, and then the daughter's wedding. Plus, almost immediately afterwards the bride and groom are going to live abroad, aren't they? That can't be easy to face.'

'Let's just leave her alone for a while,' says Minnie. 'She'll enjoy some time alone amongst the plants. I wish Viola was here. No one makes a tour of a garden centre more interesting than Viola, do they? I'm sure she could take Maisie's mind off things.'

Gwen's gaze slides away, but she says nothing.

Maisie walks aimlessly around the plant displays, hardly seeing them. The staff are busy watering the stock and trying to tidy the few remaining pots of annuals so they look as though they have some life still in them, as though the summer is not half over, as though the longest day and Frances's wedding is not hurtling like a meteorite towards them. To prove the mendacity of the illusion, potted up chrysanthemums—the classic autumn annual—are already on display.

Maisie passes, unseeing, through the area dedicated to fruit trees and hedging plants, past another with troughs and planters stacked on pallets, to a far precinct of the place where there are garden buildings, sheds, summerhouses and the like. There is no one about and, almost in a daze, she enters the shade of one of the buildings, which is furnished as a home office, with some cane furniture and a desk with a fake computer. She sinks down onto a settee. Her rage has expiated somewhat and she finds, away from the clamour of the restaurant and the insinuations of her friends, she can think more clearly.

It is unbelievable to her that Gloria has also chosen apricot—as nearly apricot as dammit—for her wedding outfit. What surprises Maisie even more, the other women who also plan to wear variations on the same shade have not cottoned on. Well, that's their business and I have enough on my plate. It feels like a conspiracy, but that's unreasonable. How could any of them have known, since I've been so reticent about my mother-of-the-bride getup? No, it's just one of those coincidences that happens sometimes. I'll have to return my own costume to the shop and choose something else. Thankfully, I didn't remove the labels, so there shouldn't be an issue. The thing was expensive, surely the boutique will have a reasonable returns policy. Perhaps they will have the same *ensemble*, but in a different colour? But the shoes and the fascinator were both bought online. I doubt they can be returned.

Maisie has no idea what style Frances's wedding dress will be. Minnie made the dresses for the whole bridal party but at Frances's insistence Maisie has not been allowed to see them. They are swathed in tissue and zipped into garment bags in one of Minnie's spare rooms. Maisie is strictly debarred from peeking.

It's all so annoying. Maisie closes her eyes and leans back against the comfortable cushion of the settee. But then the whole wedding is a source of … not annoyance, but certainly of frustration. Frances has been relentless in keeping me at arm's length, not consulting me about the venue, the menu, the cake, the cars—I suppose there will be some kind of transport provided for the wedding party—the flowers … Even my offer of funds was refused. I haven't been asked to give the speech which Clifford would have made, if he'd been here. Maisie had been pleased when Frances—deploring any archaic notion she is a chattel to be "given away"—had allocated her brother Dominic the role of walking her down the aisle, although it had occurred to Maisie that she could have done it. It would have demonstrated the closeness between her daughter and herself. But the truth is that really there isn't much closeness between herself and Frances, try as Maisie might to negotiate her daughter's awkward angles and to forgive her tendency to look down on her mother with what can only be described as scorn. Perhaps the sad truth is I will never recover from those years of drudgery, the restrictedness of life with Clifford. To Frances—used as she is to the rarefied tenor of academia, the brightest and best minds, I must seem so parochial, so dull and dim. It would explain why I was denied even the smallest concession in the matters of wedding-planning. All my ideas for the wedding—no doubt very old-fashioned—were rejected out of hand. My dream of a traditional, white, church wedding for my daughter is exactly what Frances *doesn't* want.

Maybe it would be better if I *am* lost amongst the flotilla of peach-, apricot-, orange-blossom-, coral- and rose-quartz-wearing women? Then Frances will be relieved to be able to wave an arm vaguely in my direction and say, 'My mother? Oh, over there, in that insipid shade of anaemic shrimp.'

But this fleeting moment of self-pity is swiftly followed by anger. It isn't fair. Whatever shrinking violet I may have been in the past has now been replaced by this new genre of myself—not parochial, dull or dim. This realisation is made more irksome by the fact that Maxim's mother, the redoubtable mother-of-the-groom Mrs Fothergill, has been permitted one dispensation after another. Frances's original idea—a brief and informal registry office ceremony followed by a meal at a pub—was utterly eroded in favour of what Mrs Fothergill augustly described as "proper protocol". The registry office has been replaced by the college chapel, the meal at a pub is now to be a grand wedding breakfast in the great hall of the college, and photographs are to be taken in the college quadrangle which, Maisie knows, will be beautifully abloom with a hundred different rose cultivars. All in all, for a wedding that was to have been simple and business-like, it is shaping up to be rather a sophisticated affair—which is why, Maisie concludes in misery, the matter of the dress is so important. Plus, Mrs Fothergill is clearly an appallingly superior and overbearing woman. Maisie has yet to meet her and—to tell the truth—rather fears doing so. How can I begin to compete? If I'm not careful, I will be swept entirely into the shadows. And I've only just escaped from those, so I'm damned if I'm going back!

It ought to be a comfort that her friends will be with her. She won't be left to flounder while the dons and professors hold hifalutin conversations over her head. But then doubt creeps in. Gloria can be so flirtatious. Maisie has a fleeting image of her blonded, overly made-up friend draped over an Oxford Fellow. Surely, she wouldn't ... would she? And poor farmer Val will be so out of place. And Viola ... oh dear. I hope there won't be too much free wine. But then, mercifully, she thinks of the men: of Oliver, who is adept in any situation, and James. She reminds herself that the gaggle of widows will not be let loose without some tempering, restraining influence.

Reluctantly—because it is so quiet and comfortable in the summerhouse— Maisie opens her eyes and peers at her watch. She isn't sure what time was when she stormed from the restaurant or how long she has been sitting in the secluded little arbour, but it has done her good. Her demons are identified even if they aren't defeated. Practically speaking, there is nothing to be done about them; they must be accepted. It is a pointless waste of energy to allow them to disturb her peace.

The ladies reconvene in the area of the garden centre that sells fancy kitchenalia. Maisie finds them mulling over a matching toaster and kettle as a potential gift for Frances and Maxim.

'You mustn't think of buying them a gift,' she admonishes, when she realises their intention. 'Especially not anything bulky. Remember, they'll be off to Tokyo at the end of June, and the accommodation they'll move into will be equipped with everything they'll need.'

'Will they live at the Embassy?' Gloria wonders aloud. 'I imagine it's beautiful.'

Maisie isn't quite sure, and she says so. 'Maxim will be the most junior flunkey. Just one of those suited men you see on news reports who follows the ambassador around carrying a briefcase and looking solemn.'

'But we can't go empty-handed,' says Gwen. 'That would just be rude. Don't they have a gift list? Some couples set them up at department stores.'

'I really don't know,' says Maisie, feeling wretched again. 'They haven't told me anything of their plans. Maxim's mother seems to have taken over the whole thing.'

Gwen places a sympathetic arm round Maisie's shoulders. 'That must be hurtful, Maisie,' she says. 'No wonder you're feeling upset.'

Gwen's kindness almost sets Maisie off again, so she squares her shoulders and says, 'I'll try and find something out for you. As a last resort, if you really insist on giving something, perhaps gift vouchers might be best. Now, I need a birthday card. It's my grandson Theo's first birthday next week.' She bustles off in the direction of the gift department. While perusing the cards, Maisie picks up a wedding card too—a plain, unadorned card with simple wording she hopes will not offend too much.

When she gets to the till she notices Gwen has moved off to one side and is deep in conversation on her mobile phone.

Maisie joins Amy in the queue. 'She's speaking to Val,' says Amy darkly. 'Sounds as though something's wrong.'

'Oh dear,' says Maisie, groping for her bank card. 'I hope it isn't anything serious.'

All she can hear of Gwen's side of the conversation is a stream of placatory phrases. 'I see,' she says several times and then, 'Yes. No, of course not,' and finally a whole sequence of soothing but wordless noises, 'Mmm. Ahhh. Oooh,' which eventually resolve themselves with a brisk, 'I'll be right over. Just sit tight.'

She dumps her basket of unpaid-for shopping unceremoniously onto an unoccupied checkout and marches over to Amy. 'I'm sorry, I can't run you home. Maisie, can you fit Amy in your car? Only, oh dear, something's happened at the farm and I have to get straight over.'

'Yes, of course,' says Maisie, 'only, what can have happened?'

Gwen waves the question away. 'I can't tell you now.' She bends down to Amy in her wheelchair. 'I'm so sorry, Amy,' she says. 'You must know that only an emergency would—'

But Amy only shrugs and continues to decant her goods onto the checkout from the basket balanced on her knee. 'You go, Gwen. I'm sure Val's need is greater than mine. I'll be alright with Maisie, even if she has to leave my chair behind and come back for it later.'

Gwen throws Maisie an anguished look but turns and is out of the garden centre at a half-run.

Maisie finds Amy's jibe about the wheelchair rather spiteful and wholly unnecessary. 'There'll be no problem about your chair, Amy. I don't know why you said that.'

The assistant finishes scanning Amy's shopping and packs it into a bag for her. Amy proffers her card and then makes a fuss about stowing it away in her bag. When at last she does look up her eyes are a-swim with tears. The rummaging in the handbag was a search for a handkerchief, which Amy now presses to her wrinkled old cheek. 'So disappointing,' she gets out. 'I was so looking forward to a nice afternoon with her, just the two of us. I'd bought a new jigsaw, and some macaroons to have with our tea. They're Gwen's favourites, you know—'

'Oh, Amy,' Maisie cries, bending awkwardly to gather her into a gentle hug, 'don't be upset. I know I'm a poor substitute but I have nothing at all to do for the rest of the day and I *love* macaroons.'

It isn't true that Maisie has nothing planned for what remains of the day. Now that she is living at Minnie's house she is trying to get that garden in order, in addition to maintaining her own. Trevor Vine will probably have a list of queries for her about the building works and she hasn't yet had a chance to go through the brochures she collected from the kitchen showroom in anticipation of the visit from the designer, which she thinks is a few days away although the actual date and time escape her just now. And of course, she must also return to the boutique to exchange her outfit. But she can hardly abandon Amy at her door when she's this upset. Clearly Amy is feeling lonelier since Gwen took up with Val and with Viola away. She was quite unwell a few months earlier and it is something of a miracle that, frail as she is, she managed to recover. All these things considered, Maisie resigns herself to an afternoon of jigsaws and macaroons.

Minnie asks to be dropped at home on the way to Amy's. 'Dolly's been on her own quite long enough,' she says, so it is just Maisie and Amy who settle into the lounge of the flat.

Amy says, 'Pull the curtains across will you? The sun is blinding today.' She sinks deeper into her chair and closes her eyes while Maisie, in the gloom, unpacks the few things Amy bought at the garden centre. Although she herself has absolutely no desire for it, she makes a pot of tea and arranges the macaroons onto a china plate.

It seems today's outing—or perhaps today's emotion—has tired Amy, who sits immobile and seemingly in a doze while Maisie busies herself. Even the sound of the tea tray being placed on a small table adjacent to Amy's chair does not rouse her. Maisie lowers herself into another armchair and wonders what she should do. There are so many matters needing her attention. She really doesn't have time to waste here while Amy sleeps. Perhaps she ought to just slip away. She could pop some clingfilm over the macaroons.

But then, with her eyes still closed, Amy speaks. 'Of course, I've always known about Gwen.'

'About Gwen?' Maisie repeats. Her voice is hushed, the dimness of the room somehow lending it a rarefied, sacred air.

'Yes. I've always known she is gay.'

Amy does not open her eyes and Maisie wonders if this is a dialogue Amy is really having with herself, a means by which she can come to some kind of acceptance of Gwen's new friendship with Val. Amy's face seems at rest, but in the shadow of the curtained room, it is difficult to tell for certain.

So Maisie just says, 'Oh, yes?'

'For a start,' Amy says, 'she has never shown the least interest in men. I don't know if you've noticed, but when the rest of us banter about which film actors we like, Gwen never joins in. Many years ago, she and I went on holidays for single people. Of course, the words "lonely hearts" were never spoken, but, essentially that was the idea. Gwen had her chances—let me say that—with quite nice chaps, but she was never interested.'

Maisie makes no reply, but shifts in her chair, settling in to listen.

'It's obvious, really,' Amy goes on. 'She's so capable, isn't she? And reliable. Not that those qualities are restricted to men, of course! And … well, I suppose it's a cliché … but she's very masculine in her ways. I mean, her dress and so on, but also her mannerisms.'

'I suppose so,' Maisie murmurs, but thinks to herself that being gay, being a lesbian, is rather more than preferring to wear trousers. '*You* didn't meet anyone on the singles' holidays?'

Amy smiles. 'No. I'm too picky, I'm afraid. But, looking back,' she goes on, 'I think that must have been the trouble between Gwen and Bert. Bert didn't like that Gwen always had the upper hand. You never knew Bert Barker, did you? He was a thin, rather ineffectual chap. Gwen was twice the man he was, if you know what I mean, and he didn't like it.'

Maisie says, 'I see. No, I never met Gwen's husband.'

'He turned very nasty. But his loss was my gain. You know about my fiancé, don't you? After he died I never expected to meet anyone else. I *didn't* meet anyone else. I know we were never married, as the rest of you girls were. I'm not strictly a widow and yet I do feel that perpetual ache of bereavement you all must feel. He was the only man for me.'

Maisie puts her head on one side, plumbing her own ache of bereavement which, to be truthful, isn't very deep.

'But,' Amy goes on, 'with Gwen, you see, it didn't matter. It wasn't the same, but it was … something.'

Very softly, into the gloom, Maisie says, 'Are you telling me you have feelings for Gwen, Amy?'

Amy lifts her hands, and then drops them again into her lap. A little breeze ruffles the curtains a fraction, momentarily admitting a thin shaft of sunlight. It lights up the whiteness of Amy's hair. 'Not *that* kind of feeling,' she says. 'I'm not attracted to Gwen …' she waits, as though the thought, which the next words must articulate, has not quite formed. 'I'm not in love with her … but I do love her,' she says at last. 'It's hard to explain.'

'I think I understand,' says Maisie, although half aware that Amy, in her drowsy ruminations, needs no reply. But Maisie is instantly hooked back in time to her school days. There had been a girl, one of those golden girls who are good at everything, sports as well as lessons, and who are always popular. She'd had the loveliest blonde, curly hair. In the normal run of things Maisie would never have been friends with a girl like that, but it happened they both lived at the last stop on the school bus route and so would sit together when the bus had dropped off all the others in the afternoons. The girl—Heather—would help Maisie with her homework, and not make her feel silly for being dim. And in the mornings they would wait at the bus stop together and talk about what they'd watched on television the night before. So they had become friends, although they never spent any time together in school, or out of it, except on those bus journeys. But she would always say hello to Maisie if they passed in the corridor, and that made Maisie feel special, that they had a unique friendship no one else was part of, or even knew about.

Now, remembering that girl, she thinks she had loved her. Certainly she had admired her. There had been nothing sexual about it. It had not been a crush—*those* she'd had on a series of older, utterly unobtainable boys. Maisie speaks again, but softly, into the eddying dust motes of the shaded room, 'Yes. I do understand.'

'With a friend like Gwen … ' Amy muses again, still as though speaking to herself, 'well, she's so able to do everything, and she likes to take the initiative. I have only needed to sit back and she has organised everything. I'm picked up and taken out, all my needs are considered, and …' again, a pause, while her thoughts arrange themselves, 'and she has made me feel *special.* Gwen makes me feel *valued.* What husband would do more? I'm only a spinster, a retired librarian! I mean, *there* is a cliché, if you need one! I'm one of those grey, negligible people whom no one notices or cares about. But Gwen cares about me, or she did do. With Gwen as a friend I was never short of anything a man could give me. Except sex, of course.'

The conjuring and the expression of this seems to have wearied Amy, and for a while she says nothing more.

Maisie also remains silent. She glances at the teapot. Now she *would* like a cup of tea, but it will be cold, and the act of getting up and the noise of the re-boiling kettle would disturb the confessional air.

Presently Amy says, 'And even though there has never been sex, there has been a sort of physical affection. When you're old and wrinkly and frail, people don't touch you. They must think I'll break. Or perhaps it's just too revolting a prospect. But Gwen hasn't seemed to feel any disinclination. She's helped me in the shower and washed my hair, and she's helped me get dressed and all in a perfectly business-like way but at the same time … tenderly, as though she really cared. A bit like a mother, I suppose. As though nothing about me could possibly shock or revolt her. But no, that isn't quite right because, with Gwen, I have always felt like an equal partner. Oh dear,' Amy emits a frustrated sigh. 'I'm not explaining this very well.' She takes a deep breath. 'What I'm trying to get to, Maisie, is that now I haven't got it, I realise how much I have enjoyed it. I miss it. Gwen's very tactile and, for years now, she's the only human contact I've had.'

Maisie nods. Yes. Gwen is always ready with a hug, to reach out a sympathetic hand. When the women went away on their occasional coach holidays, Gwen always shared a room with Amy to provide what she terms "personal care". Up until now, Maisie never had a very clear idea what that might entail, but she can imagine Gwen's care being adept; intimate without being erotic, assiduous but not sensual.

'We all need physical affection,' Amy adds. 'Human warmth, a sense of contact. I think people get that mixed up with sex. They think physical affection *means* sex. It doesn't though. But here's the thing: does Gwen need

Val because I didn't … because I have never …' Amy falters again, and Maisie sits forward in her chair, ready to catch whatever is to come. 'Because she needed more from me than I gave?'

Amy's eyes flare open and fix on Maisie, their pale, gimlet gaze not at all dazed by sleep but lucid and penetrating. There has been nothing idly ruminative about Amy's monologue. Her hands—age-spotted and arthritic—are clenched in her lap. 'I could never have … you know. I mean, just the mechanics of it …' she shakes her head. 'But I could have hugged. I could have held her hand.' She furrows her already wrinkled forehead into corrugations of speculation. 'I could have kissed her, in a sisterly way, without ever allowing … without ever implying …'

'If she had misconstrued,' Maisie offers, 'that would have been cruel.'

'Yes it would, but I think I could have walked that line; a platonic line between affectionate friendship and … whatever she has with Val.'

Amy sits back, exhausted by the intensity of all that has passed between them. 'I'd like some tea,' she says faintly.

Maisie stands, and bends to pick up the tea tray, but suddenly Amy's bluish, bony hand seizes her wrist.

'Maisie don't make the same mistake—with Oliver, I mean. Don't lose his friendship just for the sake of … a little tenderness.'

Chapter Five – Viola

Women—variously battered, bullied and bewildered—came and went from the upstairs flat in Viola's block, and she found herself peripherally attached to the team of volunteers who eased their passage from hell. It moved Viola that the women's aspirations were so meagre; she watched them wonder at the lack-lustre appointments of the barren little flat as though it were a palace. She saw that, to them, it was a high tower, a refuge, a burrow where they could hide. Clearly, in their own eyes, they expected little and felt they deserved less. Their situation resonated with Viola's and opened a wellhead of sympathy within her. She had never been a woman given to sensibilities but something about these women provoked a tsunami of unwonted fellow-feeling. At first she attempted to befriend them, seeing them as kindred spirits regardless of how far removed their ages, backgrounds and social situations were from hers. She assumed—wrongly—that they would feel as she did, an affinity. But forming friendships was a skill she was ill-practised at and her overtures foundered, met by one pair of glassily uncomprehending eyes after another. At length she realised that when these poor women arrived at the flat, they were still in a state of shell-shock, as she herself had been in the hospital and afterwards. What they needed was rest, quiet and kindness. They were not ready for anything new and any fragment of trust that they had retained was a shattered, storm-damaged thing.

In any case, after a day or so they were gone, taken in by family or sucked back into the maelstrom.

So, instead, Viola took on practical tasks. It became her job to clean the flat and launder the sheets, and to provide such easily-digested food that stomachs made dyspeptic with terror could assimilate. She made a lot of soup and, although she herself rarely ate sweet things, she baked buns and biscuits by the dozen—simple, nostalgic recipes from the Be-Ro book— perhaps they might remind the women of happier times. Sometimes Viola was needed to help with personal care, the victims being too catatonic to even bathe or dress themselves. Frequently there were wounds to tend. But more often than not they needed nothing more than the warm press of a kindly hand and a promise—unfailingly kept—that she would sit in watchful vigil while they slept, the two of them safely barricaded in together.

She would sit in the bedroom, where a shaded lamp cast a benign glow, and watch over the women's fitful slumbers. At these times she was overcome by anger at men's cruelty, and set her heart into a hard and obstinate stone that she determined would never be allowed to soften or to yield, never to make itself vulnerable to the stamp of another monster's boot. But eventually her ferocity tempered. There *was* kindness. After all, here *she* was, a bastion of compassion against brutality, and this gave her hope. She felt the clutch of a strange and benevolent hand around her impervious heart and did not know if it would draw off her burden of bitterness or simply remind her how heavy and obdurate it was. Although not a religious woman she would find herself ardently hoping, almost importuning some unseen and not-quite-believed-in providential power that the woman in the bed— like she herself—would see and enjoy better days.

For herself, she felt those better days edging nearer, but they were still a distant prospect whose exact dimensions and colours she could not yet make out. It was hard at times. Her Christmas with Brian had been pleasant enough, a bright beacon in the grey and dismal days before and after, but he had then been embroiled in a huge project at work that occupied all of his time, and she had not seen him since.

January and February were cold and cruel, with a raw wind blowing off the sea and a seeping dampness that chilled her to the bone. She walked aimlessly round the town, her stick abandoned now, hunched against the elements as the short hours of daylight dragged by, reluctant to go back to the flat where she felt increasingly cooped up and constrained. Her fortified chamber was becoming more prison than sanctuary—a sign, she felt, that she was ready to emerge. Her green fingers itched with idleness. In her mind's eye she designed and planted out gardens of the future: large plots with raised beds and numerous herbaceous borders; postage-stamp gardens she could make to seem bigger by clever planting and meandering paths; yards she could populate with pots and over whose unpromising walls she could cause clematis and honeysuckle to clamber. Not knowing what she would be able to afford was infuriating. The lawyers of the two sides were entrenched. Graham took sadistic pleasure in prevarication, keeping her guessing as to what he would or would not allow, although Viola's solicitor assured her that his wishes would butter no parsnips if it came to court.

From time to time Gwen or other volunteers associated with the charity would come to Viola's flat to give her notice of the imminent arrival of a "client" or tell of one who had particular needs—children in tow, a disability or a dietary requirement. Viola cherished these occasions, pressing tea and food on her guests, flapping around the flat to make it more hospitable, feeling ill-equipped yet eager for the social niceties. But usually there was no warning of a client's arrival. She would hear a car pull up late at night or there might be a muffled knock on her door and she would pull on a fleece to go and help the new-comer up the stairs, turn down the bed, offer to run a bath. She would snatch a few moments' company while the flat's new occupant settled in—she and Gwen or Uma or one of the others exchanging *sotto voce* remarks in the gloom of the little vestibule outside the bathroom, while the client stifled her sobs within. As much as she deplored the need for the charity she cherished the connection it gave her with other people. Without them, she would have been lonely indeed.

During her years with Graham she had not been a particularly sociable person but she did not recall ever being lonely. She had made herself self-sufficient, she supposed. Sammy and her plants had been all the company she needed—she had told herself then. In reality they were all she had been allowed; Graham disliked her to attend clubs, and she believed one of the reasons he was so keen on Brian going to boarding school was to deny Viola the opportunity to make friends with other mothers at the school gate. But in any case, she lacked social graces. She found it hard not to speak her mind, which had often got her into trouble with Graham—an unbitten tongue resulting in a black eye or thick ear—and that habit also hampered her ability to make friends. Was she selfish? Her troubles had caused her to grow a tough shell, a defensive autonomy. But now, seeing the camaraderie amongst the women volunteers, she began to feel the attraction of friendship. She considered going to the charity's headquarters at Millport where, she gathered, there was a drop-in centre for women and girls, a kettle perpetually on the boil and someone always available to chat. But the idea that she might encounter Graham around the town made her hesitate.

Suddenly in April, all Graham's delay tactics ceased and instead he became urgent about wrapping up the loose ends of their marriage. The house was to be sold. A cash buyer had come forward offering the asking price but only if the contracts could be exchanged within a month. Graham gave up all claim to Viola's jewellery and it was delivered by courier to her solicitor's office. He suddenly "found" the statements for various savings accounts and investments he had claimed to have no knowledge of, and was prepared to offer Viola an additional cash sum in lieu of a stake in his pension. The total of her share in their joint assets looked like it would be more than sufficient to buy a small property and to maintain her afterwards.

If she was careful, Brian said, she would not have to work. 'All in all, I think it's pretty fair,' he said when he had looked over the email she forwarded to him.

'I'll need to pay back all I owe you,' said Viola. 'The rent you've paid for this place, and all the furniture you bought.'

'That's nothing, in the scheme of things. Look what the house is going to fetch! Compared to that, it's a drop in the ocean. But you know, I can make it a lot more if you let me invest it for you, Mum. Even if you stayed put for a year in the flat, I could get you ten or even fifteen percent. That's … ' she could hear him tapping the keys of a calculator, 'a hundred grand I could add to the pot, in just twelve months!'

In her mind, Viola did a valedictory scroll through the images of the gardens she had imagined.

A thin rain beaded the glass of her patio doors but through it she could still see the bright golden daffodils that struggled up through the leaf litter beneath the pyracantha hedge. She said, 'A year?'

'Or two at the most.'

'I don't know,' she said. 'I haven't absolutely decided to accept it yet. I can't help wondering if there's something your father isn't saying. Some ulterior motive. He's been so reluctant to agree to anything, but now … do you know why he's suddenly so keen to get all this sorted?'

She could feel Brian hesitate, almost hear the debate he was having with himself.

'Brian?'

'Well,' he said at last, 'there *is* something, but it isn't related to money, or not directly. When he was in Thailand at Christmas he met someone.'

'A woman?'

Brian snorted. 'A girl. She isn't much older than me!'

'You've met her?' Viola didn't know how she felt about this development. She wasn't jealous—she no longer had any feelings for Graham other than a faint disgust—but she didn't much like the idea of a rival for Brian's affections. A young, exotic, exciting step-mother would be hard to compete with. Simmering beneath this initial reaction was a sense of concern for the young woman. What had she let herself in for? 'I hope she can take care of herself,' she said cynically. 'She may have bitten off more than she can chew with your father.'

'They're all loved-up at the moment,' said Brian, and his shudder of disgust reassured her.

'What's she like?'

'Oh, you know. Petite. Dark hair. She doesn't say much. Her English isn't great.'

'I wonder what the attraction is,' Viola mused sarcastically. 'What does she do?'

'Nothing much, I don't think, but her parents own the resort Dad stayed at: hotel, several restaurants, beach bungalows …'

'He'll be keen to get his hands on those,' Viola said. 'That explains his hurry. He has much bigger fish to fry. Well, I don't mind that. Good luck to him. And to her.'

When she finished speaking to Brian she sent an email to her solicitor accepting Graham's offer, but in a last-minute addendum stipulated he should pay all costs. It was like her; she had never been one to lie down without a fight. She liked to have the last word and wanted to punish him for the loss of her beautiful home and garden.

The rain had ceased and a watery sun struggled through the clouds, silvering the wet paving of the carpark. She edged open the sliding doors and put her hand outside to test the temperature of the air. Which coat would she need for her walk? The gravel of her little terrace was thick with moss but if she peered closely she could see, here and there, the minute scalloped leaves of aquilegia plantlets, sprouted from those seeds she had purloined the previous autumn. The sight deluged her in ridiculous happiness, and for a moment she thought she might cry.

Towards the end of that month a storm blew up, flapping open the lids of the wheelie bins and scattering rubbish all over the carpark. Viola, up early, had set to with a broom to collect it all and stow it back into the bins before the wagon came mid-morning.

She was busy sweeping when the man from the end flat came out via his patio doors and squeezed through the gap at the end of the hedge. He was dressed, as usual, in baggy grey flannel trousers, a pullover that had seen much better days, a blue anorak and much-worn boots. He hoisted the strap of a holdall over his shoulder, and would have walked past Viola if she had not said, 'Good morning. That was some storm we had last night, wasn't it?'

The man mumbled, 'Normal, for the time of year, I suppose,' and would have walked on, but some devilment in Viola, a sudden surge of frustration at her neighbours and their wilful refusal to speak to each other, made her say, '*March* is for winds. April should be for showers, or so the saying goes.'

The man's step faltered. 'Whoever said that never lived here. This coast has a will of its own. Whatever it's doing, wait ten minutes and it'll be doing something else.'

'You've lived here a long time then?' Viola leaned on her broom, disposing herself for conversation, and effectively barring his progress along the path. Now she was close to the man she could see he was older than she had imagined, the skin around his eyes like crêpe, his hair thin on his scalp. The hand that held the strap of his bag in place trembled slightly. His feet shuffled, first one way and then the other, seeking a way to pass, but she fixed him by holding out her hand towards him. 'I'm Viola,' she said.

Something seemed to soften him—her name perhaps, and the small fragile flower it represented. His eyes—wary, the lids pink-rimmed and watering in the chill breeze—relented. They did not quite meet Viola's, but he held out his hand and took hold of hers. His hand was hard, calloused, but quite warm.

'I moved in last summer,' she said. 'I don't know why we've never met. Everyone here seems to keep very much to themselves.'

'They do,' he said matter-of-factly. 'I've lived and worked in Southquay man and boy,' he offered, answering her earlier question. 'I did forty years in Parks and Gardens. I've lived here,' he indicated the dour flats with a jerk of his head, 'four years. Since the wife died. The kids thought the house would be too much for me.'

'I'm sorry,' said Viola, although thinking privately she was not sure why people said that; it was not *their* fault. 'But I see you get out and about every day.'

'So do you,' came back the quick reply. 'All times of the day and night, I see you.' His gaze strayed obliquely up, to the balcony of the middle, upper flat. 'Lots of comings and goings. All very cloak-and-dagger.'

'I can't tell you anything about it,' Viola said, adding, with an attempt at humour, 'Official Secrets Act. You didn't tell me your name.'

The man hesitated. 'Gordon,' he said at last. He cast his eyes across the pavement, where food containers, damp tissues, chicken bones and other detritus still remained to be swept up. 'This is good of you,' he allowed. 'No one else would bother. I would but, to be honest, I've done my bit over the years; litter collection, you know? You wouldn't believe the things people leave behind. And anyway, I'm in a hurry. Got somewhere to be.'

This surprised Viola, who had imagined him—much like her—counting down the hours in libraries and greasy spoons, wandering the promenade, feeding the seagulls the crusts of the sandwiches she supposed he carried in his trusty holdall. 'Oh?'

He took a sideways step, to circumnavigate Viola and her broom and the little heap of rubbish she had accumulated. He raised his hand to a hat he wasn't wearing; an old-fashioned gesture Viola hadn't seen in a long time. 'See you again, Viola,' he said. As he passed she heard the faint chink of metal against metal coming from his bag, and wondered for a wild moment if he was a burglar, off to prise open windows with a crowbar and rifle through people's drawers.

'Where are you going?' she blurted out. 'I mean, where do you go every day, Gordon?'

He paused and turned to look at her over the shoulder of his anorak. 'Community allotments,' he said.

Unfortunately, that afternoon a new client was brought to the flat who had needed Viola's undivided attention for the whole weekend, so she was too busy to Google the community allotments. She asked Gwen about them the following Monday.

Gwen said, 'Oh yes! The community allotments in Southquay are quite famous. Hadn't you heard about them? There was a fuss about them being set up in the first place. People objected because they thought it would be a commercial enterprise; you know? A market garden? Although why that should be objectionable, I can't tell you. And then there was all kinds of fuss about their entries to various flower and produce shows. People said it wasn't fair for a group to compete against individuals. But it's all blown over now. I know a few folks who are involved down there, if you're interested. I had no idea you were a gardener.'

Viola thought about telling Gwen that if she were to be sliced open the word "gardener" would be found written inside her, like "Southquay" through the local sticks of rock. She had not quite known how indelible and intrinsic gardening was to her whole character until discovering that every day her neighbour Gordon trudged off to work the soil with a bag of trowels and pruning shears. Her feeling on watching him walk away that windy April morning was envy and the kind of desperate, visceral need she imagined addicts feel when denied their next hit. Only the early hour, and the still-fluttering rubbish—and the fact that she was only wearing a pair of slippers—had stopped her from pursuing him.

'They're right at the end of the promenade,' Gwen explained. 'Past the pitch-and-putt course and then slightly inland, before you come out on the common. Do you know it?'

Viola tried to picture it. 'I'm sure I could find it. I've walked on the common a few times.' It was quite a long trek to that end of the promenade. She wondered if Gordon walked it, or if he caught a bus. 'Can anyone go?'

'In theory,' said Gwen. 'In practice, people are referred. The thing is run under the umbrella of social services. If you want to give it a try I'll call my friend Martin. He's in charge. He'll sort you out. But Viola, if you're short of things to do there are several worthy causes that need volunteers. There's an animal shelter I'm connected with …'

'No, thank you Gwen,' said Viola. 'I'm not ready for anything like that yet. But gardening …' she struggled to articulate it. On her lap, her hands crumbled invisible soil. She wanted to say that gardening was like medicine, a substance her mind and body craved, but balked at having to admit to needing anything, even to Gwen.

'Gardening is good for you in all kinds of ways,' Gwen finished for her. 'They call it "vitamin G," don't they?' She reached across and placed her hand on Viola's. It was large in comparison to Viola's, whose hands were small and dainty. 'I tend to forget,' said Gwen in a low, confidential voice, 'that you're on this journey too. Just like Cindy,' the current occupant of the upstairs flat, 'but a bit further along. You've been an absolute brick, Viola, but you must do what's right for you.'

Viola blinked away tears. She wanted to reciprocate the pressure of Gwen's hand but something held her back. Pride? Or a sense that, once she opened her shell, she did not know what atrocities might pour out.

'I'd like to go to the allotment,' she croaked out, 'if you can arrange it.'

Later, after Gwen had gone, Viola went into her bedroom and rifled about in her wardrobe until she found her gardening clothes: an old pair of denim dungarees with plentiful pockets for secateurs, bits of twine, plant labels and the like, a fleece top, and several pairs of gloves. These were particularly precious—good gloves in a small size were so hard to come by—and she had hoarded her favourites jealously, mending rents from thorns and washing them carefully after each use. She laid the items out on the bed almost reverently, as though they were vestments for a rite. Brian had managed to bring some of her things from the house and these had been at the top of her list. At the time she had worried Graham might have destroyed them; it had happened before: taking scissors to a favourite scarf and putting a mohair pullover she had knitted herself into a boil wash. Brian claimed her gardening boots were nowhere to be found; perhaps Graham had thrown them away. But she was glad of these old friends and the prospect of wearing them again—of sowing seeds and tending plants— made her heart ache with desire. She laid her hand on the fabric of the dungarees, its nap like velvet, oft-washed, its colour all but gone. There was a little tear to one of the pockets. She would mend that, she decided. She wished she had her tools. Her Niwaki Kurumi secateurs had cost over a hundred pounds, and she'd owned a lovely Farrar and Tanner fork and spade, but her favourite implement for almost any small gardening job had been an old set of bone-handled knives picked up at a junk shop, and she supposed she might find more of those in town, if she looked in charity shops and such.

She glanced at her watch. It was past three o'clock and some instinct told her that Cindy, upstairs, would be emerging from the sleep that seemed to assail most clients as soon as they gained the refuge of the flat. It was as though their bodies, minds and souls were so exhausted by the effort—sometimes of many years' duration—of keeping things together that the moment the battle was over they simply collapsed.

Viola collected a tin of shortbread biscuits she had baked that morning, a notebook and pen and a pint of milk, then headed out, but with a regretful backwards glance at the gear left on the bed.

It was a dry, wind-blown day towards the end of April when Viola made her way to the community allotment. The pitch-and-putt was deserted but for a man and his dog. Viola skirted its edge to find the sandy lane that would take her to the slight depression in the tufted common where the allotments were situated.

The whole site was enclosed by thick hedging—fuchsia, escallonia, blackthorn and gorse—and accessed by a wide gate. Just inside, a few vehicles were parked haphazardly on the rutted ground. A number of bikes lodging in a bike rack gave Viola the notion she might get one herself. It had been quite a long walk from her flat and she knew that, all being well, by the time she was ready to go home she would be shattered. Having said that, it must be thirty years since she had ridden a bike. It was said that you never forgot, but …

The allotment plots spread out left and right, with a central avenue between them. Viola walked slowly, scanning both sides. Some of the plots were prick-neat, their beds hoed and ready for the year's planting. Some were already sprouting with garlic and onions, some ragged with the remains of last year's brassicas. Some were a mess, rank with weeds, the raised beds rotten and collapsing. She saw sheds, greenhouses and make-shift polytunnels, water butts, cold frames and chicken runs, all in varying states of repair. Each plot was divided from its neighbour by some sort of fence or hedge and these too differed from site to site: chain-link fencing, post-and-rail, pallets up-ended and filling the gaps between hedging plants. Some folks were at work, their backs bent over half-dug trenches. She could see a woman inside a brightly-coloured shed, perched on a stool in front of an easel, her apron larded with paint. A man and a toddler chased an errant chicken round and round a strawberry bed. But most of the plots were empty, with no sign of any preparation being made for the spring planting season that was now almost upon them.

Viola paused to watch the eventual capture of the hen and its return to the coop before she enquired as to the location of the community plot. The man gestured further along the avenue.

Presently she came to a sign, hand-painted in colourful but not very well-formed letters, nailed askew onto a wooden gate which was itself leaning at an alarming angle. She paused before going through, to survey the situation; if she didn't like the look of it, she could walk away. The community plot was double the size of the others, at the very bottom and stretching across the whole width of the site. On the whole it was pretty tidy, except for the grass paths between the beds which were ready for mowing, and an area towards the back with a dozen or so lopsided compost enclosures, some long bits of gash wood, rolls of wire and other detritus evidently kept in case it might come in handy. Lots of the raised beds needed weeding and it didn't look to her that the trees in the little orchard had been pruned. She counted perhaps eight or ten people at work around the site, including Gordon, who was busy constructing a frame for beans or peas with the help of a very tall, much younger man and a stocky youth.

It looked fine, she thought; pretty good in fact; not such a basket-case that it would be a thankless sinkhole of work, not so well-managed that she could not make a meaningful contribution. She was, after all, pretty experienced and competent. Viola took a deep breath and reached for the latch of the gate, which was awkward and out of line because of the gate's dilapidation. She wrestled with it for a moment or two, making the gate rattle, and when she looked up it was to see the tall man striding athletically towards her through the long grass of the path.

'Let me help,' he called out. 'It will bite you if you don't know the knack of it.' Too late. The catch sprang loose, catching Viola's finger in its mechanism. She winced and put her pinched finger into her mouth, smiling round it ruefully.

The man moved with such alacrity that he almost tripped, catching his foot on some impediment, and arrived at the gate at a half-run so that, if it hadn't been for the gate, they would have collided. 'Oh, I'm sorry,' he said, opening the gate for her and beckoning her through. 'Well, that's you blooded, so you're one of us. Sort of induction. We say you can't really be a member here until the garden has inflicted some kind of injury on you. Although, to be honest,' he lowered his voice, 'lots of us come here nursing wounds of one kind or another in the first place.' He looked down at his right arm, which she now noted was in a sling, tucked inside his jumper. 'I rest my case,' he said.

Awkwardly, with one hand, he fastened the gate behind her. 'As annoying as it is, we have to keep this gate closed for health and safety reasons,' he said. 'Sometimes people bring their children, and the other allotmenteers aren't always very friendly if they escape.' He straightened and held out his left hand. 'I'm Martin,' he said, 'and I'm guessing you're Viola? Welcome.'

She took his hand. It was slender, with long fingers, but unfortunately scratched across its back, perhaps by a thorn or barbed wire. A pianist's hand, she thought, and then amended it to a gardening pianist's hand. The idea made her smile; it was an unusual pairing. He wasn't as young as she had imagined from his lithe figure and alacritous gait. She looked up at him—for Viola, who was herself taller than average, this was a novelty. She put him in his mid-forties, younger than she was, but not much. His skin had the weathered quality of someone who spent a lot of time outdoors, with creases around his eyes, which were brown and very kind, but also rather sad. His smile revealed a chipped front tooth. He had a partly-healed gash over one eyebrow.

She thought, 'My God! This place must be a death-trap!' but aloud she said, 'Yes. I'm Viola. Gwen rang you about me, I believe.' She withdrew her hand and made a show of looking over the allotment. 'This looks very promising,' she said, but then regretted it. Do I sound patronising?

Clearly, she did. Martin gave a little snort of laughter. 'Well, thanks,' he said. 'We do our best. But any help we can get is always welcome. Let me show you around.'

They toured the area, Martin cataloguing the crops they had produced the previous season, their plans for the summer, and introducing the volunteers; a fat, friendly, grey-haired woman called Brenda; Veejay, a man in a turban who had a long, grey beard, was Indian, but spoke beautiful, unaccented Queen's English; a horsey couple in expensive waxed jackets and Hunter wellingtons with a name Viola did not catch; and Gordon, of course, who expressed no surprise at seeing her but did allow his eye to droop in a knowing wink; and his assistant, Adrian, a be-spectacled young man with Down Syndrome, and three or four others. Martin pointed to a polytunnel, very productive, he said, where trays of pea. bean, onion, tomato and chilli seedlings were being pricked out by two androgynous teenagers, tattooed and pierced and clad from head to foot in black. The greenhouse—an old timber-framed one that had been second or third hand when donated to them—was in a sorry state. Martin said their fund-raising project for the past two years had been to buy a new one. 'But it serves its purpose,' he said, 'just about. We had a fantastic crop of aubergines last year, anyway.' She caught him giving her a sidelong glance, to see if he had impressed her.

'Aubergines,' she exclaimed politely. 'Amazing!' and took note of his suppressed smile.

The tour ended at a long, low wooden building that seemed to be an office, a shop, a store and a meeting place. In one corner was a battered metal desk with a scattering of papers and several dirty coffee cups strewn across it.

'My desk,' said Martin, pulling a face. 'I'm almost never to be found at it.'

A trestle table adjacent to the desk contained a box of cling-filmed sandwiches and tray-bakes, some hand-made greeting cards and other handicrafts variously priced, some old copies of *Gardeners' World* magazine, a collection of hand-tools and a box of disposable gloves. Bags of sharp sand and vermiculite and seed compost leaned against the opposite side of the room. At the back was a door Viola assumed led to a toilet but turned out to be a tool store.

'Always locked at night, but frequently broken into,' said Martin with a sigh.

There was an old sink, a fridge and another trestle with a kettle and a jumble of cups and mugs and canisters of tea, coffee and sugar. 'You help yourself,' Martin explained, 'and make a donation if you can.' He motioned towards the crafts, sandwiches, tray-bakes. 'Brenda makes those. All proceeds go to the funds. You'd be amazed how many people come for the day and forget to bring lunch. Have you brought anything? That is … if you've decided to stay.'

Viola had a large flask of soup in her bag. She brought it out. 'Plenty to share,' she said, placing it on the table.

In the centre of the space was a round plastic garden table and some chairs, and a Calor gas heater. A notice board to the left of the door had health and safety notices, a list of services for Easter—now past—at the local Methodist church, telephone numbers for the nearest hospital and a number of posters about the Samaritans, Shelter, emergency contraception and the women's refuge.

'I need to run you through the Ts and Cs,' Martin said. 'Everyone who comes here is a volunteer except me. I'm paid by the local council and I have overall responsibility for the site and for the welfare of the folks who come here. So although we make joint decisions on just about everything, the buck stops with me and so in the end I do have the deciding vote. For instance, I insist on custard creams in the biscuit ration.' He sucked his teeth. 'It doesn't make me very popular; most people would prefer digestives …' He paused.

Viola looked at him blankly. Am I supposed to say something witty? Declare a preference for one biscuit over another?

She said, 'I don't eat biscuits, generally.'

Martin nodded sagely. 'Probably very wise.' He seemed to make a readjustment, coughing slightly before going on. 'People come here for all kinds of reasons. Some, like Gordon, just miss having a garden to potter in. Some come for the company—Brenda, for instance. Some, like the pair in the polytunnel, are here as part of their community service order. Others are recovering from mental health issues, marital breakup, bereavement, illness, surgery. To an extent we don't differentiate, although of course some people have particular needs. We have several service-users who use wheelchairs and of course we do all we can to accommodate them, although we are sadly limited by our toilet facilities. On Wednesdays we have a minibus of young people from a school for differently abled kids. And then there's Adrian … but I needn't say more. We don't judge or discriminate in any way. Neither do we pry. Having said that, people do tend to open up about their problems and this is a very supportive group. We discourage gossip. What happens on the allotment stays on the allotment.'

Viola nodded. 'Of course.'

'There,' said Martin, smiling. 'That's my little peptalk done. So now, to business. What do you fancy tackling? Gordon's going to need an extra pair of hands with his wigwams.' He held up his bandaged arm. 'I'm about as much use as a chocolate teapot with this thing. Or, if you fancy keeping a bit warmer, you can help prick out those seedlings in the polytunnel. Brenda and Veejay are … I'm not sure … ' He gestured towards the kettle. 'What about a cup of tea, to begin with?'

'Oh no,' said Viola, 'thank you. I'm itching to get started. What about those raised beds at the far end? I could make a start weeding those out.'

Martin quirked an eyebrow. 'Okay,' he said, 'if you're sure. Wouldn't you rather work alongside one of the others?'

Viola shook her head. 'No. I'm used to working on my own. Only, I'll need some tools.'

Martin made a sweeping gesture with his good arm. 'Step this way.'

The day passed quickly, but Viola had little consciousness of it. She reluctantly stopped for lunch; the prospect of sitting round the table and exchanging small talk with the others made her cringe. But the business of finding clean cups and sharing her soup, a long soliloquy of soup recipes from Brenda and some banter between Adrian and Martin allowed Viola to avoid saying much at all. She drank her soup and flicked through one of the magazines while the others nattered, and escaped back to her work as soon as possible. Brenda and Veejay left after lunch and the two teenagers were collected by their probation officer around three-thirty, at which time Martin brought her a mug of tea saying, 'This is probably cold now. But if Mohammed won't come to the mountain …'

Viola scrambled to her feet. 'I'm sorry?'

'Tea is at three,' he said. 'You were called, but perhaps you didn't hear.'

'I didn't,' Viola said, taking off her glove and raking her hair back. She surveyed her handiwork. 'I've been a million miles away.'

He handed her the tea. 'It's Long-life milk, I'm afraid.'

'Any port in a storm.' She took the tea and sipped it—satisfactorily strong but lukewarm. She decided she would drink it anyway. 'What will be planted here?'

Martin considered. 'Sweetcorn, if I remember rightly. It's a good spot, sheltered from the wind.'

Viola nodded. 'They can be greedy,' she said. 'But I'm guessing there's been plenty of organic matter dug in here.' The soil in the allotment was light and loamy, very friable. It was a pleasure to work, much easier than the clay soil of her own—her previous—garden. She allowed her eyes to travel over the rest of the allotment. Gordon and Adrian had moved from wigwams to servicing the wheelbarrows but, as she watched, Adrian bade Gordon farewell and walked towards an older woman Viola assumed to be his mum, who was waiting at the gate. Martin went to speak to them both and after she had drunk her tea, Viola returned to her weeding.

After a while, Gordon came over to where Viola was just finishing her second raised bed. 'I'll be heading off in a bit,' he said. 'Martin tends to shut up shop promptly at five at this time of year. He's expected at home. I catch the shuttle bus that goes past the pitch-and-putt at quarter past. I've got a bus-pass, but …' he looked at his feet and mumbled, 'you know, if you wanted to, but you might rather walk, I don't mind …'

Viola straightened up. Her back ached. 'I'll catch the bus with you Gordon.' She glanced at her watch and was surprised to see it was gone half past four. She took off her gloves. The breeze that had blown all day was now chill, and the sun had disappeared behind a bank of cloud. 'Alright,' she said. 'I'll call it a day.'

Martin was in the long shed, leaning over his desk, scrolling through some emails on his laptop computer, occasionally typing one-handedly. He had lit the Calor gas heater and the shed was warm. The only light came from an Anglepoise lamp on his desk.

'Shall I rinse the cups and whatnot, Martin?' Gordon offered. 'I've time before my bus. Viola's going to come with me. She lives …' he faltered, 'at that end of town,' he finished.

Martin said, 'Oh, thanks Gordon.'

Gordon took the fork and trowel from Viola and returned them to the tool store before tackling the washing up. Viola wished she had offered to help. With Gordon busy at the back of the shed and Martin intent on his emails she suddenly felt spare and awkward.

Then Martin straightened up, wincing. He put his hand to the small of his back. 'I ought to sit down,' he said, half to himself.

Viola said, 'Tall people like us are martyrs to our backs.' She stroked her lower spine in sympathy. 'Welcome to my world,' she said.

Martin smiled. 'You've worked wonders today, Viola. Have you enjoyed yourself?'

'I have,' said Viola. 'I … I used to have a garden of my own but …'

'Not now?' There was barely the suggestion of a question mark, an ever-so-slightly open door of invitation for Viola to say more. Viola wondered how much Gwen had told Martin. Did he know she had been a victim of domestic violence? The idea that he—that anyone—should see her as a "victim" was appalling.

'No,' she said briskly, zipping up her fleece and rummaging in her pocket for some change. 'Not anymore. I'm on the cusp of a whole raft of new beginnings.' It was true, she thought. Her divorce would soon be finalised, her financial settlement would land in her bank—or in Brian's, which was much the same thing—and she could turn her back on the past. She found a couple of pound coins and dropped them in the jam jar where she had seen others put their donations for hot drinks and Brenda's sandwiches. When she turned back she saw Martin was still regarding her, his good arm and his injured one crossed against his rather concave chest. For something to say she asked, 'Is the allotment open every day?'

'Except Christmas Day,' he returned, 'and even then, sometimes, I'm tempted. Some of the service-users spend Christmas Day on their own. If you get the right mix of people things can turn quite jolly. In the summer, we have— Ah! Here are the stragglers. "I counted them out, and I counted them back in," as they say in the Corps.'

The couple whose name Viola could not remember had come into the shed as Martin was speaking.

The man said, 'All accounted for, Sergeant,' in a manner that might—or might not—have been tongue-in-cheek.

The woman looked bone-weary and collapsed into one of the garden chairs. She was a diminutive figure, whose blonded, expensively-styled hair, careful makeup and designer clothing did not quite hide her age, which must have been north of seventy. She had a generally harried, haggard air. She threw Viola a look that was hard to decode.

'You look like you're ready for a hot bath and a stiff gin and tonic,' said Viola, 'like me.'

'That would be nice,' said the woman weakly. 'I think I've probably overdone things today.' Her voice was thin, wavering.

'Nonsense,' said her husband, clearly—from his upright demeanour and brusque, clipped address—a military man. He was much bigger than his wife, with a florid complexion and large, beefy hands. He turned to Martin to say, 'That's all the potatoes planted Martin. I've labelled the beds with the different varieties.'

'Gosh,' said Martin, '*all* the potatoes? I'd no idea you'd do them all.'

'If we start a thing we like to finish it, don't we Vanessa?' He turned to his wife.

Vanessa summoned enough energy to say, 'Yes, Clive.'

Viola cringed at Vanessa's subservience, but a hot wave of annoyance at the man quickly swamped that, leaving the kind of compassion Viola felt for the women who came to the upstairs flat.

'Even so,' Viola said pointedly, addressing Clive. 'Gardening's no fun if you overdo it. We're not serfs, are we? We're not on piece-work.' She crossed the wooden floor of the shed and pulled a chair up so she could sit next to the exhausted woman, to whom she addressed her next remarks. 'I hope you've brought a car,' she said. 'If not, I'll ring you a taxi. You look done in.'

'Oh, Clive will drive us,' said the woman loyally, plastering a smile on her face. 'But I must say,' in a lower voice, 'that's kind and thoughtful of you.'

'But wholly unnecessary,' blustered Clive. 'I think I know what's best for my wife, madam.' He turned to Martin. 'Same time next week, Martin?'

'Certainly Clive, if you're free,' replied Martin. 'But, you know there's no need to do the whole day, if it's too much. A half day would be …'

'Uneconomical with our time,' Clive interjected. 'We committed to one day a week, and one day a week is what we'll do, isn't it Vanessa? Now let's get home. You'll hardly have time to get the supper cooked before we're due at the bridge club at seven.'

Vanessa hoisted herself to her feet.

Viola addressed her directly. 'I'll be here next week, so I'll see you then. In fact, Vanessa, I plan on coming down most days, so if you're free and you fancy a chat …'

Vanessa made a small mewing noise, half longing and half lament.

'Vanessa is far too busy for idle chat,' said her husband. 'We have a full calendar of engagements. Good evening.'

He herded his wife from the shed and Viola heard the rattle of the gate, followed by an expletive as it took a bite out of Clive's finger.

'I must get that fixed,' muttered Martin.

'Oh, I don't know,' said Viola through her teeth, 'the universe has a way of getting its own back, sometimes.'

A shadow passed over Martin's features, and he turned back to his laptop.

The bus took a long time to get them home, via convoluted detours. The promenade road was under repair. As Gwen had predicted, new storm drains were being installed along both sides of it.

Gordon said, 'You didn't like Clive, I gather?'

'No I didn't. He's a bully,' said Viola.

'You only met him for five minutes,' said Gordon. 'You're quick to judge.'

'But not usually wrong. What do you think of him?'

'Not much,' Gordon admitted. 'Behaves like he's doing us all a favour, coming along every week, but it's only so's he can crow about his "good works" to his cronies on the golf course.'

'I know the type,' said Viola. 'I felt sorry for his wife.'

'Ah yes, put-upon little body, isn't she? Last summer we all had a tipple or two of Martin's home-brew and I found her crying behind the compost heap.'

As Viola lay in the bath that evening, her hard-earned gin and tonic balancing on the tiled surround, she thought back on her day—the feel of the soil in her hands, the slight resistance of the weeds as she pried them from the earth, the smell of compost and, behind her in the hedge, the busy chatter of birds building nests. It had conjured her old life so powerfully that she almost heard the little stream running through the ghyll, felt Sammy's nose behind her knee. But seeing Vanessa, and knowing instantly how things were with her, had hoiked her right back to the present, to her life now and her connection via Gwen to the women's refuge. Perhaps, she thought, the two worlds—the then and the now—were not so incompatible after all.

May was very dry that year, with long, warm days but chilly nights. The seedlings in the polytunnel were well-advanced but everyone agreed it would be foolish to plant them out before all danger of frost was past. Consequently the allotment was in a kind of holding pattern, with nothing much to occupy the volunteers other than to keep the strawberry beds well-watered, protect the nascent fruits with netting, to mow the paths and earth up the potatoes. Martin found some wood stain from somewhere and a few people began to refurbish the shed, but quite a few said they came for gardening, not DIY, and drifted off.

Viola suggested they use the time to sow annuals, which would germinate quickly, and if they were lucky be ready come June to sell on in hanging baskets and containers. Martin seconded her idea with enthusiasm and put Viola in charge of it. She tutored the community service contingent and the pupils from the school, teaching them to sow the seeds thinly, in rows, to tamp the soil down and to water the trays from underneath. It surprised her that she could not only tolerate but actually enjoy the company of the young people. In former days she would have shied away from the surly, monosyllabic attitude of the one and the dribbly, sometimes scarcely intelligible verbosity of the other. But the fountainhead of compassion that the refuge women had uncapped had sweetened Viola's generally acerbic nature. She liked this new iteration of herself.

On Thursdays—which turned out to be Vanessa and Clive's day at the allotment—she made a point of asking Vanessa to help her with some task or other, gently leading her to some sequestered spot where private conversation would be possible. As an opener she recounted her own history, hoping it would embolden Vanessa to make reciprocal confidences, but Vanessa only blinked her anxious eyes and said, 'How perfectly awful for you.'

'So now,' Viola laboured on, 'I'm working alongside a women's refuge. We help people escape from domestic abuse. There's a centre in Millport and, for women who manage to escape, there are safe houses.'

'How splendid,' said Vanessa shrilly.

Viola left a conversational space for Vanessa to fill, but she only looked down on the task they had been working on together and said, 'There. I think that's a great improvement, don't you?' and wandered back to where Clive was working.

Viola went to the allotment as often as she could, often several days a week, riding a bike she bought from a shop in town and enjoying both the exercise and the freedom to come and go without feeling obliged to accompany Gordon. It appeared he had taken a shine to her. He had begun to wait for her in the mornings, hovering on the pavement with his holdall until she should emerge, and on their afternoon bus rides he had started suggesting alighting a stop or two early to saunter the rest of the way, 'Maybe get a drink at a pub, or even fish and chips. My treat, of course.'

One Sunday she was invited round to his flat to meet his son and daughter-in-law. They were pleasant enough people but clearly only visited as a duty. The two children, as before, rode their scooters in circles round the carpark while the adults ate the shop-bought cake and drank the weak tea that Gordon served up, and as soon as those were gone they made their excuses and left.

Viola helped Gordon wash the crockery. His kitchen was disconcertingly like hers and she had to stop herself from being surprised that his cups and saucers did not live in the same cupboards that hers did.

'You've just the one child?' she asked, to make conversation.

'Yes. Though, to be accurate, he isn't really mine. Janice had him when we met. He was born … he was a mistake.'

'Does he know?'

'Oh yes. We were always very open about it. I always thought Janice made too much of it, as though she wanted to punish herself. I mean, everyone makes mistakes, don't they? And she had been very young—'

'Some men wouldn't have taken on a woman with another man's child, in those days,' Viola remarked. 'You're a good man, Gordon.'

Gordon blushed, and picked up a saucer he had already dried to dry again. 'And you're …' he began, 'you're … on your own, are you?'

'I'm divorced,' said Viola, 'or I will be, soon.' She emptied the washing up bowl and dried it with the dishcloth.

'A bit of companionship is nice, isn't it?' suggested Gordon. 'And no harm in it, for people who are on their own.'

Viola didn't know whether to laugh or cry. Gordon must be twenty years her senior, an old man by anyone's standards, he surely couldn't intend … but the very idea of a new relationship was anathema to her, with *anyone*. The absurdity of what Gordon seemed to be suggesting was only matched by the feeling of sick fear that rose in her throat; a reminder, should she have forgotten, that she could not allow herself to be hurt again.

'It's been so nice, Gordon, thank you. But I must get home. My son always calls me on Sunday afternoons and it's almost his time.' It was a lie, but it would do. She collected her cardigan and let herself out through the patio doors.

Now that she had her bicycle she did not have to travel to the allotment with Gordon on the little bus. His disappointment that first morning had been palpable, but she made sure to be extra friendly to him while they were working round the allotment and gave him first pick of the food she took to share.

The crops were planted out in June, a full contingent of volunteers turning up over a weekend to get the seedlings into the ground, staked, watered and labelled. Every raised bed was occupied. Beforehand they had looked like elongated graves, freshly filled and rather macabre; but afterwards they glowed and danced with life; the fresh greenery making a gay haze over the dun soil. A team of people filled hanging baskets and tubs with the annuals, some of which were already beginning to flower. Martin had secured a stall in the market the following week where the baskets could be sold.

The crew paused at three for their customary tea and Brenda handed round free cake as a celebratory gift. Martin settled himself on a makeshift bench next to Viola. She was warm, stripped down to a t shirt, the bib of her dungarees undone and dangling onto her lap. She had pushed her sunglasses up onto her head.

'A good day,' he said, smiling. 'I don't know how we would have managed without you. Those hanging baskets were an inspired idea. They'll bring in quite a bit of cash, I should think. With any luck we'll be within striking distance of the new greenhouse.'

She returned his smile. His arm was better now, and he had worked tirelessly amongst the volunteers. He'd had his hair cut, but it was poorly done, with uneven tufts here and there and one side much shorter than the other. She wondered if he had done it himself or had his mother or wife do it, not that she knew if he had either. His hacked, ravaged curls lent him an oddly appealing look. The gash over his eye had healed but was replaced by another on his chin. She knew by now that he was very clumsy; there was a standing joke amongst the volunteers that he could be relied upon to trip over a blade of grass. She wanted to say something teasing about his hair. Had the hedge-trimmer fallen onto his head? But instead she said, 'I wondered about an open day. We could invite the other allotmenteers in. It's such a shame there's a "them and us" mentality. There's so much we could share. We have dozens more tomato plants than we can possibly use. On the other hand the chillies haven't germinated well at all. We could do swaps.'

'Another great idea,' said Martin, stroking the cut on his chin with an unconscious finger. He hadn't shaved, probably because of the cut, to give it chance to heal. Viola rather liked the designer stubble. 'I'd like the people from the council to come down,' he said. 'They're always carping about the running costs. They don't see what we actually *do* here. And then there are the parents of the school kids. They would be keen to see what their children have achieved, surely?'

'And we might attract more volunteers,' said Viola.

Martin put his elbow on his knee and rested his head on his hand, looking at her in a kind of awe. 'You're a marvel,' he said. 'I don't know why I never thought of it.'

Viola wondered whether to tell him she had done something similar before—long before—when she had designed and planted a garden at Brian's primary school. She'd held an open day the summer before he was due to leave, to make sure the garden would have people to run it, when she was gone. Those days seemed far away now, a dim memory of a time she did not wish to revisit. Her life wasn't in the past, but here and now.

'There's something different about you, Viola. In just a couple of months, you've changed.'

'I was going to seed, before,' she told him. 'This allotment has been just what I needed.'

Privately she added, 'And I'm happy.' She *was* happy, back where she felt she belonged. It didn't matter that the garden wasn't her own. At night she slept soundly, with fewer of the nightmares that had disturbed her at first. Her obsessive cleaning of the flat had lessened; instead she gave it a once-over now and again. Her dealings with the abused women had ceased to scrape raw her own wounds and now, although always empathetic, she felt she could aid them without becoming emotionally involved in their crises.

In pursuit of befriending Vanessa, Viola joined their bridge club as a beginner. She was put under the tutelage of a woman called Amy Snow, who turned out to be a good friend of Gwen's—a pure coincidence but no surprise to Viola. The more she knew of Southquay and of Millport the more Gwen seemed to have some hand in; the Scouts, the animal rescue, a charity shop and a church all added to the burdens she bore in addition to the women's refuge, which must have been, on its own, unwieldy enough. Viola enjoyed playing bridge very much; it appealed to her competitive spirit and fed her thirsty mind. In the evenings at home she dealt hands of cards and went round the table practising her bids and then playing out the hands.

It wasn't long before she had moved up from the beginners to the intermediate group. She saw Vanessa every week, but she and Clive played in the advanced class and, at coffee time, when Viola tried to approach, Clive always seemed to find a way of herding his wife away.

Viola put this failure into perspective, though. Generally, her circle of acquaintance had widened. She was often hailed now, in supermarkets and at the bank, by people who looked strange out of their scruffy workwear, dressed up for work or coffee with friends.

Viola stumbled across Veejay at the hospital, where she went for a final check before being discharged. In his surgical scrubs he looked almost unrecognisable, but he came to a halt in front of her as she waited outside her consultant's rooms and exchanged a few words about the watering regime on the allotment.

He said, 'I'm a cardiac surgeon. I've been recommending my patients try gardening for many years. Then last year I had a heart attack myself, so I've had to begin to take my own medicine. I'm back at work part-time now, but when I retire I'll be able to give more time to the allotment.'

Brenda turned up almost everywhere: at the market, in charity shops, walking a snappy little terrier on the promenade, and once or twice they shared a cup of tea in one of the promenade cafés. One day Viola met another volunteer, a woman called Sunita, for lunch, and another time she went for a walk with Adrian and his mother. She accustomed herself to the daily, warm embrace of Mary, a roly-poly octogenarian woman of Caribbean heritage, who could not be in anyone's company without hugging and patting them. Gradually, Viola got to know their stories. Sunita was a widow with five sons all at university. She confided in Viola that she suffered from depression and came to the allotment as part of her recovery therapy. Mary's husband had dementia. She cared for him at home six days a week, but on Tuesdays he went to a day centre and she came to the allotment for respite. Adrian's mum, Betty, was a single parent, chuffed to bits to see her son at college, learning a skill that would support him when she was no longer around. Gordon, she knew, was just lonely, and Clive and Vanessa … well, who knew what benefit they derived from it?

She could look across the allotment now and feel that she knew everyone a little. Only Martin remained a mystery.

Chapter Six - Maisie

A few days pass before Maisie learns what crisis at the farm had sent Gwen hurrying over there, and resulted in her own extraordinary conversation with Amy Snow.

Working in her garden, Maisie becomes aware of more than usual activity in the farm's rough paddocks over the hedge. She hears heavy vehicles coming and going and a lot of plaintive bleating from the goats. Intrigued, she walks to the gate in the orchard to see what's going on, and is in time to witness the whole herd being coaxed up a narrow, straw-strewn gangway and into a trailer. She can just make out Val, a diminutive figure in her habitual overalls and wellington boots, but there are several others Maisie doesn't recognise. A vet, she thinks, in professional-looking oilskin over-trousers, some men in workwear and others who might be volunteers but who look much more business-like than the usual collection of bored retirees and troubled youths who sometimes show up to help.

A new port-a-cabin has been delivered to the site as well as a nearly-new static caravan, which has been put down where Val's old one used to be, indecently close to the chalet that has been Val's home for the past four or five years. Workers are busy connecting them to the utility services. Timber for new fencing and animal shelters is stacked near the entrance. The air of bustle about the place is something entirely new. Usually the farm is rather sorry looking, the animals somehow woebegone, still weighed down by whatever trauma or mistreatment brought them there. Normally Val is the only human figure to be seen, trudging doggedly in all weathers behind a wheelbarrow loaded with manure or hay bales. Maisie uses her hand as a visor to survey the scene. Could this commotion be connected to Val's request for time off?

She looks back at *Old Farm Hall.* Work is progressing well; the fine, dry weather has gifted full days of productive work both inside and out. All the new windows are in place. The old cement render has been hacked off and is being replaced by new, which will be smooth, in the modern fashion, but painted traditionally, in brilliant white, not the battleship grey so popular nowadays. The roof is sound, the solar panels wired up to begin exporting electricity to the grid, the chimneys pointed and lined in preparation for the log-burning stoves that will be installed in the lounge and the dining room. The extension is up to its full height, ready for roof-joists and purlins. Inside, all the *ensuites* are plumbed and plastered; the installation of bathroom fixtures will begin imminently. The rewiring is on-going; Clifford's botches are proving a headache to fathom and unpick. The delicate work of restoring and repairing the ornate coving and ceiling roses will soon commence.

Only an hour earlier she had made twenty-odd cups of tea for the workmen and had a short confab with Trevor about the parquet in the hall and the panelling in the dining room, both of which are to be professionally restored and polished. She probably won't be needed again, so she goes through the gate and plods up the field to where she can see Val in consultation with a youngish, red-haired man in a suit.

Their conversation—one-sided, as Val says little or nothing—falters as Maisie approaches. 'I don't want to interrupt,' she says. 'I can see you're busy. But I wanted a word with you Val, when you have a moment to spare.'

'That's quite alright,' says the man genially. Now she is close to him, Maisie can see he isn't as young as she thought. The suit—natty, probably expensive—fits him like a glove, but is wholly unsuitable for a farm environment. 'Val and I are through, I think.' He turns to where Val stands in his shadow, picking at some indeterminate spatter of grime on the bib of her overalls with a dirty fingernail. 'Unless you wanted to circle back on anything?'

Val gives him an uncomprehending look and says, 'No,' but her tone is uncertain, as though she is not sure what she has just refused.

'That's fine then,' he says, clearly relieved their interview is over. 'I'll get back to head office and make a note of our bullet points.' He turns to Maisie. 'Goodbye. She's all yours,' then he heads to the gate and one of several cars Maisie can now see parked along the lane.

'I had to come over, Val. What on earth is going on?'

'This,' Val says dourly, 'is what comes of asking for a holiday.'

'Surely not!'

'Oh yes.' Val exhales heavily. 'You'd better come in. I'm gasping for a cuppa. That lot,' she indicates the vet and the workers who swarm round the port-a-cabin and the caravan, 'can shift for themselves.'

When they reach the chalet, Val removes her boots and her overalls in a little vestibule before venturing inside. Maisie takes off her gardening shoes, although they are not the least dirty. Underneath the overalls Val wears a pale, much-washed tee shirt and some shorts which, though Lycra, hang loosely round her skinny thighs. She dons slippers and takes Maisie across an open-plan living room to a kitchen, where she fills the kettle and puts it on to boil.

'I forgot to tell them about Crystal,' she mutters. 'Poor thing. She won't know what's happened to her.'

'Crystal?'

'The wall-eyed goat with the misshapen hoof,' Val says gloomily. 'She likes a scratch between her ears before she'll touch her breakfast. And that hoof can get infected if it isn't pared back regular.' She reaches for a torn-off sheet of paper and scribbles a note on it.

Maisie has never been inside Val's chalet before. It surprises her. Somehow she had expected it to be an extension of the farm and of Val herself: shabby and unkempt and furred with animal hair. In fact it is a bright, clean and uncluttered space with a proliferation of natural, unvarnished wood on walls and floor, a small dining table with two chairs and a modern settee upholstered in a motley of bright colours. A huge picture window, uncurtained, looks onto the farm. Over the hedge at the bottom of the paddock, Maisie can see the roof and chimneys of *Old Farm Hall*.

'Nice view,' she says.

'It has been,' grumbles Val. 'I thought I'd live out my days here, but it seems not.'

Maisie turns to where Val is standing, in the doorway to the kitchen. 'They haven't told you to leave?'

'No. Not in so many words. But things are going to change. Well,' she cocks her head, indicating the port-a-cabin and the caravan, 'you can see for yourself.'

'And this all kicked off last week, when you phoned Gwen? No wonder she dropped everything to come over.'

At the mention of Gwen's name, Val's expression—surly and resentful—softens. 'Yes,' she says, lowering her gaze. 'She did, didn't she.'

The kettle shrieks and Val goes to make the tea. Maisie perches on the settee.

'Got no biscuits,' says Val, coming in with two mugs.

'That's alright. Now, sit down and tell me what's going on.'

The situation, as far as Maisie can divine it, seems an unfortunate serendipity of a number of events. The first and most momentous of these is the local trust that historically ran the farm has within the last month or so been absorbed into Ani-Well, a much bigger, national, charitable organisation. As well as funding peripatetic animal welfare officers and providing free veterinary treatment to the less-well-off, the organisation also runs a number of facilities just like Val's. It does all the rescue work that the former trust did but in addition—and as a means of generating funds—it runs its facilities as destinations for visitors. To entice them there is to be an adventure playground, a petting shed where hapless rabbits can be fondled by children, something called hay-bale scrambling and possibly even tractor rides. An "educational facility" will focus on conservation and the environment. Also, there is to be a café and a picnic area. Val, utterly appalled, enumerates the attractions as though they were circles of Dante's inferno. 'I can't run all that,' she says. 'I don't want to. It sounds like hell. I just want to look after the animals. It's all I've ever wanted to do.'

It appears Val's farm has operated very much beneath the radar of even the local trust that purportedly ran it. 'I never asked them for anything,' Val explains. 'I suppose they paid the council tax and whatnot, and of course I got my wages, but other than that I kept my head down.'

'But what about animal feed and bedding. What about when you needed the vet?'

Val looks shifty. 'The vet never charged,' she says. 'And as for the other stuff, I got it one way or another. Folks who bring animals here, they feel bad, so they usually leave a donation. I keep it in that tin over there.' She motions towards a Cadbury's biscuit tin that sits on a shelf. 'The rangers at the country park have more hay than they know what to do with, so it's a kindness to take that off them. Other things, like the drinkers and blankets and that …'

Maisie narrows an eye. 'You pay for yourself?'

'Sometimes. I've nothing else to spend my wages on.'

Unfortunately, Val's request for a leave of absence has shaken loose the farm's cloak of invisibility. This is the second event provoking the sudden and alarming turn of things. It alerted the new organisation to her existence and as a result she has been inundated by managers, marketing experts, welfare officials, education consultants and, as Val puts it, 'interfering do-gooders of every hue. If I hadn't contacted them just when I did,' she laments, 'I might have been left alone. There was no reason why they should ever have found out about me.'

'I think,' Maisie suggests gently, 'that, in time, they might have done. Some accountant auditing the books would have queried the expenditure, slight though it may have been. But, oh dear, what an upheaval for you Val, after all these years.'

'That chap,' Val says. 'I couldn't understand a word he said. He wants me to send him a list of my "core competencies." I've no idea what he means. And what's a "customer offer" when it's at home? A kind of voucher?' she speculates. 'He asked me if I wanted to "drill down." *Drill down?* She shakes a bewildered head. 'Is he talking about fracking?'

'I'm as clueless as you are,' says Maisie, 'but, in fairness, I don't think he means that. It must be business jargon.'

Maisie can't help but wonder what the advent of the new, all-singing-all-dancing tourist attraction on the border of *Old Farm Hall* will mean for her. More noise, of course, with children coming in hordes to scramble over the playground. She worries about litter from the café and picnic area and about the traffic that will probably come down her lane in search of the farm. The lane past the farm gives access to a rear entrance to the country park but it is a very narrow, unpromising lane and people are quite likely to turn down Maisie's instead.

But then a thought assails her. 'I presume they've got planning permission. Because, surely, without it, they couldn't develop the site to this extent.'

Val shakes her head. 'I don't know. I suppose I could have asked that chap. I forget his name now. He's the new big cheese in Personnel and Marketing, came to "chat over my options".'

The advent of the big cheese is the third and concluding catalyst of Val's situation. Fresh to the role and keen to make an impression, he has come in all-guns-blazing to shake things up. Anyone can see Val is far from the cutting edge of modern commerce. Maisie doubts she has any qualifications, as such; everything she knows she has learned over long years of trial and error, hard work and dedication. But nowadays the business world is all about algorithms, globalisation, targets and stake-holders. What chance does Val have against such foes?

Maisie sips her tea. 'And what *were* your options, if you don't mind my asking?'

Val pulls a face. 'Like it or lump it.'

'And about the holiday?'

'Oh! As far as that's concerned, there's no problem. They're moving a new site manager in next door, so he'll cover me while I'm away.'

Maisie thinks about Clifford. He had kicked up such a stink when work began on the pub at the bottom of the lane, the Smithy, all to no avail. He'd be equally horrified by the prospect of a tourist attraction on his rear border. Maisie determines to consult James Armstrong. He has strong connections with the local council and the chamber of commerce. She is sure he will be able to advise on the legality of the charity's plans. As for Val's situation, she will talk to her paralegal son, Dominic. Despite his repeated failure to pass his final law exams, he really is very knowledgeable about employment law. Moving a new manager in over Val's head can't be legal, can it? All these changes to be imposed … she wonders if Val might have a case for constructive dismissal. Dominic will know.

'A new site manager?' Maisie repeats.

'Oh yes,' says Val grimly, putting her cup down on the table. 'I've met him. Captain Cruikshank. Ex-army. A proper little Captain Mainwaring, he is, if you know what I mean.'

'I do.' Of course Maisie remembers the portly, officious sit-com character. 'Oh dear,' she says.

She makes no promises to Val, but walks back down the paddock full of determination to do *something*. Really, she has so much on her plate already that it is the last thing she needs, but having nailed her colours irrevocably to the mast of *Old Farm Hall*, she must do all she can to protect it. And Val is an old friend, or would have been if Maisie had made more of an effort in the past. The proposed changes to the farm are a nuisance, but the prospect of a legitimate reason to contact James Armstrong ameliorates the bother considerably.

The donkeys, who have always shared their enclosure with the goats, bray inconsolably for hours.

Pamela, Maisie's daughter-in-law, calls while Maisie is watering the plants in the greenhouse.

'I hope you know,' she says without preamble, 'that Jessica is going to kick up a dreadful stink about this flower girl dress you want her to wear for the wedding. In fact, she's already getting the heebie-jeebies about it. I just mentioned the possibility of a matching ribbon for her hair last night and this morning Dominic only just caught her before she cut a great hank of it off.'

Pamela's accusation reignites all Maisie's anxieties about the forthcoming wedding. Of course she had wanted her two granddaughters to be flower girls, but the idea was stamped on as soon as she mentioned it. Naturally, the fearsome Mrs Fothergill has succeeded where Maisie failed. Maxim's sister is to be the bridesmaid that Frances does not want, and it is in a spirit more vengeful than gracious that Frances permitted the inclusion of her two nieces. 'But you're not to meddle, Mother,' Frances said. 'Minnie understands what's required. If I *must* have a posse of groupies, at least they'll be dressed as *I* want.' The only thing Minnie has let slip is that the outfits are plain and unfussy. Maisie relays this information to Pamela now. 'Not a frill or flounce to be seen,' she says, adding, 'you know Frances. What about you, Pamela? Will you wear that lovely dress you bought for the little garden party I had?'

'It looks as though I'll have no choice,' says Pamela dourly. 'Dominic has put an absolute embargo on further spending, for the time being. I have taken his good suit to the cleaners. It's the one he wore to the funeral. I hope the baby-sick comes out.'

Maisie tries to recall the suit in question, but fails to bring it to mind. 'I'm sure it will be fine.'

'Of course,' says Pamela, 'no one expects to outshine Gareth.'

Maisie's youngest, a commando in a special forces unit, will look splendid in his dress uniform. She has no qualms about *him*.

'Or Michael either,' Pamela adds. 'I'm sure he has a wardrobe full of designer suits.'

Maisie can't contradict her. Michael is the step-son she has only recently learned of, a person who must be shoe-horned into the family from now on. Pamela is right, he will doubtless pass the high standards of even Maxim's frighteningly posh family. But his elegance will only further undermine Dominic's low self-esteem. But perhaps this is something she need not worry about too much. Michael has a knack of bolstering Dominic's confidence. She must trust to both of them to take the oddness of their new-found association and find a way to make it work.

Maisie resists the temptation to offer funds to ease the difficulty of Dominic's sick-stained suit. 'Frances and Maxim are the last people to care about what people wear. That's why they embargoed the hired morning suits. I hope you can reassure Jessica; and if she really can't be brought to wear the flower girl outfit I don't suppose it will be the end of the world.'

'Mrs Fothergill won't think so,' says Pamela with a growl.

'Mrs Fothergill will be too appalled to see the crew of miscellaneous interlopers I'm bringing with me to notice little Jessica,' says Maisie. 'You know what they're like, my friends. I hope Frances won't live to rue the day she said I could bring them. Needless to say, they're all thrilled. None of them has a daughter … well, Gloria does, but they don't speak.'

'She's the blousy one with the blonded hair?'

'Yes.'

'I suppose you've all booked into a hotel. Dominic says we will have to drive back afterwards. He says we can't afford two nights' accommodation.'

In fact, lodging for the extended party had proved quite a problem. No hotel within a convenient distance of Frances and Maxim's college, where the ceremony was to be held, could accommodate them all. The problem had exercised their minds for some time until James Armstrong suggested they find an Airbnb. Oliver Harrington immediately volunteered to organise it. Maisie had no clue what he might have in mind to book, or at what cost. She held back on asking more after some initial stipulations—a downstairs bedroom and accessible shower for Amy, for example—had been waved away by Oliver. Even Minnie, who still has the propensity to quibble at any potentially profligate expenditure, had said, 'I'm sure Oliver will choose somewhere that suits everyone. I'm just so delighted to have been invited.'

Gloria had added, 'I hope it has a hot-tub,' She'd recently had one installed. 'I do so enjoy my daily wallow.'

'Like a hippopotamus,' Viola would have sneered, had she been there, but by that time she had disappeared off to London, so the conversation moved on.

'Oliver's booking something,' Maisie prevaricates now. 'I don't know the details.'

'*Is* he? Just for the two of you?'

'No, of course not,' she says with an artificial laugh, 'for the whole party.' She changes the subject quickly. 'You'll be going back to work soon, won't you? Have you got childcare arranged for little Theo?'

'Oh yes,' says Pamela with a sigh. 'He's got a place at Edmé's nursery. But … it may be that … I mustn't say too much. Things are not finalised yet.'

Maisie's ears prick up. 'Oh? Is change afoot?' She wonders if Pamela is expecting again.

Pamela hesitates. 'Michael came to see us last weekend. You haven't seen him since then?'

'No. Michael came to Nottingham?' What, she wonders, did he make of Dominic and Pamela's dingy little house, its scribbled-on wallpaper and dilapidated kitchen?

'Yes. He just ran down for the day and we all went out to that country house hotel for lunch. You know, the one with the alpacas and the birds of prey? He treated us all, which was good of him, I thought.'

'Goodness,' says Maisie. 'Did the children behave?'

'Beautifully, as a matter of fact, but Michael had booked the girls on an alpaca walk, so that helped. Theo ate his own weight in Yorkshire pudding, and that kept him quiet while we talked.'

'I'm delighted,' says Maisie, wondering what they had talked *about*. Pamela had been brazen, back in May, in touting for a job for Dominic at Michael's company. Perhaps she had been successful. It would be wonderful to have Dominic and the family nearer to her but it did seem a bit mercenary to take advantage of Michael's affluence. Maisie's idea, in acknowledging Michael as Clifford's son, had been that the benefits should flow all the other way, towards Michael. 'Delighted and intrigued,' she prompts.

'I've probably said too much,' Pamela admits. 'How are the renovations going?'

Maisie talks for a while of the works, downplaying their extent and certainly their expense until, abruptly, Pamela says, 'Oh! There's Theo. He's woken up from his nap. I have to go. Bye.'

Maisie returns to her watering. Usually, any activity in the garden soothes her nerves but today she finds that relief does not come. Pamela's call has threatened to tip over—again—Maisie's stack of woes. Wasn't the dress Pamela bought for the garden party a sort of orange blossom colour? Oh God! And she hates to think that Michael has been in some way manoeuvred into offering Dominic a job. She stops. No. I won't allow things to get on top of me, like they did at the garden centre. I must keep hold of the revelation that came to me then: that these things are out of my hands. But Val's situation—that is something I can help with.

She pulls out her phone and calls James Armstrong.

James Armstrong comes to the Crescent the following evening in response to Maisie's invitation. Minnie is out babysitting for a friend while Maisie has been trying to catch up with the gardening although, truth be told, she is exhausted from a day spent in her own garden. Minnie's house is to be put on the market as soon as they have moved back into *Old Farm Hall* and Maisie feels it is the least she can do to keep Minnie's grounds in trim. Also, the long, light evenings are too lovely to waste indoors.

James's house is not very far away from the Crescent, situated on a similarly exclusive road. Like Minnie's house, it borders the golf course, and has a view of the sea. Maisie has never been there, but she envisages houses of similar, ivy-encrusted grandeur, inhabited by consultant surgeons and high court judges. How James endures such solitary majesty now Elspeth is in care, she can only imagine. She wonders if, like Minnie—and to an extent like herself soon after Clifford's death—he has reduced his living down to one or two rooms. Does he live off cream crackers and stale things from the fridge, and drink milk straight from the carton? She supposes he eats out most of the time, with business contacts and friends, although who those friends might be she has no idea; he never mentions any of them by name. When she is with James she is always conscious of Elspeth's shadowy presence inhabiting him like a ghost, her weight on his shoulders. Suffering brings out Maisie's inherent kindness but her feelings for James go beyond mere compassion.

James arrives on foot, walking along the periphery of the fairway that divides Minnie's house from the cliffs and the sea. Only his shadow, falling across where she is weeding a rockery, alerts Maisie to his presence. When she looks up, the low sun is in her eyes and she can only make out his silhouette.

He is tall and well-built, with a shock of wavy brown hair that he has a habit of raking back with his hand. She struggles to her feet to greet him. He is wearing sunglasses so she can't see his eyes. Maisie takes in his attire: smart twill shorts and a monogrammed polo shirt, his feet sockless in expensive-looking boat shoes. His bare calves are shapely, tanned and furred with golden hair. His kiss—brisk and continental—is nothing like the fierce and passionate one they had shared a few weeks previously in Maisie's kitchen.

She removes her gardening gloves and runs her hands through her hair—surely it looks a mess—laughing awkwardly. Dolly, rather belatedly, runs barking from where she has been lying in an envelope of evening sun just within the French doors, but as soon as she recognises James she retreats back to the house.

'Thank you for coming,' Maisie says. She precedes him along a path towards a summerhouse that has been strategically placed to catch the last rays of the evening sun. On a little deck in front of it there are two chairs and a table. 'Do sit down,' says Maisie. 'I have some beer in the fridge. Would you like one?'

'Only if you'll join me,' James says affably. 'Is Minnie out?'

'Yes. Babysitting for a single mum who's doing something called an Alpha course. It's a church thing.'

'She's very into all of that, isn't she—Minnie, I mean?' James remarks.

'More so, recently. I think in the past she went to church just for somewhere to go. She met Peter there. Then when he died it helped with the loneliness. But since she moved to the citadel, something has changed. It's more than just a social thing, now. Let me get that beer.'

Maisie pours her own beer into a glass but knows James prefers to drink from the bottle. She adds a bowl of nuts to the tray and carries it out to the summerhouse. Once they are settled he asks, 'Has she tried to get you to … you know …'

'To convert? Not as such. She's invited me to one or two events. I helped at a bazaar and then there was a concert by a choir of people who had been homeless—reformed addicts, that kind of thing. There were "testimonies." It was very moving; I must say that. Having …' she reaches for a word that will sound neither trite nor disrespectful, '*faith* in their lives has literally saved some of them—from death I mean.'

'Christianity supplies the two needs that everyone has,' James says, reaching for some nuts. 'We all need to feel loved and we're all afraid of dying. At the home where Elspeth is—it's not specifically a Christian institution but most of the staff seem to be Christians and the local church provides a lot of support—that's the nature of the comfort that is most often meted out. The patients needn't worry; they are valued and cared for, and the future is nothing to fear.'

'I suppose,' says Maisie tentatively, 'that for patients who've lost their connection with the past and who are confused and disoriented by the present, it's the only comfort that *can* be offered.'

'I suppose so,' says James. He heaves a heavy sigh and puts his beer bottle down on the table. 'I don't know,' he says. 'I'd like to think that it's true, but there isn't a spoon big enough to hold the salt of my doubt. I'd need to see it before I could believe it.'

'Minnie says you have to believe it, *then* you can see it,' Maisie says. 'But I seem to recall the same thing was claimed for the Loch Ness monster.'

James chuckles and the mood between them lightens. 'Was there something in particular you wanted to see me about?' he asks.

'It's always a pleasure to see you James,' she says warmly, but conscious of a constriction in her throat. There are so many things she would like to offload onto James's patient, capable but already so put-upon shoulders, but how can she trouble him with such trivia as wedding outfits and her disgruntlement over being excluded from the wedding arrangements? Of course, about Oliver, she cannot say a word. She launches into a description of the situation at Val's farm, the charity's plans for development and the introduction of a new manager. James listens, nodding sagely from time to time, his legs stretched out in front of him and crossed at the ankle. The sun slips slowly down the sky and a beautiful purple twilight exudes from the earth. The heat of the day, which has been like a fist, releases. And the air of the garden is filled with the scent of roses, honeysuckle and thyme.

When Maisie's tale is done, he says, 'As far as improving the site—better housing for the animals and so on—there's no need to get permission for that. The port-a-cabin and the caravan are temporary structures, so that's okay too.' Now it is dusk and James removes his sunglasses, but Maisie, sitting at an oblique angle from him, still cannot see his eyes. 'The play equipment will need health and safety input, a risk assessment and so forth, but that's more for insurance purposes. If there's to be catering, the same thing will apply. Food standards will get involved, EHOs—'

'EHOs?'

'Sorry. Environmental Health Officers. They'll want to inspect the catering facilities as well as the procedure for pest control and the disposal of animal waste, and what measures are in place to prevent any cross-contamination. But you can bet the charity will have all this covered. Arguably, they'll need change of use from agricultural to leisure, although historically people have always been allowed to come and look at the animals, haven't they? So that may be just a formality. If you want to object ...' He turns towards her. She knows one eyebrow is raised but it is almost dark now so she can't actually see it. 'Do you want to object, Maisie?'

'I'm worried about Val, of course,' she says, 'but I am concerned about what effect the whole thing will have on my house too. Its value—I'm spending a fortune on its restoration—and its environment. If there is the opportunity I'd like to voice concerns. I suppose I'd get accused of ... what's the term for people who agree with things in principle until it affects them personally?'

'Nimbyism? Yes, you might. And we can't lose sight of the fact that the farm does a lot of good. Those animals—'

'Yes, of course. But it can do that without play equipment and cups of overpriced coffee.'

'Access might be an issue. That lane is awkward. More of a track, really. They'll need dedicated parking, otherwise the cars will block access to the country park.'

'I've seen ambulances use that track, in the past.'

'That's something you can raise, then. The council has a portal online where you can view current planning applications. I'll have a look at it in the morning, just to see if anything is pending, and if there isn't, I have the name of a planning officer I can contact, just to test the ground. Now, what about Val?'

'She's been as good as told she isn't required any longer. But I'll ask Dominic about that.'

'I know something about employment law, you know.'

'I know. But if you look at that council thing for me, you'll be doing enough. I mustn't impose.'

Maisie expects—or hopes—James will say, 'I'd do anything for you, Maisie.' But the words remain unspoken.

James finishes his beer. It is almost fully dark now, with only a frill of light remaining along the far horizon. 'I ought to go if I'm to walk back along the links,' he says. 'I don't want to fall to my death over the cliff.'

'Gosh, no,' says Maisie. 'And I can't offer to run you. Minnie has the car. Although,' she peers at her wristwatch, 'she shouldn't be too long, now.'

'Don't worry,' James says, 'I'll be fine.'

Maisie casts about for reasons to make James stay. 'Have you eaten?' she asks, doing a quick mental assessment of the contents of the fridge. 'I could probably rustle up some cheese and biscuits.'

'I ate a good lunch. I'm okay, thanks.' He reaches forward and picks up his sunglasses, folding them and making to slip them into the breast pocket of a shirt he isn't wearing. He makes a self-deprecating noise, realising his error, and places the glasses back on the table. Maisie senses he shares her reluctance to end their time together and indeed his next remark is, 'I can always walk home the long way, if it's too dark. I mean, really, what have I to go home to?'

His bleakness touches her. 'What about another beer then?' she offers.

This time she brings a wider variety of snacks on her tray—olives and some artichoke hearts decanted from a jar, some breadsticks and a tub of hummus—and a citronella candle, as well as their beers.

'Tell me about the wedding plans,' James says, when she has lit the candle. It casts a wavering, slightly eerie light on the shrubs that border the little arbour.

It is the last thing Maisie wants to talk about but her troubles spill from her mouth. 'The nearer it gets, the more I dread it,' she admits. 'Maxim's mother features in my nightmares and I worry that … I'm ashamed to say it … but Gloria and the others, they're quite giddy with excitement. I'm worried they won't behave themselves. Those are the only two things I can positively state with any degree of certainty.' This isn't quite true. She is certainly very worried that Gwen's relationship with Val is opening up a schism within the cohort of women that might well sour the wedding trip, but James won't be interested in that. And, at the back of her mind is the idea that Oliver will take the opportunity of being under the same roof to make some kind of move on her, but this is not a concern she chooses to share just now so she concludes, 'I know literally nothing about any of the arrangements. I don't even know where we're staying. Do you?'

James wafts at a mosquito Maisie can't see. 'Well, yes. I can vouch for the accommodation. It's certainly very nice. But Oliver would insist on taking charge of the arrangements so, naturally, the thing has mushroomed. Optional extras that turn out not to be optional at all … it's costing a fortune.'

'Who's paying?' Maisie is appalled.

'Not you. That's been decided.'

'Oh.' Maisie finds she is hurt, rather than grateful for this consideration. Have they all been communicating behind her back?

'The party is growing,' James tells her. 'Michael has asked if he can join us. Of course he'll fit right in, this having become a Harrington affair.'

'Oh,' Maisie says again, nonplussed. A *Harrington* affair? But this is *my* family occasion, nothing to do with the Harringtons. On the other hand, if the place is vast, I wonder if Dominic and Pamela could be saved the expense of a hotel night. And what about Gareth? But no one seems to want to know what *I* think. I've been excluded from the plans *again*. 'It sounds intriguing,' she says tersely.

Through the glimmer of the candlelight, James throws her a look. 'I've explained about the Harringtons before,' he says. 'They have their own ideas about things. Oliver certainly does. He's tenacious and a force to be reckoned with. As an employee, that's great. I can trust him to get any job done. But on a human level, he can be ... overbearing. I might go so far as to say "manic".'

Maisie takes a gulp of beer. 'Was ... was Elspeth like the others?' she ventures. James's wife is not often mentioned between them but whether that is because she is hallowed ground or quicksand, Maisie isn't sure.

James considers. 'She's the exception that proves the rule,' he says at last. 'She isn't anything like the others, or she wasn't.' He gives a harsh bark of laughter. 'Now, I suppose, she has returned to type. As you know, mental illness runs in the females of the family. But back then, when I married her, she was a quiet, self-effacing little thing, tossed backwards and forwards in the stormy currents generated by the rest of them. All she wanted was a quiet, simple life. The glamorous side of being a Harrington—Masonic dinners, golf days, charity events—those meant nothing to her. And as for the histrionics—the all too public displays of excess, especially Louisa's, and the fallings-out—she hated all that. Now ... well, it surprises me ... now Elspeth is very volatile. It's as though the illness has opened a valve and a lifetime's angst is pouring out of her. I had no idea she had stored up so much anger and—well, vitriol. She can be toxic.' He shakes his head, his eyes fixed on a point in the dark garden. 'The Elspeth I knew is gone.' Slowly, he turns to look at Maisie. In the candlelight she can see his eyes are wet. 'I'm as much a widow as you are, Maisie.'

She reaches out an instinctive hand and takes hold of his. It is warm, and returns her pressure. She feels the current of his loneliness in the soft dryness of his palm and in the way he draws her hand into his. An answering surge comes down her arm to meet it. She hadn't known how lonely she was until this moment. In fact, if she had been asked, she would have said that in the past few months she had felt more befriended than ever before. The heartfelt touch of their hands reminds her of what Amy had described—the tenderness of human contact, and its necessity.

Maisie feels her own need for such contact rising to meet his. He begins to draw her inexorably towards him and leans forward. The candlelight flickers in his eyes. Then Elspeth's shade interposes itself and Maisie pulls away. It isn't true that he is as much a widow as she is. His wife is alive, an insurmountable obstacle.

Just then the kitchen light goes on, banishing the comfortable shadows of the garden in its harsh, florescent glare.

'Minnie is home,' says Maisie.

Maisie's mind is occupied by the extraordinary conversations she is having with her friends recently. They seem intent on opening up the fissures in their histories, lifting layers of their lives to allow her a peek of their sacred interiors. In Gloria's case, a not-so-sacred interior, perhaps—there had been nothing holy about her drawer of sex toys—but even those'd had the sort of honesty that first Amy and then James has vouchsafed her. And now there appears, since Gwen's advent, a less impenetrable sheen to Val's usually crusty veneer. Only Oliver seems intent on bamboozling her with mixed signals. Viola, of course, has clammed up entirely; Maisie has received no reply to her various messages. Maisie is a relative newcomer to the forum of personal friendships. Perhaps these intimacies are normal? On the whole she feels blessed by them, but there is an element of burden too. She feels honour-bound, now, to call or visit Amy every day. And, having taken up the banner of Val's cause it would be a dereliction of duty to lay it back down. On that front, however, there is some cause for hope. James informed her that an application for change of use is pending with the council, and sent her a link so she can lodge her objections to the new management objectives of the farm. One more thing she must add to her unwieldy to-do list, at the top of which is the matter of her wedding attire.

One day soon after James's visit she manages to return to the boutique with her mother-of-the-bride outfit. It is an unprepossessing shopfront on a busy arterial road, with a doubtful looking Chinese takeaway on one side and a locksmith on the other. The nearest carpark is a good ten minutes' walk away and Maisie struggles with the awkward parcel of her outfit as a warm wind blows dust and litter in crazy eddies around her ankles and fills the large polythene bag as though it were a sail.

The inside of the shop is an oasis of calm. Her feet sink into the plush carpet which, after the hot and uncompromising pavement, feels like deep, yielding moss. The shop froths with lace and dazzles with silk and satin in every mother-of-the-bride hue. Small, beautifully upholstered chairs are positioned here and there. Lamps in pleated pink shades proliferate. French polished side tables are cluttered with silk corsages and boutonnières. A multitude of mirrors reflect Maisie's wind-blown hair and reddened face back at her before the scented air-conditioning and the effusive approach of two immaculately made-up sales assistants assail her. One of them—an artificially sculped Barbie doll of a girl with an impossibly flawless complexion—relieves Maisie of her burden and lifts out the cellophane-wrapped garment as though revealing a holy relic. She hangs it reverently on a rail. The other—more mature, with nails like talons and a face made mask-like by an excess of Botox—coos an obsequious enquiry with the degree of concern one might use when asking about an injured dog or sick child.

'Mrs Wilde, isn't it? What can be the matter? You're not … I hope there's no possibility …?' She leaves the unspeakable prospect unarticulated.

'Oh no,' Maisie assures her, sinking, as though drawn by irresistible magnetism, into the nearest velvet chair. 'The wedding is still on, don't worry. And I love the outfit. But it turns out nearly everyone I know is planning on wearing the same colour, or so close to it that—'

The end of her sentence is rendered inaudible by the women's shrieks of horror. As though choreographed, they clap their hands to their mouths, appalled. Their eyebrows levitate to their hairlines, or would have done, if either'd had sufficient elasticity of muscle to achieve such a thing. The cancelling of the wedding, an absconding groom, even the very death of the bride could not have been greeted with more abject dismay.

'So, I wondered,' Maisie goes on when their cries of consternation have ebbed, 'whether you have the same thing, but in a different colour.'

'Oh,' the botoxed woman says, suddenly wary. 'You mean, you wish to return this *tenue*?'

'This outfit, yes, and swap it for another. Is that possible?'

The women exchange a look, slightly offended. The younger one breathes in sharply through one plastic nostril. 'Have you had any alterations done to it?'

Maisie shakes her head.

'Hmm,' says the older woman, looking doubtfully to where the apparel hangs on the rail. Warily she approaches it and peers beneath the cellophane cover. 'You'd be surprised how many people wear an ensemble and then return it, with some excuse or other. We can always tell, of course. Soiling to the hem or neckline. Body odour—'

'I haven't even tried it on since I bought it,' Maisie protests. 'It is exactly as it was when you sold it to me.'

There is an awkward silence while the woman uses her talons to lift different parts of the dress to her face, sniffing suspiciously.

'It still has its tags on,' Maisie says, her indignance rising, anger boiling up, like milk in a pan. 'I paid an awful lot of money for it. You did say, when I bought it, if there were any issues I should come straight back.'

'Naturally, we always say that,' Barbie coos. 'But,' with supreme complacency, 'there never are any issues with the clothing. What we mean really is, if you find you need accessories.' She indicates the hats, bags, shawls and shoes that occupy their own section towards the rear of the shop.

'This isn't an issue with the garment itself,' Maisie says, quelling her wrath but finding that, in its stead, is a desire to burst into tears that makes her throat tight. Her next words are almost a whine. 'I'd just like to exchange it for a different colour, if you have one.'

'And what if we don't?' Botox has finished her examination and takes up a defensive stance by the till, as though Maisie might force a way past her to raid it. 'We don't offer refunds, you know. Not just because you've changed your mind.'

'I haven't changed my mind.' Maisie tries not to sound pathetic. 'Not really.' She decides to summon every woman's nightmare. 'I can't turn up in the same colour as everyone else, can I?'

'I suppose,' offers Barbie, whose heart, behind her unnaturally perky breasts, must have some human feeling, 'we could look and see.'

'There'd be a restocking fee,' her colleague says nastily.

Pure profiteering, Maisie thinks, but clamps her mouth closed on an objection. She gives a cold, cynical nod.

This time there is not—as on her first visit—a glass of sparkling wine or a platter of canapés to sweeten the bitter pill; but there is a choice of alternative colours and, at this point, that is more than Maisie could have hoped. Neither is there a hovering, obsequious assistant to tweak hemlines and offer up sycophantic exclamations, but Maisie doesn't care. She dithers between powder blue and a light, pistachio green before turning her back altogether on pastels—that seem rather insipid now she really looks at them—and opting for a rich and luxurious colour that the label describes as teal but seems more to Maisie like iridescent peacock blue. It will be just as tricky to find accessories to match it but as soon as she sees it against her tanned complexion and sun-touched hair she has that thrilling feeling of completeness. It is stunning—much more dramatic than the apricot; its layers of silk and lace make her feel exotic.

Before finally agreeing to it she makes a call.

Frances answers, irritated as always. 'Yes, Mum? I can't talk for long. We've a table booked for afternoon tea with Maxim's people.'

'That's perfect, actually,' Maisie shouts. She has stepped out of the shop, back into the heat and noise. Lorries and buses thunder past. 'I wonder if you can tell me what colour Mrs Fothergill's outfit is. I've had to change mine … it's a long story … and I want to make sure we're not going to clash. For the photographs, you know.'

'What do they matter? I'll never want to look at them. I hate seeing photographs of myself.'

'Could you just ask her, Frances please?' she says, through clenched teeth.

Frances relents. 'I don't need to ask. She showed me last week. It's sort of pastel orange.'

The traffic going back to Millport is particularly bad. Maisie calls at the Crescent to deposit her outfit and it's almost five o'clock when she gets back to *Old Farm Hall*. The men have gone home for the day and there is an air of eerie quiet about the site. She squeezes her car past the skip. It is a perpetual feature on Maisie's drive these days, stacked with off-cuts of timber, rubble, old radiators and Styrofoam cups. Sometimes she imagines Clifford's shade jealously picking through the day's trash, rescuing bits "that might come in handy."

There is a strange car parked on the drive.

The front door is boarded up and she hurries round the side of the house, ducking to avoid the scaffolding, scanning the garden, the orchard, the *parterre* for any sign of a visitor. Seeing no one, she walks across the terrace to find the back door ajar.

In the kitchen she finds Oliver and a man she doesn't recognise poring over a laptop computer on the old table.

Oliver straightens at her arrival. 'There you are at last Maisie,' he says, smiling, but with a trace of disapproval or perhaps disappointment on his handsome features. 'Mr Naidu and I had almost given up on you.'

Maisie looks from one to the other of them, nonplussed. 'Did we have an appointment?'

'Yes,' Oliver says with forced lightness. 'Mr Naidu is from the kitchen showroom. You remember, we went there a week or so ago—'

'Oh,' Maisie cries shaking her head. 'My brain,' she says. 'It's addled. Was that for today?'

Mr Naidu glances at his watch—an expensive one. 'It was. But perhaps we should re-arrange?'

'No need for that, surely,' Oliver puts in. 'We've covered a lot of ground already, between the two of us. Maisie can look over what we've sketched out. You never know,' he gives a self-deprecating laugh, 'she may think it can't be improved on.'

'That would be a first,' says Mr Naidu dryly, and the two men exchange a complicit look. 'At the very least, the ladies do like to pick the colour.'

They step aside so Maisie can see the screen. She makes no move towards it, resentful of their patronising air and offended by their presence here, uninvited, in her kitchen. It doesn't matter that the house is a building site. It's irrelevant that, all day long, it is invaded by builders and deliverymen, building inspectors and planning officers. Those people are all funnelled through the conduit of Trevor Vine's eagle attention; but these two …

'How did you get in?' she asks. Trevor has one key, she and Minnie share another. There is a spare, kept hidden—

'I used the spare key,' Oliver says. 'Gareth was locked out one night when I brought him home the worse for wear from a race meeting, so I knew where it was kept.'

'And you thought you'd—' Maisie indicates Mr Naidu. She speaks mildly, as though the thing is only of passing interest, but her rage is a fireball inside her. It surprises and rather appals her. She is not used to feeling so angry, but to some degree or other it seems to be a permanent state with her now.

'I expected you any moment,' Oliver says, 'and it seemed rude to keep Mr Naidu waiting.'

His remark quenches Maisie's indignation somewhat. Of course, it's true she is unconscionably late.

'Not to worry, Mrs Wilde,' says the salesman. 'We have made good use of the time.'

It turns out that the two men have used Maisie's tardiness to measure up the kitchen and make a close examination of the existing plumbing and electrics. They have entered it all into a program on Mr Naidu's computer and spent a long time experimenting with different configurations of larder cupboards, pan drawers, plate racks and bridging units.

'The finishes are really exceptional,' says Oliver, practically bouncing with enthusiasm. 'I particularly like this handleless design. It's so sleek and modern.' Reluctantly, Maisie approaches the screen. Her kitchen is unrecognisable—cold and ugly—with high gloss units in clinical white.

'Oh no,' she murmurs. 'We want a farmhouse-style kitchen. Painted. In cream.' It was what she had always wanted, right from the start—something Clifford had promised her "in time," and a design Minnie has also readily agreed to.

Whatever objection Oliver is about to make, he chokes it back with difficulty, his Adam's apple bobbing in his throat, like an owlet swallowing a mouse whole.

'No problem,' says Mr Naidu, reaching for his keyboard.

Oliver makes another sally. 'You thought you'd keep the sink in front of the window, I suppose,' he says, pointing to the place where Maisie's sink had been located in the old kitchen. 'But look at this.' He seizes the mouse from Mr Naidu and clicks a tab. 'If you had a kitchen island, you could have your sink in it. What do you think? Right across from the range cooker, and making a perfect triangle with the fridge, which,' he strides across to the end wall and opens his arms to indicate a large, impressive appliance, 'will go perfectly here, even one of those enormous American-style ones, which I think you're going to need. That way your guests can sit here,' he sashays across the flagstone floor to indicate the other side of the imaginary kitchen island, 'out of the way of the cooking, but still part of the social occasion.' He perches on a make-believe stool and leans his elbows on the surface of the proposed island. 'See?'

Maisie stares, trying to see—in the gloom and dereliction of the empty room—the picture Oliver has conjured, while struggling to suppress her irritation with him. Who does he think he is? Why should he have any say at all? How dare he steal from her all the fun of planning and deciding? 'A sink in the middle of the room?'

'Oh yes,' Mr Naidu chimes in. He is a dapperly dressed middle-aged man. In the dimness of the unlit kitchen his teeth and the whites of his eyes have an unnatural quality and remind Maisie of the synthetic attributes of the women in the boutique earlier. Still bruised from her encounter with them, she reminds herself not to allow her resentment of them to show in her attitude to him.

Oliver, on the other hand, has surely crossed some kind of red line and immediately proceeds to add insult to injury by crossing another. He stamps the floor experimentally with his foot. 'I presume these slabs are going,' he says. 'So old fashioned and rustic. No problem to dig a channel for drainage and water, once you've got rid of them.'

'No, indeed,' says Mr Naidu, peering down. 'Although in this light it's difficult to see.'

'There's no electricity,' Maisie tells him, 'so I can't put the light on. We're still mid re-wire.'

She looks down at the old stone slabs, lost in a wash of shadow at her feet. She doesn't need to be able to see them to know every contour, every corner of them. How many thousands of times has she mopped them? What cocktails of things have been spilt on them over the years? How many times have her own tears splashed on to them? In some ways she would be glad to be rid of them, but they are a part of the house's original fabric, like the panelling in the dining room and the cornicing in the hallway. It would be sacrilege to remove them even if they could be pried up, which she doubts.

Oliver gets his phone out and presses the torch. In its unflattering beam the slabs do look dour; dirty, of course, from the tramp of dozens of work boots, and perhaps indeed very unsophisticated. She almost hates him for exposing them in such a harsh, cruel light.

'No,' she says firmly. 'The slabs are staying. They belong with the house.'

Oliver snaps off the torch with a snort and stuffs his phone back into his pocket before folding his arms across his chest and turning to examine a cobwebby corner of the room.

Maisie, unwilling to rub anyone the wrong way, offers, 'I like the idea of an island though, so we can all work on food preparation together. The sink can stay where it was. It's quite nice to be able to—'

'Oh no, Maisie,' Oliver shouts, almost derisively, swivelling back to face her. 'Not if you want the range over here.' He strides round to the place he means and waves his arm. 'Imagine having to walk *round* the island every time you need to get to the oven!'

'I've walked from the sink to the oven round the kitchen table for twenty years,' she replies. 'It'll be no different.'

'Mrs Wilde,' says Mr Naidu, fixing her with a suggestive eye which, in the gloom, is like an iridescent marble with a dark centre. 'Different is exactly what we're looking for here, isn't it? After twenty years, I think you deserve something different, don't you? This is a large space. You have the potential for something splendid. Your … friend and I have been looking at—'

'He isn't … ' Oliver, across the room, emits an offended grunt. 'I mean, of course, he's a friend,' Maisie amends, 'but he isn't the primary decision-maker. I am.'

There is an awkward pause.

Then Oliver expectorates a strangulated, 'Naturally.'

Mr Naidu makes a little bow. 'Please won't you look at the schematics we have put together for your consideration?'

Maisie walks over to the table and puts her hand on its old, worn but achingly familiar surface while she watches the screens of her unrecognisable kitchen scroll by on Mr Naidu's laptop. Distractedly she notes the ingenuity of various rotating shelves and pull-out baskets, the capacious drawers and vast acreage of worktop, even the shaft of sunlight that comes in through the window—something that never occurs at any time of year in this northerly-facing room.

'I like the idea of the island,' she says again. 'But we could move it along a bit, couldn't we? And what about putting the Aga there.' She points to the place where Oliver had suggested they put the fridge. There is a wide alcove where, presumably in days of yore, the open fire of the ancient cooking range had been located. It has been empty for years; its chimney capped. Maisie has used it to store her ironing board and a clothes maiden. 'Would it fit?'

Mr Naidu spirits a laser measure from his pocket and projects it across the gap, squinting to see the measurement. 'Yes!' he pronounces. 'Even with the Aga companion that your ... that I am told you are considering.'

Oliver steps into the alcove and makes some experimental taps on the plaster around it. 'It would make a nice feature, I suppose,' he mumbles. 'You could put an artificial mantel up here, tile the interior ...'

Mr Naidu works at his laptop and in minutes has reconfigured the kitchen to show the Aga ensconced in its alcove, the sink in its customary location and an enormous fridge-freezer in the spot the old range had occupied. 'The golden triangle,' he declares with satisfaction. The island has two levels, one for standing and working, the other level lower, effectively a table. 'This can be as large or small as you require,' he says. 'Unless you wanted to keep this table?' He pats it gingerly. The table is indeed another of the house's "holy cows." It was there when Clifford and Maisie moved in. But she has resigned herself to its departure. Indeed, it is only here now to facilitate the making of the workmen's brews.

Maisie, catching the vision, begins to walk round the room. 'Then, on this side of the door, a big dresser arrangement,' she says, waving her arms. 'I can display my aunt's Old Blue Willow on it. Lots of storage below—'

'Yes, yes,' Mr Naidu squeaks, his hands a blur as he draws it into the plan.

Oliver goes over to the outside wall, 'And along here ... ?' he queries bullishly.

Graciously, inferring a suggestion he has not made, Maisie says, 'Yes, Oliver. Lots of cupboards and a long length of worktop. This is where the kettle will be and all the cups in a cupboard above. I expect we'll be making a lot of tea!'

'You could do away with the kettle altogether if you have one of those boiling water taps,' Oliver snipes, his unspoken addendum being that, *naturally,* Maisie will veto the idea.

To Maisie there is something primordial about the process of putting a kettle on to boil. It signals all kinds of rituals endemically entrenched in the English psyche. What visit does not begin or end with the making of tea? What heartache cannot be soothed by it? Tea is the nation's mother's milk. As foetuses we float in amniotic tea. But not wishing to provoke Oliver more than she already has, she makes a non-committal noise and the matter is left unresolved.

It is almost fully dark in the kitchen by the time they finish. The bluish glow of Mr Naidu's computer screen is the only light in the room. Then the computer is closed and there is no light at all. Outdoors, however, the evening is still bright. Maisie opens the back door as wide as it will go; it is as though she has opened a portal to a magical land of light and birdsong.

Oliver has withdrawn to a corner. Maisie knows he is there but in the past hour he has played little part in the discussion even though, to mollify him, she has from time to time asked for his opinion.

'You must think carefully about lighting,' Mr Naidu advises as he shuffles together his brochures, 'but that's for another day, I think.'

'I am really very sorry for being so late,' Maisie says, holding out her hand.

'That's no problem,' Mr Naidu assures her. His grip is firm but brief. 'We got there in the end, I think. I'll go back to the office and price all this up for you, Mrs Wilde.'

Maisie watches him walk along the terrace and turn the corner. 'Come out into the garden, Oliver. It's too dark and gloomy in here.' She has offended him, she supposes, and perhaps he feels she has shown him up in front of the salesman. His chagrin has morphed into a sulk. She sets her mind to making things right.

'I haven't time,' he says, emerging from the shadows and almost pushing past her. 'I should have been at work half an hour ago.'

She is wedged into the doorway. He looks down at her, glowering. 'I thought you were very rude.'

'To be so late?' she says, feeling herself pale under his admonition. 'Yes. To be truthful, I'd forgotten all about it. Thank you for holding the fort.'

'Yes, that,' he says, 'but also to me. You swept aside all my suggestions. I don't know why I bothered. It isn't as though I don't know a thing or two about kitchens, you know. I'm pretty clued up, as it happens. I'd have thought you'd be grateful for my input.'

'I am *very* grateful,' she cries. She lays a hand on his arm and presses it warmly, offering the platonic kind of human contact Amy had suggested he needed. 'Thank you, Oliver,' she says, looking up into his dark eyes. 'I'm so glad you were here and I do appreciate your input. I'm sorry if I seemed … if you felt … but, in the end, this will be *my* kitchen.'

He nods slowly. 'I see,' he says heavily. '*Your* kitchen.'

'Well …' She struggles to understand how the remark could be a surprise. 'Yes. Of course.'

'Of course,' he echoes.

He stands very close, almost pinioning her against the open door. She can feel his chest as he breathes in and out, the whistle of the air in his nostrils. Beneath her hand a pulse throbs in his arm.

'Oliver?' she says, very gently. 'What else did you imagine?'

He places his hands on her shoulders. They are large hands and, beneath them, her shoulders feel frail and vulnerable. 'What did I imagine?' he repeats, adding to himself with a sigh, 'Oh! What haven't I imagined?' He looks at her with eyes that burn but are unreadable to her.

'I don't know,' she bursts out at last. 'I think that's the problem, Oliver. I just don't know what you think. We talk and talk but, in the end, I can't think what we've actually *said.*'

She doesn't want a row. What she wants is to break through the veil of half-hints and the flurry of flirtation that has separated them, even though she is afraid of what she might find on the other side of it. The nature of what that might be is ambiguous to her. If only he would *say*, and then she would face it—a vacuum, a vortex, indifference, or a passion so incendiary it might turn her to ash—whatever it was. To encourage him she places her own hands on his arms, above the elbows, where the muscle is taut and bulging. 'Just talk to me,' she says.

He croaks, 'I haven't time.'

'Not now, perhaps,' she concedes, 'but soon.'

The man looking down at her is not at all the urbane and worldly man she has known up to now. There is something boyish and strangely appealing in his confusion. His lips move but no words will come. A lock of dark hair—usually swept back and gelled into place—has fallen across his brow. Even in the pouring rain of the Lake District she never saw him anything other than immaculately smart, neat and flawlessly styled. It is humbling to observe this unwonted dishevelment. It is overwhelming to entertain the suggestion that she might be the cause of it. But his very awkwardness is a siren to Maisie, who is far more likely to be moved by need than by self-sufficiency. She slides her hands up his arms and cups his face but resists the urge to push back the errant lock of hair. 'It will be alright, Oliver,' she says. 'We can work it out together if we are just honest with each other.'

For an instant they lock eyes. Oliver's are dark, then suddenly lit by a manic fire she has never seen in them before. The next moment she is caught up in a torrent, a tornado—snatched from shelter and hurled into the roaring tumult of his frenzy. She is kissed, her lips crushed beneath and between his, her body pressed against the door at her back and ground in front by the weight of his body. She is locked within the cage of his embrace, his hands now in her hair, clutching and pulling, now on her breast, then reaching down to knead her buttock. She feels his hips held hard against her. His tongue is not—as she had once imagined it would be—erotic, but hard and intrusive. Her mews of distress are lost in the abyss of his frenzy. She struggles against him, her hands against his chest, but only when he at last releases her mouth does she manage to shout, 'No! Stop it, Oliver! Stop!'

The fever is over as quickly as it began. He steps away, releasing her entirely, wiping his mouth with the back of his hand. He withdraws, panting slightly, to the centre of the terrace, but his eyes do not leave hers. 'There,' he says, his voice hoarse. 'That's me being honest with you. I hope you understand me now.'

He turns on his heel and strides across the terrace and round the corner of the house.

Maisie's legs are shaking. She staggers to the *parterre* and the stone bench where she and Minnie like to drink their morning tea. The garden is speciously benign, bathed in early evening sunshine. Birds twitter in the orchard, and from over the hedge, she can hear the rattle of a feed bucket tempting the hens back into their run.

She sits for a long time, while the shadows of the garden lengthen and the air cools. From down the lane at the Smithy there drifts the scent of cooking oil and chargrilled meat, carried on a small breeze. It sickens her.

At length, she returns to the house and locks the back door before wandering round in the dusky garden in search of a new secret location for the spare key.

Maisie avoids *Old Farm Hall* for a few days after her bruising encounter with Oliver. This goes against every instinct; the place has been her harbour for almost the whole of her adult life and she has invested in its future now, entirely and irrevocably. But the thought of meeting Oliver is more than she can countenance. She is angry at him, but beneath her anger is a vat of fear. Whatever she has unearthed in him—the power of what she must now unequivocally understand is his attraction to her—is terrifying. From being open to the idea of exploring a new terrain of friendship with him she now finds a chasm whose precipice she dares hardly approach. Maisie has been many things in her life—disappointed, frustrated and humbled—but she has never been afraid. And nor, until lately, has she been conscious of the unreasonable anger that is now her perpetual companion.

Truth be told, life as a whole is a struggle she feels ill-equipped to deal with these days. The finely tilled soil of her life has been infested by every kind of invasive weed and woe. Oliver, in her mind's eye, is an ensnaring bramble: thorny and pernicious. Her skin, where he crushed and chafed her, feels flayed. Then there is Amy, a delicate flower blighted by ill-health; she has developed a summer cold that is threatening to go to her chest and her attendance at the wedding is seriously in doubt. The renovation of the panelling in the dining room has stalled, a huge boulder in the way of progress: suspected dry rot is holding up the specialists brought in for the task. She isn't sleeping, finding it impossible to empty her mind of Oliver, the wedding, James and the enormous scope of the renovations she has put in train. Night after night she lies sleepless, hot and uncomfortable, staring at her ceiling through the brief hours of the summer nights.

One morning she and Minnie argue on finding there are neither eggs nor milk in the fridge.

'You said you would do the shopping on your way home,' Minnie says tearfully. 'I offered, but you said no. Don't you remember?'

Maisie does remember now, when it's too late. Her mind is a sieve. She is tired. Tears vie with an entirely unreasonable desire to fly off the handle. There is no avoiding a visit to *Old Farm Hall* today. Trevor has been on the phone to report an issue with the tiles that have already begun to be installed into one of the bathrooms. Did she really order *callow green*? No! Of course not. She'd chosen *cloudy grey*. She drives to the house fulminating at herself, the tile centre, the traffic and even the weather—it is another beautiful day. But when she arrives, Trevor is dealing with a plastering issue so she decides to walk to the farm to buy eggs.

The farm seems unusually quiet. Val's beaten-up old Land Rover is nowhere to be seen but the hens are out and scratching at the dry mud of the yard and Maisie can see strews of fresh hay in the donkey paddock.

Reports have filtered down—via Gloria and Gwen—of more atrocities being meted out onto Val. A full audit of accounts is threatened. It has been darkly suggested Val's tax affairs might be awry if she has not listed the benefit-in-kind of her living accommodation. The red-haired man has been back, apparently, with a manual as thick as a doorstep of the charity's policies, work-in-practices, aims and objectives—very daunting for anyone, let alone a woman like Val. The hint has been dropped, casually, that she might feel happier with a position elsewhere. Dominic's opinion is that Val would have a strong case for unfair dismissal, but it would be against the former trust, which is now dissolved. Her best hope in her situation is for breach of contract, should she be effectively debarred from her home. But he warns that these cases can take years to resolve and, of course, cost money to pursue.

Maisie and Minnie have penned what they hope will be a compelling letter of objection to the site's change of use. The more she thinks about it the more she dislikes the idea of a busy tourist attraction right on her border. While she has been able to ignore or at least tolerate the light industrial estate and the pub at the front of *Old Farm Hall*, she has always enjoyed the feeling of being in the country that its rear aspect afforded. Of course she has not mentioned this in her letter, sticking to concerns about access, noise and pollution. But the whole affair is yet another branch to add to the pyre of Maisie's anger. It is no wonder that, by the time she gains the top of the paddock, she is ready to let fire at anyone who steps out of line.

Captain Cruikshank is not as Maisie has imagined him, physically at least. Far from being portly and dumpy he is of middling height and of a remarkably athletic build for a man of his years, which must be north of sixty. He has a full head of grey hair, neatly trimmed, bushy eyebrows over penetratingly blue eyes, and is closely shaven. He emerges from the narrow gap between his caravan and Val's chalet, which immediately arouses Maisie's suspicions. What can he be doing, lurking down there?

'Can I help you?' He is very well-spoken, his accent what Maisie would describe as Home Counties. He isn't wearing a uniform but his khaki trousers, checked shirt and many-pocketed twill gilet are certainly very military in style, expertly laundered and ironed to pristine smoothness.

'I'm Maisie Wilde,' she says, holding out her hand stiffly. 'Your neighbour from over the hedge.' She waves down the paddock to where the roof of *Old Farm Hall* can be seen in the mist of the early morning. She nods towards the caravan. 'I see you're making yourself at home.'

'I'm Cruikshank. A pleasure to meet you, Mrs Wilde,' says the captain, taking Maisie's hand and giving it a perfunctory shake. 'Indeed. Sheer luxury compared to some of the billets I've had.' He pulls his lips back to reveal white, even and patently false teeth in a smile that is equally artificial. 'Active service you know, prepares you for anything.'

'My son's with Special Forces,' she says, trumping his remark. She turns and surveys the paddocks. Already the tumbledown housing of the donkeys has been replaced with much sturdier shelters. The wonky wire fences are now more solid post-and-rail. Two old horses bend their necks over a new water trough. 'You've been busy,' she allows, 'but the place seems empty, without the goats. Why did they have to be moved?'

'To make room for our new raw recruits. They'll be with us next week.'

'Oh?' Maisie imagines delinquent pigs, escaping from their enclosure and rampaging over her vegetable plot, or antisocial birds—peacocks, guineafowl—screeching night and day.

'Alpacas. Tricky customers, I'm told, but popular with Joe public, and that's what we're after.'

'Are we?'

Captain Cruikshank beetles an eyebrow. 'Of course! People come to see animals, pay money, money funds rescue and upkeep of animals. Mission accomplished. Now, what can I do you for?'

Maisie holds out her egg box. 'I buy my eggs from Val,' she says. 'I'll take a dozen if you can spare them.'

'Buy?'

'Yes.' Maisie shakes the box to show it contains coins and also to communicate her frustration. She is becoming sick to death of being messed around. '£1.50 a dozen.'

'Hmm.' He fixes her with a gimlet eye. 'Goes in the petty cash, does it? Or straight into the pocket?' He takes the box from her, but rather in the manner of someone who suspects it will detonate. He holds it gingerly at arm's length.

Maisie thinks about the Cadbury's tin in Val's chalet. She says, 'I'm sure it's all above board. Val will know. She's not here though, by the looks of things.'

'No, gone AWOL with that ...' one eye droops in a conspiratorial wink, 'friend of hers.'

His term and his insinuation rile Maisie even further. 'AWOL? That's not Val's style at all. And Gwen's a friend of mine.'

'Is she?' This information seems to exacerbate, rather than to quell, the captain's suspicions. Now Maisie can see where Val's comparison came from. The man is officious and hateful.

He appears to ruminate for a while. Then he says, 'I'll be upfront with you, Mrs Wilde. This unit has been allowed to go pretty much rogue. Chain of command tied round a tree and left to rot, if you get my meaning. Discipline non-existent. Sloppy bookkeeping, maverick tendencies, animal welfare issues …' he sucks his teeth ominously.

Maisie has had enough. 'You'll excuse me if I contradict you.' She knows she sounds like a fish-wife but she can't stop. 'Val has been left to run this place single-handedly, without any support from the trust, for years. I know for a fact that she has funded some of its upkeep from her own pocket and I don't think she has had a single day off *ever*. I've seen her out in all weathers and never, *never* was any animal allowed to suffer under her care.'

The captain draws himself up. She can tell he is not used to being contradicted—certainly not by a civilian—but rather than being angered by it he is wrong-footed. She presses her advantage by adding, 'And since we are being upfront with one another, I will add that I have lodged an objection to the development of this site into a tourist destination. Just so we know where we stand. It's nothing personal.'

She reaches out and snatches the box from him. 'Forget the eggs. I'll get them elsewhere from now on.'

She stalks back down the paddock and through her gate, her anger at the captain's pomposity by no means expiated by her outburst. Who does he think he is, maligning Val's character so easily? And I *still* have no bloody eggs. It is already hot, although barely nine in the morning. The churning cement mixer, the sound of hammers and drills, saws and planes, and the laddish banter of the men at work makes her want to scream.

James, sitting on the stone bench in the *parterre*, is the hapless receptacle of her fury. 'That man,' she fumes, waving an arm toward the farm, 'is *horrible!* He badmouthed Val's character to my face, and he's a homophobe to boot. It's very clear to me the charity wants Val off the site as soon as possible and they've sent that … that Rottweiler to do their dirty work. The poor woman! But he's going to make it impossible for her to stay.'

Maisie's anger and frustration on behalf of her friend, and a catalogue of all her other woes push the raw and bewildering tumult of her temper to crisis point. She clenches her fists and emits a noise that is half a cry for help and half a war cry. Then she bursts into tears.

James, calm as ever, leads her to the bench and pulls a clean handkerchief from his pocket. He places an arm gently around her shoulder and allows her to sob into his shirt for a few minutes.

Presently she blows her nose and wipes her eyes, but offers neither apology nor explanation. It isn't necessary.

'I wasn't expecting you,' she says, balling his handkerchief up in her hands.

'I came just on the off-chance. I was passing anyway. I've had a meeting with Oliver.' If he feels her stiffen at the name, he doesn't say anything.

'Oh?'

'But I wanted you to know, I think I've come up with a pretty good idea, about,' he cocks his head to indicate the farm. 'My friend in the planning department says there's not much hope of the application being turned down, I'm afraid.'

'Oh,' Maisie says again, thinking of the wasted evening she and Minnie spent constructing their letter of objection.

'No. The promise of employment for local people is pretty compelling, and then there are the animal welfare issues, plus they've offered to pay for the alterations to the access—to widen the lane, put up signage and provide dedicated car parking.'

Maisie sighs, her shoulders slumping still further beneath James's arm, which he has not removed. 'It's hopeless then.'

'Not quite. My idea is that we harness the power of the most explosive force in the modern world.'

'A nuclear bomb?' she suggests dryly.

James chuckles. 'More powerful even than that. We're going to use the media.'

Chapter Seven – Viola

Brian invested almost the whole of Viola's divorce settlement into a number of high-risk, high-yielding funds, holding back only a comparatively small amount to generate an income that would supply her needs day-to-day. The one to two years he had predicted it would take to augment her funds stretched to three, but Viola found she was perfectly content with her life. The little flat no longer felt bland and dour, it felt like home, and when she got back to it after a day at the allotment she valued its spartan, no-nonsense character. It was tidy, unfussy and undemanding.

She had a social life, albeit a small one, seeing a few of the volunteers from the allotments for coffee or lunch, and once or twice being asked by some of the people at the bridge club to fill a spare seat at a dinner party. On the surface, the bridge club members were very different from the volunteers, they did not seem to have the psychological fractures or historic calamities that characterised the folks at the allotment. They were generally retired after successful careers, living mortgage-free in bungalows or senior-living complexes, untroubled by memories of failure or unhappiness. They seemed to be what Viola herself should have been, or would have been without Graham's malicious impact, but somehow she felt more affinity with the gardeners than she did with the bridge players; they had scars in common.

The dinner parties were perfectly nice—three or four courses prepared by private chefs or by the host and hostess themselves—but in some cases, Viola suspected, decanted from Waitrose containers. Fine wines eased the talk of golf handicaps and the problems of owning property abroad, of troublesome grandchildren and the health issues of aged dogs and cats. Viola, usually invited as a spare female to balance the table, found herself seated beside widowed ex-lawyers and divorced former businessmen, all well-to-do and perfectly eligible. Several of them asked to see her again, promising weekends away in exclusive hotels, sojourns in friends' chateaux, participation at regattas on some acquaintance's yacht, but she always declined. What would be the point? Outwardly her life might have broadened its scope, and her harder edges had softened, but her heart necessarily remained a stone—impervious, never to be broken or abused again.

She continued to assist the women's refuge. The clients came and went from the upstairs flat and often she never heard where they went or how they did. She was a staging post in their journeys, and that was all. None of them did she count as friends. Even Gwen—whom she probably saw more of, knew better and who knew her better than any of the others—was a fickle friend in that she had so many plates to spin; she always had to leave one to tend to another. Viola learned to be grateful for the time Gwen allowed her, knowing how limited it was.

The seasons turned at the allotment. Springs were busy as crops were sown and nurtured. In summer there was watering and weeding, harvesting and processing. Viola, Brenda, Mary and some of the others made countless jars of beetroot relish, chutney, pickles and preserves, using up the surplus vegetables that were not wanted or needed by the volunteers, or could not be pressed upon friends and neighbours. The jars were sold on a market stall that the allotment had every week from June to October, manned by Martin, Viola or other volunteers. Often they would be at the allotment until seven or eight o'clock at night, the long, warm hours of summer enticing them to remain outdoors. Martin would linger, although it must have exceeded his official hours of employment. Occasionally she was aware of a reluctance in him, an edginess, a feeling he would rather be elsewhere. But the volunteers were all eager to stay and he could not leave the site until everyone had left and it was secured. Someone would bring food and wine or beer, or Mary would cook up some delicious dish from the allotment's plenty, seasoned with spices and served with flatbreads she would cook on a large skillet over an open fire. Viola, with nothing particular to go home for, would remain behind to clear up as the long shadows crept over the raised beds. The last of the volunteers would wobble off into the gloaming, leaving only herself and Martin behind. Then, in near-darkness, they would part ways beyond the gate, she to pedal back along the promenade, he to disappear with long and urgent strides in another direction, somewhere beyond the common, his canvas bag weighing down his stooping shoulders. She supposed he was eager to get home.

Autumn was a time for tidying, leaf raking and for digging compost into the raised beds. Viola adored the smell of damp leaves burning on the bonfire. Martin acquired a cider press and they collected windfalls and laid down hundreds of litres of sharp, potent cider. Parsnips and Brussels sprouts were nurtured, to be eaten on Christmas Day. They repaired infrastructure and installed more water butts, washed and fumigated the polytunnel and greenhouse.

Winter was a quiet time. Only a few volunteers continued to turn up at the allotment. Often Martin and Viola were there alone during the short daylight hours, planning the next year's crops, extracting and drying seed from desiccated pea- and bean-pods, withered chillies and shrivelled capsicums. The shed was quiet but for the hiss of the Calor gas fire and the two worked in companionable silence as the hours passed. Viola liked it—the fact that they did not need to talk. Although wary of men in general she never felt uncomfortable in Martin's company; indeed she sensed in him a reflection of her own circumspection. In all the time she had been going to the allotment she had learned scant information about his private life. He was married—to Susanne—but they had no children; this much she gleaned from Adrian, who was not shy about asking personal questions or relaying the answers to anyone who was interested. Martin and Susanne holidayed early or late in the year to avoid school vacations. Apparently Susanne enjoyed extreme sports like caving and potholing—hobbies that, due to his size, Martin found difficult. Certainly he returned from them nursing injuries, but expressed no dissatisfaction with the situation.

While he was away, a social worker was seconded to open the allotment and oversee the volunteers. It surprised Viola that the council considered it appropriate to deploy someone from social services, but then it occurred to her that this was Martin's profession; he was not—as she had supposed—someone brought over from Parks and Gardens, simply a bloke with a green thumb and an affinity for people. The realisation threatened to change her view of him; perhaps his easy temper, his patient, affable manner were simply professional ploys and not the real man at all. She watched him, alert for some inkling that, in his private life, he was just like other men. She sought hypocrisy, but found none.

The year after Viola joined—thanks to the extra income generated by the hanging baskets—the new greenhouse was purchased and erected, and was a valuable addition to the allotment. They grew annuals for hanging baskets every year after that, taking orders from local businesses and individuals, ploughing the proceeds into new tools, a much better wheelchair-accessible port-a-loo, a marquee where they could hold their annual summer open day when the weather was wet. They dabbled in cut flowers, partly to encourage pollinators, partly as another potential income stream. The beds of delphinium, hollyhocks, gypsophila and cosmos looked amazing, but difficulties in getting them fresh to market proved insurmountable, and so instead they dedicated an area behind the compost heaps to wildflowers, which attracted innumerable bees and butterflies. An apiarist brought a hive and soon they had honey as well as preserves to sell. Martin said it was yet another triumph of Viola's, to add to the open days, which had proved so popular, and the improved relations with other allotment-holders, which, he said, was bearing fruit in lots of ways.

Susanne never appeared at the allotment, even when, for their second open day, they had been asked if a crew from the local television company could come and do a piece about the project. For that, the world and his wife declared their intention of showing up: the mayor and mayoress and various other council worthies, the head teacher and half the governors of the special school and some of the lecturers from Adrian's college. Viola expected that on such a momentous day, Susanne would show her face, and was mildly curious to see what kind of woman she was, but was to be disappointed.

Martin was keen that Viola should speak on behalf of the volunteers but of course she declined, and in fact spent most of the two or three hours the crew were present skulking behind the compost heap or hiding in the polytunnel; she didn't want Graham to see her on the screen. Even now, after more than two years, she had not got over a sense of trepidation that he might find her and hurt her again. His spectre hovered in a far recess of her consciousness, often hardly there at all, but never entirely absent either.

Viola thought it would be natural for Martin to be the one to be interviewed, but he too seemed reluctant, and in the end it was Clive who stepped forward. He had been interviewed "dozens of times" he said, although in what context he did not state. Viola would not have been surprised to find it was whilst under caution in police custody. He arrived at the open day clad in tweeds and expensive brogues with a pocket watch and heavy gold chain. Viola thought he looked like a facsimile of a lord of the manor escaped from a low-budget situation comedy. Vanessa was similarly dressed up, her usual gardening gear replaced by a dress and jacket that would have been suitable for a garden party at Buckingham Palace, her hair freshly coloured and set and heavily lacquered. She wore high heeled shoes wholly unsuitable for the soft, grassy paths of the allotment and wobbled along on them unsteadily as Clive sauntered round the beds expanding on their crop rotation, compost production and organic credentials.

The interviewer went on to ask about the volunteers.

'Oh yes,' said Clive, 'all are welcome. We have people from all backgrounds, including immigrants.'

Both the interviewer and, off camera, Martin, looked uncomfortable. Viola, in the shadow of the hedge, suppressed a cry of dismay.

The interviewer said, 'Your volunteers are ethnically diverse?'

'Indeed,' said Clive, oblivious to his blunder. 'And we have children from the handicapped—'

'I'm sorry,' said Martin abruptly, stepping in. 'We'll have to cut that and do a retake. Can we start from when you asked about the volunteers?'

The interviewer and her camera operator had a brief discussion.

Martin said, 'Clive, just to remind you, our volunteers represent many ethnic minorities, they aren't "immigrants" and the children have complex educational needs. Nobody uses the term "handicapped" anymore. It's insulting.'

'Stupid political correctness,' muttered Clive. 'They *are* handicapped.'

'They have learning differences,' said Martin firmly. 'If you can't see the distinction then perhaps you're not the best person to represent us here.'

Clive looked as though he would object. Vanessa cowered behind him, her heavily ringed hand pressed to her mouth. Only an intervention from the mayor saved the situation; he stepped forward and offered to take over. Faced with being so ignominiously up-staged, Clive said, 'No need, Mayor. Ethnic minorities, learning differences. Got it. Let's go again.'

Afterwards Sunita and Viola served tea and cake to the visiting dignitaries. Aside, Sunita said, 'I was waiting for Clive to describe those of us with mental health issues as "basket-cases".'

'Me too,' admitted Viola. 'He's a hateful man. I can't stand him.'

The two of them looked over to a group near the greenhouse. Clive and Vanessa had attached themselves to the contingent of bigwigs but their association was tenuous; they looked awkward, out of place. Clive spoke too loudly, gesticulated too emphatically, imposing himself upon them by main force. Vanessa, in his shadow as always, sipped and sipped and sipped her tea until Viola was sure the cup was drained dry, but still Vanessa lifted it to her lips, her concentration absolute on the polite, pointless exercise. Viola found herself engulfed with sympathy for her. How often had she—Viola—stood thus in Graham's lee at one of his initially tedious but then increasingly debauched office parties?

In another part of the allotment the band of volunteers huddled together and discussed the day's events with animation. What kind of benefit might accrue from their exposure on local television? A regular gardening feature, one speculated. A contract with a local supermarket, suggested another. To a man they wondered when Martin would break out the cider. The cameraman had remained after the interviewer had departed, seemingly genuinely interested in the project. Adrian had him cornered and was asking for a minute explanation of the equipment, whilst at the same time dropping heavy hints about his aspirations to work in the media.

'You go for it, mate,' said the cameraman. 'Nothing you can't do if you set your mind to it.'

The school children's parents allowed themselves to be led in and out of the greenhouse and all around the raised beds whilst their offspring explained their own individual part in the season's abundance. Afterwards they bought Brenda's crocheted bookmarks, doilies and bags of *potpourri*.

Somewhere midway between the VIPs and the volunteers hovered Martin, as though trying to make a bridge between these two utterly divergent groups. He stood head and shoulders above both and yet managed to be almost invisible, his cup and saucer balanced awkwardly in his hands. His head, on its long stem of neck, swivelled from one group to another, a smile plastered on his face. His hair—generally disorderly—had been combed for the occasion. But against the smart attire of the dignitaries his clothes were sadly lacking, his flannel trousers a little short in the leg, his jacket threadbare at the elbows. Beside the volunteers, though, he looked formal, far different from his usual approachable self and as a result he was not, as he would normally have been, absorbed into their number.

Sunita said, 'Poor Martin. He needs rescuing.'

'Why isn't his wife here?' Viola wondered.

'At least he's managed not to trip up or anything,' said Sunita. 'I never knew a more accident-prone man, did you?'

And then Gordon emerged from the polytunnel with his family and Martin, like a man in a desert spying water, hurried over to join them.

After that open day, Clive and Vanessa stopped coming to the allotment. More pressing claims on their time, they said, alternative outlets for their energies.

'I can't say I'm sorry,' said Martin.

'Neither can I,' Viola agreed.

Although Clive and Vanessa did not come to the allotment anymore, it was not the last that Viola saw of them. She met them at one of the bridge club dinners, some months after the open day at which Clive had so nearly caused such offence.

The dinner was held at a large, Edwardian property on the promenade. Viola's hosts were retired dentists, both avid bridge players who also, like so many of their ilk, played golf. Justin was also a member of a local shoot and his wife, Penny, dabbled in amateur theatricals. They had a wide circle of acquaintance and Viola had been surprised to receive an invitation to their party until she entered the large and lavishly furnished drawing room to find Veejay hovering diffidently in the bay window, clutching a glass of orange juice. He wore a beautifully tailored suit and a crimson turban. His beard, combed and oiled, flowed down his chest.

On seeing her he put down his glass and hurried over to meet her. 'Delighted you were free,' he said. 'I hope you don't mind, but I asked Penny if she would invite you. Being a single male means being lumbered with all kinds of random females, and I didn't think I could face another maiden cousin or widowed sister. I made your being invited a condition of my own attendance.'

Viola laughed. 'It's the same for single women, you know,' she said, taking a glass of sparkling wine from a passing waiter. 'We have to take potluck, too. But I'm very happy to see you.'

A booming voice alerted them to more arrivals and they moved further into the room. 'Oh no,' hissed Viola, 'it's Clive and Vanessa.'

'Oh yes,' Veejay told her, 'Clive goes shooting with Justin, I think.'

'I'm amazed he's allowed to own a gun,' said Viola under her breath.

Then Clive and Vanessa were in the room—he, as always, striding out in front, she scampering in his wake. She saw Viola and raised a hand in greeting, and would have stepped across the richly figured carpet had Clive not barked out, 'Vanessa! Will you have a glass of sherry? I think you might allow yourself just one, you know.' He added to the room in general, 'Vanessa is driving, of course. You know she will insist on it.'

Vanessa veered off her intended course and hurried over to Clive. Viola heard her say, 'Just a very small one, please.'

Viola and Veejay exchanged looks. 'I bet she does insist on it, if the alternative is being driven home by Clive when he's over the limit,' she whispered.

'Clive drinks?' Veejay's eyebrows shot up to the rim of his turban.

'Oh yes,' said Viola sagely. 'Trust me. I know the type.'

Twelve guests sat down to dinner, which was prepared by, Penny boasted, a chef who had made it to the semi-finals of Professional MasterChef. It was served by white-coated waiters. A succession of courses came and went. Veejay was offered vegetarian alternatives to the meat and supplied with sparkling water because he did not drink alcohol. 'It's a religious thing,' he admitted, 'but, in my profession, alcohol's a real stumbling block, so I've been glad of the excuse to forego it. I've seen many an excellent surgeon founder on the Scotch rocks.'

Across the table from Viola, Clive was on his third or fourth whisky, having waved away the selection of aperitifs and the wine. He had avoided speaking to her, but had been friendly enough towards Veejay. Vanessa, marooned between her husband on one side and a monosyllabic ex-orthodontist on the other, picked miserably at her food and spoke only when called upon by Clive to second his conversational assertions.

Whilst they waited for the fish course, Viola attempted to engage Vanessa by enquiring what they did now they had given up the allotment.

'Oh,' faltered Vanessa, so startled to have been addressed that she almost dropped her glass. 'Oh, we … er … we …'

'We help out at the charity shop,' Clive supplied. 'You'd be amazed at the quality of person who comes in. People you wouldn't think would lower themselves. Last week we had the rural dean's wife in. She bought—'

'Oh, but Clive,' stammered Vanessa, laying a tentative hand on his arm, 'perhaps we ought not to—'

'Don't be ridiculous,' said Clive, shaking her off. 'Nobody *here's* going to say anything. In any case, it doesn't matter what she bought, really. It's the fact that she came in at all.'

Someone said, 'I don't think the clergy get paid as well as all that.'

'Humph,' Clive snorted. 'Free housing and utilities though, and they no doubt eat out *gratis* every day of the week courtesy of their parishioners.'

'If you're speaking of the man I think you are,' put in Veejay, 'I can vouch for him being at the hospital three or four days a week. He's a tireless visitor to the sick.'

Clive glared at him. 'This is his wife, though. It was his wife who was in the shop.'

'Perhaps she just believes in buying second-hand,' mused Viola. 'Lots of people do, nowadays. It's considered not only perfectly acceptable but preferable—'

'Well, of course,' said Clive with a sneer. He drained his glass and held it up to get the attention of one of the waiters. 'And that's the whole point of the charity shop.'

'I think not,' said Veejay quietly. 'The main point is to raise funds for … which charity is it?'

'The British Heart Foundation,' crowed Clive, 'so put *that* in your pipe and smoke it.'

There was a titter—but an awkward one—round the table.

Viola laboured on. 'So, Vanessa, do you find the shop a bit less gruelling than the allotment? I used to worry about you. Sometimes you went home absolutely done in.'

'She certainly did not,' replied Clive. 'She was more than equal to it. Good Lord, when *is* the next course coming, Justin? Has the chef gone out on a trawler?'

Later, with Clive well and truly in his cups, the party moved back to the drawing room where coffee and *petits fours* were served. Four guests, including Clive, made up a table for bridge and the rest disposed themselves for conversation. Viola managed to get a seat on a small settee, next to Vanessa.

'Delicious dinner,' she said. 'Did you enjoy yours?'

'Oh very much,' said Vanessa, 'yes, thank you. Penny is a wonderful hostess, isn't she?'

'We could both be just as good, with a private chef and a team of waiters,' said Viola. 'Do you entertain very often?'

'Oh no,' said Vanessa. 'Clive says I'm not up to it. And he's right, of course. I've never been much good in the kitchen.'

'Is he any better? It isn't set in stone that women have to cook, you know.'

'Oh goodness me,' cried Vanessa, her little eyes wide with astonishment, as though Viola had uttered some blasphemy. 'Gosh no. Clive would never … and even when I came home with the babies … but thankfully my sister …' she dissolved into incoherence.

Viola looked up to see Clive eying them narrowly from across the room. 'He can't hear you,' she muttered.

Vanessa whispered, 'But he can see. And afterwards he'll ask me what we were talking about.' Her hands moved restlessly in her lap.

Viola gave her head a little shake. 'Just the lovely dinner,' she said lightly, 'especially the soufflé. That was divine, wasn't it? We exchanged recipes, perhaps.'

'Oh, but I've never made a soufflé,' gasped Vanessa.

Viola laughed. 'Neither have I. But as far as he needs to know—'

'Oh yes, I see.' Vanessa threw her a look, complicit, laced with mischief.

Viola leaned a little closer, pretending to admire Vanessa's earrings. 'You haven't forgotten what I told you that day on the allotment? About the refuge?'

Vanessa's head shrank into her neck. 'No,' she said, in a voice so low it was little more than a murmur. 'But I couldn't do it. Where would I go?'

'Just to the place I told you about in Millport. They would look after you. They have places where you can stay. Secret places where he couldn't find you. Perhaps, after that, your children might help you? My son …'

Vanessa's face began to crumble. A tear oozed from her eye and began to run down her cheek. Viola sat forward, blocking Vanessa from Clive's view.

Vanessa shook her head. 'They wouldn't; not if their father said they mustn't.'

'Your sister, then. You mentioned you had one? But even if there's no one, the refuge will help you. You won't be left to cope alone, I promise.'

Gently, Viola took Vanessa's hand in hers, pretending, now, to examine a gold bracelet that was so heavy it seemed to weigh down its wearer's thin little wrist. She turned Vanessa's hand over. On the wrist, beneath the bracelet, was the faint trace of a scar.

'You poor thing,' Viola crooned. 'I understand. I do, really.'

'What are you saying to my wife?'

Viola's head shot up. Clive was standing before them unsteadily, his eyes bloodshot and bleary, his hand of cards still clutched in his fist. Vanessa made a frightened mewing noise and pressed herself back in her seat.

'You're upsetting her!' said Clive, leaning so far over them that he almost toppled.

Someone at the bridge table called, 'Clive, it's your bid. You're in three no-trumps.'

'Vanessa was showing me her lovely bracelet,' said Viola lightly. 'Such a generous gift.'

Vanessa choked out, 'For our wedding anniversary, wasn't it Clive?' but she removed her hand from Viola's and buried it back in her lap. 'Are you ready to go home, Clive? I'm ready when you are.'

Clive looked from one to the other of them suspiciously, swaying all the while.

'Clive!' his partner called again. 'What's your bid?'

'I don't like you speaking to my wife,' Clive enunciated. 'I'd like you to go and sit somewhere else.'

'I certainly will not,' said Viola firmly. 'I'm quite comfortable here, thank you.' To emphasise her point she sat back against the cushion and crossed her ankles. She threw him a smile that was half smirk, half challenge. 'Nobody tells me what to do.'

Clive flushed beetroot and breathed heavily through his nostrils. Clearly, he was not used to being gainsaid.

Vanessa, seeing what was to come, made a small whimpering noise.

Suddenly Clive's hand shot out, his hand of cards fluttering to the carpet. He grasped his wife's wrist and wrenched her bodily from her seat. A small table in front of her that held her empty coffee cup and a small, beaded bag fell over. Several guests leapt to their feet.

'Vanessa is unwell,' snarled Clive, frogmarching his poor, harried wife across the room. 'She needs to visit the powder room.'

'Oh poor Vanessa,' shrilled Penny. 'I hope it isn't anything she's eaten. Let me show you the way.'

'That's quite alright,' growled Clive, pushing past her. 'I know the way.'

The two disappeared into the hallway. There was an awkward silence. One of the bridge players laid down her hand with a sigh. 'Nineteen points,' she said ruefully, 'and all four aces. What are the chances?'

Viola said, 'Perhaps someone should call them a taxi? I'm not sure Vanessa will be up to driving.'

Someone gave a hollow laugh. 'You don't know Clive very well, do you? He'll make her sit here for as long as he wants to stay, ill or not.'

'It's dreadful behaviour,' Viola said. 'As their friends, I'm amazed you stand by.' She scanned the room, searching for a sympathetic eye, but found none.

'It isn't any of our business,' a man said.

'Except,' added his wife, 'it does get rather tiresome. They had a scuffle at our house once and he broke a rather expensive decanter. I've said I won't invite them again.' She glared at her husband, daring him to undermine her, but he occupied himself with a *petit four*.

'It's so awkward,' wailed Penny. 'He has to be invited at least once; he's the club captain this year.'

'So that makes it alright for him to bully his wife?' Viola retorted.

Penny went white. Justin's brow contracted, his face dark with anger, or perhaps embarrassment. Viola couldn't tell.

Veejay gave a little cough. 'I think I'll be heading off,' he said. 'I have surgery in the morning. Viola, I wonder if you'd like me to give you a lift?'

Viola got to her feet. 'Yes,' she said. 'That's very kind. I'll go and find my jacket.'

In the small cloakroom Clive and Vanessa were locked in combat. He had her up against the wall, his hands at her throat. Her hands flapped uselessly against his huge chest.

As Viola opened the door they sprang apart. Vanessa leaned over the toilet and began to retch. Soon her gourmet dinner splattered the peach-coloured porcelain.

In a theatrical voice Clive said, 'There. That will mend things. You've over-indulged yourself again Vanessa. I've warned you again and again about being gluttonous but you just can't control yourself, can you? I'm ashamed of you.'

He turned to leave the room, a look of supreme disgust on his face. Viola's instinct was to back off and let him through. Her own dinner rose in her gorge. The toxic atmosphere in the cramped little room was too familiar to her.

'I should call the police,' she stammered out. 'I've just witnessed an assault.'

She wasn't surprised when her threat was swept aside. 'Don't be ridiculous,' said Clive. 'Now let me past.' He stumbled towards her. His attitude would have been menacing except that he was so patently drunk. All in all he presented a pathetic figure, but Viola wasn't too naive to know that even a drunk could pose a threat, and she certainly didn't want to make things worse for Vanessa. She stepped to one side, disappointed in herself but powerless to face up to him; the past and all she had gone through with Graham constricted her like a straitjacket. As he passed her in the narrow doorway Clive hissed, 'You bitch. You keep away from my wife in future.' She could smell the whisky on his breath, read the dazed myopia of drunkenness in his protuberant eyes. It was all so familiar, well-rehearsed. As though Clive had seen the show and knew the script he reached out and grasped her wrist, squeezing until it hurt. Then, at last, her paralysis fell away and she saw red. Nancy's training came back to her. She lifted one foot and planted her stiletto heel onto the toe of his shoe, leaning all her weight upon it. He let go of her wrist abruptly, lurching violently to one side to escape the cruel point on his toe. It only needed a little push from Viola to send him sprawling into a little hall table that stood just outside the cloakroom. The table contained a plethora of little nick-nacks: glass ornaments and miniature china figurines. They all hit the polished parquet of the hall floor and splintered into a million smithereens. Clive hit the floor on top of them, sprawling his full length, shards of glass and pottery embedding themselves in the skin of his cheek and hands.

Viola called, 'Oh dear. Clive has stumbled. Can someone help?'

Veejay drove her home and parked his car outside her flat. 'Would you like me to come in?' he asked. 'Or at least see you to the door?'

In the darkness of the car the whites of his eyes had a luminous quality. She saw the flash of teeth; white and suspiciously even.

Fleetingly, Viola wondered what it would be like to be made love to by a man with surgeon's hands—gentle, expert. Veejay was by no means an ill-looking man and what little she knew of him, she liked. But the idea of becoming lost in the softness of his beard was faintly appalling, and who knew what his turban hid? Greasy hanks of greying hair? Or lustrous, aromatic skeins? In any case, she could not risk it. The clasp of her heart which had, in the last few moments, shifted infinitesimally, snapped shut again.

'No, thank you Veejay, I'm fine.'

Viola continued to attend the bridge club, honing her aptitude at the game until she was a true proficient. Amy Snow had remained as a tutor for beginners, so Viola partnered any player who arrived singly. Often she was far above them in skill, but occasionally she would find herself playing with one of the more talented members. She loved these opportunities, sharpening her wit, trying to match their competence, learning all she could. There was talk of her representing the club at competition level.

If her partner was an expert player she would find herself in the rarefied atmosphere of the advanced group, where Clive and Vanessa played. Playing against Clive was a challenge Viola relished; she delighted in tripping him up, forcing him into error, putting him down both socially and in the game. To be truthful, Vanessa was an indifferent player, afraid of making errors and very anxious not to displease her husband. Only consideration of her, and what she might suffer once the evening was over, curbed Viola's venom.

After their brief but telling encounter at the dinner party, Vanessa had ceased all pretence about the state of her marriage as far as Viola was concerned. They snatched half sentences of communication in the ladies' loo, Viola pressing Vanessa to make the break, while holding her thin, shaking shoulders. Vanessa wept, and dabbed at her eyes with a ball of makeup-smeared tissue, but could not be persuaded.

One day in early January, Martin and Viola were at work alone in the shed, the Calor gas heater throwing off an orange light, the ground outside hard and white with an unusually heavy frost that had lasted for over a week. The Christmas decorations, which everyone had been so keen to put up, but that Viola knew no one would be available to help put away, winked amongst the rafters; tatty tinsel, cast-off baubles, innumerable paper chains made by the kids.

She and Martin pored over a plan of the allotment's beds. They had been deciding how best to rotate the crops, whether to give sweet potatoes a try, if Jerusalem artichokes would be considered too socially compromising.

Once they had a plan to present to the rest of the group, Martin boiled the kettle and set about making tea. Over his shoulder he said, 'I saw Vanessa and Clive the other day. They do a stint at the charity shop now.'

'Yes, I knew that,' said Viola, and went on to tell him about the disastrous dinner party. 'I'm absolutely sure she's a victim of domestic abuse,' she said. 'She admitted as much and I saw him assault her with my own eyes.'

Martin busied himself at the tea table. 'You didn't tell the police?'

'No,' said Viola, shamefacedly. 'It would have been his word against mine. Vanessa would have denied it, so what would have been the point?'

'You did all you could,' said Martin, bringing the tea over. 'Vanessa knows there is help if she chooses to take it. But these situations can be more complicated than we realise.'

'Don't I know it,' muttered Viola into her tea. It was strong, just the way she liked it.

Martin raised an eyebrow.

'Oh come on,' said Viola, 'don't pretend you don't know my history. I'm sure Gwen gave you chapter and verse.'

Martin dunked a biscuit in his tea. 'You don't know Gwen very well if you think she would betray a confidence,' he said. 'She certainly never said a word to me about it. So … you … in the past?'

Viola nodded. 'Yes. For twenty-five years.'

Martin's expression was a complex litany of anger and sadness, sympathy and concern. 'So that's how you come to know Gwen?'

'Yes. She came to see me in the hospital and now I help out with the women who use the refuge.'

He nodded. 'That must give you a sense of karma. Re-adjusting the balance, I mean.'

'Maybe. But I know how it feels to be trapped. I want the clients to see that escape is possible and life afterwards can be good.'

'Life afterwards,' echoed Martin to himself. 'Yes, I suppose believing that is half the battle.'

'More than half.'

Martin sighed. 'When you're so deep in the pit, though—'

'Oh yes, all you can see are the walls. The little disc of sky at the top seems impossibly far away. I suppose that's how Vanessa feels.'

'I suppose so,' said Martin, toying with his cup. 'But then, you can't help wondering how *he* feels.'

'Clive?' The notion surprised Viola. She had not wasted any consideration on Clive.

'Yes. I mean, to be like that—violent, and so angry—there must be something fundamentally wrong with him. Some unresolved trauma, something going back years … Beneath all that vitriol there must be someone who needs help, just as much as she does.'

Viola thought about it, but found it hard to summon even an ounce of sympathy. Graham hadn't experienced any trauma that she knew of, but she recalled his inner-demon—his temper. Perhaps Clive was possessed by something similar. Not that that was any excuse. She said, 'That's very fair-minded of you, Martin.'

Martin finished his tea. 'If you don't mind me asking,' he said, 'how did you get out?'

Viola took a deep breath. 'My husband attacked me so badly that I was hospitalised,' she said. 'I decided I wouldn't go back. So, in a way, he did me a favour. Before that I just kept hoping things would improve, that *I* would improve because, of course, I was constantly told it was all my fault. Life was like walking a tightrope, a constant balancing act, pre-handling every situation that might arise. What would annoy him? What would placate him? But then again, I'm afraid I sometimes provoked him on purpose. I *had* to just to prove that I … that I wasn't—'

'Utterly crushed?'

'Yes.'

Viola looked at Martin across the table. His eyes didn't shy away from hers. He nodded, slowly, sagely. He understood. She felt ridiculously proud of herself for having summoned the courage to tell someone, and a man at that.

'I haven't told anyone else any of that,' she said. 'I don't know why I told you, really.'

'I'm glad you did,' he said. 'I'm very honoured.'

Viola looked at her watch. 'I don't suppose,' she said, 'you'd be interested in a late pub lunch? There's a place in town I went to with Sunita that did the most amazing steak pie I've ever tasted. And I haven't much in for supper.'

It was hard to see, in the half-light of the shed, but it seemed to Viola that Martin blushed. 'I haven't brought my wallet, I'm afraid, and if I eat a big lunch I won't manage whatever Susanne has prepared for supper.'

It had been on the tip of Viola's tongue to offer to pay, but Martin's second remark made her seal her lips. He was being diplomatic, she realised. It would be unprofessional of him to be seen in town socialising with what, she supposed, would be considered a service user. Her pride of only a moment before dissipated in the humid air of the shed. Now she felt ashamed of what she had told him. She had spoken as she would to a friend, to a confidante, but he was neither of those; he was a man who was paid to supervise the halt and the lame, the broken and abused. He was a social worker, probably trained in counselling. He had drawn her out, she realised, with his sympathetic eyes and his pretence of understanding. How could he possibly understand what she had been through? She felt cheated and exposed.

She got up abruptly and grabbed her coat off the back of her chair. 'Of course,' she said. 'I forget that other people have lives outside the allotment. I'll just go to the butchers on my way back and make myself a nice steak pie.' She busied herself with the zip, with gloves, with the tying of her scarf. 'I might take Gordon some,' she said, spooling out inconsequential talk to displace the atmosphere that had suddenly materialised in the shed. 'He doesn't like this icy ground. He's frightened to death of falling and breaking a hip, so I don't suppose he's been shopping this week. Shall I tell him you said hello?'

'Yes please.'

Martin had also risen to his feet. He looked bewildered at the sudden change between them, but there was a guilty light in his eye. He knew he had been caught out. For a moment she thought she saw remorse also; he was sorry, but that's how things had to be.

She relented a little, offering a placatory smile. She had transgressed, not he. 'I'll see you tomorrow,' she said. 'We can look through the seed catalogue.'

She walked to the door but at the last minute she looked back. Even with his height, his head almost amongst the rafters of the shed, the fleeting impression she got of Martin was of a man who was dwarfed. He stood awkwardly on the spot, his eyes wide and staring in the dim.

'Viola,' he said, 'I would have come for lunch if it hadn't been for—'

'Oh,' she cut him off. 'No need to explain. I quite understand. I shouldn't have asked. Bye!' She wrenched open the door and stepped out into the crystalline wonderland that was the frost-encrusted allotment. The sun shone in a pale blue sky, illuminating every twig in the icy fire of the thick hoar frost. After the gloom of the shed it was dazzling. Either that, or the sudden shock of cold, brought tears to Viola's eyes and she brushed them away with the back of her gloved hand.

The handlebars of her bike were icy cold, even through her gloves. She jolted down the track towards the entrance. It was rutted, solid as iron, making it hard to pedal. A single car, just inside the gate, had its engine running; a plume of exhaust fumes clouded the air. Its windows were misted from the inside. Viola swerved to avoid the toxic gasses, supposing the car belonged to one of the allotment holders who had just popped down to make sure all was well, perhaps leaving a wife or child in the warmth of the car. She rode out of the gate and took the lane past the pitch-and-putt, then out on to the promenade. Council works along there had been completed at last. The kerb was punctuated by a rhythm of metal storm drains that would draw water from the road if there was to be another flood. The dull metal contrasted with the road and the pavement, which were a-glitter with ice, like strewn diamonds, bright almost beyond bearing. A woman walked a reluctant terrier along the promenade. As Viola passed her, the woman raised a hand. In greeting? As a warning? The next thing Viola knew was a roar at her back, a maelstrom of air that made her bike veer dangerously towards the kerb, throwing her to the ground mercifully clear of the nearest storm drain, but almost on top of the startled dog walker. The car shot away at speed down the wide, deserted road.

The woman found her voice and yelled, 'Stupid idiot!' at the retreating car. She came and knelt by Viola. 'Are you alright?' she gasped. 'Let me call an ambulance.'

Viola struggled to a sitting position. 'I'm okay, I think. More shaken than hurt. What did he think he was doing?'

'He was probably blinded by the sun,' said the woman. 'It's so low, at this time of year. He can't have seen you. Are you sure you're alright?'

They both looked at Viola's bike. The front wheel was buckled where it had hit the kerb. The woman got out her phone. 'I'm calling my husband,' she said. 'He's got a Land Rover. He can get your bike in it and we'll run you home.'

'I'm very grateful,' said Viola. Her left knee hurt badly, and so did her wrists, which had taken the impact of the fall. Ridiculously, she wanted to cry, but she did not know if it was because of the fall, or because of what had happened before, with Martin.

When she was safely home, after a soak in a hot bath and two pain-killers, Viola sat in the gloom. It could have been an accident, she told herself; the low sun, the frost's dazzle blinding the driver. But she couldn't get out of her head the idea that the driver had been Graham, that he had been waiting for her in the car at the entrance to the allotments, that he had followed her and ...

All her old terror flooded back. She had let her guard down. Who did she think she was, cycling around town, lunching with friends, as though she did not need to maintain, at all times, a strict vigilance? She had abandoned all her fortifications, outwardly and inwardly. What had all that emotion been that afternoon? Tears? Because a man had rebuffed her? How ridiculous! She could not afford to become emotionally attached; she could not afford to *feel*. No. Not ever again.

After her accident, Viola went back to avoiding others, retreating to the bastion she had inhabited during her marriage to Graham. For the first week or two, she used her buckled bike as an excuse, but the truth was the anxious stone she thought had melted away from her solar plexus had returned with a vengeance. She was watchful, guarded, alert always for movement at the periphery of her vision, an unfamiliar car in the carpark at the flat, a bulky stranger following at a suspicious distance. One day Gordon wheeled her bike into town for repair, so after that it was harder to think of excuses. She resumed her work at the allotment, but went less often. When there, she worked alone in sequestered corners. But the weeks passed and there was no further incident to suggest Graham was stalking her. In fact she learned from Brian that his father was busy setting up home with his new girlfriend, who at last had a visa and could stay indefinitely in the UK.

Gradually Viola convinced herself the accident had been just that. Little by little she stopped finding reasons to be separate, and by April she was back in the thick of it, kids to either side of her at the wide, slatted bench of the polytunnel pricking out seedlings and potting them on.

The other—perhaps more real—threat to her well-being had been harder to overcome but she was mastering it—deliberately cauterising the weakness she had allowed to develop in herself. Of course Martin was a great bloke, amiable and kind, but she could not afford to be vulnerable, to relax her personal vigilance. Look how just a little compassion on his part had undermined her! She kept her distance from him and especially avoided situations when they might find themselves alone. It made her sad. She missed his quiet, unruffled companionship. She caught herself thinking, 'I must tell Martin that,' or, 'Wait till Martin hears this,' before remembering she had no right to think of him in that familiar, comfortable way. She fought, tooth and claw, the natural draw she felt towards him. No. She could not let him in. She was sure Martin had noted the change in her, the abrupt withdrawal, the determined ways in which she made sure there was always a third person present or at least within earshot. Sometimes she sensed in him a perplexed curiosity at her litany of excuses, her tardiness in the mornings, when formerly she had been the first there, her anxiousness to be off promptly each day when before she had lingered until the last. He seemed to respect it though, whatever it was, and so his request, one day, was doubly surprising.

'I'd like to have a word with you, Viola, if you have a moment.'

She looked around the polytunnel to make sure everyone was happily occupied, and then said, 'Okay, sure.'

He took her to one side, to a circle of mismatched benches and old garden seats that had been placed behind the shed where they were sheltered from the wind, and where the last rays of the summer sun lingered. It was where the volunteers gathered at the end of the day for food or cider, but now it was deserted as everyone got on with their allotted tasks.

Martin sat on one of the benches and indicated to Viola that she should sit next to him, but she perched on a chair across from him instead.

He said, 'From next month, our numbers are going to increase. I've been approached by a local care home to see if some of their residents could come down and help out, and there's a rehabilitation centre for wounded military personnel which is also interested.'

'I see,' said Viola, relieved this was to be a professional, rather than a personal conversation. 'Well I can see why they'd be keen.' She cast her eye over the allotment. There were always tasks to be done but it was hard to see how they could meaningfully occupy many more volunteers. Of course, many of them might not be up to much physically, but even the dodderiest old person could pick peas or raspberries, or sit at a table and prick out seedlings. She knew from her own experience that people in rehab were desperate to get away from the stench of antiseptic and agony that pervaded the wards.

'You're thinking we won't be able to keep them all busy,' said Martin.

'I am,' admitted Viola. 'We seem to tick over pretty well with our current numbers.'

'I agree,' said Martin, 'and that's why I've stipulated we can only accommodate them if we adopt two more plots. Thankfully, the two immediately adjacent are available, so we won't have many logistics to contend with. We can break through the hedge at either side of the gate.'

Viola pulled a face. One of the adjacent plots was in a parlous state, choked with bramble and infested with Japanese knotweed. The other was better, and had a useful shed. It wouldn't take too much work to get back into order. She nodded. 'I see. Yes, I can see how that might work.'

'Can you?' Martin sat forward and placed his elbows on his knees. His sleeves were rolled up. His forearms were fuzzed with golden, downy hair. Just above his wrist, on the underside of his arm, there was a livid welt.

Viola pointed at it and said, 'What have you done to yourself now?' but immediately regretted it; it was just the kind of personal enquiry she had no business making.

He glanced down at his arm. 'Burned it on the iron,' he said. 'My own fault. I'd left it on and then I knocked against it.'

She rolled her eyes.

'But here's the thing, Viola,' Martin pressed on. 'I've told the council I can't manage more volunteers *and* a bigger site, and they have told me I can recruit an assistant. I'm offering you the job. What do you think?'

'Me?'

He nodded. 'Yes. You're here nearly every day in any case, or you *were* …' he left the clause hanging for a moment, leaving space for her to fill in some explanation, but she sealed her lips. 'And you're good with the volunteers,' he added. 'You're clearly a very experienced gardener. Who better? It would only be part time to begin with, twenty hours a week …' He regarded her intently, as though to read her thoughts while she considered his proposition.

'I don't know,' she prevaricated. 'There's my work with the women. It might interfere, sometimes …'

He waved that away. 'So long as you put in the hours it wouldn't matter to me if you fitted them round other things. I know how important the refuge is to you.'

His remark conjured up their conversation the previous winter, her imprudent confession. Its awkwardness blossomed briefly between them. Wouldn't *this*—the arrangement he now proposed—make *that* kind of recklessness even more likely?

'I haven't any formal training … with vulnerable people, I mean. Surely you'd need someone with a degree in psychology, or social work?'

Martin shook his head. 'I've got that covered. Yours will be a more practical role, planning a scheme of works, organising volunteers. All the things you do now, in fact, except you'll get paid for it.'

Viola considered. She didn't need the money, and if Martin had asked her to take on one—or both—of the new allotment plots as a specific voluntary project she would probably have agreed. Already her mind was on fire with potential uses for the very neglected plot. Essentially she would be starting from scratch, because everything would have to be cleared, every nettle, bramble and ragwort eradicated—

'What are you thinking?' Martin broke into her thoughts. 'Talk to me, Viola.'

'I'm excited by the possibilities,' she admitted, 'especially for that plot on the right. But Martin, you wouldn't have to employ me. I could do it as a volunteer.' That, she thought, would be so much safer. She understood, now, the need for a professional distance between them. It protected him. As the person in charge he had a responsibility, a duty of care; but he also had to protect himself from any hint of inappropriate behaviour. It also safeguarded her, assuming her rigorous self-discipline—the steely armour she kept clamped around her heart—was not sufficient.

But Martin shook his head. 'That wouldn't quite work for me, Viola. I need someone who would be a partner in this project, someone to share the load of the volunteers, and the more … shall we say, sensitive aspects of working with people who have all kinds of baggage. I know you know what I mean. For that I'd need you *not* to be one of them.' He gave her a direct look. She narrowed her eyes; it was her turn now to try to divine, not so much his thoughts as his intentions. What was behind this? He tried to help her. 'There has to be a divide, between me—the professional—and the service users,' he said. 'Oh! I try to muck in, of course, and be one of the crowd, but I can only do that to a point. Do you see what I mean? There has to be a distinction, no matter how fine, and … well …' He held out his hands, palms up. 'It's lonely over this side of the Rubicon, Viola.'

All her own loneliness—for that, now, is what she recognised it to be—of the past few weeks resurfaced in Viola's heart. The resolute eradication of Martin from her consciousness had resulted only in the proliferation of heartache, as the clearing of one weed will only allow for the establishment of another.

His kind, brown eyes held hers intently. She tried to read them, to discern sub-text, if there was any. It was worrying—but also somehow comforting—to know he had missed her too.

'I don't know,' she said lamely.

'I can't tell you how great it would be to have someone to share the load a bit.'

Viola felt the gentle tap on the fount of her compassion. His appeal to it was calculated to move her; of course, she would like to help him. She thought again of the overgrown allotment—a garden, with accessible flower beds and wide pathways that the wheelchair-users could navigate with ease; a sensory area, with lavender and rosemary, a summerhouse, perhaps, with a shady pergola, where there could be art classes, book groups, therapy sessions … the vision hovered before her.

But actually before her was Martin, his hands clasped on his lap, his eager eyes on her face.

'I worry that … that …' she tried again, but how could she complete her sentence? How admit to him the vulnerability of her heart?

'You'd have nothing to worry about,' he said. He regarded her with frank, guileless eyes. 'Don't you think it could all work pretty well? I do.'

She felt her grip on the snake of temptation loosen. A community *garden* would be a wonderful resource. So soothing to the wounded soul, a place of respite and balm.

Her resistance crumbled. 'Yes,' she said. 'I think we can make it work.'

Chapter Eight – Maisie

Evangeline Ogden has been dispatched by the editor of the *Millport Observer* to investigate the proposed attraction behind *Old Farm Hall*, and especially to probe the charity's treatment of Val. She is a tall, angular woman, thin to the point of emaciation, with eyes of a grey so pale they are almost colourless.

When she arrives at Minnie's house on the Crescent she seems confused. 'I can't possibly have the right address,' she says, scrolling a scarlet-taloned thumb over the screen of her mobile phone. 'This is nowhere near the animal rescue site.'

Maisie motions her in. 'You're from the newspaper? Yes, this is the right place. Come in and I'll try to explain.'

The day has brought a merciful decrease in temperature. A light rain fell overnight and now a breeze brings more grey clouds from the sea, like a dirty curtain being drawn over the land. For the first time in weeks it isn't pleasant enough to sit outdoors so the small committee gathered to explain things to Evangeline convenes in the lounge of Minnie's house.

James is present, hot-foot from some important business meeting that he had to cut short to be at Minnie's at the appointed time. He is immaculate in suit and tie, gold cufflinks and tiepin glinting. He looks like someone to be reckoned with. In comparison Val, although the very epicentre of the story, looks like a bag lady brought in off the street. She has not changed from her farm clothes, which are smeared with ordure. Her hair has not seen a comb. She removed her boots, to Maisie's relief until she sees the state of Val's socks—holey and the greyish hue of sewer water. Val perches on the very edge of Minnie's plush settee, her hands sandwiched between her knees. Gwen sits alongside her, a proprietorial arm snaked into the space where Val's bottom would be if she were sitting properly on the settee. Gwen is her usual no-nonsense self, and although Maisie fears her new emotional connection with Val might muddy the waters somewhat, she would rather have Gwen here than not. Minnie is present of course, but more as a functionary than with the view of making any contribution. She makes and serves coffee and offers biscuits and tries to restrain Dolly, who has taken a dislike to Evangeline and crouches on the hearthrug, snarling.

Maisie introduces the principals while Evangeline chooses her seat and gets out the tools of her trade: a little tape recorder, a notebook and her pen. James mentions the editor—and also the newspaper's proprietor—by name, in the context of some swanky chamber of commerce event they all attended, to leave Evangeline in no doubt that she stands to gain kudos with her superiors at the paper by a correct handling of this story. Gwen reels off her credentials—innumerable charities, committees, church affiliations and other altruistic connections that cannot fail to impress Evangeline—when it comes to "good works" Gwen knows what she's talking about.

'Minnie and I will live next door to the site,' says Maisie. 'At present our place is undergoing renovation, so we're living here. That's why we suggested meeting here, and not there.' It occurs to her that Evangeline might get the impression that this is a "gay" issue, that she and Minnie are … the same as Gwen and Val. She struggles to think of a way to quash this misconception but nothing suggests itself that would not make her seem homophobic.

James says, 'I do encourage you to visit the site though, Ms Ogden, to see for yourself the alterations that are being put in train, *before* planning permission has even been granted.'

'Oh, I have done,' says the reporter. 'I met with …' she consults her notes, 'a Captain Cruikshank and he referred me to …' more leafing through her spiral-bound book, 'Mark Scholey, Personnel Manager. So far he hasn't returned my calls. But I'm here to hear *your* side of this story, so if you want to start from the beginning …'

Maisie does her best to describe the farm's history; its establishment years before by a bequest and its administration by a trust. Val's herculean, often lone, efforts to house and nurse the animals, her relationship with local vets and suppliers—

'Stakeholders and partners,' James supplies.

… the selfless years Val has spent on the farm, many of them in a cold and dilapidated caravan …

'It was alright,' mutters Val, unhelpfully.

… so as to be on hand day and night … the fact that she has never taken a holiday or been off sick … the calm, caring atmosphere provided for traumatised animals, retired horses and injured wildlife … the second chance given to animals when their owners have tired of them …

'Pot-bellied pigs,' says Val, 'and pygmy goats. Bantams. They were all fashionable at one time, as pets. Of course, it was doomed. Bantams can be as vicious as pit-bulls.'

Evangeline's pen covers sheets of paper, even though the whole interview is recorded on tape. 'I think I've got the picture,' she says. 'Now, about this new project. How is that going to be different?'

'Much more commercial,' says Gwen. 'It's all about the money.'

Maisie confirms this. 'Captain Cruikshank told me the goats have been sent away because alpacas are a better attraction and will bring in more money.'

'Alpacas.' Val snorts derisively. 'There's nothing wrong with goats.'

'There's nothing wrong with alpacas,' suggests James judiciously. 'I suppose they can be just as vulnerable to mistreatment as goats. The point is that it could hardly have been in the goats' best interest to be transported halfway across the country when they were settled, well-cared for and *loved* where they were.'

'I *did* love those goats,' mutters Val. 'Especially Crystal. I worry about them.'

James waits a moment to make sure Evangeline has noted Val's heartfelt remark before he concludes. 'The removal of the goats calls into question the charity's intentions, I think. I'd be interested to see their charter, wouldn't you?'

'I would,' says Evangeline, making a note. Then she turns to Maisie. 'I take it you've objected to the planning application?'

'I have,' admits Maisie.

'It could be argued this whole story is just about you wanting to scupper the development.'

'Maisie's name should be kept out of this,' says James firmly. 'This is a story primarily about the possible compromise of animal welfare for the sake of commercial enterprise. The animals will be at the farm as *attractions*. Their well-being will be secondary, that's our fear. Up to now the farm has housed *any* animal in need, even the ones who are not very sociable. That's right, isn't it?' He turns to Val, who nods.

'I've got the scars to prove it,' she says. 'I had a cockerel once—Hannibal, I called him—he was a *fiend*. He took chunks out of me on a regular basis.'

'But that kind of animal couldn't be let loose on the public, could it?' says James. 'Under this new regime, it is our contention that animals like Hannibal will be turned away. Not very inclusive, is it, Ms Ogden?'

Evangeline writes "inclusive" on her pad.

'Then there's the human angle,' says Gwen. 'In my view it's at least as important as the animal welfare issue. Val is being effectively evicted. They have brought a new manager in over her head, and sited his accommodation indecently close to Val's. There's no privacy … and she is undermined at every turn.'

Evangeline turns to Val. 'And how do you feel about that?'

'Well,' Val says, 'it's a kick in the teeth, if I'm honest.'

'Of course it is.' Evangeline scrawls on her pad. 'I suppose they've brought in a whole raft of new working practices?'

'You've got that right,' says Val. 'I'm expected to be able to use a computer, and there are volumes of stuff on health and safety I'm supposed to read. Administration … reams on that, accounts …' She shakes her head. 'I just want to look after the animals.'

'They've threatened an audit of her tax affairs, for goodness' sake!' Gwen butts in. 'She hasn't any tax affairs. If the trust didn't fill in her P60 properly that's no fault of hers. She has been as good as told to resign. This is constructive dismissal, that's the long and short of it.'

'Have you felt under pressure to resign?' Evangeline addresses Val again, pen poised.

'Well … yes,' says Val, her eyes suddenly large and glassy. 'I don't see any other option. I can't do things the way the new people want, so I'll have to leave.' A fat tear oozes from her eye and she wipes it away with her hand.

'Oh, sweetheart,' says Gwen, passing her a handkerchief. 'Try not to upset yourself.'

'Have you taken legal advice?' Evangeline queries.

'Not yet—not officially, at least,' Maisie replies. 'But informally, we understand Val might have a case.'

'Got it, got it,' says Evangeline, scribbling. 'Long-time servant of the community, animal-champion, extreme altruism …' she nibbles the end of her pen for a moment, 'Mrs Doolittle? Animal-whisperer? *War Horse? Black Beauty?* There must be an angle here somewhere. Leave that with me.'

Gwen goes on. 'And her sexuality is clearly an issue. She only came out a few weeks ago and *immediately,* it seems to me, she is being targeted. That can't be coincidence.'

Evangeline's eyes light up. 'Oh *really?* Now that *is* interesting. Tell me more about that.'

Val looks uncomfortable and mutters, 'I don't want you writing about that though.'

Evangeline's eyes narrow. She is not going to relinquish this juicy aspect of the story. 'I can say it without actually saying it,' she says reassuringly. 'The charity doesn't approve of your "lifestyle choices." Which could be anything. You could be a naturist, a vegan, a druid. It covers a multitude of … of things.'

'However you couch it, Val is a victim,' declares Gwen, putting her arm round Val's shoulders. 'But her friends will stand by her. Public opinion must be mobilised.'

'Indeed,' says James.

'A victim of …?' Evangeline hovers.

'Discrimination,' says Gwen.

Evangeline switches off her recorder and puts it away in her bag. It appears she has what she needs. 'That's all great,' she says, standing up and smoothing her skirt down over her skeleton. 'I'll be in touch to organise a photo shoot,' she says. 'Val with some of the animals in her care, especially the cute ones. If nothing else we'll call the charity to account, and if we can get you a decent settlement, so much the better. But I must warn you the charity won't take this lying down and as a journalist it's my job to present both sides of the story without prejudice. If they agree to an interview, which I am sure they will, I'll have to offer their angle in an unbiassed way. I won't mention you, Maisie, but it won't take a Miss Marple to find out that you've objected to the development and that you're closely associated with Val.'

'My association with Val is just as a friend and a neighbour,' says Maisie, slightly panicked. 'It isn't … it isn't a matter of lifestyle choices.'

Evangeline glances across at Minnie. 'If you say so,' she says.

Maisie turns to James, but his face is a picture of suppressed mirth.

When Evangeline has gone he says, 'We'll have lesbians tumbling out of their closets and flocking to our cause.'

Val looks stricken. 'I hope not.'

'I don't care,' says Gwen, taking Val's hand and patting it tenderly. 'Really, I don't care what anyone thinks. I'm way beyond all that. You're all that matters to me, Val. You're being treated appallingly and I won't stand for it.'

Val, appeased, gives a wan smile.

As she is seeing them out, Maisie asks, 'What became of Hannibal, Val? Did you manage to tame him in the end?'

Val grins. 'No chance with that one. He went in the pot.'

'Let's not mention that to Evangeline,' says James.

The respite in the heatwave does nothing to calm Maisie's over-wrought mind or ease her beleaguered physiology; sleep continues to be elusive, her body still troubled by heat and restlessness despite the lower temperatures.

In the small hours she tries to counterbalance her worries with the things that are going well. The issue with the bathroom tiles has been remedied and the *ensuites* are now almost complete. The panelling in the dining room has been reprieved, the suspected dry rot pronounced to be simple age and decay. Their restoration will require more remedial work than planned—and, of course, be more costly—but Maisie is way beyond being bothered by that.

Amy is slightly better after a course of antibiotics. She is optimistic about being able to attend the nuptials.

Maisie is happy with her new outfit. She gets it out of the wardrobe from time to time and holds it against her, admiring its rich colour and the way its lacey over-layer drapes her body. Somehow, she has found shoes to match, on eBay of all places. Worn once to a prom and then put up for sale at half the original price, they nestle in tissue paper at the bottom of the closet— satin, with pearl embellishments and a heel that will not be too uncomfortable.

But these positives by no means outweigh the negatives. Mr Naidu's kitchen quote is, quite simply, staggering. Minnie and Maisie stared at it agog, until Trevor eased it from their hands and said, 'Know a few blokes in the kitchen trade. Ask around.' Thinking of the quote in the small hours, Maisie doesn't know what troubles her most: the enormity of the estimate, its association with her tangle with Oliver or a sense that in rejecting it she will stir up more troubled water between them. The question is by no means resolved.

Oliver himself has been away—attending an advanced sommelier course, according to James—so the necessity of encountering him has also been deferred. What will happen at the wedding, when they will be under the same roof, seated at the same table, in daily proximity? She is still disturbed by the memory of his embrace—the violence of it, its unexpectedness. If he had persisted, could she have repulsed him? The intensity of feeling that must have engendered his ardour is also worrisome. To be desired with such passion … it is humbling. And Maisie's instinctive, inherent kindness could not refuse a need of such intensity. If only she could be sure that, beneath the ferocity, there is a hollow well of longing that she, with her abundance of love and caring, could actually fill.

Wedding logistics are still a plague. There is so much I don't know and can't prepare for. It seems ridiculous that although I'm close to the crux of the occasion I'm being left out of all the planning. Frances has excluded me, and now some of my friends also seem determined to leave me out of their decision-making. How come I have no idea where we'll be staying? Why is it I'm the only person whose transport is not fixed?

They have agreed Minnie will drive the car they now share, but there will be no room in it for Maisie because a wedding dress, a bridesmaid's dress and two flower girl frocks will occupy all the space. Minnie is anxious about the drive but it has been arranged that she will follow in close convoy behind Gwen, who will transport Amy, Val and Gloria. Viola is to meet them in Oxford. So far Maisie has made no arrangements for her own transport and no one has offered her a lift. Oliver's is the only car without passengers and ordinarily she would have had no qualm about sitting beside him for the trip, but now …

The obvious solution is James; but James comes too easily to her mind as the first and flawless solution to everything.

The wedding is ten days away when Frances announces she is coming up for a few days, by train. 'Minnie says we should have a fitting,' she says with a sigh, 'to check the hem length and so on. I suppose I ought to see what she's made, just in case.'

It is news to Maisie that Minnie is in independent communication with Frances, but the brief taste of jealousy is somewhat sweetened by the prospect of seeing her daughter. She wishes she had thought of the idea herself. 'How long will you stay for?' she asks.

'A couple of nights. Minnie says that will give her time to make any tweaks and for me to have a final fitting before the wedding. Is there room for me at her place? I know I can't stay at home.'

'Plenty of room. It will be *lovely* to see you, Frances. I suppose, at the wedding, you'll be taken up with all your guests, and then, immediately afterwards—'

'Yes, we'll be off to Tokyo,' Frances says carelessly, as though she was moving to Tewkesbury or Taunton.

'You might want to … I don't know … while you're here … revisit your old school? Or see some old—'

'Whatever for?' Frances's tone of voice is scathing. 'I'll only be away three years. It isn't a life sentence, you know. I wouldn't mind looking over the house, though. I suppose it's pretty much unrecognisable, isn't it?'

Maisie chews a fingernail. 'Just now, it's a building site,' she admits. 'It will seem very strange to you, I suppose, but what *I'm* seeing is—'

'Your commune. Yes, I know.'

'No, Frances, that isn't what I was going to say. I wish you wouldn't interrupt. What I'm seeing is the vision your dad and I had right at the start, now coming to life.'

'Mmm.' Frances is sceptical. 'Well, I wouldn't mind having a look, but, to be honest, even in May it didn't feel like home. With all dad's stuff gone—'

'Those things didn't *make* it home,' Maisie objects, 'they *prevented* it from being home.'

'My train gets in at four on Friday. Can you pick me up? It will just be me. Maxim's got his final briefing at the Foreign Office. Dominic says he'll bring the girls up for their fitting on Saturday, but just inside the day. They won't stay. Pamela has other fish to fry, seemingly, so she won't be coming at all. Is Gareth home?'

'No, he's still at his boot camp. He's travelling directly to Oxford from there.'

'Oh.' Frances hesitates. 'And Michael?'

Maisie's annoyance of the moment before evaporates. It is significant that Frances mentions Michael in the same breath as her other brothers. 'I'm sure he'd be delighted to see you,' she says. 'Shall I arrange for him to come over?'

'If you like,' Frances replies. 'Although, to be honest, it will be nice to have some peace and quiet. Things have been hectic here—packing up the flat, and so on. And Oxford is teeming with tourists. You can hardly move for Americans. Did you organise somewhere to stay? I hope so. Every hotel is bursting at the seams. Margot's having the devil of a job finding beds for all their relatives, but then she has left it rather late. All the hotels within striking distance are full.'

'Margot?'

'Maxim's mother. We're on first name terms now. And he's Frank, just so's you know.'

'Frank Fothergill?' Maisie smothers a giggle. 'That's rather unfortunate.'

'I'll be Frances Fothergill. What's funny about it?' Frances does not like to be laughed at.

Maisie swallows her mirth. 'Nothing at all. It's just my nerves, I'm afraid. To be honest, I'm terrified of meeting them.'

'You should be,' Frances says with a hollow laugh. 'Not him, he's rather sweet, but she's a *tour de force*. So, where are you staying for the wedding?'

'Oliver's organised somewhere for our group,' says Maisie. It is on the tip of her tongue to mention its likely spare capacity, to offer to accommodate any waifs and strays, but she bites back the impulse. She mustn't interfere. 'I don't know anything about it,' she concludes.

'How mysterious,' says Frances. 'Will there be room for me? Since we must have a song-and-dance about it, I might as well get ready with you and the girls. I suppose one of your friends can drive us to the college chapel. Unless you've booked a minibus?'

'Frances,' says Maisie, more sharply than she intends. 'You can't suddenly start making these arrangements *now*. I've been asking for *weeks* what your plans are, only to be told again and again that it's all in hand and I mustn't interfere. Next thing you'll want me to arrange a hairdresser. At this late stage! And which girls do you mean? Jessica and Edmé? They aren't staying with us, so far as I know. Maxim's sister *definitely* isn't. And, as for transport, I haven't given it any thought. For all I know our accommodation will be in walking distance of the college. If not, I'll get a taxi.'

'Well if you want to be awkward about it,' snaps Frances, 'I won't bother. I thought you'd like it. Maxim suggested you would. I'm doing my best here, Mum. If you recall, I wanted a no-fuss affair. I didn't even care about an outfit. Any summer dress would have done for me, but oh no, you and Margot have wheedled and manipulated things until the wedding I wanted is obliterated in lace and confetti and speeches and wedding favours … all the flummery I specifically did not want.'

Maisie is stung. 'That's not fair, Frances. My sole contribution was the suggestion that you have a dress made, rather than bought. You didn't have to agree to it. Yes, I *wanted* you to ask the girls to be bridesmaids or something, but I didn't suggest it. I haven't volunteered myself to walk you down the aisle or to make a speech … I might have liked to, but wild horses wouldn't have made me ask … ' She is close to tears.

Frances says, 'What on earth's the matter with you, Mother? You sound … not like you. I've never known you so snappy.'

'I'm sorry,' Maisie sniffles. 'I'll try to find out about the place we're staying. You can always share with me. And then, when I know where it is, we can think about transport.'

Frances flings out, 'Only if it's no bother.'

Evangeline Ogden's article appears in the *Millport Observer* the following day. It is the front-page story, accompanied by a picture of Val holding a hen. It is difficult to say which of the two looks more uncomfortable.

Profit or Protection?

Local residents are concerned that changes to the long-established and much-loved animal shelter located on the outskirts of the country park may have negative consequences for animals, neighbours and employees alike.

Following its surprise absorption into the national charity Ani-Well, recent weeks have seen wholesale changes at the refuge, although an official planning application has yet to be considered.

A representative from the planning department said, 'The application is due to be discussed in the next few weeks. In the meantime we are carefully monitoring the works that are being done on the site.'

The animal sanctuary has long been an important part of the local community, well-known for its work with sick, injured and abandoned animals.

'Up to now the farm has housed any animal in need,' a local resident said.

But neighbours fear its takeover by Ani-Well will bring a change in balance from animal welfare to tourism. An unnamed source told me the goats will be replaced by alpacas because they are more appealing to visitors. Neighbours fear that a café and an adventure play area, whilst generating more profit for the charity, will characterise the site primarily as a tourist destination. They worry the farm will no longer, as formerly, accept all injured, mistreated or unwanted animals but only those deemed most appealing to potential visitors.

Questions have been raised about entry to the site, which has always been free for local families and groups of schoolchildren.

Local head-teacher, Mrs Lewis, expressed concern. 'The children enjoy visiting the farm. In these cash-strapped times, a place that makes no charge, where we can teach our pupils about social responsibility and zoology, is a god-send.'

Mother-of-four Fatima Rasheed said, 'I bring the children here two or three times a week. They like to feed the horses. But that will have to stop if I need to pay to get in.'

Likewise, it is suggested that help from the voluntary sector—students from special schools, the retired and other community groups—which the farm has previously enjoyed—might no longer be welcome.

'That would be a blow,' said Arnold Banks, pensioner. 'Coming to lend a hand on the farm gives me a reason to get out. I enjoy the fresh air and exercise, not to mention the company. I like the donkeys. They're retired old codgers, like me.'

Objections to the planning application have already been lodged by neighbours, who mention concerns about noise, litter and increased traffic.

A spokesperson for Ani-Well confirmed they intend to install vastly improved housing for the animals in their care, an education suite to promote greater understanding of animal welfare and the environment, plus recreational facilities for visitors. They would not confirm whether visitors such as local schoolchildren and families would be welcome free of charge, as formerly. The question of voluntary help is 'still in discussion', raising issues of training, safeguarding and health and safety. No one was available for interview but in a statement they told us: 'Ani-Well's core objectives are the rescue, welfare and rehabilitation of animals, public education and the essential fund-raising that will enable us to fulfil our aims.'

It seems the goats are not the only ones threatened by the new regime. Up to the present, the day-to-day work has been largely undertaken by a single employee, who has resided on-site for twenty years. It is universally acknowledged that Ms Fletcher [65] has shown selfless dedication to the animals in her care. She is *lauded as the area's go-to authority on injured wildlife and at-risk animals and no one who has seen her amongst the animals can doubt her affection for them.*

Asked for her response to the recent removal of the goats she said, 'I loved those goats. I worry about them.'

But in a sinister turn of events it would appear Ms Fletcher's position is itself under threat. When approached for comment she agreed the introduction of a new supervisor, 'has been a kick in the teeth,' and that she has felt under pressure to resign because of the charity's expectations regarding administration, accounting, health and safety, and computer literacy. 'I just want to look after the animals,' she said. 'I can't do things the way they want, so I'll have to leave.'

Ms Fletcher intends to seek legal advice as to whether she would have a case for constructive dismissal.

A very close friend accused the charity of 'discriminating' against Ms Fletcher on the grounds of recently-revealed lifestyle choices. 'It can't be a coincidence that this has happened now,' she said. 'She is a victim.'

Ani-Well told us: 'The charity is an equal opportunities employer. Ms Fletcher's sexuality is irrelevant, as far as we are concerned.'

Ms Fletcher stands to lose not just her job, but also her home.

'Not bad,' says Gwen, having read the article several times. She, Gloria and James have come hot-foot to Minnie's house with copies of the paper.

'It's quite a nice picture of Val,' Gloria concedes. 'But didn't you suggest she change out of her overalls?'

'They wanted a natural shot,' said Gwen.

'They've certainly got that.'

Maisie is worried about the repeated reference to "neighbours." It won't take a Sherlock Holmes to identify her as the source of much of the article's information. But instead she says, 'How does Val feel about the reference to her "lifestyle choices"? It's pretty plain what's meant, even though it isn't spelt out.'

'The charity spells it out,' says Gloria. She quotes, "'Ms Fletcher's *sexuality* is irrelevant, as far as we are concerned." I think that nails Val's "lifestyle choices," don't you?'

Gwen shrugs. 'It is what it is,' she says, helping herself to a slice of millionaire's shortbread.

James folds his copy of the paper and puts it on the table. 'On the face of it, she's been pretty even handed,' he says. 'But the statements from the charity are fairly damning, aren't they?'

'So cold and official,' Maisie agrees. 'Really as though they don't care at all.'

'They don't,' Gwen cries, spraying crumbs. 'That's the point.'

Minnie speaks up. 'I don't know how anyone can mistreat an animal of any kind, do you?' She strokes Dolly, who is perched on her lap. Dolly had been a rescue, starved and neglected by her first owners.

'I don't think we can accuse the charity of *mistreating* animals,' says James gently. 'There's no doubt that they do a great deal of good. What we're suggesting here is that they're being *selective*. I think Evangeline's got that point over pretty well.'

'Oh yes,' says Minnie. 'Yes, she has.' She finds the place in the article and reads it out, "'They fear the farm will no longer, as formerly, accept all injured, mistreated or unwanted animals but only those deemed most appealing to potential visitors." That's clear enough, I think.'

'The comments from the headteacher and so on are very telling, aren't they?' says Gloria. 'I think I might know Arnold Banks. I've an idea he attended my salsa class for a while. Quite a looker, if you can get past the squint.'

'So now we just have to wait,' says James. 'See if public opinion is roused.' He checks his watch. 'I must be going. I said I'd call in at the Smithy. Oliver's back at work today. Can I offer you a lift, Maisie?'

Maisie is conscious of a churn of anxiety in her gut. Oliver being away has postponed an encounter that must, sooner or later, take place. She considers accepting James's offer. Meeting Oliver in James's company will mean there can be no repeat of Oliver's assault … she checks herself. Perhaps that is too inflammatory a term to use … Oliver's attentions, she amends. But today is the day Frances is due, and she has a bed to make up and shopping to do.

'I'm not going to the house today,' she says. 'Trevor has everything in hand and the grass will be too wet to cut. But look, while you're all here, there are things I need to know about the place we're staying for the wedding. What are the details? Does anyone know? Frances would like to stay on the eve of the wedding—'

'It would be odd if she wanted to stay on the *night* of it,' Gloria chortled.

'So I wondered if there would be room. And then, how *close* is it to the college? Will we need transport? Because, if Frances does stay, there will be her and the bridesmaids, I suppose.'

'I think the bridesmaids usually arrive with the bride's mother,' says Minnie. 'Although in this case, of course …' she trails off.

'No father to accompany the bride,' Maisie agrees. 'Dominic is to do that, I think. Oh really, it infuriates me that none of this has been considered until now.'

James gets up. 'I can't help you, I'm afraid. Oliver has organised everything and insists that the details are to be kept hush-hush. You'll have to ask him. I'm happy to drive anyone anywhere, if the need arises.'

Maisie busies herself with collecting the coffee cups. 'That's kind,' she says. 'I might need a lift to Oxford if you've room.'

'Certainly. I'm taking Michael, too. Just let me know.'

Everyone disperses and Maisie goes upstairs to make up the bed in one of Minnie's guest rooms. It is a single room that looks out to the front of the house. She picks it because it has a knee-hole desk where, she speculates, Frances might like to read or write, although, quite *what*, she can't think, as Frances's studies are now complete.

Will she be lost without them? Frances's university career spanned six years, and it is almost impossible to conceive of her without a book in her hand or a smear of ink on her cheek. Maisie shakes the duvet into its cover and smooths it onto the bed before finding towels in the airing cupboard.

Frances's new life will be different in so many ways. The room, despite the homely touches Maisie has introduced—a posy of flowers from the garden, a scented soap—looks characterless and bland. Frances is to teach at the international school, so in some respect her academic life will continue—but in Tokyo! Maisie can hardly picture the place. Exotic, she thinks, busy with traffic, possibly very polluted. But no. That's Beijing, isn't it? She imagines cherry blossom trees and women in kimonos, but acknowledges this is probably a hackneyed and old-fashioned image. The truth is that she is ignorant of what her daughter's life will be like from now on. Frances will be absorbed into the Fothergills, into Tokyo, into married life, into a new job— and there will be nothing she needs from me. I will lose her. Of all her children, Frances is the one Maisie has struggled most to connect with. She has always been surly, angular, a breed apart. Even so Maisie is suddenly engulfed by utter despair, a shock of loneliness she has not experienced since the very early days of her widowhood. Almost grief. It is so visceral it throws her onto the bed she has just so painstakingly made. She buries her head in the pristinely-ironed pillow and howls.

After a while the fit passes. She gets up and straightens the bed, and swaps the pillows so the one that has absorbed her outburst is underneath, hiding any trace of emotion.

What on earth is the matter with me? I hardly know myself these days. I've never been given to eruptions of emotion, tears, anger …

She glances out the window to see Minnie hurrying up the Crescent with Dolly. They have been to visit Minnie's neighbour, Irene, who will look after Dolly while the party is away in Oxford.

Maisie takes a deep breath, gives the room a last look over and goes downstairs.

Minnie bursts in, panting, 'Haven't you heard your phone ringing? James has been trying to get in touch with you. In the end he rang *me*.'

'No …' Maisie pats her pockets, casts around her for her mobile. 'I can't remember where I left it.'

They search together. Maisie upends her handbag while Minnie looks under the cushions on the settee, all the while repeating, 'He says you ought to go over. Something at the house. Or at the farm … I can't remember. But he says you ought to drop everything and go.'

'But *why?*' Maisie shouts. She is at the coat hooks in the cloakroom searching the pockets of her various jackets. 'Is the house on fire? Has someone been hurt? Is it Val?'

'He didn't say,' Minnie wails. 'Just that you ought to *go.*'

At last they find Maisie's phone under a basket of ironing in the utility room. There are several missed calls from James as well as two from Gwen. There is a voicemail but Maisie's phone battery expires as soon as she tries to retrieve it.

'Oh for God's sake,' she fumes, throwing the phone back into the laundry basket. 'This bloody thing. The *one time* I actually need it, it gives up on me.'

'Use mine,' says Minnie, holding it out. 'I don't know why we didn't think about it sooner.'

But James's phone goes to voicemail and there is no reply from Gwen.

'Well, I suppose I'll just have to go over,' Maisie says. 'Where are the car keys? You had them last, Minnie.'

'Here.' Minnie holds them out. 'Shall I come with you?'

'No,' says Maisie. 'I'll go by myself.' It is on the tip of her tongue to say whatever the crisis is, Minnie will be no earthly help, but she bites it back. 'Thank you,' she adds belatedly. 'I wonder if you wouldn't mind throwing a batch of scones together. The millionaire's shortbread all got scoffed and I'd like to have something homemade to offer Frances, after her journey. You have a much better hand with scones than I do, Minnie.'

'Alright,' says Minnie, mollified, but only just. 'Call me, though, when you find out what's afoot. I suppose …' she glances at her watch. It is already midday. ' … I suppose you'll do the shopping afterwards. We're low on milk and—'

'Yes, yes. I've got the list.'

The lane to Maisie's house is lined with vehicles parked alongside the pavement on one side, and up against the hedge on the other. She steers carefully between them, her eyes drawn to the crowd gathered on the lane outside the gates of *Old Farm Hall*. She estimates about forty people, many of whom hold placards, squares of cardboard hastily tacked onto broom handles and the like. They are chanting, but she can't make out the words.

As she gets nearer she makes out the writing on some of the signs: 'Animals, not NIMBYs!' reads one. 'Animals have Rights!' says another. '100,000 animals a year SAVED!' declares a third.

Many of the protesters wear Ani-Well tee shirts. Several have dogs on leads—three-legged, torn-eared—presumably adopted through Ani-Well's famous rehoming scheme. Amongst them, Maisie is horrified to see a man wielding a huge television camera. Maisie spots the well-known presenter of the local television news mingling with the protestors, asking questions, but the woman is hardly able to make herself heard over the cries of, 'We speak for the animals!' and, 'Ani-Well is a National Treasure!'

Maisie's face is aflame, her heart in her mouth as she noses the car carefully past the crowds. They peer in through the window as she goes by. 'Maisie Wilde?' shouts one woman. Her hair is a roiling mass of dreadlocks and she has several facial piercings. She presses her face against the window of Maisie's car. 'Are you Maisie Wilde? How dare you jeopardise the animals! Where will they go if they close the farm? How can you be so selfish?'

Cravenly, Maisie shakes her head and drives on. The builders have closed the wrought iron gates across the entrance to her house and stand behind them, forming an implacable phalanx, denying any of the protestors or journalists access to the property. They surely recognise Maisie's car but they give no sign. They are stalwart. She is deluged with gratitude as she had earlier been swamped with woe.

The pub carpark is almost full. A large van emblazoned with the logo of the local TV company takes up two spaces, but Maisie manages to find a spot, grabs her bag and hurries into the pub.

James and Oliver stand at the end of the bar. Both step forward and sweep her into a secluded booth. They must have reserved it. The pub is busy with lunchtime trade. For the first time in her life Maisie feels she really *needs* a drink.

'Well,' says James dryly, 'I think we can say we've succeeded in mobilising public opinion.'

'But all against *me*,' Maisie wails. 'They think I'm against animal welfare.'

'Keep your voice down,' Oliver says. 'There are several reporters here. They all want to speak to you. I've been fielding enquiries all morning. I suggest we come up with a statement. I don't mind reading it out, if you don't want to.'

She looks at him. He is concerned, attentive. There is no trace of the anguished man she last encountered but frankly that horror has been completely superseded by this new one.

'Oh Oliver, would you?' she says.

He looks at her then, a penetrating, speaking look, and between them his words in May echo: 'Don't you know, Maisie? I'd do anything for you.'

Out loud he says, 'Of course, if you like.'

'I can't face them,' she says. 'I love animals, and I've lived next to the farm for years … those people have got completely the wrong end of the stick.'

'We know,' says James. He rests his hand on her arm. 'We hadn't expected this but, you know, they say all publicity is good publicity. We need to keep focused on what we're trying to achieve here.'

'I feel a bit out of the loop,' says Oliver, and Maisie can't help but see how his eye is fixed on the familiarity of James's hand on her arm. 'What *are* you trying to achieve?'

Maisie's eyes dart about the room. The idea that she might be overheard—or misquoted—by a reporter is terrifying. Her tongue is welded to the roof of her mouth.

James helps her out. 'We're concerned the new regime at the farm will be more about generating profit than about rescuing animals. The emphasis seems to be much more on its commercial potential than its humanitarian one. If it *is* going to be a commercial enterprise, Maisie is worried about noise and traffic. Plus, there is a strong feeling Val Fletcher is being poorly treated on account of her being gay.'

Their confab is interrupted by the arrival of Gwen. She is beaming, brimming over with delight. 'There you are!' she cries, sliding into the booth next to Maisie. 'Minnie said you'd be here. Well, I must say, this is all *very* satisfactory, isn't it?'

'Satisfactory?' Maisie turns to face her. 'How can you say that? My house is besieged by protestors accusing me of animal cruelty!'

'Oh?' Gwen's eyebrows beetle. 'Are you sure? How odd. No, I meant what's going on at the farm. There are dozens of gay rights activists picketing the entrance. Cruikshank is holed up in his caravan. Val's been approached by two different lawyers offering to represent her *pro bono*.'

'Another protest? At the farm?'

'Apparently so. I came the back way, along the green walk from the estate. I didn't know you had your own campaigners.'

'They aren't mine,' says Maisie bitterly. 'What if things turn nasty? What if they smash my new windows?'

Oliver reaches for his phone. 'I'm going to call the local police station,' he says. 'You should get to work on a statement for the press. We need to calm this down.'

'On the contrary,' says Gwen, 'we need to work it for all it's worth. Isn't this exactly what we wanted? Those animal-rights people are on our side, if you think about it. I'll have a pint of shandy, Oliver, when you have a moment. I'm parched.'

'They don't seem to be on *my* side,' grumbles Maisie. 'They think I'm arch enemy number one.'

'You care about the welfare of the animals at the farm, and so do they,' Gwen explains. 'It's because you're concerned that you've objected to the development. Isn't that right?'

'I suppose so, partly.'

James reaches underneath the table and brings out a briefcase, from which he slides a slimline laptop computer. 'Let's get some of this on the page,' he says.

While they come up with a pithily worded statement, Oliver gets a text message from a reporter friend stationed at the farm to say that the gay rights people have been joined by representatives of community groups who have been involved in the farm over the years: parents of local schoolchildren and residents on the nearby housing estate. Other journalists loitering in the pub must get wind of the escalation too. They hurry off to get a handle on events.

Gwen, between gulps of shandy, reports that feelings against the proposed new version of the farm are running pretty high. 'Nobody wants it to turn into a commercial site. Naturally, Val is very much the focus of their concern. Rather touching, isn't it? People are appalled that she may not be on hand to care for the animals. The idea that she is to be evicted is even worse. One woman described her as "a treasure." Someone else said she should get an OBE. Wouldn't that be something? That personnel chap was in attendance, of course. I'm afraid someone threw an egg at him, but the highlight was a little girl wearing an ankle-foot orthotic. She went right up to him and demanded to know where Crystal has gone. "'I'm sad the goats have gone away," she said, bold as brass. "I liked Crystal. She had a poorly foot, like me." Oh! There wasn't a dry eye.'

It is almost two o'clock before arrangements for a statement can be made with the various newspaper reporters and the television crew. Other journalists are summoned from the farm site and are followed by demonstrators, all wishing to hear the statement. The crowd of animal rights protestors has been augmented by people who work in the commercial units across the lane. Having seen the hubbub develop they have left their desks to see what's going on. Together with the local contingent and the gay-rights people they make a considerable horde. They all convene outside the Smithy.

Maisie cowers behind the curtain at one of the pub's windows, eager to hear how their statement will be received but desperate not to be recognised. Through the partly open window she can see and hear most of what transpires.

'The woman who lives at that house up there wants the urban farm closed down,' the newcomers are told—wrongly. 'She's lodged an objection. I mean, what kind of person wants animals to suffer? Where will they go, if not here?'

'Pure nimbyism,' says another. 'Doing up her house, after all these years. Suddenly she's too good to live next to a farm. I wonder she didn't move. That farm's been here longer than she has and I know that for a fact.'

A police patrol car arrives, adding to—rather than decreasing—the unrest.

At last Oliver appears with a printed statement, which he hands around to members of the press before reading it out aloud, filmed by the TV crew.

'About time we got something in the can,' the cameramen mutter to each other. 'Only three hours before the teatime bulletin.'

Oliver stands head-and-shoulders above most of the crowd but gains further advantage by climbing easily onto a low wall. 'I have been authorised to make this statement on behalf of Mrs Wilde, who is the owner of the house across the car park,' he begins. 'It is true she has lodged an objection to the proposed alterations to the animal refuge behind her property.'

Cries of, 'Shame!' ripple around the crowd.

'If you read the text of her objection,' Oliver goes on, 'you will see her objections are *not* to the farm,' he pauses, then repeats, 'NOT to the farm. No. They are concerned with the possible noise, litter and road safety issues occasioned by the proposed *development* of the farm into a more commercial enterprise.' Oliver lets the distinction he has made sink in. Most people have not bothered to research the basis of Maisie's objection and the realisation that they probably should have done cools their spleen. They look decidedly less sure of their ground, even the ones with placards. Oliver goes on, 'There is no suggestion whatsoever that Mrs Wilde objects to the urban farm itself, either in its current form or in its future guise *provided that* animal welfare is at the heart of its operation.' The crowd is virtually silent now. Placards are gradually lowered. Oliver eyes them all from his vantage point. 'Mrs Wilde, like you, like all right-thinking people, is an advocate for the continuance of the refuge, for the continued rescue and rehabilitation of *all* animals in distress. *All* animals.'

The throng shifts uneasily. All animals. Yes, that's the point, even the goats that were sent away. Well, *that* wasn't right, was it?

An equality advocate shouts, 'Sheep *and* goats! Sheep *and* goats!' and her cry is taken up for a few moments.

When that has subsided Oliver says, 'Of course, we all recognise the vital necessity of fundraising to carry on this important work, but the opinion of Mrs Wilde and of everyone here is that the *animals must come first.*'

His words are taken up and repeated. 'Yes, yes,' they tell each other. 'That goes without saying. The animals must come first.'

One of the animal rights people produces a collection bucket and people begin to fling their change into it.

Maeve Morely, presenter of the local TV news, calls out, 'Isn't it true the owner of that property has objected to the planning application?'

Oliver bends a superior eye on her. 'Yes,' he says patiently. 'As I said, she has objected to the development of the site for commercial purposes. She has no objection to its use for animal welfare.'

'Ani-Well is a charity,' Maeve points out. 'A not-for-profit organisation. Any money they make funds their programme of animal rescue and rehabilitation.'

'Profit is not a dirty word,' allows Oliver. 'But, as I said, the animals must come first. This is a sanctuary, not a circus.'

Maeve turns and addresses a few concluding remarks to the camera. Maisie scans the crowd. It looks as though they are readjusting the object of their outrage. She is almost limp with relief.

Oliver steps down from the wall and shoulders his way back into the pub like a triumphant gladiator. He is pumped up and imperious. The glance he bounces off Maisie as he returns to his station behind the bar is exultant. She throws him a look that she hopes will convey her gratitude.

The place is a jostle of journalists shouting into their mobile phones. The TV crew begin to pack up their gear.

In the melee, Maisie slips away and joins the exodus from the carpark. She needs to do her shopping and be at the railway station by four.

Chapter Nine – Viola

Viola's new role at the allotment was a game-changer. The work became not just something she did to scratch her horticultural itch, but an activity with a purpose. She had things to do. People were depending on her. She was expected. She woke early, bright and eager for the day, and was often cycling along the promenade before the sun was fully up. Her physical and intellectual lives were productive. If her emotional life remained barren, Viola—a pragmatist—was nevertheless satisfied.

She had her own set of keys to the padlocks now, and a council-issue mobile phone to use for professional contact with the service-users: sending texts, making gentle enquiries after their well-being, encouraging their attendance and picking up on clues when some respite or a personal visit might be beneficial. She and Martin communicated confidentially when necessary, restricting their interaction to the site and its community: Sheila is struggling—it's the anniversary of her accident; Pavel's mother is deteriorating—he won't be on site this week; Ben's physio says he's overdoing things—let's use him on the market stall for a day or two. There were times—but not many—when they found themselves alone at the beginning or the end of the day, but Viola guarded herself against any but a purely professional connection.

Sometimes it seemed that Martin wanted more. He made conversational openings that invited her to stray from the professional to the personal: How was her bridge playing? Had she seen Vanessa? Was the women's refuge keeping Viola busy? How was she, now, looking back? Or, did she know Gwen had taken on yet another charitable role? He supposed Viola was still involved with the refuge. Was it as busy as ever? And how was she, now, looking back? It seemed to Viola that his gambits brought him from various points, along different pathways, but always ended at the same destination—her own experience as a survivor of abuse, her victory over it, her success in sloughing off the mire of the past. Was this a continuation of the stewardship that had existed when she herself had been a service-user? The disinterested concern of one colleague for another? Or something more? Whatever it was, she shielded herself against it. She was friendly, up-beat and cheerful, but kept her feelings in tight check. Viola would not admit to liking him more than was wise; she would not *allow* herself to like him. She rooted out with an iron-clad fist the tenacious tendrils of instinctive affinity that threatened to inveigle her heart, and welcomed the numbness an extra glass of wine in the evening provided.

Viola and Martin worked companionably alongside each other in the new, weed-choked allotment, thickly gauntleted and in protective eyewear, hacking day after day at nettle and thorn, ground elder and couch grass and especially at Japanese knotweed, which had got a stranglehold on the plot. It was as pernicious as a triffid, invasive and persistent. They pulled it out by the roots and threw it on the fire that burned perpetually in a corner of the plot, then dug out the soil as well, to remove the sprouting nodes that would recolonise the area in weeks. The weeds' persistence could not be allowed to prevail. If permitted they would soon resurge and run rampant. If Viola saw the irony of the metaphor, she assured herself that Martin did not.

The new cohort of volunteers was an assorted crew, largely lacking in any gardening know-how. The ex-service men and women were variously abled; some were amputees, some partially sighted, some bore facial disfigurements with fortitude and resilience. Others were coping with the psychological impact of conflict: PTSD, anxiety, depression and panic attacks. All, however, set to with the energy and discipline borne of their rigorous military training. They attacked the overgrown allotment, eradicating insidious briar, nettle and rosebay willowherb, pulling out tangled skeins of barbed wire, rotten wood and broken bricks. It amazed Viola how quickly they gelled as a unit, though hailing from various military arms; and how the weakness of one was made up for by the strength of another. They were easy to organise, if sometimes a little over-zealous; more than once she had to call a halt for their own good, lest they overstretch themselves. She monitored them like a mother hen, insisting on frequent breaks for water and food and especially for social interaction which was, she told them, more than half the benefit the garden could offer.

The old folks were a different matter. Physically frail and yet very eager, she set them to more sedentary tasks such as sowing the seeds for the plants that would one day be set out in the new garden, gentle weeding in the established plot, tending the tomatoes in the greenhouse. They needed frequent reminders of their task, which they often forgot in favour of cosy chats and nostalgic reminiscences.

At the end of the day, when their minibus made its halting way up the rutted track to the allotment, the senior citizens would climb aboard, weary but happy. The military personnel, on the other hand, would wave away their transport in favour of a trip to the pub.

Often Viola was left to lock away the tools and secure the sheds. Martin would hurry off as soon as five o'clock came, anxious to be home. She might watch him from the corner of her eye as he loped off down the track, his shoulders stooped and vulnerable in his loose old jacket. Sometimes she experienced a stab of jealousy, for the companionship Susanne would get and she would not, for the meal they would share, for the details of their days that they would exchange. Her flat seemed dull and uninviting, and she wished she had accepted the squaddies' invitation to the pub. But no, that wouldn't be professional.

Thursday was Viola's night at the bridge club. She had been a member there for three years and now regularly played in the advanced class, as well as representing the club at competition level. She had acquired a permanent partner in Justin, the retired dentist at whose house she had witnessed Clive's assault on Vanessa. Penny, Justin's wife, had given up bridge in favour of a greater involvement at the amateur dramatic group, leaving Justin partnerless, and it had seemed natural the two should pair up. Justin was a good player—Viola's match—and the two soon learned one another's playing ticks. But beyond bridge Viola found him rather dull, and was glad to find other companionship at coffee time. Vanessa was her usual quarry, and it pleased her to circumnavigate Clive's attempts to keep the two asunder. She would slip into the seat he had temporarily left vacant at the table and then smile beatifically at him when he returned to find his place taken. Or she might waylay Vanessa in the ladies to listen patiently while she poured out her litany of sorrows, offering consolation and gentle encouragement to Vanessa to trust herself to the women's refuge. All the while, Clive paced and fulminated in the corridor, barking out reminders that Vanessa's coffee was going cold, or that play would soon recommence, or inventing some imperative why his wife should come out *immediately* unless—darkly menacing— she wanted him to *come in and get her.*

One Thursday Clive and Vanessa were late—an almost unpardonable *faux pas* at the bridge club—hurrying in five minutes past the hour, Vanessa being prodded and harried from behind although, in all conscience, eager enough to get to her seat. From her place across the room, Viola eyed her friend with concern. Although always rather heavily applied, Vanessa's foundation and powder seemed even thicker than usual, and her manner was decidedly agitated. It was obvious her mind was not on the game; Clive's harrumphs of annoyance rang out again and again, echoed by Vanessa's antiphonic apologies. At coffee time Viola lost no opportunity in seeking Vanessa out, meeting her in the middle of the room, Vanessa clearly having the same intention.

'Oh! Viola,' Vanessa began, reaching out a thin and trembling hand. Her voice, always weak and wavering, was choked and whimpering to the point of being almost incomprehensible. 'I want you to help me. I've decided … oh dear! But it really must be, this time …' Tears welled up in her eyes. Now she was closer, Viola could see the makeup hid a livid bruise on the forehead and, above the hairline, a fresh cut.

Following Viola's gaze, Vanessa put her other hand up to it. 'Yes, I'm to say I banged it on the lid of the boot this afternoon, as we unloaded the shopping. It's true, in a way, but … Clive—'

'He brought it down on your head?'

Vanessa nodded miserably. 'I've only a few minutes,' she squeaked, scanning the room anxiously. 'He's queueing for coffee. I asked for decaffeinated because I know they have to make that specially, and I asked him to buy us some raffle tickets as well. I hoped that might give you and I a few minutes. Tell me, Viola, what do I have to do? Oh, I can't bear it. I'm so afraid, so *afraid* …' She gripped Viola's arm so hard it made her want to cry out. Vanessa's face, beneath the makeup, was gaunt and haggard. '*Please* help me,' she sobbed out.

Viola led her gently to a quieter part of the room. 'What have you brought with you?'

'Nothing! Nothing!' Vanessa motioned towards her handbag. 'I've only a few pounds in my purse; five at most. It's all he allows me. He keeps my passport and driving licence locked up in the safe. I need my blood pressure tablets.'

'You can get more of those from the doctor. I could take you with me right now. We'll call a taxi and walk out of here this moment.'

'Oh no, oh no,' Vanessa snivelled. 'There's poor Kitty. I can't leave her or Clive will drown her. He hates her.'

Viola nodded. 'Okay then. So, what happens on Fridays?'

Vanessa chewed her lip. Her eyes were wide and restless, the makeup around them smudged and gloopy. 'Golf,' she said at last. 'He plays golf.'

'And what do you do, while he's playing?'

'I stay in, of course. He locks me in. I'm supposed to knit, or do the ironing. And when he gets back, he checks. He measures my knitting, to see how many rows I've done. He looks in the airing cupboard and counts the shirts … oh!' She pressed her hands to her mouth, a fruitless attempt to stem rising panic.

They were sitting in a quiet corner of the beginners' room. Viola could see Amy Snow at one of the tables, patiently re-playing a hand with one of her students. She must have been aware of Viola's scrutiny. She looked up, saw Viola and Vanessa huddled together, gathered immediately what was going on and gave Viola a discreet nod.

Viola took both Vanessa's hands in her own. 'Tomorrow morning, as soon as he is out of the house and his car has driven away, I'll come,' she said. 'I'll break a window if necessary. In the meantime, tonight, do nothing out of the ordinary. Don't try and pack anything. Don't try and get in the safe. Do nothing you wouldn't usually do. But do think. Make a list in your head of what you want to take. It doesn't have to be much. Any jewellery, photos of the children, things that can't be replaced.'

'A cheque book?' Vanessa asked falteringly. 'A bank card?'

'Tomorrow, but only if you can get them easily. Chances are he will close the account anyway, so your cheque book and bank card will be useless—unless they're in your sole name?'

Vanessa shook her head.

'I thought not. Now, repeat back to me, what are you going to do tonight?'

'Nothing,' Vanessa squeaked out, 'but just plan, in my head.'

'That's right. You mustn't arouse suspicion.'

Across the room, Amy Snow stood up suddenly. 'Clive!' she called out. 'Perhaps you can advise. This player has been dealt a yarborough—not a single card above a nine. Is that a misdeal? I'm never sure.'

Viola whispered, 'I'll be there tomorrow morning, Vanessa, I promise,' before slipping out of the room. Behind her she heard Clive boom, 'There you are, Vanessa! What are you doing lurking in here? Here's your coffee and your tickets. Now sit there while I help Miss Snow.'

When she got home Viola rang Gwen but got no reply. The phone at the refuge rang out as well. She would need someone with a car to effect Vanessa's extraction in the morning; she could not very well manage Vanessa, her chattels and a cat on her bike. It was almost eleven o'clock— much too late to be ringing anyone—but there would not be time in the morning to make arrangements. She did not know what time Clive left home but she would have to be ready early, just in case. She paced her flat for ten minutes or so, tried Gwen and the refuge once more, before swapping phones and using her council-issue phone to call Martin. It was something she had almost never done before. She didn't like to disturb him at home, or to establish any connection between them that might expand the parameters of their working relationship. On just a few occasions it had been necessary; she'd had a puncture the previous winter and needed him to meet a bulk delivery of potting compost and vermiculite. On another occasion she thought he ought to know that Adrian's mother had found a lump in her breast and that the young man would need extra support. But this was different. Vanessa was no longer a volunteer at the allotment and therefore her situation was beyond Martin's purview. And yet, who else was there?

Martin answered quickly but his voice was little more than a whisper, conspiratorial, even secret, in a way that rapped a knuckle on the impregnable fortress of Viola's heart. 'Hello Viola,' he said.

She met Martin at seven-thirty the following morning, reasoning this would be the earliest Clive might leave home as the first tee was at eight. She waited on the promenade in the mist of the autumn morning, chary of giving Martin her home address although she supposed he could find it somewhere in a file if he really wanted to. The mist draped itself over the beach and the sea in a cloak of subterfuge that was oddly in keeping with their errand.

He pulled up in the old but solid-looking Volvo he used to transport produce to their market stall. She climbed in and fastened her seat belt.

'I'm so sorry to have involved you in this,' she began. 'It's really nothing to do with you, but I couldn't reach anyone else.'

'That's alright,' he said, putting the car into gear and pulling away from the kerb. 'I told Susanne one of the service-users was in crisis and had been sectioned. It wasn't a lie, exactly.'

'No,' said Viola. Why had he not just told Susanne the truth? Surely any woman, knowing another was in danger, would do anything to help? But it's none of my business. She directed him to Vanessa's address on a row of bungalows on a cul-de-sac some four or five streets back from the seafront.

'I know it,' he said.

All the bungalows were identical, pebble-dashed, with net curtains at their over-sized picture windows. 'I wonder why the windows are so big,' mused Martin. 'It isn't as though they have a view.'

Viola agreed. If she was honest, the road did not at all have the éclat she had expected. Clive gave the impression of being very wealthy, well-travelled, a retired CEO at least, but these dwellings suggested middle-management at best; they were small and boxy.

They cruised past number twelve—Vanessa's house—to see that Clive's car was still on the drive. She recognised it with a sick churn deep in her belly. 'That's the car that knocked me off my bike,' she gasped. 'I'm almost sure of it.'

'You didn't tell me about that.' Martin swivelled in his seat to look at her.

'No.' Viola looked down at her hands. 'I didn't tell anyone. I was afraid it was my ex.'

Martin tutted. 'You should have told me.'

Viola made no reply.

When it was clear she wasn't going to say any more on the subject, Martin said, 'We'll go to the end and turn around. I'll park well up the road, not that I suppose he'd recognise this car.'

'You're very adept at cloak-and-dagger,' Viola was desperate to lighten the mood in the car, which had become suddenly layered with reproach. 'Anyone would think you did stakeouts for fun every weekend. Oh, we might have to break in. Have you got a crowbar or something?'

Martin nodded. 'I've got a hammer. You?'

She opened her bag to reveal a rolling pin. They both stifled guffaws. 'We're hysterical,' said Viola, relieved. 'It's the adrenalin. But this really isn't funny.'

Martin pulled up with two wheels on the pavement, beneath a starved-looking rowan tree. Viola brought out a flask of coffee and tried to pour it, but her hands were shaking. Martin cupped his hands around hers to steady them. He said, 'Careful, or you'll scald yourself.'

'Pot and kettle,' Viola retorted.

The steam from the coffee made the windows mist up, so he turned the engine back on. 'Or we might miss him.'

Viola was glad of the engine, which pumped heat into the car. In spite of that and the coffee, she was cold. It was all she could do to stop her teeth from chattering. She looked across at Martin. If he was similarly agitated, he showed no sign. He sat still as stone in his seat, hands in his lap, his eyes on some distant point.

They waited in silence. A paperboy cycled along the pavement, whistling loudly. The post van pulled up and the postie began his trek up drive after drive. He gave them a sidelong glance as he passed by.

'We must look suspicious,' said Viola. 'A strange car parked up, and us two just sitting here.'

'Yes, we must,' he said.

After a while, Viola said, 'Did you notice, as we drove by, if the curtains were open?'

Martin shook his head. 'Do you want to go past again?'

Viola looked at her watch. It was quarter past eight. 'No,' she said. 'We'll wait. I don't want to risk him coming out and seeing us.'

Another quarter of an hour passed. There were signs of life at the other houses. A woman took her dog for a walk. A man in his dressing gown and slippers took rubbish to his bin. Someone else fetched in their milk. Plumes of steam rose eerily from the vents of various central heating boilers, adding to the white miasma that lingered in the chill air.

Viola shared out the last of the coffee.

'You make good coffee,' Martin commented. 'Strong, like your tea. Susanne likes it weak.'

'Like Graham used to,' she said. 'Even after twenty-five years, he couldn't get it the way I liked it.'

'He didn't care,' Martin threw out heavily. 'That's the truth of it. People like that, they just don't care enough to bother.'

The door of Clive and Vanessa's bungalow opened and Clive emerged, dressed in checked golf trousers, a warm jacket and a flat cap. They both stiffened. Unconsciously, Viola reached over and took Martin's hand. He squeezed it tightly. 'Here we go,' he said, making for the door handle.

'Wait.' Viola cautioned. 'Wait until he's gone, and even then, we must wait longer to make sure he doesn't come back. It's what they do. They pretend to go out, and then they suddenly come back, to see if they can catch you.'

Martin nodded.

Clive opened the garage using a key, extracted his golf clubs and loaded them hastily into the car. He locked the garage again and then returned to the front of the house, checking the door handle to make sure it was locked. He looked up and down the road.

'Duck!' Martin cried, and they slid down in their seats, but a delivery van that was crawling along the road must have blocked them from Clive's view. They peered over the dash to see his car reverse from his drive and pull away.

'We'll wait five minutes,' said Viola, her voice unnecessarily hushed. 'Vanessa will be getting her things together. I told her not to pack much. She wants to bring the cat. Oh God, I hope he doesn't come back and catch her packing.'

'If he does, we'll deal with it,' said Martin. His voice was calm but she could see his jaw was tight. A pulse throbbed in his cheek. 'And where will we take her? To the refuge?'

'Yes,' said Viola, her eyes fixed on her watch. 'I think that will be best. It's in Millport, will that be alright? I know it's a bit of a drive.'

'I know where it is,' said Martin. 'Yes, of course. I'll take her anywhere she wants to go.'

'She has children, somewhere,' said Viola distractedly, willing the hands on her watch to move more quickly. How could time move so slowly? 'But she seems to think they won't support her in opposition to their father. There's a sister apparently, but I don't know where she lives. It would be better if she can move far away.'

'Like you did?'

'Yes. Well, I didn't move *so* far away. The point is, in cases like these, what matters is that he doesn't know where she is.'

'Yes,' said Martin. 'That's the point. You have to be able to disappear. Vanessa's lucky. At least she doesn't have a job or anything—something that would *tie* her here.'

At last the five minutes were up, and they both got out of the car. Martin reached into the back for his hammer, which he put into the belt of his trousers.

'People will think we're burglars,' said Viola, clutching her handbag. 'Probably just having these things without good cause is an offence.'

'I can say Vanessa has asked me to put up a shelf, or something,' said Martin. 'God knows how you'll explain a rolling pin.'

'A pastry emergency?'

They approached Vanessa's house and walked up the drive. Martin kept his eyes on the end of the road while Viola knocked.

There was no reply. She knocked again and bent down to call through the letterbox, 'Vanessa, it's me, Viola. I've brought Martin with me. He's going to help us.'

She listened for a sound from within, the sound of frantic packing or a muffled cry. The curtains of the front window were closed with no chink between them.

'Let's go round the back,' she said.

Viola led the way down the narrow gap between Vanessa's bungalow and the one next door, through a wooden gate—not locked—and into a small but immaculately neat garden. The back of the house had a conservatory-style lean-to that stretched its entire width, in one end of which was a glazed door. Viola knocked again, and tried the handle which, surprisingly, yielded. She looked at Martin. 'It's open,' she hissed. 'I didn't expect that.'

'Let me go first,' he said.

They stepped into the porch. A maiden of tidily arranged laundry stood next to a washing machine which had been plumbed in through the wall. Several pairs of boots and shoes stood in regimented order. There was a cat litter tray and two upholstered cane armchairs either side of a matching coffee table. The door from the porch to the main house was ajar.

'This is very odd,' said Viola.

Martin stepped through the door into a room that turned out to be the kitchen. Its surfaces were clean, entirely uncluttered, the stove top without blemish, the taps polished to a high shine.

'You could eat your dinner from this floor,' said Martin.

'I expect she has had to, sometimes,' replied Viola.

She called again through the kitchen door, forcing her voice so it would penetrate every room in the place. 'Vanessa! It's Viola. Are you there? Answer me. Make a sound, so we can find you.'

They began to open doors. A dining room—cold and dour, a study and the front room, both furnished with remarkable blandness and immaculately tidy. There was no sign in the house of Vanessa herself or indeed that she had ever inhabited the place. Even her knitting was absent. They looked into the bathroom—white and institutional—and a spare bedroom furnished only with a single bed and a chest of drawers. Then, in what was clearly the master bedroom, they found her.

Vanessa lay immobile, face down on the carpet, her head at an awkward angle, her feet spread widely apart and her nightdress rucked up so that the backs of her thighs and the crotch of her knickers were visible. Near to her was a scatter of rings and bracelets, a silver-framed photograph of two gawky-looking children and the body of a dead cat.

Martin crouched down and put a tentative hand on Vanessa's bare foot. 'She's cold,' he said. 'Stone cold.'

Viola gasped and clapped her hand to her mouth. Her entire body began to convulse; she thought her legs would collapse from under her or that she might be sick.

Martin stood and swiftly pulled her into an embrace, deftly turning her so Vanessa's body was shielded from view. He put his hand behind her head and pressed her face to his shoulder, holding her tightly until the initial spasm of shock had passed. Then he said, 'I'll call the police.'

It was past midday when Martin and Viola were released from the police station. Viola had been catatonic—stiff and oddly numb—while Martin gave their details, answered the officers' questions, called his superior to arrange for cover at the allotment and occasionally patted her hand. He pressed cup after cup of tea upon her—execrable stuff, weak, lukewarm and served in polystyrene cups that made her teeth ache. As they descended the steps of the station they found the mist of the morning had not dissipated, the windless day allowing it to lie like a shroud over the town. When they arrived at the allotment it was locked up and deserted. The eeriness of that, and the horrific events of the day, made Viola feel she was trapped in a terrible and disorienting fog.

Martin opened the shed, lit the Calor gas fire and brewed them proper, strong tea.

'I blame myself,' she said to Martin, when they had both settled in the sodium glow of the fire, 'I should have told her to sod the cat and taken her with me, there and then, at the bridge club. Called a taxi and just spirited her away. It's my fault.' She hated womanish weeping but now the initial shock had subsided tears pressed against her the back of her eyes.

'It isn't,' he said. 'She had to do it her own way, in her own time. Imagine, if you'd precipitated things and then she'd changed her mind! She'd have blamed you, and, more importantly, so would he.'

Viola gave a shudder. 'I shouldn't have liked that,' she said. 'Did you hear him, kicking off in the interview room? Talk about righteous indignation!'

Martin nodded. 'If they needed evidence that he's a man with a temper, they've got it right there.'

Viola stared into the gloom of the shed. 'Seeing her lying there … it reminded me of myself. I could have died, you know. My injuries were so bad, and then I had hypothermia as well. He left me on the floor with the door open all night.'

'Oh Viola,' said Martin, his voice breaking, 'I'm so sorry.'

She blew her nose into a tissue. 'What do you suppose happened? Did he hit her so hard that she fell? It looked to me like her neck was broken—'

'Don't think about it,' said Martin. 'There'll be a post-mortem and then an inquest. All the facts will come out. It's useless to speculate until then.'

'I suppose so. Oh! But what a waste of a life. I suppose she's been miserable for years but she could have had peace at long last, somewhere safe.'

'Like you?'

Viola considered. Am I at peace? She supposed she was, a two-thirds peace, at least, but there was no denying a gaping hole in her equilibrium, a cold and desolate place of stone and iron. It had never been so starkly apparent to her that she was squandering the opportunity she had been given. It was exactly the kind of thing she ought not to discuss with Martin and yet their experience that day, the entwining bond it must inevitably make between them, made it impossible for her to hold back.

'You know those weeds we've been pulling out of the plot next door?'

'The knotweed?' Martin frowned, unclear as to how this could answer his question.

'Yes. Rampant, isn't it? Bright green, with those spear-shaped leaves, full of life and energy and … mischief. Its will to survive and thrive is remarkable, when you think about it. But—I don't know if you've ever noticed—its stem is hollow. Inside its tough, fibrous stalk, at the heart of it … there's nothing at all.' She looked up, across the corona of artificial orange light from the heater that held the shed's dimness at bay. Martin's eyes were dark, unfathomable hollows.

Slowly, he put his empty cup on the table and steepled his hands. 'That's how you feel?' His voice, in the emptiness, was heavy and oddly resonant.

She nodded, and then shook her head in a sort of wonderment. 'The legacy of an unhappy marriage—let alone an abusive one—is hard to shake. You can never quite get rid of the fear that you will be hurt again—not physically, but emotionally. And the heart is alike any organism, really. If you don't feed it, if you don't water it, if you don't let it see the light—'

'It will die.'

'Yes. It just becomes a pump—mechanical and inanimate. That knotweed, it's vigorous … but it hasn't much in the way of beauty, has it? Its flowers are unimpressive and its fruit is black and papery. It's hard to think of any good it does, except for itself.' She sighed. 'I don't think that's the life I want for myself; otherwise, like poor Vanessa, I might as well be dead.'

Martin rose abruptly, as though jolted from his seat, his expression an undecipherable meld of appalled understanding and sympathetic aversion, but before he could act on whatever intention he might have had, there was a soft knock on the door. It opened a crack and Gwen put her head in. 'Oh good,' she said, 'you *are* here. Viola, I've come to take you home dear.'

Martin snatched the cups off the table and veered towards the sink at the back of the room. 'I called Gwen,' he said over his shoulder. 'I hope that's okay. I thought you needed someone …'

Viola stood and picked up her bag. It still contained the rolling pin but the humour of that was entirely lost now. She allowed Gwen to envelop her in a warm hug before walking placidly to the door. At the last moment she turned. Martin remained at the back of the shed, rinsing their cups, his back to her. 'Thank you, Martin,' she said.

He waved his hand in acknowledgement, but did not turn round.

Clive insisted his wife had been killed by burglars. It was his regular habit, he said, to play golf on Friday mornings. His routine was unvarying and no doubt the criminals had been watching the house for some time. Had there not been a spate of burglaries in Southquay of late? He was always reminding his wife, he asserted, to lock the back door of the house. It looked like she had disregarded his instructions, which explained why there was no sign of a break in. His disgusting insinuation was that Vanessa was to blame for her own death.

Viola attested Vanessa had been the victim of domestic abuse for years. She had planned, with Viola's aid, to leave her husband. Viola had gone to the house on purpose, with a friend, to assist Vanessa in that. Clive must have found out, lost his temper and killed her.

The detective constable who took her statement noted the facts as she gave them. Had she evidence of abuse that wasn't anecdotal or circumstantial? Viola mentioned the cut on the victim's head and the bruising to her temple, but admitted Vanessa herself would have declared this to be a simple accident. 'Victims of abuse are conditioned to blame themselves,' she said dourly.

The medical examiner's initial opinion was that Vanessa had been dead for some hours, probably since midnight or one in the morning—casting doubt on Clive's theory—but this could not be categorically established until a full post-mortem was performed. Forensics would have to determine the pattern of events, and eradicate the potential presence of other individuals within the property before they could point to Clive's guilt with any certainty. In pursuance of this Viola and Martin were asked for fingerprint samples so that they could be excluded. There was talk of building a profile. Had Clive a criminal record? Was the man known to be violent? Then there was witness testimony. Had the suspect's golf cronies discerned anything unusual in his behaviour that day? A man who had killed his wife would hardly play eighteen holes with equanimity. True, the jewellery on the carpet was a conundrum. Why had it been left behind? And then there was the cat. A yapping dog, perhaps, might have annoyed thieves, but why would they kill a cat?

'Vanessa told me Clive hated the cat,' Viola said.

All in all the police concluded that, at this stage, they had more questions than answers. Clive was not thought to be a flight risk, and until his violent tendencies were proved he was not counted as a danger to others. He was bailed pending further investigation and was still at large some three weeks later, when Vanessa was cremated. He spared no expense for her funeral, with a cortège of funeral cars and abundant flower displays as well as requests for donations to the many and varied charities he and Vanessa had 'tirelessly supported' over their time in Southquay. The ceremony was well-attended and covered by the local press.

Clive had booked a function room at the Majestic Hotel, Southquay's most prestigious and venerable venue for occasions of the type; but of their many golf- and bridge-playing friends, their fellows in charitable endeavours, the council worthies whose acquaintance Clive had fostered, and the dozens of former colleagues he had contacted with the event's details, only a scant handful made an appearance; three-quarters of the lavish buffet went to waste.

Life at the allotment went on as usual for a few weeks, hampered by the autumn weather, which turned chill and wet. Most of the volunteers did not remember Clive and Vanessa; there was only Mary, Sunita, Gordon and of course Martin to whom her name meant anything at all.

Gordon spoke to Viola about it one morning. 'You never did like Clive, did you? You were right about him, it turns out.'

'It gives me no pleasure,' said Viola. 'Of course, they haven't charged him yet.'

Clive did not show his face at the bridge club and Justin told Viola he had allowed his membership of the golf club to lapse. 'Everyone was reluctant to give him a game,' he said.

'Understandably,' Viola replied, sorting her hand deftly. 'I hope they lock him up and throw away the key.'

But Justin muttered, 'Innocent until proven guilty, Viola.'

She was tempted to throw her hand of cards in his face and walk out, even though it was a good one, long in trumps with a singleton heart, but she suppressed the impulse.

Her snappishness toward Justin was part and parcel of a general sense of disquiet that troubled Viola in the aftermath of Vanessa's death. Everything Viola had been doing, all the ways she had been helping, now seemed useless. Her mind was mired in a bog. Vanessa was gone. I failed her. It doesn't matter how many women I've helped through the refuge; I failed *her*. And that revelation in the shed? I *am* wasting my life. I'm only half alive. The need to unlock her heart from its iron fastenings was becoming imperative; she must let it expand and grow and *feel*. She wanted love, to recognise it and to receive it. But the desire was tempered with fear—a quaking vulnerability that made her hands tremble at the thought of turning that key.

That evening Viola cycled home in a downpour. Water blurred her vision, making her squint at the headlights of on-coming cars. The road, in spite of the new storm drains, was submerged in several places and water soaked her shoes and trousers as she ploughed through lagoons. Her long, waxed coat proved inadequate to the driving rain and her hair was plastered to her head. To her left she heard the pound and shudder of waves on shingle; the tide was high. The promenade was deserted, of course, and the ornate streetlamps cast opaque pools onto the empty esplanade.

She turned into the carpark of her block, preparing to dismount and wheel her bicycle under the overhang when the headlights of one of the parked cars suddenly dazzled her in its full beam. She threw her arm across her eyes. The bicycle wobbled dangerously. Then, a figure—she recognised Gordon's familiar silhouette—burst out from the hedge and seized the doorhandle of the car just as the engine revved and it shot forward. Gordon was thrown to the ground. Viola launched herself off her bike to the grass verge. The oncoming vehicle hit the bike with a sickening crunch. Behind her, flashing lights and the screech of brakes announced the arrival of the police, blocking the exit of the carpark. Officers spilled from their vehicle, wrenched open the door and pulled Clive from the driver's seat.

Viola scrambled to her feet, unhurt, and hurried over to find Gordon on his back. He was soaked, and bleeding from a cut on his head, but did not appear seriously injured.

Even so, she yelled, 'Call an ambulance,' to the policemen, before taking off her coat—soaked though it was—and laying it over Gordon.

'I saw him pull up,' he croaked. 'He tried your door. I knew you'd be out. You always are on Thursdays. But then he got back in his car and waited so I called 999. I knew what he was about. They'll arrest him now. Murder and attempted murder.'

'You're a life-saver, Gordon.' Then Viola began to cry, because someone had been watching out for her, and because Vanessa could finally be at peace.

It was November and another rain-lashed night. The deluge pelted Viola's patio windows, almost drowning out the radio program she was listening to. Her heating pipes creaked and ticked. The flat was warm and she was tired, and thought that she would soon go to bed.

She must have dozed off in the chair. She was disturbed by a soft knock on her door—a knock she recognised. It presaged the arrival of another poor battered soul in the flat upstairs, another trampled shred of life that had managed, in great fortitude, to tear itself from the boot of its oppressor.

She opened the door, keeping the chain in place.

Gwen kept her voice low. 'If you wouldn't mind, dear. It's unconscionably late, I know. Something … well, a bit unusual. I think … I'm sure you'll be able to help.'

'Of course,' said Viola, dragging her hand over her face. 'From the hospital?'

'No, not this time. A self-referral but … oh my goodness … the courage it's taken.'

Viola nodded. 'I'll just get my shoes on.'

She ran the length of her block to the door at the other end. Gwen had gone but that was not unusual. Some clients preferred to be left quite alone, to burrow into the sanctuary of the flat, to lock the door, close the curtains and hibernate in the luxury of safety. Others needed to talk, and would do so for hours, a skein of bruised memory spilling out onto the utilitarian carpet of the flat. Viola had the time and patience for it. She could make herself a receptacle where all the bitter herbs and wounding thorns of a woman's abuse could be deposited. She expected to be up all night. She didn't mind. Her tiredness had gone, leaving her wired and receptive.

She wrenched open the door and took the stairs two at a time. Wet footprints marked the linoleum along the corridor. The door of the upstairs flat opened with a slight push. There was no light in the vestibule, the kitchen was empty and when she peeped into the bedroom the bed was smooth and unused, just as she'd left it a few days earlier. She put her hand on the radiator; it was warm to the touch.

She called, 'Hello!' her voice light and friendly. 'I'm Viola. I'm one of the volunteers.' She opened the door to the lounge, which was also shrouded in darkness. The lurid glow of a streetlight in the carpark sliced through a gap between the closed curtains, illuminating a segment of the squashy settee and a corner of the crocheted throw on its arm. Had the client left? Regretted their flight or—worse—doubted anywhere could offer them refuge? She put her hand out towards the light switch.

A voice spoke from the shadows. 'Don't switch the light on, Viola.'

A man's voice.

Martin's voice.

'Martin?' Her mind went into overdrive. What was he doing here? But then, like tumbling dominoes in an intricate and exquisitely wrought chain reaction, things began to fall into place. The room remained dark but her mind was clear, brightly illuminated as at high noon. How could she not have realised? It was all plain, written in letters a mile high.

She reached out her hands. 'Where are you?'

'Here,' he said. 'In the corner.'

He had pressed himself into the recess beyond the settee. She groped towards him and her hands met his. They were cold and trembling.

'I've got you,' she said, drawing him forward and folding the long length of his stiff, tall, awkward frame down onto the settee. 'We don't need to say anything,' she told him. 'We don't need to talk at all. I'll just sit here and hold your hand.'

'Yes,' he said in a faint voice. 'I'd like that.'

Time passed. An hour? Two? Viola had no clue. The flat's heating went off and she pulled the throw across their knees, tucking it around them.

'Like old people,' Martin murmured.

Gradually, his grip on her hands relaxed. She felt him sink more deeply into the cushions beside her. His hands became warm, as warm as her own, and after a while it was impossible to tell which were hers and which his.

Presently he said, 'You didn't know. No one did.'

'I've been blind.'

'No. No. I've learned to be deceitful. I'm sorry. You were so honest with me and I—'

'You weren't ready,' she finished for him.

'No. But now ...'

'Now you are?'

'I've told her, Susanne, I mean. I've told her that I ... that it must stop.'

This gave Viola pause. 'There's a chance you'll go back? Sometimes counselling—'

'Oh God, no,' he barked out, recoiling from the idea. 'I'll never go back. How can I, when ...?'

Gently, she reached up and let her fingers explore his face, his tufted, untidy hair, his furrowed brow, his moist eyes, his unshaven jaw. 'Are you injured? Has she hurt you today?'

'She doesn't hurt me physically. She rages, she throws things, she trashes the house, but the injuries ... I do that to myself, mainly.'

'They make us believe it's our fault—'

Martin cut her off. 'No, it isn't like that. Maybe it's different for a woman, but for a man … I could easily restrain her, even retaliate, but that wouldn't be right.'

Understanding dawned. 'Ah! So you hurt yourself instead of potentially hurting her.'

She could feel him nod. 'It seems to satisfy her,' he said, 'to … assuage her hostility, if I burn myself on the iron or crack my head on the wall.'

Viola groaned. 'Oh, Martin.'

'And there's so much violence in the air. It sparks like static. Sometimes it feels good to bring it into being. It's a relief.' He gave a harsh, bitter laugh. 'Pathetic, isn't it?'

'No. *No.*' She gave his hand a little shake. 'You mustn't think that. You've been brave and longsuffering and loyal and *strong* and … and all the things …' She wanted to say, all the things she loved about him; but that wouldn't have been appropriate, so she concluded, 'all the things that are admirable in a man.'

He seemed to ponder her words. At last he said, 'I wish I could believe that's what you think. I think I've been pitiful, weak …'

She felt him turn slightly beside her, his eyes scrutinising her in the darkness.

'I don't,' she said quietly.

Later, she made tea—good and strong—groping in the unlit kitchen because he preferred the darkness. 'I'm afraid its Long-life milk,' she said, handing him his cup, waiting until she was sure he had a firm hold before releasing it to him.

'Any port in a storm,' he said. 'You said that to me once, do you remember?'

'Yes, at the allotment, that first day.' She took a sip of her brew. 'Do you want to tell me what brought things to a head today?' Her enquiry was light, almost casual, offering a chink of a conversational opening.

He sighed. 'An accumulation of things,' he said. 'Vanessa, first of all. I mean, I don't think Susanne could kill me, unless she poisoned me or something. But it was a shock, wasn't it? Seeing what the end result of all this can so easily be? And then, more powerfully, it was what you said afterwards, about being hollow, and only living half a life.'

'Did I say that?'

'Yes, or something like it. It made me realise I've been living under a stone and … I want to come out.'

In the darkness, his hand had found hers again. She squeezed it. 'That's good.'

He breathed out, a big exhale of tension. 'But there's something else,' he said. 'Really, the biggest imperative of all …'

'Yes?'

She could feel him wrestling with it, trying to shape his mind around it—whatever it was—his mouth groping for the words. 'It's difficult,' she said. 'I know.'

'Do you?' He turned to her. The darkness was lighter now. Perhaps, as the writer of the greeting card had promised, dawn *was* coming. She could see his face in the dimness, his kind eyes, a smear of trembling shadow where his lips struggled to hold back whatever confession was on his tongue. She wanted to prompt him, to repeat, 'The biggest imperative of all?' but knew she mustn't hurry him. This must come from him voluntarily, so she waited, and held his gaze.

When it came it was easy, small. Like giving birth to a perfect pearl. 'I love *you*, Viola,' he said, 'and I don't love her.'

'Ah!' She let it soak in, like honey, its sweetness unfastening all the bitter bolts and bindings.

She put her hand up to his face. 'Thank you.' Then she drew his face towards her, and rested her forehead against his.

Chapter Ten – Maisie

Frances flings her holdall into the back of the car before settling herself into the passenger seat. 'You're late,' she says waspishly. 'I've been waiting at least twenty minutes. We did say four o'clock, you know, and for once the train was on time.'

'I know, I'm sorry darling. I got held up at the supermarket. I'd left my phone at home so I couldn't call.'

'Well that's pretty hopeless. There's no point having it if you don't take it out with you.'

'I know darling,' Maisie repeats. 'Don't be cross. I've had a tricky day.'

'Have you? What's been happening?'

'Oh …' says Maisie. The last thing she wants is to rehearse the near-riot at *Old Farm Hall,* or indeed to trouble Frances with any of the affairs that have been weighing so heavily on her of late. There would be no point. Frances lacks both sympathy and empathy. 'Just stuff. I think we won't go to the house today if you don't mind. I have frozens in the back that need to go into Minnie's freezer.'

'That's fine,' says Frances. 'I'm ready for a decent cup of tea. The stuff on the train was undrinkable.'

'Tell me what you've been up to.'

Frances enumerates a list, encompassing packing up their belongings to be shipped to Tokyo, various meetings with Maxim's extended family, her course in Japanese and her correspondence with the head of the International School. Her tone suggests they are weighty affairs indeed but, to Maisie, they seem relatively trivial.

'They wanted me to teach the youngsters.' Frances gives an involuntary shudder. 'But I've said I'll only teach the older ones. To be honest, the International School is only a temporary position until I find my feet. I'm hoping for a teaching post at Todai—that's the University of Tokyo. It's the most prestigious university in Japan and it has a large international department, so I should be a shoo-in.'

'I'm sure they'll welcome you with open arms,' says Maisie, negotiating a roundabout. 'I was thinking about it earlier. I can't imagine you in any other sphere than academia.'

'Can't you?' Frances has taken Maisie's intended compliment amiss. 'I think I'm pretty adaptable. I could fit in anywhere.'

Maisie says, 'Of course darling,' but doubtfully. Frances is uncompromising and austere. There are many round holes in which she would be a very irritating square peg. 'How is Maxim?'

'Oh, he's as fed up as I am about the wedding.'

Maisie is sceptical but says, 'It will be a wonderful day, just wait and see.'

'As long as everyone else enjoys it, I suppose it will be alright. Margot's really got the bit between her teeth now. There's no stopping her. She's engaged a florist! What a waste! The college chapel is so gloomy you'll hardly be able to see the extravagant arrangements she's ordered, and she wants me to hold a bouquet.' Frances mashes her hands together. 'I'm sure to drop it or sit on it. It just isn't me.'

'It's traditional,' Maisie suggests.

'Exactly. She says the men have to have buttonholes and the women—you and she, at the very least—should have corsages. And there are to be little baskets of flowers for Jessica and Edmé.'

'Oh dear. Pamela says Jessica is already having nightmares. I don't know what she'll do if she's asked to carry a basket of flowers.'

'She can throw them in the Cherwell for all I care, and if she turns up to the wedding in her vest and pants it will be fine with me. I might just do the same.'

'That's just what I told Pamela.'

Maisie pulls up at some traffic lights. From the corner of her eye she sees a man walking along the pavement with an 'If not in YOUR back yard, then where?' placard propped disconsolately over his shoulder.

In spite of herself Maisie says, 'Poor Val's having a bad time of it at the moment,' and goes on to sketch out the situation at the farm. She mentions—but skips lightly over—the new relationship between Val and Gwen. 'Quite a surprise,' she says, 'but very sweet.'

'*I'm* not surprised,' says Frances. 'I could tell at that party you had they were attracted to each other.'

'Did you know Val was gay? I didn't.'

'I hadn't given it any thought. You're in the wrong lane, Mum. Surely we need to go left here?'

'I'm staying at Minnie's remember? It's on the Crescent, up by the golf course.'

'Oh yes. I'd forgotten.'

The lights change and Maisie approaches the junction. 'To be fair,' she says, 'I don't think their relationship has much to do with sex.'

'Eww, Mum!'

'Don't be silly, Frances. You're hardly a teenager and I don't think you're a prude.'

'No, but it feels odd having this conversation with you.'

'I don't know why. I'm not a prude either and I'm not as naive as people think.'

'Not now, you're not.' Frances sighs. 'Dad wouldn't have liked you mixing with lesbians though.'

'Your dad's not here.'

'That's plain enough. You've changed since he died. We all think so.'

'Do you?' It takes Maisie aback, that her children have been discussing her.

Frances nods. 'It's these new friends of yours. They've brought you out of your shell.'

'But, in a good way.'

'Gareth thinks so. Dominic isn't so sure.'

'And you?'

'I don't have an opinion about it. It's a fact.'

Maisie doesn't know whether to be hurt. Not having an opinion about something is the same as not caring, isn't it?

Perhaps the same idea occurs to Frances. She turns in her seat and says, 'You're happier. That's a fact too. I suppose I'm glad about that.'

It isn't an apology but Maisie decides to settle for it. 'About Val and Gwen,' she says, going back to her earlier thread, 'I think it's about friendship, companionship … connection. When you're older, a hug or the touch of a hand can be as good as sex.'

'I'll take your word for it.'

'Oh, well I …' Maisie doesn't think of herself as 'older'. She is only forty-seven. If she and James were ever to … well she does not think a hug or the touch of a hand would be enough. But she really mustn't think of James that way. It is obvious to her now Oliver has much more than friendship on his agenda. 'Anyway,' she goes on, pushing both men from her mind, 'I think it's sweet.'

'Pamela wonders if you and Minnie are an item,' says Frances. 'I told her I didn't think so. Do you know Michael has offered Dominic a job?'

'No, and no,' gasps Maisie. They have taken the turn into the Crescent. The road rises in a slight incline, with wide grass verges either side, studded with long-established trees. The entrance to Minnie's driveway is about halfway along, on the right—the better, golf club side of the road. Maisie presses a fob on her keyring and the large, wrought iron gates swing open.

'Goodness,' says Frances. 'I had no idea you were living in such splendour. *Old Farm Hall* will seem like a hovel after this, no matter how much you've spent on it.'

'I think you'll be surprised,' says Maisie, pulling on the handbrake. 'Here we are then. Let's get in and get the kettle on.'

The smell of freshly baked scones greets them as they step indoors. Dolly rushes up to them, squeaking with pleasure at Maisie's return but also barking, because Frances is a stranger.

Frances recoils. 'A dog?' she says. 'Is it yours? Don't let it near me. You know I have allergies.' She abandons her holdall on the mat, clearly expecting someone else to deal with it. She holds her jacket out to Maisie even though the cloakroom with its comprehensive array of hooks is right next to her.

'Minnie's,' says Maisie, bending to stroke the dog's warm, woolly back. 'She's sweet, and non-allergenic. All poodles are. Hang your coat up in there, Frances. I have the shopping to carry.'

Minnie is in the kitchen, dithering. She and Frances met once, for measuring, and clearly they have communicated with each other since then, but they both look slightly awkward. Maisie supposes Minnie is afraid Frances won't like her wedding dress, even though she has been consulted at every stage, but the reason for Frances's discomfort eludes her, unless she's afraid she might like it too much.

Minnie busies herself with tea-making while Maisie puts away the shopping. Frances seats herself at the kitchen table and fends off Dolly's curious advances with her foot. 'This is a lovely house, Minnie,' she says. 'I'm surprised you want to leave it.'

Maisie rolls her eyes. Doesn't Frances remember what happened in May?

Minnie says, 'It was never really my home, and Peter's children need to sell it. The year I spent here by myself was absolutely miserable.'

'So you'll be Mum's first—'

'Housemate,' Maisie supplies quickly, before Frances can describe Minnie as a charity case or even an inmate. 'Yes. In fact, *Old Farm Hall* is already Minnie's home. She lived there with me before the works began. In your old room, in fact.'

'I hope you don't mind,' says Minnie, all awkwardness. 'I could easily pick another.'

'It hasn't been my room since I went to Oxford,' says Frances, a touch sourly. 'The moment my train left the station Dad started populating it with his stuff, and when I came home for the first vacation I could hardly get into it. You're welcome to it, Minnie. I hope you'll be happy.'

'Let's have tea,' shrills Maisie, appalled at her daughter's churlish, sour-grapes attitude, 'and then I can show you to your room. When will you have your fitting?'

'Later,' says Frances.

'But not too late,' Minnie says tentatively. 'If there are alterations ...' she eyes Frances with professional expertise. 'It looks like you've lost weight. All brides do, and so we make allowances, but I see a few tucks being required.'

'Frances has always been slim,' Maisie says quickly. Thin, bony, lanky would all have been more accurate, but Frances has always been touchy about her figure. 'These scones look amazing, Minnie. I'm starving; I missed lunch. Let's tuck in. Even if I begin straight away dinner can't be ready for another two hours. I'm doing that casserole you like, Frances, but one way or another I got so behind today.'

Minnie has only been sketchily filled in on the day's events. She opens her mouth to ask a question but Maisie silences her with a frown and slight shake of the head. She doesn't know why it is, but being with Frances is always like walking on eggshells. Maisie always fears to offend, or to summon scorn. It's all about Frances, with Frances. It's best to pander to her self-centeredness; so although Maisie knows Minnie is eager for a report on the afternoon's events, and she herself is desperate for more details on Michael's job offer to Dominic, she says, 'Tell me about your flat. When do you have to give the keys back? Has it been *very* trying, packing all your stuff up?' She can't imagine Frances and Maxim have had much time to accumulate many belongings in the flat—they have only rented it since they moved out of college in May.

'My stuff is mainly books,' Frances says, smearing butter on her scone but refusing homemade jam. 'As you know, I'm not much of a one for personal belongings. Most of our clutter is Maxim's, so he saw to all of that.'

Maisie could picture Frances's contribution as grumbling and getting in the way. 'Maxim is such a treasure,' she says. 'But it must be all but done now?'

'Yes. It's scorched-earth at our place. That's why we're spending so much time at Margot and Frank's.'

'They live near Oxford?'

'They have a place at Broadway. It's in the Cotswolds, so not far. Of course, it's just a weekend place really. I don't know how they think they're going to accommodate all Maxim's relations for the wedding. It seems they *all* expect Margot and Frank to put them up. By Friday it will be standing room only, I should think. Their main house is in Chelsea; that's *much* larger. They have a flat in Poole too, for the sailing. Poole has some of the most expensive real estate in the country, they tell me. Of course I don't care about that, and I don't like sailing.'

'No.' Maisie recalls a disastrous boat trip across Lake Windermere. Frances had clung to the taffrail looking green and whimpering for the duration of the two-hour trip. 'Thank goodness you're flying to Japan. In the olden days you'd have gone by boat, wouldn't you? It would have taken weeks.'

'Peter always intended to take me on a round-the-world cruise,' says Minnie wistfully. 'I think I would have enjoyed it. I don't suppose I shall ever go on a cruise now.'

'You never know,' says Maisie. 'Gloria might decide to take us all on one of hers. I wouldn't mind.'

'I shouldn't like to leave Dolly for that long,' says Minnie. 'Of course, you should go if you like. We don't have to do everything together, do we?'

'Not at all. And speaking of that, I assume I'm to be excluded from the dress fitting?'

'Yes you are,' says Frances. She has finished her scone. She stands and addresses Minnie, who is still eating hers. 'Shall we get it over with?'

Maisie gets on with the casserole although she burns to peep in on the dress fitting. What can Minnie have come up with that will be sufficiently elegant for the occasion, but still satisfy Frances's no-frills requirements? Her head is a tumult of things she wants to ask Frances about, but daren't: shoes, a headdress, a veil, bridesmaids' gifts, arrangements for inclement weather, speeches. She chops carrots briskly. It's no good worrying about it. Before Clifford's death I'd had little hope of providing Frances with a fairy-tale wedding, no matter how I might have dreamed of it, so this—whatever this turns out to be—can only be an improvement. I ought to feel grateful for Mrs Fothergill's influence, rather than resentful. Maxim's mother is simply putting in place what I would have arranged, if I'd had a free hand and could have braved Frances's disinclination. It is galling to think Maxim's mother will have the satisfaction of it all, but so long as things fall into place with just a modicum of celebratory flourish—the merest tinkle of bells, a tiny flurry of confetti—I suppose I can be glad.

Her mind goes back to her conversation with Frances in the car. Her life has certainly changed since Clifford's death, but has *she*? Her children think so, apparently. She is only eight months a widow, and yet the years spent entombed at *Old Farm Hall* feel like a world away, a different life altogether. Do I miss Clifford? I suppose I do. He had taken care of things, in his own way, and he loved me, I know that. But his care and love were suffocating and restricting.

These past weeks organising the renovations of *Old Farm Hall* have been gruelling. What she would have given for someone—for Clifford, she supposes—to share the load. Not the Clifford she had been married to but some other iteration of him—a man not damaged by his childhood, a man not obsessed with penny-pinching and waste. But what was the point of thinking that way? Clifford had been Clifford, and she had not been happy, not really. But now …

She puts the casserole in the oven and checks her watch. It is past six o'clock. Michael will be arriving at seven. She ought to have a shower, but instead she gets a bottle of Pinot Grigio from Minnie's wine fridge, pours herself a glass and takes it into the garden. The sky is veiled by thin, high cloud but it isn't cold. In a lilac bush, a blackbird sings. Maisie climbs the shallow steps to the summerhouse and sits on one of the chairs. Her eye is drawn to the window of the bedroom where Frances will be trying on her dress, but the curtains have been pulled closed. She stretches her legs and closes her eyes to pick up the thread of her earlier thoughts.

Yes, I *am* happy, on the whole. Minnie lost Peter over a year ago and yet she still cries for him in the night. Minnie's grief is still a raw and bitter wound that will take months or even years to heal whereas mine … she searches herself for pain, for loss, for loneliness, but finds only guilt at their absence. Frequently there is anger; it surges up from some unsuspected ventricle like a gout of acrid bile, deluging her in a level of vexation she had not known herself capable of. She is sometimes impatient—she who had cultivated forbearance with Clifford's endless procrastination and obsessive hoarding, she who had perfected an ability to rise beyond these annoyances. Now she finds tolerance in critically short supply. Look how I snapped at Captain Cruikshank! And I've become forgetful. That is worrying. Sometimes I feel as though my head is filled with wool. Am I getting dementia?

She reaches for her wine and takes a long sip.

My feet have hardly touched the ground since the publication of the newspaper article this morning. Those demonstrators outside *Old Farm Hall!* It's no wonder I hardly registered being in the company of James and Oliver at the same time. My unfinished business with Oliver is still unfinished, but I have to admit he was marvellous at handling the press and reading out our statement. But that's Oliver all over: super-confident to the point of arrogance. Great, until you're standing on the opposite side. She resented his interference in the planning of the kitchen but he had been a real sounding board for other issues, pretty much filling the role Clifford—in another life—would have occupied. Perhaps that was what he wanted, what he had "imagined."

Actions speak louder than words, but oh! What I wouldn't give for a few unambiguous words from Oliver! If only we could talk. If only he would tell me, in plain words, what his feelings and his intentions are. That's old-fashioned, I know, but it is what I need. Sex, even *good* sex will never be enough if it is not undergirded by emotional connection. But that's just what, with Oliver, I can't fathom. If only he would *talk* to me.

She shakes the conundrum away and opens her eyes to look up at the house. The curtains at the bedroom window are open again; the fitting must be over. Presently she is joined by Minnie at the summerhouse table.

'Frances is having a bath,' she says.

'Did she like the dress?'

Minnie nods. 'I think so. What a relief! She allowed herself to shed a tear. Just one. But that's always a good sign. I need to raise the hem by a centimetre; her shoes have no heel, apparently. I can't persuade her to wear a decent bra and so the bust is going to be pretty sheer. I'd hoped to make a few darts to … you know …' Minnie cups her hands to indicate a bosom, 'but she says no. However, the fall of the overcoat will make a nice profile. All in all, I think you'll be pleased.'

'So long as Frances is,' says Maisie. She indicates her glass. 'Can I pour you a glass of wine, Minnie?'

'Oh no. I'll wait until our guest arrives. Speaking of which, I should go and get changed. I hope there's some hot water left.'

Maisie is left alone once more. The weather is fairing up after a week of clouds and intermittent drizzle. The forecast is for more of the hot, dry weather that has characterised the summer so far. But the rain has revived the dry and sun-blanched garden. The parched lawn has regreened and she can see new buds on the little violas that have self-seeded around the paving slabs. They remind her of her friend Viola. Although she can be prickly and argumentative, Maisie misses the companionship they enjoyed in the garden of *Old Farm Hall* where Viola had, until her sudden trip away, been a more and more frequent assistant. Bending over the raised beds, their hands and eyes occupied with weeding or planting out, she and Viola had begun to forge, if not a friendship, then certainly a meeting of minds. They thought alike about horticulture. Their enthusiasm was equal even if Viola's knowledge was greater. At the end of the day they had not infrequently shared a glass or two of wine. In those moments Maisie sensed a lowering of Viola's guard, finding—between glasses two and three—a place where their shared interest began to look a lot like friendship, where their eyes might meet, where they could share a joke, where Viola's barbs were blunted. Viola drank too much, there was no doubt about that. Without the lubrication of alcohol she could be as closed as a tomb. When she'd had too much, she was maudlin, self-pitying and unconsolably tearful. Between those two places was a land bristling with thorn and sting, and if Maisie misjudged things she might come away scratched from the encounter. There was also, however, a brief and golden glade where Viola could be kind, where she could smile, and seemed, albeit briefly, at peace. In that oasis, between sobriety and intoxication, resided the friend Maisie really wanted. But all too soon, the drink would swamp in and drown their budding friendship, snatching Viola away to briar and thistle or into a slough of despair.

Why doesn't Viola reply to any of our messages? The widows have a group chat where they make their arrangements to meet and share details of their lives, but Viola hasn't commented for weeks. What would she make of today's shenanigans?

Maisie remembers her phone, presumably still languishing in the laundry basket where she had flung it earlier. She checks her watch. Six forty. Time to go in and change. She drains her wineglass and then goes to retrieve her phone and plug it in. Maybe there will be a message from Viola.

Maisie's step-son Michael arrives on the dot of seven. Whatever misgivings Maisie felt upon opening her family to encompass Michael, she has dismissed them. Michael is a perfectly affable man, uncomplicated and open. He understands his position in relation to the Wildes. He certainly will not trespass and if Frances is to be believed, he has both the power and the desire to offer as much good as he can possibly derive from their association.

She holds out a welcome hand to her guest, and Michael stoops to press a kiss to her cheek as he enters. He is not at all like his uncle Oliver. He has not Oliver's height or presence and he certainly does not have that quality of brash entitlement that she sometimes finds intimidating.

Michael is dapper, slim, self-contained, with a shy but infectious smile. He proffers a large bouquet of flowers and a be-ribboned gift bag that contains a bottle of expensive wine. 'These are for you,' he says. 'Thank you so much for inviting me.'

'Thank you for coming! And for these. Frances will be down in a moment.' She turns to where Minnie hovers diffidently in the kitchen doorway. 'I'm sure you remember Minnie,' she says. 'From when you came to her aid at the beginning of May. She's our real hostess today.'

'I certainly do,' says Michael, shaking Minnie warmly by the hand. 'I hope I see you in much happier circumstances today.'

'Oh, you do,' says Minnie, her eyes filling with tears at the memory of that terrible evening. 'I can't tell you how much I … really, if you hadn't come, I can't bear to think—'

'Then don't think of it,' Michael says gently, and so kindly. 'Really, it's in the past. A nightmare, and now you've woken up.'

'That's just how I feel,' Minnie says. 'Thank you. Yes.'

Seemingly from nowhere, Michael spirits a second gift bag. 'These are for you, Mrs Price,' he says. 'I hope you like truffles. I spent half an hour in the *chocolatier's* trying to decide, and probably ate my own weight in chocolate while I did it. I like hard centres myself, but I decided these would be more *you.*'

'Oh thank you,' Minnie breathes. 'Such a treat. And please, call me Minnie.'

She blots her eyes with a tissue while Maisie says, 'It's turning into a lovely evening. I thought we'd have drinks in the garden, if that's alright. I'm afraid dinner won't be ready for another hour. Please follow me.'

Maisie leads them through the kitchen and out of the French doors, up to the little patio by the summerhouse.

While Maisie was getting changed, Minnie brought out more chairs and some cushions, and lit a citronella candle or two. Some soft, indeterminate music plays from a CD player inside the summerhouse. The two women scamper up and down the steps bringing drinks and snacks in between setting the table and checking the dinner. Once all the work is done, Frances makes her appearance. She wears a creased linen skirt and a shapeless, collarless blouse that might once have been white. She is shod with ugly leather sandals and her legs need shaving. Her hair—still damp—is tied back into an unbecoming ponytail. 'Oh, hello,' she says, 'I don't think I knew we were expecting company.'

'I'm sure I mentioned Michael was coming,' says Maisie.

Frances shakes her head. 'No, you didn't. You're getting scattier by the day, Mother. But never mind. Now we can have the story from the horse's mouth.' She plonks herself into one of the chairs. 'I'll have a glass of that wine, if there is any left.'

Michael looks as though he might have liked to hug or even kiss Frances, but he takes his cue from her indifferent air. 'How are the pre-wedding nerves?' he asks.

'I'm not nervous,' says Frances with a careless shrug. 'Or I wouldn't be. Everyone is making such a fuss. I wouldn't have bothered at all, but the foreign office insists on it and so does my fiancé's mother. Of the two, she's the more intimidating.'

'I'm dreading meeting her,' says Maisie, bringing Frances's wine.

'You should be,' says Frances darkly.

Michael frowns at Frances's remark. 'I'm sure your mum's equal to anyone,' he says, before turning to Maisie. 'And even if the lady's a complete harridan, you will have your friends around you Maisie.'

His words send a *frisson* through Maisie, as perhaps he had intended.

Friends. Yes. I have my friends.

Presently Maisie makes an excuse to go into the kitchen to see to the meal and asks Minnie to join her, leaving Michael and Frances alone for a few moments. From what she can see through the kitchen window, they converse easily. Frances has either forgotten or did not recognise Michael's earlier reprimand. As she watches, Michael brings an envelope from his inside jacket pocket and hands it to Frances. For an appalled moment Maisie thinks the envelope contains cash, but Frances withdraws a slim wallet, glances at it briefly and then returns it to the envelope. It is impossible to tell whether Frances is pleased. If she thanks Michael, Maisie cannot discern it.

When she goes back outdoors the envelope lies on the table. 'Oh,' says Maisie. 'A gift?'

Michael says, 'A small—'

'None of your business, Mother,' Frances says. 'Is dinner ready? I'm starving.'

They eat in the kitchen, both Maisie and Minnie apologising profusely. 'The dining room is full of boxes. The things from here, that will come with us to *Old Farm Hall* when the renovations are done.'

'Please don't apologise,' says Michael. 'If you think I live in any kind of grand style, you've got things wrong. I haven't a butler or a housekeeper, or a maid-of-all work, you know. In fact, I regularly eat off a tray, on my knees,' he confesses, a twinkle in his eye.

'We've all done alright for ourselves,' says Frances, 'considering our father was born on the wrong side of the blanket. We all know his mother was knocked up and then abandoned.'

'Frances!' Maisie cries, appalled.

'We mustn't judge,' says Michael diplomatically. 'This casserole smells delicious, Maisie.'

During dinner, Frances interrogates Michael about the job he has offered Dominic. 'I expect Pamela bullied you into it,' she says. 'She set her sights on you the moment she found out you were in a position to do something for Dominic.'

'She can be persuasive,' says Michael, 'but in fact Dominic was his own recommendation. I was impressed with the way he handled Minnie's step-children. I need a company secretary who is up to date with the law. It doesn't matter that he isn't licensed; we have a firm who represents us, if it comes to that. Employment law is a minefield, and the union representative is quite a firebrand; she keeps us on our toes. I need someone in my corner who is quick on his feet, as Dominic was that night. Grandfather's ethos has always centred on the company as "family," so it felt like a shoo-in, to me.'

'Did you interview him?' Frances flashes a cynical smile. 'I bet he was all sweaty-palmed. Did he have a psoriasis outbreak? Oh God, I can just imagine it!'

'Frances,' says Maisie with a frown, 'that isn't very kind.'

Frances sniffs. 'The truth isn't always very kind, Mother.'

'I wish you'd stop calling me that,' says Maisie abruptly. She knows she is snapping but can't help it. 'You make me sound like an old biddy in a nursing home. You've never called me "Mother." I've been "Mum" since you were ten.'

Frances pulls a face.

Michael makes a disapproving noise and then goes on. 'We interviewed him informally, yes. He came up and we all went out to lunch.'

'Did he?' This is news to Maisie. 'Dominic came to Millport? When? I didn't know.'

'About … a couple of weeks ago?'

Maisie tries to cast her mind back, but the recent past is an impenetrable mire of confusion. 'And Pamela plans to find a teaching post here, does she?'

Michael shrugs. 'It's an option. But you'd have to ask her. Will you like having them back locally?'

'Oh yes,' says Maisie. 'I'll see more of the children, which is always lovely.'

'Free babysitting,' remarks Frances under her breath.

Maisie ignores her. 'I can have them to stay over,' she says.

'Can you though?' Frances puts in. 'Are you sure Pamela will allow that, with your …' she flicks her eyes at Minnie, 'your other guests? Pamela imagines guttersnipes and ne'er-do-wells … she may not think they're trustworthy.'

'Frances!' Maisie barks, blushing furiously. Her daughter's rudeness to Minnie is unconscionable.

'Pamela can trust Maisie's judgement on that,' says Michael, 'surely?'

'The jury on Maisie's judgement,' says Frances superciliously, 'is decidedly still out.'

'What on earth do you mean by that?' Maisie says, laying her cutlery down with a clatter. 'I suppose you mean you don't approve of my plans. You think this is something I've just plucked from the air. Well, it might surprise you to know that I've had twenty-odd years to think about it; the renovations, certainly, if not the use I'm going to put them to. Your dad and I had a clear vision for the place right from the start. As for the children—my apartment will be separate from the rest of the house,' she says. 'I'm to have my own stair, my own facilities, and a dressing room where the children—or any other guests who think they're too good for the main house—can easily sleep. I planned it that way on purpose. Not that I foresee any issues at all. Guttersnipes and ne'er-do-wells! I never heard such nonsense! I've tried to explain it. To me, it's crystal clear.'

'And to me,' says Michael. 'And to Gareth, if I can be so bold as to speak for him. We discussed it at your party. He's all in favour. Of course, I know it isn't any of my business. May I have another bread roll? Thank you.'

There is an awkward silence for a few moments. Minnie offers the vegetable tureen round but no one seems to want any more.

At last, Michael says, 'Anyway, where were we? Oh yes. Pamela hopes the move can be done by September, so she can get Jessica into her new school at the beginning of term. I know they've had estate agents round to value their house.'

'A pittance, I expect,' Frances mutters, 'but Pamela will be able to put all that behind her, I suppose. You'll be paying Dominic much more than he's on at the moment.'

'That, I'm not prepared to discuss,' says Michael. He lays down his cutlery. 'That was delicious,' he says. 'Thank you very much.'

Frances hasn't eaten much of her casserole. She pushes her plate aside. 'Yes,' she says. 'Very nice. But I shouldn't have eaten that scone earlier. It took the edge off my appetite, I'm afraid.'

After dessert the others go through to the lounge for coffee while Minnie loads the dishwasher. The change of setting seems to restore the balance and Frances manages to be almost pleasant while coffee is drunk and Minnie hands round her box of chocolates.

Minnie lets Dolly out for a final tour of the garden and then bids them goodnight. 'I must be up bright and early to make those alterations.'

Michael, Frances and Maisie remain in the lounge. Two lamps cast a soporific glow. They sip brandy—a gift to Minnie from a satisfied customer. Maisie itches to take Frances to task for her earlier rudeness. If either Dominic or Gareth were present, she would not hesitate to do so, but in front of Michael, she falters. She has determined to treat him as family, and yet …

But it is Michael who challenges Frances. 'You seem to be rather out of sorts, if you don't mind my saying so. Quite on edge. I thought you said you weren't worried about the wedding. What else is bothering you?'

Frances blows out a great breath of pent-up air, and all at once she is deflated, like a balloon, the tautness gone out of her. 'It *is* the wedding,' she says.

'You're not having second thoughts?'

'*I'm* not.'

'But Maxim is?' Michael suggests.

Privately, Maisie thinks if Frances's behaviour over the last few hours is anything to go by, she is not surprised. 'He must have an awful lot on his plate,' she says aloud. 'New job, new language, new country—'

'So have I,' retorts Frances sulkily. 'I have all those things to face too.'

'And, *together,* you don't feel—?' Michael leans forward and steeples his hands.

'Well, I'd hardly be putting myself through this *alone.*'

Michael glances at Maisie. 'That's what I thought when I … when I gave you that envelope, earlier.'

Maisie looks from one to the other. 'The envelope?'

Frances reaches into the pocket of her skirt and brings it out. She pushes it at Maisie. 'It's for you, really,' she says. 'You may as well open it now although Michael suggested I wait until next weekend.'

Maisie opens the envelope. Inside is an open round-trip ticket—first class—to Tokyo.

'I didn't know what to get as a wedding gift,' Michael explains, 'and so I thought the best gift I could give to a young bride, far from home, would be her mum.'

Maisie's sight blurs with tears. Even Frances's eyes are glassy. 'I don't suppose you'll want to come, will you?' Frances gets out. There is shame in her voice, but also accusation. 'You'll be so busy now, with all your new friends.'

Ah, thinks Maisie. Here is the nub of it: not the wedding, not Maxim, but me. She reaches a hand across to Frances, but tentatively, because even *in extremis* Frances is not one to welcome physical affection. 'I'll never be too busy for you,' she says.

Frances allows her hand to be clasped, but then withdraws it. 'I don't know,' she says. 'You're so different now, Mum. It will be like having a stranger to stay.'

Her jibe stabs Maisie's heart. 'How am I different?'

'Well, look at yourself.'

Maisie glances down. She is wearing a light dress in a pastel floral design, belted, with short sleeves. 'What's wrong with me?'

Frances names—correctly—the dress' designer brand. 'When did you ever buy their clothes? When had you ever even heard of them? I've looked in your wardrobe. It's *full* of designer gear.'

'They couldn't be afforded before,' Maisie says, 'but now they can. And anyway, they're just clothes. They're not *me*.'

'It goes deeper than the clothes. There's something different about *you*. Like earlier, the old you would never have snapped at me like that. You were the same on the phone the other day.'

Michael says, 'Of course there's something different about her. She's a widow. She's grieving.'

Frances snorts. 'She isn't grieving. She doesn't miss Dad at all. Minnie, now she's grieving. She talks about her husband all the time. I never hear Mum mention Dad's name. She doesn't miss him. She isn't sad. She's … *happy* he's dead.'

Maisie is thrown backwards by the accusation, but finds herself awash with guilt. I can't deny it. Hadn't I thought the same thing earlier? She hopes the low light will disguise her blush of shame.

Michael breathes out through his nose. 'People told me you couldn't miss what you'd never had,' he begins. 'They said because I'd never had siblings, parents, a normal family life, I couldn't possibly miss it. But they were wrong. I felt the lack of it my whole life without even being conscious of it. It was just there, like a limb that I had never had and had just adapted myself to live without. Then, when your dad—*our* dad—died last year, I was swamped with grief. It came upon me like a tsunami, the moment Grandfather told me that Clifford—the odd man in the company stores I had known *without* knowing since I was about ten years of age—*that* man had been my father. And he had a wife and three other children. It poleaxed me, if I'm honest. I went off the rails a bit. That's why Grandfather took me to the funeral and introduced me. He assumed you'd all know about me and he wanted to break through the gulf that had divided us, for my benefit. As it turned out, you were all as ignorant as I had been. But here's my point. I didn't know Clifford properly and so I couldn't really grieve for him as a person. As an image—an icon, a figurehead—I could, and I did, but what I was really grieving was the father I'd never known, the brothers and sister I'd missed out on … the life I could have—*should* have had.'

'I get all that,' says Frances huffily, 'but what has it to do with Mum?'

Michael creases his brow. 'Can't you see it? Can you really not make the connection?' He turns to Maisie. 'Forgive me, Maisie, if I'm speaking out of turn. You can speak for yourself, I'm sure. I can go on but I don't want to trespass.'

'No,' Maisie says faintly, 'do go on, Michael.' She has the strange sense he is about to interpret something she has been struggling to decipher for weeks.

Michael sits back in his chair. 'It's cost me hundreds, probably thousands of pounds to get this far,' he says, half laughing. 'My therapist doesn't come cheap! And she says there is more work to be done. We haven't for example, even *begun* to talk about my mother! But here's the link I'm making between you, Maisie, and me. When I say you're grieving, what you're grieving is the life—the married life, I suppose—you never had. Forgive me, but from what I gather about Clifford he was … not the easiest to live with.'

Frances lets out a hard, cynical laugh. 'You can say that again!'

'Maisie's life was difficult, a constant compromise. Look at her nature, Frances. She's kind. She's outgoing and sociable. She's brave. She has vision.'

'Oh, stop it,' says Maisie, welling up.

'Well you are!' Michael insists. 'I can see that and I've only met you a handful of times. How much more must Frances know it?'

'Well …' Frances demurs, clearly struggling to see the version of her mother that Michael has described. 'I suppose …'

'And yet, while Clifford was alive, all of that had to be quashed. Take me. When I was a kid I wanted to build dens, go tadpoling, climb trees—but with only Grandfather for a playmate none of that was possible. He was too busy at the factory, too old to climb a tree, too proud to roll his trouser legs up and wade into a pond. So, instead, we did jigsaws and played scrabble, visited museums and stately homes. I mean, it was interesting and fun, in its way, but it wasn't what I really wanted. I had to quash what I wanted because of the circumstances I was in. Like you did, Maisie. And so, as a consequence I couldn't really be *me*. Now, I can be. Well … I'm learning who I am, who I want to be, and you're both part of that. You could say I'm going too far, too quickly, but that's part of my grieving process. That's my reaction to what's gone before. Grief is recognising the absence of something. Not necessarily a person.'

Frances blots her nose with a tissue. 'So, this new you, Mum, is really the person you've been all along? And you were miserable with Dad?'

'I wasn't miserable,' Maisie qualifies, 'but Michael is right. I wasn't really me. And,' she considers for a moment, 'if I'm honest, I think that part of what I'm doing to the house is a sort of reaction. I'm going further and spending more. It's a kind of a—'

'Revenge?' Frances puts in.

'No. An antidote.'

'Yes,' says Michael, sitting back in his chair. 'An antidote. That's right.'

Later, after Michael has left, Maisie says, 'There isn't anything *really* wrong between you and Maxim, is there?'

'I've been a cow,' Frances says. 'I have tested his patience, and the more we have seen of Margot the worse it has been. Maxim doesn't like his mother much. When you meet her, you'll see why. He's keener on you, if I'm honest! But she's his mother and, for better or worse, he knows her. I think that's made me envious because, ever since that party in May, I haven't been able to say the same. I literally didn't recognise you, Mum. Your hair and your face … the clothes … and this new idea for the house … those *men!* And then, the way you're acting. So confident. A woman of the world whereas before—'

'I was nobody.'

Frances does not contradict her.

Would Frances really prefer the old, unseen shadow of a woman who had cooked and cleaned and mopped the fevered brow? But it is no good because *that* woman is gone.

Maisie says, 'Whoever I am now, I can't go back to the person I was. So I suppose we'll have to move forward with this new me. Can you do that?'

'I don't know,' says Frances glumly. 'It looks like I'll have to try.'

Dominic arrives early the following day bringing both girls and also the baby, Theo, who has learned to walk since Maisie last saw him. The weather is warm and pleasant, and the children have fun with Dolly in the garden while Maisie makes coffee. The whirr of Minnie's sewing machine can be heard from the open window of an upper room. So far there has been no sound from Frances's room.

'I'm afraid your secret is out,' Maisie says. 'Michael came to dinner and Frances interrogated him until he told all. I must say, I'm delighted for you. Well done, darling.'

Dominic is visibly boosted by his new, improved prospects. He holds himself more upright. He smiles more. His scalp—usually scaly with psoriasis beneath his thinning hair—is quite clear. 'Ah yes,' he says. 'I was surprised, but Pamela says it's the obvious solution to all our problems. Michael saw it, even if I didn't.'

'Frances thinks Pamela will have helped to … how can I put it … *clarify* Michael's vision.'

Dominic laughs ruefully, saying 'Undoubtedly she did,' before becoming more serious. 'I know it can sometimes appear Pamela isn't my number one cheerleader,' he says, 'but she really is on my side, you know.'

'I'm glad things are better between you.' At her party in May, Dominic had voiced fears his marriage might be over.

A shadow of the anguished conversation they'd had in the greenhouse passes momentarily across Dominic's face before he says, 'Much better, Mum.'

Maisie recalls Frances's words of the day before. It has troubled her, overnight, that her children never saw—in her dowdy, caterpillar days—the brighter and more vibrant butterfly she has now become. Had they not at least seen the potential of it?

She blurts out, 'Frances says she hardly recognises me these days. She seems to resent the fact that I'm happy.'

'Oh?' Like many men—but not, Maisie notes distractedly, like Michael— Dominic is uneasy speaking about feelings. He gets out his phone and begins to scroll his thumb across the screen.

Maisie labours on. 'Michael's been having counselling, apparently. He told us last night he's grieving, not so much your dad, but the family life he never had. He drew an interesting parallel. He suggested that I'm grieving *obviously* your dad, but *also* the life I've never had because of your father's ... habits. It would explain so much ... the way I've been feeling recently ... but now ...'

She waits for Dominic to say something, but he looks resolutely at his phone. 'Dominic!' she almost snaps. 'I'm trying to speak to you.'

'Sorry.' Reluctantly, he lays his phone down on the kitchen table. 'What do you want me to say?'

Maisie casts about. 'I suppose,' she says at last, 'I want to know you don't resent it, that I'm ... moving on.'

Dominic squirms, awkward. 'I guess,' he gets out at last, 'I feel ashamed that I never realised how dad squashed you. We all escaped and left you behind, and now I wonder why one of us didn't think to take you with us.' At last his eyes meet hers. They are red-rimmed and swollen with suppressed tears, and explain the frantic but spurious scrolling.

The moment is shattered by a yell from outside. Edmé appears in the doorway. 'Theo has fallen down,' she says.

Dominic goes out to pick up the pieces. Edmé says, 'Will Aunty Frances stay in bed all day? I want to see my flower girl frock even if Jessica doesn't.'

'I'll take her this coffee,' says Maisie. 'That will wake her up.'

Frances appears in an old dressing gown and they all eat bacon sandwiches at the table in the garden. 'This is my second breakfast,' says Jessica gleefully. 'We stopped for McDonald's on the motorway.'

'That's a secret, remember,' warns Dominic. 'Mummy wouldn't approve.'

'You're turning into a hobbit,' says Frances to Jessica. 'They always eat two breakfasts.'

Jessica's eyes are round with admiration. 'Do they? I'm definitely going to be a hobbit when I grow up. What do they do?'

'They do all the ordinary things,' says Maisie, seizing the opportunity, 'like wearing dresses to weddings, but they do it with two breakfasts.'

Frances rolls her eyes but doesn't contradict her.

Jessica narrows an eye. 'Mummy's told me about the dress,' she says. 'But I don't want to wear a ribbon in my hair. She said we might reach a …' she struggles to recall the word, 'count the size?'

'Compromise,' Dominic offers.

'Let's agree, shall we,' says Frances heavily, 'that on the day of the wedding we will eat two breakfasts, wear a dress, but absolutely refuse ribbons.'

'Alright.'

Jessica finishes her sandwich and runs off to play with Theo.

'That was easier than I thought it would be,' says Maisie.

Edmé, seated on Dominic's knee, begins to cry. 'I w … w… want to wear ribbons,' she hiccoughs.

Once the children's faces have been mopped clean of tears and tomato ketchup, Minnie takes them up to the sewing room to try on their dresses. Frances enquires as to the possible location of Dominic's new house.

'Pamela fancies Southquay,' he says. 'Apparently she's always wanted to live by the sea. It would make my commute about thirty minutes, but I don't mind that.'

'I expect property is quite pricey in Southquay,' says Frances nastily. 'How much do you think you'll get for your place?'

'Not much,' Dominic admits, 'but I'll be on a much better salary, and add that to Pamela's earnings—'

'She'll continue to work?' Clearly, Frances doubts it.

Dominic's eyes slide away. 'Even if she doesn't, I think we'll be able to afford somewhere nice. There's a new estate behind the common she rather fancies. They haven't released the first phase yet, but she's poised to pounce when they do. In the meantime, we'll rent somewhere in the school catchment. Michael has offered generous relocation expenses.'

Maisie says, 'We haven't really had the chance to talk about Michael, have we, since I dropped that bombshell in May. How are you both feeling about all of that?'

'I was pretty shaken by it, if I'm honest,' says Dominic, 'but he's a nice bloke and now I'm getting to know him I feel a lot better about it. Pamela likes him, and so do the kids. I wouldn't have entertained the idea of working with him if I had any reservations.'

Frances says, 'I found him a bit insufferable last night. He seems to think he knows mum better than we do.'

'I don't think that's fair, Frances,' says Maisie. 'He was speaking of grief, of his own grief, and making parallels with mine, that's all.'

Frances turns to Dominic. 'Do you think Mum's grieving?'

'Yes,' Dominic says stoutly. 'Of course she is.'

'Hmm,' Frances says with a sceptical frown. 'She has an odd way of showing it. I don't think I've ever seen her look happier.'

'And doesn't that please you? It pleases me.'

Frances flushes and Maisie half-expects her to admit—as Dominic had earlier—to a sense of shame, but Frances's lips remain sealed. Maisie gathers up the crockery to hide her annoyance. It occurs to her that it is possible to love someone and to dislike them at the same time, even when that someone is your daughter. But while she stacks the dishwasher she relents. She is happier, but her happiness is not unalloyed. She hasn't been entirely honest with Frances—with anyone—about her mental state, hasn't described the sleeplessness, the sudden waves of anger, the forgetfulness. Now, she recognises these symptoms as grief. Perhaps, if Frances really knew what Maisie has been going through, she would not be so cruel. But then, if Dominic knew, he would not be so happy for her. She can't please both of them and so must remain lost in the maze of her own confusion. If she doesn't understand herself, how can she expect others to do so?

In the afternoon Maisie takes them to *Old Farm Hall* and shows them round the house. The site is deserted; the men do not work on Saturdays. There is much still to be done in terms of the décor and of course the kitchen is still a shell, but much of the remedial work has now been completed and the children run through the house shrieking at its empty strangeness while Maisie points out the *ensuite* shower rooms, the modernised electrics and plumbing, the freshly plastered walls and the new windows. They climb the ladder to the upper floor of the extension, where Maisie's bedroom and dressing room and bathroom will be located. 'There will be room for the children to sleep over,' she tells Dominic, mindful of Frances's jibe the night before. 'I shall have a pull-out day bed for them, and if you want to stay, you can have the whole space and I can sleep in Gareth's room, or one of the others.'

'I'm surprised,' says Frances huffily, 'in the light of developments, that you don't give up the entire scheme and just have Dominic and Pamela come to live with you. They could have the main house and you'd have this. It's the perfect granny flat.'

'But what about Minnie?' says Maisie. 'And, in any case, I don't suppose Pamela would want to live here. She's never especially liked the house. But put all that to one side, Frances, that isn't what I want.' She turns apologetically to Dominic. 'I'm sorry, Dominic. I'm thrilled you'll be nearer to me, but I'm not ready for a granny flat. I have plans and ideas—'

'That's okay, Mum,' says Dominic. 'I understand. I'm excited for you.'

Frances sniffs. 'I'll have to go outside,' she says. 'This dust is aggravating my rhinitis.'

They go down to the Smithy for an early supper before Dominic has to set off home with the children. Oliver is working behind the bar, schmoozing the customers, pulling pints and mixing cocktails with elegant flair. His dark hair is slicked back off his face, his white shirt is pristine. His smile, upon seeing her, is wide and genuine. He ushers them to a quiet table in a booth and finds a highchair for Theo. As he hands Maisie a menu their hands touch and she is conscious of a quick heat between them.

Emboldened, she says, 'I know you're working, Oliver, but if you had a few moments there are some things I'd like to ask you.'

He says, 'I've always got time for you, Maisie. Let me put your order through and I'll come and join you briefly. These drinks are on me, by the way.'

Maisie orders a glass of wine and when it comes it is a large one. Frances has a soft drink and, because he is driving, so does Dominic. The children have apple juice but Oliver presents them like cocktails, with cherries and umbrellas, which pleases them no end. He distributes colouring books and crayons for the children, before seating himself diffidently at their table.

'Let me just say,' he begins, addressing Frances, 'that next weekend, if you find you need any help with the arrangements—the caterers, master of ceremonies, anything of that nature—I'd be delighted to help out. I used to be the banqueting manager of a large hotel and before that, on the cruise line we often had weddings, so I know what I'm doing.'

'Oh,' says Frances, as though the wedding is nothing to do with her, 'I expect things will work themselves out. My mother-in-law seems to have it all in hand.'

'But it's a kind offer, Frances, isn't it?' Maisie prompts.

'Oh yes,' she says insincerely, 'very kind.'

'Well,' Oliver beams, 'I can't say I'm sorry. I'm looking forward to devoting my whole attention to this lady.' He places a proprietorial hand on Maisie's shoulder. 'But I thought I ought to offer.'

Maisie squirms in her seat, her innards both liquescent and furious at his presumption. She wishes he would remove his arm but it remains stubbornly in place.

Jessica looks up from her colouring. 'Granny, is this your new boyfriend?'

Maisie laughs, but it comes out a shrill, hyena-like shriek. 'You do make me laugh, Jessica, you funny thing.'

Oliver sails serenely over the awkwardness. 'So, what did you want to ask me?'

Maisie tries to get a grip. 'About the accommodation,' she gets out weakly. 'Frances wants to stay on the night before the wedding. Will there be room? I don't mind sharing my room with her, if it comes to it.'

Oliver allows himself a complacent smile. 'I think we'll be able to squeeze her in,' he says.

'And where is it, exactly? Is it close to the college? Will we need transport?'

Oliver gives her a squeeze. 'All that is arranged,' he says. 'You will travel in style.'

Maisie suppresses irritation. It is nice to be looked after, of course, but she will not be patronised. 'That sounds wonderful,' she says, 'but have you allowed for Frances? And the bridesmaids?' She looks to Frances for confirmation. 'I suppose you'll want to arrive at the college chapel with them. Or, would you rather they were there waiting for you? Dominic, where are you staying? Will you bring the girls to … wherever we are for them to get dressed?'

'We're at the Premier Inn,' says Dominic. 'I assumed we'd collect the dresses the night before, and then make our own way to the venue. I didn't know there was to be a convoy.'

'There isn't,' shouts Frances, smacking her glass onto the table and making Theo jump. 'For God's sake, why can't everyone just *stop* trying to organise things? I shall make my own way to the chapel. If I have to call an Uber, I will do. I don't care. Can't you see? The more fuss you're all making the worse I feel about it. You're as bad as Margot. Between the two of you you'll just about ruin the whole day.'

Maisie bridles but manages her next remark to sound genuinely contrite. 'I'm sorry, Frances. It sounds like you can stay with my party the night before, if you wish to, but I'll leave it entirely up to you.' She throws Oliver an apologetic look and he gives her the smallest possible nod. She needn't worry. He's got this. Whatever plans he has put in place can include Frances, or not, just as she wants. Maisie is swamped by relief. At least he is organised, no matter how chaotic everything else might be. But then her relief is checked. Can she really trust him?

Chapter Eleven – Viola

Martin and Viola were married quietly the following June, the twenty-first, the longest day, which fell on a Friday. His divorce had been relatively easy; he agreed that Susanne should cite his adultery. Their house was rented so there was no property to divide and he allowed her all their savings and shared possessions apart from his books, of which he possessed a great many.

'She earned all the money anyway,' he said. 'And I want a clean break.'

Viola did not blame him. Susanne made a nuisance of herself for a while, phoning up at all hours of the night, turning up at the flat to shout obscenities and hurl clumps of filth at the patio windows, making an official complaint about Viola to the board of the refuge and also to the social services department in charge of the allotment project. It all came to nothing. It could have soured their first few weeks together, but in truth they were so blissfully happy they were almost immune. Only in the darkest hours of the night did they allow themselves to dredge their chambers of horror, to exchange accounts of abuse, to lay their nightmares out on the benevolence of the cool, white sheet.

'We don't need the money,' Viola assured him. Brian's investments had come good—*very* good—and if they wanted they could both retire, although neither was much past their fiftieth birthdays.

They were married in the registry office, with Brian and Gwen as their witnesses. Afterwards there was a party at the allotment, a casual affair with food provided by the service-users and a good deal of homemade cider. The weather was kind—a blessing, as the rest of the summer had been uncooperative. The marquee, erected just in case, was not required. Adrian, egged on by the squaddies, had too much to drink and was found passed out behind the polytunnel. Mary's husband—quite batty but utterly harmless—stripped nearly every raspberry from the raspberry canes and gorged himself so that his face and clothes looked like he'd been in a chainsaw massacre.

Afterwards, they walked back along the promenade to Viola's flat, where Martin had been living since the previous November. His books were still in boxes, the boxes stacked in every corner, their suitcases packed and ready for their honeymoon, which was to begin the following day.

'When we get back from Croatia,' said Viola, reaching for the zip of her dress, 'we'll begin to look for a new place.'

He said, 'Don't do that, Viola, I want to undress you.'

She turned her back to him so that he could begin. Their lovemaking had been slow and very gentle. For the first few weeks they had not progressed beyond holding each other. Viola found her body fitted perfectly into his, the curve of his side accommodating her shoulder, breast and hip, a dip in his shoulder just right for her nestling head. They were both too raw—too flayed—for more. Their scars lay between them. They explored and named them, one by one, telling their histories. When they kissed it was almost reverent, light as whispers, and Martin often could not hold back tears. His emotions, once unlocked, were an unstoppable faucet. She loved his honesty almost as much as she loved the spare litheness of his figure, which was such a welcome contrast to Graham's stocky shoulders and pendulous gut.

'You're so beautiful,' she told him.

Susanne, Martin told her, was bony and sharp. 'Not like you,' he said, stroking her thigh. 'You're soft and warm. I knew you would be.'

Their very hesitancy added to their desire; they held back, respectful and mindful of one another's hurts until gradually their confidence strengthened and their reticence slipped away. At last, Viola opened herself and Martin brought her again and again to orgasm and finally, when she thought herself utterly spent, he slid himself inside her to achieve for them both a high, fine, exquisite peak.

They honeymooned in Croatia, touring the gardens of the Adriatic, which are beautiful but also productive. 'Land is food,' they were told repeatedly. It was exactly their own philosophy. They noted planting schemes and ideas for companion planting. They admired irrigation systems and fruit cordons.

They stayed in out-of-the-way places, little *pensions,* where aproned women served them local melon and sheep's yoghurt drizzled with honey that tasted of the small Alpines and native succulents that covered the craggy hillsides. They clambered down rocky screes and bathed in pure blue waters.

Martin read voraciously while Viola explored the shoreline. It transpired Susanne had always resented his books and interfered with his reading. He confessed to Viola he would like to try and write.

'That's what you'll do then,' she said.

When they got home, they gave three months' notice of their intention to resign and began to look for a house that would be their own. There was plenty of money, and although the bigger Victorian and Edwardian properties of Southquay were well within their means—not to mention the architect-designed new-builds further out of town—they chose a crumbling old manse in a coastal village halfway between Southquay and the next town along. The manse was square and solid, much too big for them really, with ancient plumbing and rotten windows and a hole in its roof, but it had an acre of ground, an orchard and a wild, walled garden where Viola could lay out vegetable beds and espalier fruit trees while Martin sat in a nicely fitted-out study and wrote his first bestseller.

On their first viewing Martin looked around it doubtfully. 'I've a fair skill in DIY,' he told her. 'But this is way out of my league.'

'We'll get builders in,' she said gaily. 'We can stay in the flat until it's ready, or we can move in and camp while they work round us. I don't mind.' She inserted herself into his arms. 'So long as we're together.'

One late July evening they cycled home from the allotment. Martin's Volvo had shuddered to a halt on the motorway as they had returned from their honeymoon and they were awaiting delivery of a spanking new four-by-four. In the meantime, he had acquired a bicycle and the couple took pleasure in their morning and evening rides along the esplanade.

The future lay before them as smooth and wide as the broad sea-front road. They were working out their notice at the allotment project. A new appointee was due to begin in September. To everyone's delight, Adrian had been given Viola's position as assistant. Contracts were due to be exchanged on the manse the following week, and Viola had builders lined up to begin work immediately. They hoped to be installed in their new home by Christmas.

Summer had arrived at last, a torrid affair of scorching temperatures and sudden, violent thunderstorms. The new allotment was, alternatively, a baked, impenetrable pancake or a quagmire of ankle-deep sludge. The hard landscaping had been delayed pending more equitable weather. Viola was sorry she would not see the project through to fruition, but her thoughts had moved on to her walled garden. Peach trees, she thought, would not be out of the question on its sheltered, south-facing wall.

Martin said, 'Shall we get fish and chips? I don't think I've the energy to cook.'

Viola nodded and they both cruised to a standstill near a vacant bench.

'There's a shop over there,' said Martin, pointing across the road. 'You sit tight, I'll be back in a minute.'

Viola leaned their bicycles against the bench and removed her helmet and backpack. The sun was warm on her shoulders. She sat and closed her eyes, breathing in the salt tang of the sea and the warm, slightly humid air that was overlaid by fumes of summer visitors' cars as they searched for parking spots on the front. Very faintly, a piquant top-note, she discerned the vinegary whiff of the fish and chip shop. Two boys rumbled past her on skateboards. A dog barked on the beach. Gulls screeched in the sky above her.

Afterwards, she learned Martin had left the chip shop with his purchases and stepped into the road. The driver, busy admiring the view, did not see him, but he had been travelling at a low speed and the impact would not have been fatal if it had not been for the weighty iron storm grille in the kerb. Martin was thrown backwards, his body landing flat on the road but his head hitting the grille with such impact that it snapped his neck.

He died instantly. He knew nothing, he would have felt nothing, she was told.

'No, you're wrong,' she sobbed out. 'He knew everything. He *felt* everything. That's why I loved him.'

Chapter Twelve – Maisie

Evangeline Ogden's newspaper article had opened a can of worms for Ani-Well, with repercussions well beyond the little urban farm in Millport. Several of their more commercialised sanctuary sites are the subject of investigations by council inspectors and independent animal welfare specialists. Some have pickets at their gates—bands of activists from both gay- and animal-rights communities who brandish placards and shout slogans. Their head office is besieged by a twenty-four-hour protest. A nation-wide investigation is launched as to the whereabouts of Crystal, the wall-eyed goat. Eventually Crystal and the other goats from Millport are discovered safe and well at a refuge in the midlands, and a breakfast television show makes a big deal of connecting Val with the supervisor there, so that Crystal's particular requirements regarding ear-scratching can be passed on.

Val hates all the publicity, of course. Her morning television appearance is excruciating for all concerned. However, her legal advisor has been able to make significant progress on her behalf and Gwen lets their women friends know that some resolution looks likely.

Maisie is surprised to arrive at *Old Farm Hall* one morning to find Captain Cruikshank hovering diffidently in the *parterre* clutching a box of eggs.

'A peace offering,' he says stiffly. 'Egg money in petty cash, all accounted for.' He holds the box out to Maisie. She senses a battle of will. His eyes widen while his lips press themselves together. He flushes beetroot and then, as though laying a square egg himself, he squeezes out, 'My mistake.'

'I never doubted it,' says Maisie, taking the box. 'But Val's been treated dreadfully, in my opinion.'

The captain barks out a few staccato phrases. 'Changing times,' he says, and 'market share. Out-of-the-box-thinking. Innovation.' Maisie can see that these are his final flurries of hot air. His shoulders droop.

Maisie's reply is trenchant, but gentle. 'Animal welfare,' she says. 'Human rights. Kindness.'

The captain lowers himself gingerly onto the stone bench. 'Yes,' he mumbles. 'Fact is, been out of the loop, in clink. Drunk-driving. Killed a man.' He shakes his head. 'Dreadful.'

Maisie's innate sympathy wells forth. She perches next to him. 'All the more reason,' she offers, laying a tentative hand on his crisply-ironed shirtsleeve.

He nods. 'Yes, you're right. And so …' his shoulders square themselves again, but with determination this time, not arrogance, 'you're invited to a meeting. All the interested parties: Ms Fletcher and myself, Mark Scholey and you. To see a way through.'

'Oh.' Maisie is taken aback. 'I see. When?'

'Tomorrow afternoon, if that suits.'

The following day will be Wednesday, two days away from the women's trip to Oxford for the wedding. Maisie has a hundred things to do: an appointment at the hairdresser and another at the nail bar. She *still* has to find a handbag to match her new outfit. The lawns here at *Old Farm Hall* and the ones at Minnie's house need mowing. There are peas and beans to pick and process and Trevor wants her to go through the kitchen quote with a fine-toothed comb so he can brief his preferred kitchen-fitting company. But none of these things seem very important in comparison to Val's future, not to mention that of the farm, and so she says, 'Yes. But can it be later on in the day? Say four o'clock?'

The next day Maisie rises early and goes into town for her hair appointment. She is a client of the hairdresser situated in a large department store, and hurries between the makeup concessions to the escalator that will take her to the top floor.

Halfway up, she glances down to spy a flash of peacock blue in a basket of sundry items apparently on sale. The colour is so exact to her mother-of-the-bride outfit that as soon as she gets to the top she does a U turn and takes the opposite escalator back down.

She rummages in the basket, pulling out scarves and hair accessories to find a small, beaded handbag, the perfect size, shape and colour. It has a long, finely-wrought chain shoulder strap and a clasp formed from two mother-of-pearl beads. She holds it to herself in a kind of ecstasy. At last!

The stylist chats as she snips and combs Maisie's hair into shape but Maisie pays little attention, her thoughts focussed on the afternoon's meeting at the farm. Gwen is also to be present in order to "support" Val, but when asked she has no idea what might be on the agenda. 'I'm as clueless as you are,' she had said on the telephone the previous day. 'But it looks like there is progress, so that's got to be a good thing. Our campaign is bearing fruit.'

'Speaking of fruit,' Maisie had said, 'I know you're terribly busy, but if you had an hour or two before Friday, I'd be so glad of a hand in the garden.'

Accordingly, when she returns to *Old Farm Hall* after lunch it is to find Gwen striding up and down the lawn behind the mower, Val and Gloria amongst the broad beans and Minnie on her hands and knees weeding the *parterre*. The house is a-buzz with workmen. The new render is done and the first coat of primer is being put on. Every window in the main house is open, to allow the reek of wood-preservative to escape the rooms; the refurbishment of the panelling is underway. In the extension, the new stairs are being manoeuvred into place.

Another—but less welcome—sight is that of Mr Naidu, the man from the kitchen outlet. He sits on the stone bench clutching his briefcase, his smart suit and highly polished shoes out of place amongst the workwear. Maisie takes a deep breath as she approaches him. The fact is she has no intention of accepting his outrageous quote and although she feels bad about his wasted time and effort, she knows she has to be business-like.

He stands at her approach, a wide, white smile stretching his lips. 'Mrs Wilde,' he says pleasantly. 'How nice to see you.'

She takes his hand but says, 'I know we didn't have an appointment today, Mr Naidu, so I don't need to apologise for being late.'

'No indeed,' he agrees. 'I called by in hope. I haven't heard from you and I wondered if there was anything you wished to discuss. Any point you needed clarification on?'

Maisie runs a freshly manicured hand through her newly-styled hair. 'I am sorry,' she says, 'but your quote was so much more than I had expected. I ought to have let you know, but I won't be proceeding.'

His face falls. 'Oh,' he says. 'That's a disappointment. But our quality, you know … and your kitchen is very large … so many units required.'

She holds up her hand. 'I don't question the quality, or the volume,' she says. 'But the cost is simply beyond my budget.'

'I see,' he says. 'And, may I ask, what is Mr Oliver Harrington's view? Does he share your opinion?'

Maisie bridles at this. 'I haven't discussed it with him,' she says stiffly. 'To be frank, it has nothing whatever to do with him.'

'I see.' Mr Naidu quirks a curious eyebrow. 'That's … not quite what I understood from him. But never mind. Have you already chosen an alternative supplier?'

'I haven't,' she admits. 'And, to be truthful, it breaks my heart because the kitchen you designed for me was everything I wanted. But I have to be practical. My resources are not bottomless. So I've left it to my project manager, Mr Vine. He's making some enquiries amongst the trade suppliers.'

Mr Naidu's face brightens at this news. 'Is he? We do have a trade counter. Maybe I can snatch triumph from the jaws of failure here. Is he inside, this Mr Vine?'

Maisie indicates the house. 'Go ahead,' she says.

While he is gone, Maisie gazes around the garden, at Gwen's bowling-green neatness with the mower, at the industry of the others, even Gloria—though impractically dressed for gardening, in a peasant-style skirt that keeps getting snagged on the plants—has managed to pick quite a quantity of beans in between flirting with the builders. Maisie feels deluged with gratitude. She goes inside to make tea.

They all work until just before four, when Gwen, Val and Maisie make their way up to the farm. Mark Scholey's car is already there. He and the captain are deep in conversation, perched on one of the picnic benches presumably supplied for the proposed café. They both stand as the women approach.

Mark looks apprehensively at Gwen. 'I'm not sure—' he begins.

'I'm here to support Val,' Gwen says. 'I shan't make any contribution to the meeting, unless I feel she is being coerced or brow-beaten in any way, but she feels better if I'm here.'

'I won't allow that either,' says Maisie.

Mark says, 'There is no question of any intimidation. That is certainly not what this meeting is about. On the contrary, it is our desire to find common ground and to move forward in a way that suits everyone. Shall we sit down? Would anyone care for refreshment?'

His offer of bottled water is waved away and everyone takes a seat. Mark takes a sheaf of papers from his briefcase and taps them into order.

'With your permission,' he says, 'I will record this meeting. It will mean I can also chair it. Unless someone wants to take minutes?'

They all shake their heads.

For the benefit of the recording, Mark introduces the attendees, then goes on. 'We are here to discuss the future of the Millport project. As I understand it there are two matters arising. Firstly, the role going forward of Ms Fletcher. Secondly, the balance that can be struck between the twin aims of the generation of funds and animal rescue. There is concern that the achievement of the one might be at the expense of the other. Am I right?'

Maisie says, 'Yes. That's my worry. To be clear, I support the work of the farm. I always have done. But it seems to me the new project will be much more about making money than it is about caring for animals.'

'Noted,' says Mark.

'It might be a better plan,' puts in Gwen, 'to discuss *that* first. I think the way things are going to be run will impact whether Val—Ms Fletcher—decides to stay.'

Val nods. 'Yes,' she says, 'that's right.'

'Very well.' Mark leafs through his documents. 'The charity has had another look at its proposals, in the light of concerns raised by the media and objections lodged with the council.' He glances at Maisie. 'We recognise the perceived imbalance, and propose to scrap the idea of the adventure playground and the café, neither of which directly improves the welfare of the animals. However, we propose to continue with plans for the education centre. This will, albeit indirectly, affect understanding and attitudes going forward, and will provide an income stream.' He looks around the table to see how his statements have been received. Maisie is clearly pleased. Captain Cruikshank looks stoic. Val's expression is unreadable. 'Any comments?' he prompts.

'It sounds much better,' says Maisie. 'It would address my concerns about noise and litter, anyway. But how will this slimmed-down project be able to support two employees?'

Mark refers to his notes again. 'That brings us to the second matter,' he says. 'It is suggested that Captain Cruikshank concern himself primarily with the educational facility. His role will be public relations, promotion, bookings and course delivery. He will also take over the accounts, health and safety, and liaison with head office. That will leave Ms Fletcher with her former role virtually unaltered. She will continue to care for the animals day to day and to interact informally with members of the public who visit. No administration will fall on her shoulders except for occasional holiday cover.' He turns to Val. 'How does that sound?'

Val casts a glance at Gwen, who nods encouragingly. 'Better,' Val concedes. She turns to Captain Cruikshank. 'Do you think we can get along?'

The captain fidgets on his seat for a moment. 'I think so,' he says, 'but I believe my accommodations should be moved. They're indecently close to Ms Fletcher's chalet. There isn't any privacy for either of us.'

'Very well,' says Mark, the hectic flush which has suffused his face since the meeting commenced lightening by a shade or two. 'I think we can agree to that.' He turns to Val once more. 'Do you need to consult your legal team or your ...' he flicks his eyes at Gwen, 'your partner?'

It is Val's turn to blush, but she holds his eye. 'No,' she says. 'I want to look after the animals. I want the animals to come first.'

'So,' Mark labours on, 'I can assume that any suit ... any suggestion that the charity is not inclusive, or has discriminated in any way, and any claim for constructive dismissal ...?'

Val croaks, 'Finished.'

Mark's relief is palpable. 'Excellent,' he says. 'Any other matters? Is everyone happy?'

There is general nodding, and Mark switches off the tape. He stands and reaches out a hand to each of them in turn. 'Thank you,' he says, 'Thank you. Thank you. An excellent outcome.'

'Now we can go away and enjoy ourselves,' cries Gwen, clasping Val momentarily to her bosom. 'A proper holiday, just the two of us.'

'And when you get back,' says the captain, 'my place will be …' he waves to a point far removed from Val's chalet, 'way over there.' He offers his hand to Val, and of course she takes it. Maisie has no clue whether the thing he confessed to her the previous day is generally known, but naturally her lips are sealed. She says, 'Don't be a stranger at *Old Farm Hall*, Captain Cruikshank. You're welcome at any time.'

Mark checks his watch. 'What do you all say to a quick drink at the pub? It's five o'clock so the sun is well over the yardarm.'

'They say it's always five o'clock somewhere,' says Gwen merrily. 'I'm game if you are.'

The captain blanches. 'I don't drink,' he says. 'Ought to make that clear. On the wagon. Nine months sober.'

'That's alright,' says Maisie gently. 'Would you rather we didn't go to the pub? I'm just as happy with tea.'

'Don't mind the pub,' the captain said, 'but just a soft drink for me.'

'And me,' says Mark. 'I've got to drive home.'

They take the green walk down to the Smithy, the two men walking ahead while Val, Gwen and Maisie follow on.

'We had them bang to rights,' says Gwen gleefully. 'Did you see, in his pile of papers, that letter from your solicitor, Val? That will have shocked them, I bet. A claim for tens of thousands in severance pay and holidays owing, not to mention a further … how much was it Val? A hundred grand for mental anguish and loss of domicile! No wonder they've had a rethink!'

'The captain seems a different man,' remarks Maisie. 'Much more approachable.'

'He can't have liked being the butt of all that negative publicity,' says Gwen. 'The gay-rights people gave him a hard time.'

'It wasn't really his fault,' says Maisie. 'Oh! But I'm so happy we can put this whole thing behind us. Now we can look forward to the wedding. You two are all packed? And then you're off on your holiday. And I have my outfit complete!' Maisie sighs happily.

When they arrive at the pub, Minnie and Gloria are already seated at an outside table, enjoying a drink in the sunshine. Maisie introduces Mark and the captain. Predictably, Gloria throws herself into a paroxysm of hair-twirling and eyelash fluttering, patting the seat next to her with what she thinks is sultry allure to encourage the captain to sit next to her.

'I'm Gloria,' she says, oozing charisma. 'A captain? I've always fancied a military man.'

Maisie goes inside to order the drinks.

After the bright sunlight, the interior of the pub seems dark. Maisie blinks to accustom her eyes. There are few customers inside. Oliver leans against the end of the bar scrolling through his mobile phone, but on seeing her he straightens, puts his phone away and comes to greet her.

'Maisie,' he says fondly. 'What a lovely surprise.'

While he gets their order, Maisie fills him in briefly on the meeting at the farm. 'A happy result for all concerned,' she says. 'I'm hugely relieved, I don't mind telling you.'

'So am I then, on your behalf,' says Oliver.

'Mr Naidu called today,' she risks telling him. 'I had to inform him I wouldn't be accepting his quote.'

Oliver pauses, a bottle of wine hovering over a glass. 'You won't …?'

'No.' She fixes him with a determined eye. 'Much too pricey, although of course I loved the design. Trevor is going to see if he can get something similar through the trade, at a more reasonable price.'

'I see.' Oliver finishes pouring the wine. 'Well, I won't pretend that isn't a disappointment.'

'Why?'

Oliver shrugs. 'I expected that my recommendation would be sufficient inducement to you. You've allowed me to guide you on other issues. But of course, you must do what you want. Now. Is that everything? No, don't you carry the tray Maisie, I'll do it.'

Outside there is a pleasant hum of conversation from drinkers at nearby tables. The stream tinkles merrily through the undergrowth along the periphery of the pub's gardens and birds clamour in the shrubbery. Oliver distributes the drinks amongst Maisie's friends, pausing to shake hands with the captain and Mark Scholey, saying, 'Any friend of Maisie's …'

When he is gone, Gloria leans over to Maisie to say, 'You'd be mad to let that one go, Maisie. You do know he's crazy about you?'

'Oh,' says Maisie, waving a dismissive hand, 'I'm too focussed on the wedding at the moment. I can't think about romance.'

'You're kidding,' says Gloria, giving a little shimmy. 'Weddings are all about romance.' Seamlessly, she turns to Captain Cruikshank. 'So, Captain,' she says through pouted lips, 'are you married?'

Soon Mark finishes his drink and bids them goodbye, promising a letter in the post or an email to confirm the points agreed on at the meeting. To Gloria's disappointment, the captain walks back to the farm, where there are animals to be fed, but Val remains at the table, and in fact she and Gwen agree to a bite of supper while they are there.

Oliver brings menus, and stoops down to say in Maisie's ear, 'I wanted to have a word about our travel plans, for Oxford.'

'Oh yes,' says Maisie. 'I'm to go with James and Michael.'

'No. That's been changed. Michael has a meeting last thing on Friday he can't get out of, so they won't be setting off until after five. You can imagine the traffic at that time. So if you go with them you won't get to our accommodation until …' he sucks his teeth, 'eight, at the earliest. Didn't I understand you're to meet Maxim's people on Friday evening?'

'Yes,' says Maisie. 'We're to have dinner somewhere.'

Oliver nods. 'Various alternatives have been considered,' he says.

Have they? By whom? When?

'There won't be room in your car because of the *couture,* and Gwen's is fully occupied, so that leaves mine.' His eyes sparkle with mischief. Maisie's heart drops. She knows what's coming.

'I'll happily take you, but it will have to be tomorrow.'

'Tomorrow?' Maisie is aghast.

Oliver nods sagely. 'Yep. I took the place from Thursday so I could go down ahead of the rest of you and get things organised. We're self-catering, so there are provisions to be sourced … and a few other things I wanted to put in place.' He looks shifty for a moment. 'Oh! But I mustn't spoil the surprise.'

'I see.' Maisie's mind is racing. A four-hour drive with Oliver is one thing, but a night alone with him in … whatever the place is he has booked. But to miss the meal with Maxim's parents! That's unthinkable. She chews her lips while Oliver regards her.

'Speak to me,' he says. 'Tell me what's on your mind.'

She looks at him, his anxious, eager expression, the deferential way he squats by her side, and thinks about all he has done for her in the last few weeks. Yes, he has advised her about the house and helped her to come to decisions on a hundred things. And it looks as though he has gone to so much trouble over this accommodation. But the memory of his face that afternoon— suffused, almost violent—the roughness of his embrace. She doubts.

Then, a solution comes to her and she clutches it to her as she had earlier clasped her new bag. 'Of course, that will be fine,' she says. 'Thank you Oliver. I'll tell Frances to meet us there. She'll be glad of it, I'm sure.

Maxim's parents' house is full to busting with all his relatives. Oh! She'll be delighted. I can't wait to tell her.'

A shadow crosses Oliver's face, but is immediately gone. 'Splendid,' he says, standing up. 'I'll pick you up straight after lunch.'

Chapter Thirteen – Viola

Viola had little recollection of Martin's funeral. She had lain in bed for a fortnight after his death, refusing food and drink, visitors and comfort, other than the out-of-body stupor afforded by the diazepam prescribed by her GP.

She had a hazy memory of being washed and dressed by Gwen, and driven to the crematorium, of walking woodenly between ranks of faceless mourners, of a man intoning meaningless platitudes, of a weak and wavering rendition of *Abide with Me*. But she did not think of it, preferring the oblivion of the tablets and, when these were withdrawn, alcohol.

When she emerged from the void she found herself in the spare room of Gwen's shabby little semi-detached house in Millport. There was a note on her pillow—she got the impression it had been placed there on many mornings—telling her to get up and shower, dress, eat and sit in the garden, and call Gwen to let her know that she was alive.

'I'm not alive,' Viola groused, but for some reason she could not fathom— perhaps the drone of a builder's drill in the neighbouring house, perhaps the chatter of a blackbird in the garden, perhaps a realisation that the sheets of the bed were stiff and rank—on this morning she found the courage to follow Gwen's directions.

Gwen's garden was a poor and neglected patch of grass that had been ruined by a succession of rescue dogs and, when untenanted by dogs, was used as the communal toilet for the neighbourhood's many cats. Viola sat on a wonky wooden garden chair with her coffee. She surveyed the ravages of a border riddled with couch grass and the woeful state of a ragged, untrimmed hedge. Her eyes hurt in the unaccustomed brightness. When she ran her hand over her face the skin felt rough and crusty. Her hair was thin and lifeless. She pulled at a hank of it and it came away in her hand. She opened her fist and let it blow away. Looking down at herself she saw skin and bone. She wished even that poor remnant of herself would disintegrate and drift away on the little breeze.

The calendar in Gwen's kitchen told her it was August. Where had the weeks gone? And why had more of them not passed? She wished that months, years, decades, eons could have gone by, and that she could be in the ground with Martin, an insentient life-force feeding plants and flowers in the far future. But—with a sigh—that time had not passed, and she was still breathing, and must, she supposed, go forward.

She could not again entomb her heart. It was a poor, amorphous and weakly thing, too viscous to be scooped up and locked away. And look, she thought bitterly, how easily it had escaped its imprisonment before! Instead, she set about forming a bodily armour, walling up her whole self within an encompassing shield. She had her hair cut punitively short and dyed jet black. She bought clothes that were tight and stark, uncomfortable, a penance to wear, in black also. She adopted a gothic style of makeup: black kohl and eyeliner and mascara that made her lashes as stiff as bristles; a mask she hoped would intimidate others and disguise the vulnerable woman it belied. She ate little, retaining the skeletal state her mourning weeks had wrought. She denied herself pleasure because to enjoy anything, even for a moment, was to betray Martin.

She bought a penthouse on Millport Quays—the top-most, sea-facing apartment that caught the brunt of the relentless wind and looked out across a vast expanse of turbulent brown ocean. It was never silent; the wind howled as it tore like harridans around the block; the sea below ceaselessly surged and moaned; seabirds emitted a cacophony of plangent lament as they were hurled across the sky. At night, any respite was split asunder as emergency vehicles sped to the aid of drunken revellers, antisocial hoodlums, fires and accidents. The sounds of unhappiness, of crisis and pain rose up to Viola in her eyrie and melded with the pall of her misery that hung like a cloud on every horizon.

The flat had no garden. No plant, however hardy, could tolerate its narrow, glass-encased veranda and she would not permit herself the indulgence of even a houseplant. She furnished the flat starkly in black and white, with tortured stick sculptures and moody black-and-white abstract art. Her kitchen units—white—were clinical and cold. Her sofa likewise. She brought nothing—nothing at all—from the flat in Southquay; she would not be enfeebled by the indulgence of remembrance.

Under sufferance, she permitted herself to be introduced to a small circle of Gwen's acquaintance. One of them, Amy Snow, brought Viola's former life in Southquay—especially Vanessa—so powerfully to mind that Viola doubted she could endure it. Thankfully, Amy understood the soreness of the connection and made no reference to their prior days at the Southquay bridge club. There was a woman called Gloria, also a widow, but a relatively cheerful one already keenly seeking her late husband's replacement. She was the yin to Viola's yang; buxom and epicurean where Viola was bony and ascetic, giggly where Viola was grim, sociable where Viola was sullen. Gloria wore vibrant colours—often clashing—and blonded, elaborately-styled hair. She was tactless and childish and would have been everything Viola despised if it had not been for Minnie Price, another—much more recent—widow, who became the target of Viola's most vitriolic scorn. Minnie was a dithering, ineffectual woman, mean with money in spite of every appearance of wealth. Her vacillating over the spending of every penny drove Viola to distraction, but what really enraged Viola was Minnie's shameless vulnerability—she was helpless, hopeless, incapacitated by widowhood. Really, she was just like Viola herself; the messed-up Viola that quivered inside the stiff, penal carapace of disparagement she had constructed.

For a few months the peculiar and mis-matched coterie met up for lunch and trips to shopping outlets. They met in one another's homes for whist and twee little suppers that would have been stifling and insufferable to Viola had she not lubricated them with plentiful wine. Then, in the spring, Gwen gathered yet another new widow into the shelter of her ample wing. Viola might have felt supplanted; this new woman, Maisie Wilde, was now the focus of the group's pastoral concern. But somehow Viola could not generate sufficient spleen against the newcomer. She liked Maisie although it distressed and intimidated her to admit it. There was nothing to *dis*like about her, anyway.

Amy had abandoned the Southquay bridge club in favour of one in Millport, and eventually Viola was persuaded to go along. She played the game with scowling concentration and was viciously competitive. If not for Amy, it was doubtful she could have found a partner.

The vat of grief perpetually a-brim within her fermented itself into a brew that was sour and unpleasant. She knew she was cruel and caustic, prickly—making snide remarks and unkind jibes, curdling the atmosphere between the women friends. She just could not stop; her venom rose up like vomit and forced itself into her mouth. It gave her grim pleasure, aiding her in the construction of her defences. Any day she expected the women to exclude her. She was astonished when, in March, she was invited to join them on a trip to the Lakes. She was lured by promises of stately homes' gardens—something that, in this new and crusty manifestation of herself, would normally have been out of bounds. Against her better judgement she had accepted the invitation, but the trip was a disaster in every way.

Throughout her mourning—before the trip to the Lakes, during it and afterwards, alone and in company, Viola drank. In the beginning, drinking was an attempt to recapture the analgesic haze of her days in the hospital and the opioid stupor of the diazepam. Alcohol dulled the sharp agony of her grief by locking it in a far room to which she had lost the key. She drank excessively, stupidly, finding herself in the early hours on the cold tile floor of her flat, her face in a pool of sick. Her dreadful hangovers—sometimes lasting days—were a distraction from the maw of her grief. She resorted to Vodka as a kind of anaesthetic, a pre-med that could help her face the ordeal of being alive; she invariably had two or three stiff measures before she went out anywhere. It was like surgical spirit, numbing, hardening and tightening the skin of her sensibilities. Chardonnay made her nasty, aiding the production of her careless poison and dulling the little kernel of guilt that sometimes came when she saw her arrows had hit the mark. She took a bottle to the women's little soirées and usually drank the whole thing herself. She didn't even like the taste of it much. Its oaky flavour was like tree sap; it was like swallowing down nasty medicine, a punishment that was part and parcel of her cold, comfortless flat—a place it was a penance to be—and the new smoking habit she had imposed upon herself, which required her to stand outside in all weathers. They were different elements of her self-castigation. She did not dislike the taste of Whisky but it made her dangerous, scouring off her abrasive corners and really allowing her demons out. She might turn violent, especially towards herself, recalling Martin's methods of exorcising Susanne's ire. She found out-of-the-way little clubs in Millport's back streets where hardened drinkers gathered: disillusioned businessmen, gamblers, bankrupts and degenerates. They drank steadily at their separate tables in an atmosphere heavy with despair, staring morosely at nothing until some imagined slight, some slurred remark would have them all on their feet and at one another's throats. Viola relished the physical manifestation of her misery and anger: the hair-pulling, the broken teeth. It was a death-wish she embraced whole-heartedly, but often, even in their inebriated state, she—a woman—was spared the worst of the assault.

April came, offering an antidote to the dreadful March that had preceded it. Bright warm days brought forth maliciously rampant verdure. Viola observed the nodding daffodils and trumpet-like tulips with both a resentful and an appreciative eye. Bluebells bloomed in woodland, replacing the white umbels of wild garlic. How could nature be so cruel, so quick to forget? Before long it would be June, and the anniversary of her marriage to Martin. She could not believe twelve whole months had almost passed, and that she had survived it, albeit in bile and bitterness. Then again she could not comprehend how little the time was, and would she—could she—really endure more? Year after interminable year of that empty and pointless existence?

It was amid this ruthless perplexity that Maisie came to Viola with a request she would help out from time to time in the garden. What had prompted this request, Viola did not know. It was easy to suspect some interference from Gwen, a sly prompting that *this* would help poor Viola emerge from her bereavement. It seemed unlikely to Viola that Maisie really *wanted* her company. Who would? She was such a cow. But Maisie's garden called to Viola, a siren cry she could not ignore. She found herself there almost against her will, hefting the wooden handles of Maisie's second- and third-hand tools, plunging her hands into the well-dug soil but then upbraiding herself for her weakness, for allowing herself such indulgence. When the day was done she would produce a bottle of wine from a cooler, and pour them both a glass. It was a way of gathering back to herself the armour she might have shed amongst the raised beds or in the balmy air of the greenhouse. She needed to re-infuse herself with the wine's treacly protection, to remind herself that *this*—this spiteful and imperviously-skinned woman—was the real Viola. But sometimes, between the naked soberness of the garden and the full metal jacket of inebriation there was a tranquil place of friendship with Maisie she was loath to relinquish. Could it be—before the hot pincers of spite got their grip on her again—that she could allow the garden to reclaim her? That Maisie, and Maisie's garden, might save her yet? The very question appalled her. How could she even contemplate it? And yet, at night, on her hard mattress, she pictured it through mazed, drink-dulled eyes. A garden, and her in it. She prised open the narrow aperture just a little, gasping at her own audacity, quailing at the risk, but daring anyway to see the bright vision projected on the ceiling of her imagination.

Then, one evening at *Old Farm Hall*, Maisie said, 'You're all invited to my daughter's wedding. It's in Oxford, in June. The twenty-first. Longest day,' and the little thread of hope that Viola had been clutching was snatched from her hand.

She snuck away from the group as they toured the empty rooms of Maisie's house, trying to see her vision for the place as she projected it for them onto its damp plaster. What did Viola care for renovated ceiling roses or refitted kitchens? What was the point of any of it while the mine of her grief was so deep and cruel, and her wedding anniversary—June twenty-first—was a few short weeks away, a clamouring reminder of all the happiness she had lost?

At the top of the lane she flagged down a taxi. 'Take me to town.'

It was almost three in the morning when Viola stumbled out of the lift on the top floor of the building where her penthouse apartment was located. Her eyes—dark hollows of smudged kohl and mascara—were swollen with weeping and bleary with alcohol. Her tight designer jeans were filthy. One shoe was absent. She leant against the wall and peered into the corridor where she thought—but could not be certain—a figure was lurking near the door to her flat. Eventually she shook her woozy head. It must have been a trick of the light, or of the booze which, that night, had failed her. No amount of it had succeeded in dulling her pain.

She groped in her pocket for her door key, failed to find it, tried the other pocket with the same result, and then the first pocket again, in a routine that would have been comic were it not so utterly pathetic.

'Shit,' she mumbled through numb, dry lips.

Her body began to slide down the wall. Soon she would be sitting on the floor, could easily sleep there, she thought, until … well, until *something* … As she resigned herself to spending what little remained of the night on the cold tiles, the hazy figure at the end of the corridor gathered itself and began to come into focus. Gwen finally materialised from the skewed and unreliable field of Viola's vision and gripped her in a firm embrace.

'There you are at last,' said Gwen. 'I've been looking everywhere for you. Where have you been?'

'A club,' Viola got out. She showed no surprise at Gwen's appearance. 'I've lost my key.'

'I know,' said Gwen. 'Luckily, I have the one you gave me. Come on, let's get you inside.'

Gwen half-carried Viola along the corridor and opened the door of her apartment. They moved through to the bedroom and Viola collapsed on the bed.

'You must drink some water,' said Gwen. 'Do you think you might be sick?'

'Been sick,' Viola muttered into the pillow.

'Is that what's on your jeans? Let's try and get them off.'

Removing the one remaining shoe, Gwen peeled the jeans from Viola's unresisting body.

'Oh, Gwen,' Viola moaned. She rolled onto her side and began to cry; great, heaving sobs. Presently she said, 'Why did it have to be …? Why did it …?'

'I know, I know. It's a cruel coincidence. A year to the day. Maisie didn't know.'

Viola cried some more, tears and mucus smeared over her face, her body thrashing as though in agony. Her sharp nails scrabbled her chest above the V-shaped neckline of her top as though to tear out her heart, leaving livid wheals. 'It hurts too much,' she cried. 'I can't bear it! It hurts too much!' At last she said, 'Gwen! Oh Gwen I tried … I went to the … and I tried—'

Gwen sat on the bed next to Viola and took her hand. 'What did you try, dear?'

The alcohol, the overwhelming deluge of her misery and her emotional exhaustion formed a thick layer through which Gwen's question could hardly penetrate. A few moments ticked by and Gwen thought Viola had passed out, but then she murmured, 'Went to the railway station. But,' with a hard, dark, bitter shout of laughter, 'no bloody trains came.'

'I see.' Gwen patted Viola's hand.

'I can't … I *can't* …' Viola gasped out. 'I can't go on.' She fixed Gwen with a look that was a mixture of agony, apology and shame. 'I *can't.*'

'Not like this,' said Gwen. 'You need help, Viola. If I organise it for you, will you go somewhere they can help you?'

Viola looked doubtful. 'There *is* no help,' she moaned out.

Gwen said, 'There *is*, dear.'

Chapter Fourteen – Maisie

The weather forecast for the weekend of Frances and Maxim's wedding is splendid: warm sunshine and cloudless skies. But as Maisie watches Oliver stow her suitcase and dress carrier into the space behind the seats of his sporty little car, her mood is overcast, heavy with things unspoken. Her mind crackles with thunderous static.

Oliver is his usual suave and affable self, and if Maisie's initial sulkiness bothers him, he gives no sign.

'You've eaten lunch?' he asks as they wait for a gap in the traffic. 'I'm happy to stop, if not.'

'I had a late breakfast,' says Maisie, 'thank you.'

Oliver drives with the top of the car down. The wind plays havoc with Maisie's hair while Oliver's is protected by a driving cap. Its peak, and his impenetrable sunglasses, make it impossible for her to read his eyes, but the rest of his face is utterly benign; there is no hint of self-congratulation at a scheme that has come to fruition. Maisie feels manipulated but he shows no indication of having consciously manipulated her. He is the epitome of a man facing, with pleasure, the prospect of a long weekend away with friends. After a while Maisie pushes away the wild and probably unreasonable phantoms that have haunted her all night.

A quick call to James had confirmed Oliver's assertion that if she travelled with them she could not hope to be in Oxford until eight o'clock on Friday night.

'I shall be sorry to lose your company on the drive,' he had said, 'but if you want to meet Maxim's people on Friday evening you had much better go with Oliver.'

Frances had responded positively to Maisie's suggestion that she come to their accommodation on Thursday instead of Friday. In fact, she had sounded uncharacteristically carefree. 'Oh yes, if you like,' she had said.

'Frank's brother and his wife arrived today and Margot's sisters are coming tomorrow; they're flying in from Florida. Why they couldn't all book into a hotel I just don't know. Margot is making up sofa beds in every room. She expects Maxim to sleep on the floor the night before his wedding, if you can believe it. The room we're using is to be given over to some aged aunt. Maxim says he won't stand for it and will probably decamp. The best man might put him up.'

'The only thing is,' Maisie had concluded, 'I haven't a clue where we're staying, so I can't give you an address or anything.'

'That's alright. Oliver set up a group WhatsApp. I can find out from there.'

'There's a group WhatsApp? How come I don't know about it?'

She could hear Frances's eyeballs rolling. 'Because apparently this whole weekend is a super-duper surprise for *you*, Mother. My wedding is simply a sideshow.'

'But *why?*'

'Don't ask me. I have to go. Bye!'

Maisie had mulled this development over while she packed her case. No wonder Frances is aggrieved, if Oliver's been making this whole weekend about *me*. What can he have planned that requires such subterfuge? She collected her toiletries and tucked them into a space between her nightdress and a light dressing gown. I really will have to head him off at the pass before Frances arrives later. We *must* talk. I can't stand the mystery of it.

Now, as the motorway slides effortlessly beneath the wheels of Oliver's car, Maisie attempts to grasp the nettle. She turns to Oliver and, speaking above the roar of the car's engine and the growl of other traffic, says, 'So Oliver, now we're actually on our way, surely you can tell me something about where we're going? If I'm honest, it's really unsettled me. You've been so mysterious about it.'

Immediately his face lights up, the cautionary note she has tried to sound quashed by his eagerness. 'I think you're going to like it. I hope so, anyway. I pulled in a favour from a friend. The place we're going to has spent the last eighteen months undergoing wholesale renovations, so I thought that would interest you, to see how a house can be transformed, as yours is going to be. They hoped to have it ready for lettings this summer but there were weeks of delay after the discovery of bat droppings in the attics. It seems there are all kinds of protection orders in place for bats. Anyway, the schedule slipped and so it's only just finished. We will be the first guests. How will you like that?'

'I'm sure it will be marvellous,' she says, envisaging still-wet paint and untested plumbing. 'So long as everything works,'

'Of course it will work,' Oliver says sharply, adding in a more conciliatory tone, 'it's all been thoroughly tested. Last week my friend said the builder's still-to-do list ran to four pages, but now he assures me that everything's perfect. We can have confidence in a fully-functioning house.'

'Perfect.' Maisie hopes he does not discern the falseness in her voice. 'And, you say we'll be the first ones to use it?'

'That's right. It's listed now, and apparently the bookings are flooding in, but we'll be the first. That's what I wanted, for us. For you.'

'That's kind, but quite unnecessary,' says Maisie. 'I'm a second-hand rose, you know.'

'Not to me, Maisie.'

Their route takes them off the motorway much sooner than Maisie expects and for a few miles, as they pass road signs with every place name but Oxford on them, Maisie briefly entertains the possibility that she is being abducted, that their destination is not Oxford at all, but some remote and unfindable farmhouse where she is to be held for ransom. She eyes Oliver obliquely. She has known him only a few months, and what a conundrum he is. Sometimes she senses an ego that is much more fragile than his arrogance would imply. It is ridiculous to harbour any suspicion of him and yet … that one time, when he had just briefly abandoned himself to his passion, it had added a bitter flavour to an otherwise highly palatable repast.

She decides to tackle the issue. 'Oliver,' she says, swivelling in her seat so she can look at him properly. 'Where are we going, here, you and I?'

He glances at her quizzically. 'Oxford,' he says. 'Of course. Where else?'

There is a beat. Well, if *that's* the way he wants to play it. 'I don't recognise any of these place-names,' she says, 'and this road, I'm sure it isn't the one I've used before.'

'We've a way to go yet,' he says. 'This is a longer route, but more scenic. It takes us into the Cotswolds. I thought you'd like that. There's a little tea shop I'm hoping we can get to and still be at our destination by five-thirty. I have a supermarket delivery booked—Waitrose. Only the best for you.'

'My goodness.' Maisie is impressed in spite of herself. 'You really have put a lot of thought into this, haven't you?'

Oliver's hand leaves the steering wheel and he places it momentarily on her knee. 'Of course I have,' he says warmly. 'It's all I've thought about for weeks. I want everything to be perfect for you.'

A swift jolt of electricity—pleasure? foreboding?—presses Maisie into the back of her seat. 'Watch the road, Oliver,' she cries.

He chuckles. 'Don't worry,' he says, 'I've got it all under control.'

They pass villages with honey stone cottages, thatched roofs, greens dimpled by duck ponds. In the distance some soft, green-gold hills rise up to a perfect blue sky. Birds—kites, Maisie identifies—wheel in lazy circles. They are awe-inspiringly elegant, consummate navigators of the air, yet ultimately, they are predators, searching for things to eat. The analogy is not lost on Maisie and brings home to her with a drench of cold dread the ambiguity of her situation.

Her uncertainty wells up again until it is intolerable. She can't continue without knowing, without understanding exactly where Oliver is coming from. Clearly, it won't do to beat around the bush.

She turns to him again. 'Oliver,' she says, her voice firmly tremulous. 'We never had that little chat we promised ourselves, did we?'

'Little chat?' His eyes remain fixed on the road.

'Don't you remember, after my appointment with Mr Naidu …?'

His face betrays no recollection of the incident.

She labours on, squirming in her seat. 'Yes, we had a … well, you kissed me and afterwards we agreed we needed to *talk*.'

'Talk?' He almost shouts.

'Yes. So we can properly understand each other.'

He turns to face her but, maddeningly, she can't read his eyes. 'I think,' he says slowly, 'that we're way past *talking* Maisie, aren't we?'

She frowns, one eye narrowed. What does he mean? 'No,' she stammers out, her face still furrowed with incomprehension. '*I'm* not, anyway. I need us to talk to each other because I don't know … I don't understand,' she concludes miserably.

Oliver smiles, and she can't tell if it is a kindly, sympathetic smile or a cynical, patronising one. 'What you need, Maisie,' he says, 'is tea.' His hand flicks the indicator and she looks up to see they are pulling into the carpark of a pretty, bay-fronted tea shop.

Oliver parks, and is out of his door and round to her side of the car before she can unfasten her seatbelt. He assists her out of the car and offers his arm. 'Perfect timing,' he says. 'I wanted to be here by three-thirty, and here we are. Afternoon tea awaits.'

They go into the tea shop, which is impossibly twee, with a proliferation of gingham, lace doilies, horse brasses and rag rugs, and a solitary, lonely-looking budgerigar in an ornate Victorian cage. Oliver ushers them straight to the table in the window. It bears a card with his name inscribed upon it in calligraphed handwriting. A waitress in a white apron busies herself immediately with the makings of tea, fetching neatly-cut sandwiches on a bone china plate, scones, jam and cream.

'I wanted us to have something pretty substantial now, so we can be at leisure later,' says Oliver. 'I shall be cooking, but something light. A soufflé omelette, I thought. How does that sound?'

'Frances doesn't eat eggs,' says Maisie. But Oliver is busy arranging the tea things and doesn't acknowledge her remark.

They reach their destination just before five. From what Maisie can tell it is not close to Oxford city centre at all. The surrounding area is all leafy hamlets, affluent commuter belt communities and farmland. She imagines travel into Oxford for the wedding has been organised by taxi or minibus, and gives a passing thought to Amy, whose wheelchair will have to be accommodated somehow. But Oliver has obviously put so much thought and planning into the whole occasion, thrown so much money at it, and is clearly so pleased with himself about it, that she hesitates to question him on any detail. Her role, it appears, is to be passive and delighted. It riles her, to tell the truth, that the wedding of her own daughter has been so thoroughly usurped, but she is powerless to do anything about it now.

The house is approached through stately gates and along an extensive, deeply-gravelled drive. It curls around a thick plantation of laurels and rhododendrons and an area of neatly mown lawn before allowing the house to come into view. The house itself is beautiful, and Maisie cannot help but gasp at the sight of it. It is Georgian, she thinks, with twin, rounded wings at either end. It is three-storeyed, partly built of the warm, golden stone she sees is indigenous to the area and partly rendered. Ivy smothers a good portion of the house, so although the windows and paintwork are patently new, the place retains an old-world charm.

Oliver brings the car to a halt in front of the door. The silence, after the buffeting wind and the engine's high-pitched squeal, is delightful, but soon filled with birdsong and the distant sound of lowing cattle. Maisie allows her eyes to travel over the house's impressive frontage to the gardens: formal, with clipped yew, old stone urns and topiary. There are a number of classical statues: ladies in various stages of undress. Part of Maisie longs to wander in it, to stretch her legs and to take in the grandeur of the place, to draw out the mounting anticipation because, if it is this wonderful outside, what beauties must it hold within? At the same time she is uneasy, powerfully desirous of putting off what is increasingly feeling like an inevitable culmination. But what?

Oliver has removed his hat and sunglasses. He watches her, his face a picture of gleeful expectation. 'Well?' he says at last. 'What do you think?'

'Oh, Oliver,' she breathes. 'It's … well it's splendid. I can't imagine what it's costing.'

His face darkens at this, and she realises she has hit a wrong note. 'Such generosity,' she amends. 'I'm humbled. And you? You're pleased?'

'Oh, I've been here before,' he says. 'I bobbed in on my way home from that sommelier course I did. There was still a skip outside then and, at the back, the walled garden … but I mustn't spoil the surprise. Suffice it to say I was assured that for today, for *you,* it would be ready. And it looks like it is. Shall we go in?'

The house is simply superb, room after room of opulent good taste, beautifully furnished and appointed. There are two sitting rooms, a library, an enormous breakfast room with a vaulted ceiling and French doors opening onto a terrace. The kitchen, Maisie notes with joy, is a similar style to the one she wants: painted, shaker-style units and exactly the configuration of Aga and companion that she hopes to have. There are plentiful bedrooms on both upper floors and one on the ground floor, perfect for Amy. Maisie tries to apportion the rooms as they peek into each one, murmuring, 'I suppose Gwen and Val will share, but this room has a double and single, so, if they aren't sleeping together … Viola likes a room on her own. This one will suit her, I think. She'll enjoy the view of the garden … Minnie will love this … she likes a deep bath … I wonder if James and Michael will object to sharing a bathroom. What do you think, Oliver? And what about *you?* Which room will you choose?'

He has gone in front of her, throwing open door after door to reveal virgin carpets, beds draped in luxurious linens, and ornately curtained windows framing views of bucolic farmland. Every bathroom is a dazzle of fresh tile and glinting chrome, with pristine white sanitaryware, fluffy towels and thick, enveloping dressing gowns.

At her question he turns to face her. 'Never mind about me,' he says. 'I think you're forgetting the most important person. Where will *she* sleep?'

Maisie gasps. 'Frances! Oh yes, of course. Now, let me see—' Her mind retraces its steps along the thickly-carpeted landings, revisiting the blue room with the brocade bed hangings, the yellow room with its impressive shower, but Oliver says, 'No Maisie, not Frances. You! Which room do *you* like?'

'Oh! *I* don't matter. They're all so lovely,' Maisie demurs. I wish Oliver wouldn't constantly put me front and centre. I'm not used to it. I don't want it. 'Anywhere is good enough for me,' she concludes.

He frowns again; a dark cloud blotting out his good humour as effectively as an eclipse blots out the sun. The sudden chill in the room makes Maisie shiver.

He steps towards her, blocking the sun that streams in through the mullioned window, casting her in his long shadow. He leans over her, towering above her. 'You *do* matter,' he says emphatically. 'All this is for you, and I want you to choose. Before the others come, before your kindness allows everyone else the best of everything. That's why I brought you here today, to give you that chance.'

She looks up into his face. His expression is penetrating; his eyes burn into hers. She can see his eagerness to please her but she still cannot read what is behind it. And they still have not had their 'little chat.'

He moves an iota nearer, and she does not know whether to hug him for his single-minded kindness or to shrink from his intensity.

Then a horn blares outside on the drive.

'That'll be the Waitrose delivery van,' he says.

Maisie fetches her luggage while Oliver supervises the unloading of the grocery order. She notes cases of Prosecco and wine, baguettes, jars of olives, breakfast goods. When she offers to help put things away in the cavernous fridge he waves her away.

'Go and choose,' he says.

She mounts the stairs again and looks into the rooms. She will not take the best one, she decides. It would be too awful to be thought selfish or proud. But she dares not take anything too modest for fear of incurring Oliver's wrath, although 'modest' here, is relative. At last she finds—up a half-stair and along a galleried landing that looks down on the breakfast room—a room that is smaller than some of the others but boasts a full bathroom with a claw footed bath. It has a dressing room annex, with a single bed in it.

I can sleep there tonight and tomorrow. Frances can have the double.

She unpacks her case, hanging her wedding outfit in the wardrobe with her shoes and bag, putting her other things in a small chest of drawers under the window. She puts her toiletries in the bathroom, glad that she stocked up on the expensive brand she uses nowadays. Vaguely, she hears the delivery van drive off. It is almost six. When will Frances arrive? Her phone shows no messages but, when she looks closely, it has no signal either. What if Frances gets lost? How will she get in touch?

When she gets back downstairs there is no sign of Oliver. She assumes he is unpacking in whichever room he has chosen for himself.

Maisie wanders through the rooms again, taking in smaller details this time: the canvasses on the walls, the personal mementoes that make the house feel more like a home than a holiday let. The library is full of interesting-looking books and there is a leather wing-back chair by the fire. She makes a mental note to provide books in an alcove of her drawing room back home, but she decides she will have two chairs, to provide a place for confidential chat.

The French doors in the breakfast room have been thrown open and she steps onto the broad expanse of terrace. It is bathed in late afternoon sunshine—something her terrace will never manage—and even through her thin-soled shoes she can feel the warmth of the flagstones. A number of garden chairs and some loungers invite her to sit, but she has been sitting for most of the day so, instead, she walks down the three or four shallow steps onto the lawn.

There is no sign that the house was recently a building site, or, indeed, that there has been a drought. The grass is lush and green, unmarked, and she wishes now she had made more of an effort to protect hers from the constant tramp of the builders, from pallets of cement blocks and bags of sand. A long herbaceous border lies down one side of the garden, with a tall stone wall behind it providing protection for the blousy hollyhocks, delphinium, coreopsis and lobelia, and support for the rambling roses that fill the air with perfume.

She has just reached the end of the flowerbed when a door in the wall opens and Oliver steps through. Somehow, he has had time to shower and change.

His chinos and shirt have been replaced by shorts and a tee shirt. His dark hair glistens with moisture.

'Ah, there you are,' he says, holding out his hand. 'Perfect timing. Come and see the surprise.'

Unthinking, she takes his hand and follows him through the door into what must at one time have been a walled vegetable garden but which now contains a swimming pool, hot tub and ornate summerhouse. Outside the summerhouse, on a wrought iron table, sits an ice bucket containing a bottle of champagne, and two glasses. There is a double swing seat with towels laid over the back.

'Surprise!' cries Oliver, as delighted as a child at Christmas. He scans her face. 'You weren't expecting *this* were you?'

'I certainly wasn't! My goodness! Is there no end to this place's delights?' She walks across the smooth square paving slabs to the edge of the pool, bends and dips her hand into the water. It is cool, but not cold, very enticing in fact, after the day spent in the cramped car and the fumes of the road. 'What a pity I didn't bring swimwear,' she says, turning to look back at where Oliver still stands by the door. 'But we must message the others and let them know.'

Oliver puts his head on one side and quirks an eyebrow.

'But of course,' she realises, 'they *do* already know.'

'Indeed they do.'

Oliver crosses the terrace and heads for the champagne, which he opens with a flourish and a carefully suppressed 'pssst', allowing the golden wine to froth into their glasses. He brings her one and then produces a gift bag from behind his back, his eyes sparkling.

Maisie looks at the bag, aghast. Her understanding has made a sudden leap and the idea that lights up her jumbled mind is so shocking that she fears to reach out and take the bag from him. Is he … does he … could it be that all *this*—the manoeuvring to get her alone, the splendid house in all its virgin bloom, the champagne—is all leading to a marriage proposal? She stares at him, her mouth agape, as all his oddly proactive interest in the house's renovation, his attempt to impose his suggestions concerning kitchen design, even his offer to represent her at the impromptu press conference all begin to look like a scheme calculated to inveigle himself into her life. It explains everything! He thinks … he imagines …

While her brain clicks and whirs itself through this astonishing idea, Oliver continues to hold out the bag, his delighted expression not diminishing in spite of the pause in her reaching out and taking hold. 'Well,' he says at last, shaking the bag. 'Aren't you going to look?'

In trepidation she takes the bag and peeps into it. Then, she almost shouts in relief. No ring box. She pulls out a two-piece swimming costume in emerald-green, just the right size. She recognises it. 'Didn't I look at something similar that day we went to the outlet village?'

He nods. 'You did. I went all the way back to get it.'

Maisie's relief is so overwhelming she feels like weeping. She feels badly now for attributing Oliver with such connivance, until it occurs to her that just because *this* is not the moment, does not mean that it is not coming. She gets out, 'Thank you, Oliver. Thank you *so* much.'

He lunges at her, and she braces herself for his kiss, but he grasps her shoulders and swivels her in the direction of the summerhouse, sending her in that direction with a little pat on her bottom.

'Go and get changed,' he says. 'You can do it in there. There's a shower, if you want to use it. I'll test the water, shall I?'

He strips off his tee shirt, kicks off his Birkenstocks and dives smoothly into the pool.

When Maisie emerges he is swimming vigorous lengths up and down the pool, his stroke practised and effortless as she somehow knew it would be. The desire to introduce other people to this awkward tête-à-tête is imperative. *When* will Frances arrive? Could Gareth be brought to Oxford a day early? She gives a brief thought to Dominic and Pamela. Surely it would be possible to fit them in somewhere. The children will *love* the pool. Later,

I'll tour the house properly—there were some rooms on the top floor I barely glanced into—and do an assessment of the accommodation to see if they can be fitted in without giving trouble to anyone else. I'll have to suggest it cautiously. Oliver won't like to have his plans trespassed upon. It might be better coming from Frances. When she comes, I'll mention it.

Maisie eases herself into the pool, using the steps. She isn't a strong swimmer and so stays in the shallow end, idly sculling and looking at the plants that have been trained up the walls. Oliver swims doggedly and there isn't the opportunity to speak to him for quite a while. When he eventually emerges from beneath the surface and hauls himself on to the side, he is breathing heavily.

'A good workout,' he says, checking his fitness watch. 'I've burned off that afternoon tea, anyway.'

'I hope Frances will be able to find us, when she comes,' says Maisie. 'She'll think the place is deserted. We should have left a note on the door, or something. Perhaps you did, Oliver? You've thought of everything else.'

He makes a non-committal noise, seizing his champagne and drinking it down.

The pool is delightful, and so is the hot tub. They spend over an hour in the walled garden, swimming and drinking champagne, not speaking much. Maisie's pleasure in it is soured by the moment-by-moment expectation of Oliver's declaration, but he says nothing and makes no move and she begins to question her suspicion. Perhaps she has got it entirely wrong. Presently, Maisie finds herself on the swing seat, her towel wrapped around her, watching the shadows that are beginning to creep across the warm slabs.

'It will be time to go indoors soon,' she says. 'Is there a Wi-Fi code? My phone has no signal and I ought to contact Frances, to see if she's on her way.'

'No,' says Oliver. He is stretched out on a lounger. 'I don't think so. We are cut off from the world, Maisie. Cast adrift, like two lost souls.' He turns his head to look at her. 'Never mind, eh?'

Maisie smiles, but is conscious of the enlargement of her pocket of disquiet, because Oliver is quite right. They *are* cut off, with no phone signal and no Wi-Fi. She has no means of knowing whether Frances's arrival is imminent and she is *still* unsure what Oliver's intentions are. They have not talked. The signals are so mixed. Everything about his manner and certainly everything about this house seems calculated either to impress or to seduce. On the other hand, she might have things entirely wrong. His only intention might be to please and indulge her. If only he would *tell* me. I need to know where I stand.

She shivers. 'I think I'll go in and get changed,' she says, struggling to get off the seat. 'I wonder what time it is?'

Oliver, though wearing his watch, makes no effort to look at it. 'Is there any more champagne?' he asks. 'While you're on your feet.'

She checks the bottle. 'No,' she says. 'Unbelievably, we've drunk it all. No wonder I feel wobbly.'

He smiles. 'I could carry you upstairs.'

'You offered to do that once before, at my party. Dominic was incredibly shocked.'

'*Was* he?' Oliver's voice is wistful. How much of the champagne has he drunk? She can't be sure, but she thinks she's only had a couple of glasses.

He must be tired. All that driving and then such a lot of lengths in the pool.

'I wish Frances would come,' she says briskly. 'Then I could take us all out to dinner. She's sure to know somewhere nice.'

Oliver sits up. 'I said I'd cook.' His dreamy detachment of a moment before is utterly gone.

'I know. So thoughtful. But I'd like to treat you, to say thank you. You wouldn't have to drive. We'll call one of those things Frances talks about. An Oover?'

'Uber.'

'Yes. It's like a taxi, right?'

'Yes, but …' he swings his legs off the lounger and gropes for his shoe, 'this house … we oughtn't to waste a minute of the time that it's ours.' He looks first down at his watch, giving a satisfied little nod, then up at where she stands beside the lounger, her damp towel clutched to her. 'I know it's embarrassing,' he says, smiling coyly, 'but I have *literally* planned nearly every minute we'll be here, especially the minutes when it will be just the two of us.'

He stands. Suddenly, he looms over her. His puts an arm around her shoulders and draws her in. His chest is bare and warm, whereas her towel is damp and probably cold, but he does not flinch. He drops his head so his face is beside her ear and seems to inhale the scent of her. His voice is low when he speaks again, and gravelly, as though something is caught in his throat. 'And just now is the time I planned to do this.'

Then his mouth is on hers. Not as forcefully as before, but still too hard. Inexorably, her lips are prised open and his tongue is in her mouth. Her body rises to meet him while her mind shrinks away, an ambivalence too complex to analyse, and before she can make any effort of her own she is released.

'There,' he says, as though he has just completed a satisfactory job of work. 'Now run and get changed into something pretty.'

Maisie spends a long time shampooing her hair and then blow-drying it. She chooses the floral dress she wore for the dinner with Michael, adds a quick sweep of lipstick and a spray of perfume. Will these touches send a wrong message? She tries to analyse her mental and emotional state. Have I had too much to drink? And if not, what is this peculiar sensation in my stomach? It is a warm flutter of anxious wings. Am I ready to be swept off my feet by Oliver? Her mind speaks sense: she must be on her guard. Until I know what he intends in the medium to long term I mustn't do anything reckless. Her body, on the other hand, importunes with restless desire. When she examines her heart, however, she finds it mute—and its silence is perhaps more telling than the clamour of either voice.

Thank goodness Frances is to come. She will be the cold dousing of sense we all need.

Maisie is ready, but hesitates to go downstairs. Instead, she fusses around the room, turning down the double bed for Frances, closing the curtains, switching on a bedside light in the dressing room, where she has left her book and reading glasses for later. Finally, she takes her phone and carries it over the two upper floors of the house, searching for a signal. On the top floor, in a corner of a pretty, vaulted bedroom—a double and two singles, room for a cot, Maisie notes distractedly—she finds a flickering bar or two, but when she dials Frances's number it goes to voicemail, and as soon as she begins to gabble out a message, what small amount of connectivity she has found is lost.

She can put the moment off no longer. With grim determination she collects her bag and phone—for all the good it is—and goes downstairs.

Dusk has fallen while she has been prevaricating upstairs. Oliver has switched on a few lamps in various rooms, and from the kitchen comes the soft melody of some smooth jazz. The French doors to the terrace are still open. He has set a table for two—just two? Does he not intend to provide Frances with any dinner?—and lit some tea lights. The air is still and balmy, the sky a shade of pearly mauve, and across it she can see late-roosting birds, or possibly bats, flit in dizzying acrobatics. When she tunes her ears she can hear almost nothing except the dull drone of Oliver's music.

'Ah, here you are,' says Oliver in a low voice. She turns to find him beside her. He hands her a glass of something and then he too looks out into the beautiful evening. 'Just perfect, isn't it?' he murmurs. 'Cheers. To us.'

His proximity intensifies the unsettled feeling in her solar plexus. She takes the drink and, because his glass is poised, waiting for her response, she says, 'Cheers,' but avoids the necessity of echoing the second part of his toast by taking a long drink. The cocktail tastes sweet and innocuous but she suspects it is strong. Almost immediately she feels a glow in her stomach. Its effect is welcome, a sudden bolster to her confused feelings, a slight quelling of those fluttering wings.

'That's delicious,' she says, taking another pull at it.

He looks ridiculously pleased. 'It's called a "summer sunset." There was a seminar on cocktails at the sommelier course I did. As soon as I tasted this one, I knew I'd make it for you.'

She smiles and takes another drink. The memory of their earlier kiss lingers like a flavour on the tongue—as potent as the cocktail, and as potentially dangerous.

'Is it very strong?'

He winks. 'Dynamite.'

She gabbles out, 'I love my house and, when all the work on it is done I think I'll love it even more. But it will always be a house in a town, with traffic noise and commerce. This …' she struggles to describe it. 'It's like a slice of heaven, isn't it? I don't think I've ever heard such intense silence. Do you think it's silent in heaven?' She knows she is wittering. She can feel a nervous flush rising from her chest to her throat, a peculiar hot shiver. She can feel the alcohol begin to ooze through her veins—lovely, but alarming.

Oliver looks at her quizzically. 'In heaven?' he says. 'How would I know?'

It is the kind of question she might have asked James, and he would have humoured her in it. To cover her confusion, she drains her glass.

'Another?' Oliver offers. 'Naughty, aren't they? But what have we got to lose?'

He returns with another cocktail for each of them, and a tray laden with little bowls of olives, neatly curled slivers of Parma ham and asparagus spears, which are her favourite. He says, '*Antipasto!*' and decants the nibbles onto the table.

She pounces on the asparagus. 'Oh, I *love* asparagus.'

'I know,' he replies complacently. 'In fact, there isn't much about you I *don't* know, if I'm honest.'

'Oh? Such as?' She lowers herself onto one of the chairs and takes another sip of her drink before putting it on the table, determined to make this one last. He remains standing but moves half a pace so as still to be at her side.

He considers. 'I know you prefer chicken thigh to breast,' he begins, 'and a wine sauce to a cream sauce. You like shoes with small heels. These,' he lifts a hand to brush her hair away from her ear to reveal the simple, gold-hoop earrings she is wearing, 'are your favourite earrings. You wear them *all* the time. You favour practical underwear over pretty, but,' with a wink, 'we can change that.'

Maisie's mouth flaps in astonishment. It isn't the least bit funny but she finds a giggle has risen up and burst out. 'How do you know anything about my underwear?' she gasps out.

He turns his mouth down at the corners. 'You hang it on the line,' he says. 'Anyone can *see*. It's just that I *look*.'

She allows this to sink in. 'I don't know what to think about that,' she admits with an astonished laugh. In spite of her earlier resolution, she reaches for her cocktail and takes another sip.

'I really mustn't drink too much,' she says, but she is already a bit tipsy. Their afternoon tea feels like a long time ago and drinking on an empty stomach is madness. She helps herself to some of the ham.

'Why not?' he says.

'Because it will spoil tomorrow,' she says, 'and the excitement when the others come. I can't wait to show them around the house, can you? And the next day, the wedding. I don't want to make myself ill for that.'

'I'll look after you,' he says in a tone that manages to be both avuncular and roguish. 'Anyway,' he throws out a bit huffily, 'I'm not thinking about tomorrow. *I'm* in no hurry for this evening to end. I'm focussed on now.' His implication is that she ought to do the same. Suddenly she feels rather selfish to have relegated this—his oh-so-carefully wrought production—into a context in which it is merely one in a sequence of things and by no means the most important one.

'Yes,' she says. 'I suppose you're right. We should take our pleasures one at a time.'

This seems to satisfy him. They drink in silence for a while, as the moon rises in the sky. Somewhere across the fields, an owl hoots. The night air is beautifully still and warm. The potent liquor permeates Maisie's flesh and bone and seeps into her spirit. She feels buoyed up, afloat, her earlier doubts shrivelled to a thin thread of misgiving from which she cannot quite free herself.

Presently Oliver gets up and passes behind her, resting his hands momentarily on her shoulders as he goes. 'You're not cold?' he murmurs. 'You don't need a shawl or anything?'

She shakes her head. She feels quite warm, almost entirely enrobed in a delightful sense of serenity from the cocktails and the tranquillity of the evening. She wishes Frances would come. Perhaps a "summer sunset" or two will smooth her sharp edges. Maisie's own reservations are reduced to a niggling qualm.

Oliver goes indoors and, after a while, emerges again with two glasses of white wine. 'I've beaten the eggs,' he says, 'and made a salad. Supper can be ready in a jiffy, just say the word.'

Maisie takes the wine even though she knows she's already drunk enough. It is crisp and fruity and very cold, a pleasing antidote to the sweet and slightly cloying flavour of the cocktail. It is perfect; just as she likes it.

Oliver reads her mind. 'Yes,' he says, taking a drink from his glass. 'It's a New Zealand Sauvignon Blanc. Do you remember I introduced you to it in the Lakes? Viola was surprised. She likes a dry white wine but even she thought Sauvignon Blanc was virtually undrinkable until I suggested this.'

'I miss Viola,' Maisie blurts out, and finds it is so true she could easily cry. 'To be truthful, I'm quite worried about her. I haven't heard anything for weeks. Have you? I know there's a WhatsApp group I'm not part of. Is she active on there, at least?' She drinks some more of the wine.

Oliver shrugs. 'I can't recall. Most of it is the cardiganed crusaders reminding each other to bring their pills and spare pairs of glasses, who's bringing heated rollers … I hardly glance at it. Are you ready to eat?' His cynicism tweaks the filament of Maisie's uncertainty, reminding her again that beneath Oliver's glassy surface, something volatile lurks.

Maisie looks at the table. Oliver has set it simply, but elegantly. 'We ought to wait for Frances,' she says. 'Surely, she can't be long now. She mentioned something about Maxim's aunts arriving from Florida. Perhaps she's been delayed—'

'She isn't coming,' says Oliver. He turns away from her and saunters to the other end of the terrace. His face is in shadow. She cannot see if he is pleased or sorry, or disappointed for her.

'Not coming?' The pleasant sensation in her stomach suddenly curdles. The thread of doubt becomes a hawser of suspicion. 'Why not?'

He swivels to look at her from the far end of the terrace. 'I told her not to,' he says. 'Drink your wine. It will get warm. It's so sultry this evening, isn't it? Even this Sauvignon Blanc won't stand being above fifty degrees.' To prove his point, he drains his own glass.

Obediently, Maisie reaches her hand to her own glass, but then checks herself. She doesn't have to do what he says, does she? What she wants to do is rise to her feet. She wants to advance on Oliver and face him. Some imperative struggles beneath the oily slick of the alcohol. Is it anger? Fear? Outrage? Whatever it is, she finds she is pinioned to her seat, stupefied. Although as Oliver has stated, the night is warm, her flesh puckers into goosebumps. 'You told her not to come?' she gets out. 'Why?'

His eyebrows quirk in swift confusion. 'Isn't it obvious?'

She prises her hands from where they grip the arms of her chair. 'It's becoming more obvious,' she croaks out.

'That's good,' he says, his forehead clearing. 'I'll go and begin dinner, shall I?'

Maisie feels as though all the blood has drained from her head. When she looks into the garden all is shadow and dim, the scene hazed at its edges. She scans the terrace but there is no sign of Oliver. She presumes he is in the kitchen, making omelettes. Panic seizes her. She is tempted to run, speculating wildly that this terrace will take her along the side of the house and out onto the drive. But it was a long driveway, she recalls, with deep gravel, impossible to run along with stealth—or even at all, given her footwear. Even as she stares down at her strappy, impractical sandals, they wooze in and out of focus. I'm drunk. What possessed me to drink so much? She swallows down her dread. All I need to do is *tell* him. She summons the words but her thoughts are disordered and her mouth woolly. She's flattered ... she grasps hold of that one and tucks it away. And she's incredibly grateful. Yes, he will need to hear that too. She likes him *very* much ... but she mustn't emphasise that one too much. The main thing is ... she rummages until she finds it ... she isn't ready ... she knows that now. After the confusion of the last few weeks, the restless probing through the mist of Oliver's intentions … now at last his objective is clear: this is a seduction, pure and simple. And it is not what she wants.

The need to get up takes hold of her again, the need to pace, to get some warmth into her limbs, which are really chilly now. But when she tries to stand her legs are unreliable, with that numbness that sometimes presages pins-and-needles. *If I get up I might well fall.* She grapples in her bag for her phone. There is still no signal. And, to make matters worse, she is almost out of battery. She wants to hurl the thing into the garden, but what good would that do? She puts it back into her bag.

Oliver emerges with another glass of wine for her although the previous one remains unfinished. In his usual way—she recognises it now—he muddies the water by replacing the heavy inference of their last exchange with small talk. 'I've got the glasses in the wine fridge,' he explains conversationally, straightening her knife and centring the cruet with the deft efficiency she has seen him use countless times in the Smithy, 'to keep them chilled. It makes such a difference, I find. Do you plan to have a wine fridge in your new kitchen? I'd recommend one.' He spirits her half-finished glass of wine away with a slight frown. 'This will be too warm to drink now, unfortunately. But I mustn't stand here nattering. The omelettes require precision timing. Back in a moment.'

He is gone, and Maisie picks up her fresh wine glass and pours more than half of the wine into a nearby flower tub. She tries to summon some acuity but it is slippery and avoids her grasp. She is angry—at the sheer ego of the man, that he has manoeuvred her into this corner and prepared, planned, organised and decided all this without ever *once* asking her if this is what she wants. Her acquiescence has been taken utterly for granted. Such hubris! Her anger, though, like her common sense, is hard to actuate. It flails and ricochets in her head and her abdomen like an irate bee that won't, even for its own good, be caught and released. And undergirding the anger is a sense that Oliver must not be provoked. His self-assurance seems impregnable but she feels that, within its shell, there quivers a much frailer man. It isn't that she fears to hurt his feelings; it is the realisation that his feelings, once hurt, will hurt back.

He returns bearing two plates, which he sets gently onto the table. A soft, impossibly light pillow of creamy yellow omelette, sprinkled with chopped chives, sits alongside a neat scatter of salad leaves. He whips a folded napkin she had not noticed before from the table, flaps it open and lays it across her knee. His hand, as it passes the vee of her groin, exerts the slightest possible pressure. She thinks she might be sick.

Oliver seats himself opposite to her. '*Bon appetit*,' he says, raising his glass. She lifts hers to her lips but does not drink. She sees him eyeing it. 'You're enjoying the wine?' he asks.

'Very much,' she says stiffly.

He begins to eat but Maisie's food remains untasted. 'Oliver,' she says, 'I'm disappointed Frances isn't coming. I wanted her here.'

'Oh?' He continues to chew, apparently unconcerned, but she sees a flash of annoyance in his eyes.

'She's going away for such a long time,' Maisie spells out. 'And she's to be married, arguably the most important day of her life. Really, I wanted to focus my attention on her for these last few days.' In her own ears her voice is slurred and silly, the voice of intoxication.

So far as she knows Oliver has drunk as much as she has, but his voice is its usual, articulate self. 'I see.' He puts down his cutlery and daps at his mouth with his napkin. 'But when I explained, she was fine about it.'

'What did you explain?'

'Oh, how hard you've been working these past weeks. What a strain you've been under. And she agreed with me that you're not your normal self. She's worried about you. We all are. She thought—as I do—that a day of perfect rest, of being pampered and treated and looked after like a queen would do you the power of good. Eat your omelette, Maisie, since I've gone to the trouble of making it.'

Automatically, she cuts off a square of omelette and puts it in her mouth, but it tastes of nothing, and the feeling of nausea has not subsided. 'Delicious,' she offers, swallowing with difficulty and putting down her cutlery. She reaches for her wine glass but then thinks better of it. 'I wonder if I might have a glass of water,' she says.

'In a minute,' Oliver snaps. He nods at his plate. 'If I get you one now my supper will spoil. I'm enjoying it, even if you're not.'

'I'm sorry,' Maisie mumbles. 'I think I've had too much wine. My appetite has gone.'

'Have some bread, at least.' He motions to a basket of rolls. She takes one and tears a morsel off, but when she puts it in her mouth it is like ash. She chokes it down.

'Oliver,' she tries, 'we really must talk. We must understand each other. I think … I fear … I'm afraid …' Her thought processes are in disarray and her mouth seems unable to convey what little perspicacity she can conjure.

'Oh, spit it out, woman.' Oliver throws his cutlery down onto his empty plate and leans back in his chair.

'Don't be angry with me,' Maisie says, her voice a squeak. Unaccountably, although outraged and wishing to defend herself with righteous vim, she finds her eyes a-brim with tears. She brushes them away and quashes the timorousness that threatens to overpower her. Why should I beg? Why should I be afraid? Oh! If only I had stayed sober. 'You've got the wrong impression,' she says, with as much forcefulness as her flaccid mouth will allow. 'You're taking things too far, too fast. I'm not ready for … what you have planned.'

'Not ready?' His voice is a roar. 'Not ready? You're not seriously …' He narrows an eye, trying—but failing—to grasp the possibility that she might be rejecting him. 'After all I've done? Oh, the hours—the days and *weeks* I've spent planning! If you only knew! And all the while burning …' He clenches his fists in front of him, shaking some invisible foe. 'But no. I've "taken my time." "Taken it *slowly.*"'

The way he says these things makes it clear he is probing an old wound. He thrashes in his seat as though tortured, his hands raking his hair. 'Don't you realise?' he barks out, leaning across the table now, thrusting his face into hers. 'Don't you realise what you're being offered here? I mean,' he leans back and holds his hands out to indicate himself: his handsome face, his honed physique. He allows a moment for her to take him in. 'And you tell me you're not *ready?*' His voice is a shout, fierce and intimidating. 'Good God, woman! If not now, then when? I mean, what do you *need?* What the *fuck* will it take, if not *this?* He throws his arms wider, to encapsulate the house in all its splendour, the romance of the gardens and by implication everything else he has accumulated for her enjoyment: the luxury, the thoughtfulness, the exquisite perfection of it all. His gesture—sudden and expansive—knocks the table so a wine glass falls to the terrace and smashes into a million fragments. Oliver leaps to his feet and they both look down, appalled. 'Now look what you've made me do,' he shouts. 'Have you any notion what the damage deposit is on this place?'

Maisie tries to gather her limbs together but they feel made of lead. She squints at the shards of glass. They seem impossibly far away, down a long tunnel. 'I'll find a dustpan,' she says, but hopelessly. 'I'll pay whatever—'

He says, 'Forget it. It doesn't matter.'

'I'm sorry,' she says, without being quite sure what she's sorry for. She presses her hand to her head. The terrace slopes at an impossible kilter. The lawn, beyond it, is a heaving sea.

'Oh!' he cries out. 'Everything's going wrong. This isn't what I wanted at all.'

'What *you* wanted ...' She intends to tell him that what *he* wants has to be what *she* wants too, but isn't, and that if they had only *talked,* as she wished, if they had only been able to understand each other ... but her words are swept away.

He is at her side, on his knees amongst the broken glass, which must be cutting into him but he seems unconscious of it. He snakes his arms around her waist and buries his head in her lap. It is hard to make out his words. They come out in hard sobs at first. She catches only slurred phrases and garbled words—'It isn't fair,' and 'I deserve,' and 'so special,' but gradually his voice becomes steely, determination and some imperative impulse overcoming his dismay.

She takes advantage of a break in his outpourings to say, 'What *I* want—'

'Oh!' He lifts his head from her lap and although his eyes are glazed they are also full of flint. 'I know what you want,' he spits out, 'and you shall have it.'

He seizes her and lifts her roughly into his arms. She struggles, but she seems to have left her strength behind her on the seat, in the shower, in the pool, or even back at Millport. Her mind is so fuzzy, crackling with static, her limbs like jelly. She looks back, as though down a long corridor, but her sovereignty is a small and ineffectual thing, too far away to harness. She is helpless in his arms, no matter how powerful the absolute resistance of her will.

If Oliver had hoped for the masterfulness of a Rhett Butler, he falls short. He struggles to carry her through the breakfast room and up the stairs. Perhaps he is drunker than he thought. He sways, stumbles, almost drops her. She is unwieldy, drunk but not unconscious, and her faint but unambiguous words, 'No, Oliver. No. Please, no,' are not what he anticipated. But he is not to be deterred, not now, and the last thing Maisie recalls is being brought into a room that is bathed in flickering, golden, celestial light, overpoweringly warm and filled with the scent of roses.

Chapter Fifteen – Viola

Tilbury Hall looked like the epitome of genteel living. A Georgian mansion surrounded by deciduous woodland and neatly patchworked fields, it was accessed via a long driveway and through beautifully landscaped grounds. Residents were encouraged to gather on the plush lawns at eight every morning for Tai Chi. There were circuitous paths through the trees for jogging. Pagodas strewn with cushions invited meditation in the restorative outdoor air. There was a pool, a wood-fired sauna and an ice-plunge.

Indoors, the high-ceilinged rooms on the ground floor were given over to group therapy, Pilates and Zumba. The library hosted a weekly book group and the kitchen served up gourmet meals. Each individually-styled room was gorgeous with velvets and brocades, sparkling chandeliers and canvasses displaying pastoral scenes.

For the first week of her stay, Viola thought she had arrived in hell. There was no alcohol, naturally, but neither was there caffeine or tobacco. Weak herbal or fruit infusions took the place of a proper brew. The cigarettes she had thought she only tolerated suddenly became urgently necessary to her now she was denied them. And there was no contact with the outside world; she had surrendered her mobile phone and tablet. No newspaper, television or radio informed the residents of life outside their charmed—but beleaguered—enclave. She was permitted Sudoku and crossword books, but could settle to neither. The first week she paced—round and round her elegantly furnished room, then up and down the long landing. She could not sit, could not rest. Her limbs twitched and spasmed. She bit her nails. At night she thrashed in the overly soft bed and hurled the too-heavy quilt from her flailing body. Sweat poured off her. The night nurse—a constant presence with cool, efficient but impersonal hands—would cleanse Viola's body with flannels then sit her in an upholstered chair, shivering and wrapped in a blanket while deftly changing the sheets. When sleep came to Viola it was fitful and peopled by dreams: Graham loomed at her from the shadows with a clenched fist; Vanessa sprawled on the carpet with her head at an impossible angle, then swivelled an agonised eye and fixed Viola with a reproachful stare; Martin ran towards her as he had that first day, his arm in a sling. And always, accompanying her remembrance of him, came the sharp bite of the gate catch on her hand; it seemed she could savour no happy memory of him without a savage accompaniment of pain.

More than once she threatened to leave, getting so far as packing her case and carrying it down the shallow steps.

'Of course,' the maddeningly unflappable receptionist said, 'you can leave if you like. Your problems are waiting for you just beyond the gate.'

All the staff were calm, kind, and impervious. No amount of Viola's sarcasm could move them. She wore herself out producing sally after sally. They smiled beatifically and said, 'It's beautiful today, Viola. What about a walk in the garden?'

The other residents walked like ghosts from room to room, or sat and stared through the prolifically curtained windows to the arcadian scene beyond. Each, Viola supposed, was in their own purgatory, each battling their own demon. One or two would smile wanly at her as they passed in their ceaseless pacing. Some who were perhaps further along in the programme would take the time to lay a sympathetic hand on hers, to nod encouragement and say, 'It gets better.' Viola was brought powerfully to mind of the greeting card she had seen on her first visit to the upstairs flat: *Look forward. Dawn is coming.* She could not see it—the dawn. No. To her jaundiced eye the prospect beyond her window of pristine flowerbeds and artfully clipped yew, the verdant tree line and beyond, the undulating fields of ripening wheat and barley were all monotone, a blur of dim on dim, smudged shadow and glowering storm. From her window she looked down sneeringly at the slow and controlled movements of the Tai Chi class and wondered what the point of it was.

During the second week Kemi emerged from the blur of faces that had loomed in and out of Viola's consciousness during her detox. Kemi was a youngish woman, very dark, with an aureole of magnificent hair that she bound back in a selection of bright, exotic scarves. Like all the staff she wore a quasi-uniform: a short-sleeved tunic in pale yellow, tights—despite the soaring temperatures—and flat, functional shoes. She approached the table where Viola was eating breakfast—a requirement for all residents; there was no escaping the selections of fruit and muesli, yoghurt and wholemeal breads, although Viola had tried.

'I just want coffee,' she said, day after day. 'Just coffee for me. I never eat breakfast.'

'Here, you do,' they said patiently. 'We have green tea, or Lady Grey.'

'It's all decaffeinated,' Viola grumbled. 'It tastes like cat pee.'

'Yes,' they said, smiling kindly, 'we know.'

Kemi said, 'Good morning Viola. I'm going to be your counsellor. How would you like to take a walk with me?'

Viola opened her mouth to make some cutting remark, but found she could not rise to it. Her storehouse of ripostes was empty. 'Alright,' she said, getting up, glad at least to escape the table where her damned fruit and muesli lay half-eaten.

Kemi began by telling Viola a little about herself. An unremarkable story of an ordinary upbringing by hardworking but typical second-generation immigrants, a degree in psychology followed by a masters in rehabilitation counselling. She had been married, was now divorced and the single mother of a nine-year-old son.

'We have lots in common,' Viola admitted. 'I did a degree, although I never used it for anything. My husband's career had to come first. I'm divorced, like you. And I have a child, a son. Mine's twenty-seven, though. I'm also a widow.'

Kemi nodded. 'That's an experience I haven't had. But there's something else we share.'

'Oh?'

They had come to a place in the garden where a wooden bench gave them the opportunity to contemplate a long avenue of trees to the far horizon. By mutual consent they sat down, Kemi resting easily against the back of the bench, Viola perched on its edge, as though poised for flight. Kemi said, 'Can you think what it might be?'

Viola scrutinised her. She was young, healthy, enjoying what she supposed was a fulfilling and—given the fees—lucrative career. Divorce was never easy, and she supposed raising a child alone was a struggle. It was a shameful fact that even in this day and age, being a black woman meant encountering racial discrimination—something Viola, a white, middle-aged, middle-class woman would never experience. There was something else about Kemi. She was open, at peace within herself. Her clear eyes and level gaze, her easy smile spoke of a person who would never fall prey to the cynicism and toxic fatalism that had withered Viola's soul. 'No,' she said at last. 'You're not like me, and you never will be.'

'You're wrong,' said Kemi. 'Four years ago I was just like you. Alcohol-dependent, I mean. I don't pretend to know what brought you to this place, but I can tell you what took me there. It was simply this: I lost my belief that a better life was available to me. To *me*. To others, yes, but not to me. My solution was to try and make life a better place from within the confines of my mind—to console myself, to cauterize myself with alcohol. But oddly, it never seemed to work.'

Viola breathed out, a long, slow exhaling. Wasn't that just what she'd been doing?

'So then,' she said, 'how is this going to work? How are you going to fix me?'

'That's the first thing we need to establish,' said Kemi, taking her hand. 'I'm not going to fix you at all. You're going to fix yourself. Nothing, *nothing* will work until you decide that this is what you want to do. You, Viola. We call it "individual sovereignty".'

Viola's rehabilitation was a gentle thing, of quiet talks and tearful remembering. She told Kemi everything—of Graham and her life of abuse; of the refuge and her failure to save Vanessa; and at last, of Martin, the sweet but oh-so-brief oasis in her life of struggle and trauma. She had dreaded sessions in a sequestered room, the bombardment of questions, the accusations and reminders of failure. She had expected to be bullied, cajoled and reasoned into sobriety. But none of this occurred. She and Kemi met outdoors, in different locations of the grounds, and it seemed to Viola that as she unearthed each noxious detail from her ample store to Kemi's compassionate probing and deft excision, she was able to leave the cadaver of it behind her on the annealing ground.

Occasionally Kemi shored up aspects of Viola's history with details from her own. It was not about trumping them but simply a way of saying, 'Yes. I understand this. I have felt this, too.' Her shared experience helped Viola traverse the challenge of confronting her addiction, and also her grief. It was easier, she found, to tread in the footsteps of one who had gone before. Kemi understood the colossal effort it was to lift oneself up.

Sometimes they did not discuss Viola's condition at all, but looked at the plants and flowers, the produce in the kitchen garden and the budding fruits in the orchard. Kemi knew nothing of gardening, but seemed interested. Being amongst plants, speaking of them, touching, smelling and tasting them was as good a balm to Viola's wounded spirit as any cocktail, and in the absence of a cocktail of course she drank it in. Kemi saw the beneficial effect of it. 'You're different, when you talk about gardening,' she said.

'They call it vitamin G,' Viola said with a smile. Gwen had told her that, she recalled. She'd never heard it before. Lovely Gwen, how kind she was, how loyal, such a stalwart friend.

At night Viola slept more easily, her curtains and windows open to the still night air. The very silence was a salve. How troubled the soundscape of her high-rise flat seemed in comparison—no wonder it had robbed her of sleep. Here in the countryside, she heard only the screech of owls and the bark of foxes, the slough of wind in the trees and, in the blue gloaming of dawn, the chitter of sparrows in the ivy below her sill. It took her back to the farmhouse in the gash in the plain. She had been happy there, in between Graham's onslaughts. The pain of those episodes had been less than the agony of losing Martin, and sometimes she wished she had gone back to Graham from the hospital and picked up the reins of the life she had known there. She might have resumed her relationship with Douglas. How bad had it been really, in comparison with the blitzkrieg of her life since? She comforted herself by imagining she had never met Martin; that he remained in another life, in the Southquay allotment, jollying along the volunteers; and that some other woman—perhaps Vanessa, perhaps Gwen—would eventually rescue him from Susanne's coercive control. The trajectory of his life would go differently. No cycling along the prom, no sudden yen for fish and chips, no car accident, no death.

She sighed and turned over. These 'what-ifs' were fruitless—just another panacea to numb the pain and confusion of life. Kemi would say that her freedom would come from the ability to reconcile herself with life as it is, not life as it could or should have been.

Presently Viola was invited to join a group therapy session. She resisted. She did not want to sit through the self-indulgent lamentations of others.

But Kemi said, 'This is all part of it, Viola. Rehabilitation can be a lonely road. Why travel alone when there are others on the same path? You never know, they may teach you something, or you may teach them? The group will allow you to create bonds that can last far beyond Tilbury Hall; I'm still in contact with several people from my group, and that's four years on. They're the only ones who really understand.'

Viola looked askance at the residents at their various tables in the dining room. 'I'm not sure,' she said.

'You don't have to like them,' said Kemi. 'You just have to trust them. A group is a circle of trust—'

'Oh stop it, you'll make me throw up.'

'A safe space for sharing and for practising our social skills. Be honest—are you the guest on the top of everyone's list?'

'Probably not,' said Viola, thinking of her dreadful behaviour in the Lakes, and afterwards. 'But I don't think I'll have anything in common with these people.'

'You'll have one thing, at least. Come on. You might even enjoy it.'

Viola thought suddenly of her friends—of Maisie and Gloria and Minnie, all widows, all of whom had passed through the fire of bereavement, just as she had. There, if anywhere, she could have found compassion. But instead of taking the comfort they offered she had ridiculed and belittled them. She had bullied Minnie, there was no other way of describing it. Viola felt ashamed, and allowed herself to be led to the session.

The group met in one of the pagodas—eight residents and two counsellors. Viola lowered herself onto one of the cushions and leaned her back against a pillar. The residents introduced themselves: Rick, a thin, long-haired thirty-odd year old with tobacco-rimed fingers spoke first. He was both a drug addict and an alcoholic. He admitted this was his second stay at Tilbury. Eric went next. He was a fat, balding man in his fifties who enumerated a long list of business credentials before bursting into tears at the confession that his wife and three daughters had threatened to disown him if he didn't get sober. Sophie was the youngest of the group, a party-girl, she said, who had almost killed herself with an overdose of methamphetamine and whose sugar daddy was paying for her to get clean. Marcus was a dentist who had become addicted to ketamine. Victor said he was a sex addict. Bob and Clarissa were a husband-and-wife combo who had decided their nightly gin-and-tonic-and-bottle-of-wine-apiece habit had got out of hand. 'We're not addicts,' they said gaily. 'We're not even dependent. But we're looking for ways to curb our consumption.'

Viola said, 'I'm Viola. I'm here to get sober. I began to drink after I lost my husband. That's all I want to say, just now.'

The counsellors probed the group regarding their various triggers; what situations were likely to make them resort to drugs or alcohol or, in Victor's case, sex? Later, they moved on to challenge the group to share strategies for avoiding temptation in the future. Eric said his colleagues would prove a stumbling block because boozy conference dinners were part of the work environment. He supposed in future he just wouldn't attend. Marcus said he would surrender his key to the drug cabinet at the practice. Victor said he supposed he could cut his dick off. Rick said none of those things would work. 'It's about willpower,' he said, 'not about making it impossible. You have to *choose* not to do it, even when its right there. If it isn't there, it's easy. Right? Nobody promised this would be easy.'

'Very good, Rick,' said the counsellor. 'I think we'll leave things there.'

Later, Viola said to Kemi, 'I think I understand drinking won't make things better, and in fact will make them worse. It won't bring Martin back and it won't ease the pain of losing him. He died. That's it. It was awful, cruel and I miss him, or … I miss what I never got to have with him, the years and years we should have had. But others have had it worse. Think of soldiers who got married one day and went off to the front the next. And died. Their wives had them for just one night. It's sickening, but it happened. I did better than they did. When I look at it that way, I ought to feel blessed.'

'Counting your blessings,' said Kemi, 'is excellent therapy. But you don't need to minimise what happened to you. It was truly awful and you're justified in feeling angry, cheated and very, very sad. The point is, as you say, drinking won't make it better, or different. It won't make it go away. Nothing can do that, unfortunately.'

Viola began to cry. Kemi passed her a tissue.

'It isn't fair,' Viola choked out. 'It isn't fair, it isn't fair.'

Some of Viola's sessions with Kemi were like walking over hot coals. It hurt to dredge up the past, and there were times when she felt she was reopening wounds so old their scars hardly showed.

'But they're there,' said Kemi gently. 'Our psyche is like a sieve. Some traumas pass right through and some stay enmeshed for years, to the point that they get grown-over and almost assimilated into the fabric, like the ivy on that tree over there. What a sorry, gnarly old thing it is! It's more ivy than tree, isn't it? It looks like the ivy is the only thing holding it up! But, in fact, the ivy is what's killing the tree. It has to be excised.'

Their talk went back to Viola's childhood. She had been an only child and a lonely child, desperate for friends but seemingly unable to make or keep them. 'I wanted a *best* friend,' Viola admitted, 'someone to share secrets with, someone who would always save a place for me. But I was no good at being tactful. If someone didn't look nice, I wouldn't say they did.' Instead, she had attracted the attention of bullies. 'After that,' she said, 'no one would go near me. No one wanted to ally themselves with me against those tormenters.'

At university she had been a loner, working in the library until it closed, and then going back to her chilly bedsit to study some more. 'Occasionally I went to the Union,' she remembered, 'where there were discos. I drank until I could be brave enough to get onto the dance floor. I suppose that's where it began—my idea that alcohol could change my reality.'

There came a point when Viola had no more rotten secrets to tell, no more shame, no more festering resentments. The chips on her shoulders were offloaded. She was scoured, but clean.

She felt bruised but liberated; her step was lighter, her sleep deeper. She ate better, and with more enjoyment of the healthy food and, yes, even the breakfast fare that was served up at the Hall. She found, in her own company, not the dogged, punitive adequacy that had characterised her early days in the Southquay flat, but a peaceful kind of self-sufficiency that was almost enjoyable. She walked slowly round the grounds and admired the view. She breathed the air. She even joined in the Tai Chi, stretching her muscles as she expanded her mind to contemplate life without alcohol *and* without Martin.

Her tight clothes grew tighter, and when she was weighed she found she had gained a stone. Her hair grew longer and she neither cut nor dyed it. It was utterly unlike its former self, its mousiness bleached pure white. She left off the black eye makeup and faced the world as she was, in all her vulnerable nakedness.

She found she could tolerate Sophie's companionship even though she was a confirmed airhead, ineffectual and thoughtless. She reminded Viola of many a young waif who had come and gone from the upstairs flat, a pawn in the game of control and abuse. 'Oh yes,' said Sophie, when Viola broached the subject, 'I've been hit more times than I can count.' She said it as though she expected—as though she deserved—no better.

Rick turned out to be a deeply thinking soul, a poet who had drifted into rock 'n' roll as an outlet for his creativity. He read some of his verses to Viola one evening as they sat on the long terrace and watched the sun sink below the horizon. They made her cry.

'Were you drunk when you wrote those? Or high?'

'No.' He shook his head. 'I was sober. I write when I'm wasted, and it seems fantastic, but then I look at it when I'm sober and I see it's rubbish. It's all screwed up. It isn't *true.*'

She disliked Bob and Clarissa, seeing in them all she had despised in the bridge- and golf-club cronies of Vanessa and Clive, and she avoided Victor, who she felt was far from conquering his addiction, but she found a place of sympathy with Eric. His recourse to alcohol had been all about a sense of inferiority amongst his colleagues. 'My sales figures were never enough,' he said. 'I couldn't outsell them but I could outdrink them.'

'Did you ever hit your wife?'

'Yes,' he sobbed, breaking down. 'I did.'

At one time Viola would have castigated him, pouring onto him all her contempt. He was Graham, he was Clive, he was every man who had laid a violent hand on a woman. But no, he was just a weak and pitiful man who had tried to make others pay for his own sense of inferiority. She could not forgive him, but she could understand.

Her talks with Kemi were all about the future, about what she would do when she went home, about the support network she would gather around her.

'I have friends,' she said, 'and I think I'll have a place to live, with two of them. My friend is doing up her house for … for people like me, who don't want to live alone. She has a garden …'

Viola's time at Tilbury came to an end on the Thursday before Frances's wedding and, of course before the anniversary of her own. She and Kemi had spoken of the upcoming event and she had discussed it in the group.

'Your anniversary is no different to any other day,' said Clarissa, reaching out for Bob's hand. 'Our anniversary often gets forgotten, doesn't it, Bob? But I don't make a fuss. Every day is a blessing.'

'I'm not sure that's very helpful,' said Rick. 'What I'd suggest to Viola is that she focusses on these friends of hers. Introspection—feeling sorry for ourselves—is counter-productive. This is *their* day. You being off your face won't improve it.'

'Being off my face doesn't improve anything,' said Viola. 'I've learnt that much.'

Kemi spread her hands. 'Our work here is done,' she said.

Viola was given her phone and tablet back at reception, along with a card with useful telephone numbers on it. Both the phone and the tablet were out of battery and she had to use the telephone at reception to call a taxi to take her to the station.

While they waited for it to come, Kemi said, 'You're having a baptism of fire, Viola, going straight from here to a wedding, especially in the circumstances. The temptations to be maudlin and to drink will be legion.'

'But I shan't give in to them,' said Viola. 'I miss Martin every day. Saturday will be no different, neither worse nor better. And drinking doesn't help.'

Kemi gave her a hug. 'Don't be a stranger,' she said.

Being out of Tilbury was strange at first. The world seemed a large and noisy place after its sequestered atmosphere, and she half wished she had asked Brian to pick her up. She arrived in Oxford at just after three o'clock. It was teeming with people, mainly tourists, all burdened with cameras and backpacks. She soldiered forth, getting a walk-in appointment at a hairdresser, who trimmed off the still-black tips of Viola's hair and styled it into a soft elfin bob. She visited three or four clothes boutiques to buy outfits that would fit her newly fleshed-out figure and accord with her new, more optimistic mood. She bought several pairs of loose linen trousers in pastel colours, and a floaty skirt and matching top in white that she decided to keep on; it was so cool and comfortable. She bought some soft, flat, comfortable shoes to replace her crippling high heels, which she deposited at a nearby charity shop. She chose a dress to wear for the wedding: textured organza, A-line, sleeveless, with a flared skirt. In peach.

She was booked into a small hotel in the outskirts of Oxford, but she did not wish to go there so soon. It was past five when she finished her shopping. She went into a pizzeria and ordered food, pushing away the proffered wine list and asking for sparkling water. She ate slowly, watching the activity on the pavement as she did, exchanging pleasantries with the staff. After her dinner she had coffee, black—no one ever died of a coffee overdose. Afterwards she wandered the streets, peering in through the college gates at the neatly mown quadrangles and the old stone buildings.

By the time her taxi deposited her at her hotel it was well past seven; the sky
was a rich mauve tinged with orange. She checked in and carried her bags up
a flight of stairs to her room. It was a small single room, the bathroom
cramped and in need of a good clean, but it would do. She spent some time
unpacking her new clothes and putting them in the wardrobe. Then she
plugged in her phone and connected it to the hotel's Wi-Fi.

There were dozens of messages. Many missed calls, voice messages and texts
from the widows enquiring after her well-being and asking if she was having
a good time with Brian. The women's WhatsApp group chat had spiels of
interactions—lots of stuff about Amy, who had been unwell, Val and the
farm, a journalist, some protest or other, the progress of Maisie's works, a
sale at their favourite department store, endless debate about hair rollers and
handbags, who would travel with whom … The messages spooled into the
in-box like pennies falling from heaven. Viola scrolled through it all, feeling
distanced from it and yet oddly grounded. This was her tribe; these were the
women who would bring her back to herself.

Then, as the messages became more recent, she became concerned. She
gathered that Maisie was already in Oxford, at their eye-wateringly expensive
Airbnb, with Oliver. Their travel plans had changed—or *been* changed—
brought forward by a day. She had a sudden and almost visceral yearning to
be reunited with her friends. If Maisie was here, in Oxford, and the house
was available to them, why should Viola not join them? She had committed
to paying her share. She looked around the depressing little hotel room with
a sinking heart. But then another sense, more pressing still, was that Maisie
needed her. She could not clarify it. It was a dull but urgent sensation—the
kind that had, in former times, sent her scurrying up the stairs to the upper
flat in Southquay to find the woman there in tears, or on the phone being
talked into going back to her abusive partner. Maisie and Oliver … the
coupling was uncomfortable; it didn't sit right. She was not sure, could not
tell … but something was wrong.

She repacked her bags and hurried back down the stairs. 'I'm sorry,' she told
the bored receptionist. 'I can't stay after all. I don't care about a refund.
Please, will you call me a taxi?'

She had the taxi drop her at the bottom of the drive and trudged the quarter mile or so up to the rental property, dragging her suitcase with difficulty through the deep gravel. The house, when she reached it, was charmingly illuminated by the soft glow of lamps from within and the subtle glow of exterior lighting hidden amongst the clinging ivy. Oliver's little sports car was parked on the drive.

Viola climbed the steps and turned the handle of the door, which opened silently onto a shadowy hall. She parked her case. Music drifted from behind a door. She pushed that open to reveal a cavernous kitchen where the makings of a meal—eggshells, cheese parings, some shreds of lettuce—had been abandoned on the black granite worktop. She moved to the stove and touched it gingerly: still quite hot. At the far end of the room French doors were propped open to the balmy night. She walked over, her soft shoes making no sound on the Italian tiles, but the lugubrious strains of the jazz would have masked them anyway. The sound of voices wafted to her through the night air. Oliver and Maisie. The soft scrape of cutlery on china suggested they were eating a meal.

She paused. She had given no thought until this moment of how or when she would explain to her friends where she had been. There was no doubt that she had a great deal of explaining to do, and about the same quantity of apologies to make. She thought that on balance it would be easier to get it all over with in one fell swoop, to wait until the whole crew were assembled and then eat the vast portions of humble pie that were her due. But that could not be until tomorrow. In the meantime, she would be forced to perpetuate the cover story that she had spent the past weeks at Brian's house. They would want to know what museums, galleries and theatres she had visited, what Brian's new girl-friend was like, details of his swanky flat in Dulwich village. Of course, she would refuse a drink. That, on its own, would arouse a tsunami of suspicion. She dithered as she considered her options.

Then, penetrating her deliberations, she heard Oliver say, 'In a minute! If I get you one now my supper will spoil. I'm enjoying it, even if you're not.' His voice was razor-edged, peevish and cold. Viola stiffened. That was not like Oliver, she thought. He was usually all oily smoothness.

She craned to hear Maisie's reply, but it was a mumble, inaudible.

She edged round the door. The two were seated at a pretty iron table. Tea lights flickered between them, pushing back the darkness that pressed in from beyond the terrace. A light from one of the rooms pooled onto the slabs and on to Oliver. His face was flushed, his eyes glittering, his whole demeanour buoyed up by some inner energy whose source Viola could not divine. Maisie had her back to the lamp light and Viola could only see her in profile, but even in the wavering candlelight her face was ashen. Her lips were moving but Viola couldn't make out what she said. Her face was oddly immobile. Her body, in her chair, seemed half-slumped. She looked drunk, but this was unlikely. Maisie liked a glass of wine or two, but she never drank to excess. Maisie's tone was strangled, pleading. She was afraid.

All of a sudden Oliver threw his knife and fork onto his plate. 'Oh, spit it out, woman,' he said sharply, and then, after more inaudible mutterings from Maisie, a great roar of, 'Not ready? Not ready? After all I've done? All I've *spent?*' His fists were clenched, his body a paroxysm of fury. Viola shrank back against the opulent curtain. She was drenched in sweat, paralysed, seized by dread. She heard snatches of Oliver's tirade. 'What do you *need?*' and, 'What the *fuck!*' and then the smash of a falling glass. Viola pressed her hands to her ears and burrowed into the enveloping folds of the curtain. Memories crowded back at her—Graham inflated by hubris, wielding his fist or whatever implement came to hand. She pressed her palm against her mouth to stifle the sound of her own whimpers.

The playlist came to a halt, leaving only the tick of an enormous clock on the wall and the soft plink of water falling from the tap into a bowl. The drama on the terrace played on, the voices lower now, but Viola's own clamouring demons would have drowned them out in any case.

Then, with a flurry of movement and a quick draught of warm night air, they were through the doorway and across the room, oblivious of Viola who had curled herself into the ample pleats of the curtain so effectively that she was invisible. Oliver had Maisie in his arms, awkwardly; she seemed as limp as a rag doll. He struggled with the unwieldiness of her unresisting body as he bore her with difficulty through the hall and up the stairs.

Viola followed, her heart in her throat, her feet silent on the thick carpets. She scurried in his wake along the gloom of the half-lit landing.

She heard Maisie's faintly protesting, 'No, Oliver. No. Please, no,' but Oliver's step did not falter as he turned into a room which was ablaze with a hundred flickering tea lights and scattered with rose petals. The heat and the smell were overpowering. Viola looked on from the open doorway aghast, as he laid Maisie across the bed and began to tear at the buttons of her dress. His face was dark, suffused with his evil intention, but his eyes shone in the lurid glow of the candles, wet with tears. She recognised it, this agonised confluence of emotion that hijacked the abuser at the moment of their transgression; absolute determination to commit the crime and a deep and sincerely held regret that it should be necessary.

Viola's paralysis released its grip, replaced by anger and a primitive need to prevent what was about to occur. For Maisie, for herself and for Vanessa, but also for Cindy and Shakira, for Carole and Helen, for all the women who had suffered abuse and also for Martin and men like him. She cast about her for some means of restraining Oliver, saw and rejected the thick cords of the curtain tie-backs and the fire irons on the ornate hearth before seizing a heavy Satsuma Ware vase that stood atop a chest of drawers. She crossed the carpet and smashed the vase onto the back of Oliver's head.

It was not like in the cinema, where the bad guy is knocked out cold. Oliver was stunned and down, but by no means out. He struggled from the bed, where Viola's blow had sent him sprawling beside Maisie who was, mercifully, unconscious. They faced each other across the hotly scented room. She readied herself for a blow, but none came. Panting, he said, 'What the hell …?' and raised a curious hand to the back of his head. It came away bloody. Viola stood her ground, her breathing also laboured.

'Maisie said no,' she spat out. 'I heard her distinctly. No is no, Oliver.'

He waved a dismissive hand, but feebly. 'She's drunk,' he said. 'I was helping—'

'No.' She fixed a steely eye upon him. 'I know what I saw.'

He breathed out, a deflation, and she allowed herself to do the same. She wondered what she should do next. Call the police? But on what charge? Is that what Maisie would want?

Oliver spat, 'Since you're here, I suppose you can look after Maisie.' He took a step towards the door, his feet crunching on the shards of china scattered over the carpet. 'You'll have to pay for this though. The damage deposit is sky high—'

'I don't care,' she flung out. She planted her feet firmly on the carpet and folded her arms. 'You should leave.'

He moved another few paces, his eyes straying to where Maisie lay across the bed, her dress open to the navel, a little glass bead in the middle of her bra winking in the candlelight. Viola could hear his mind cogitating ways to explain what had just occurred, fabricating a train of events that would make the outcome seem perfectly reasonable, that would exonerate him and make Viola's accusations seem laughably histrionic. 'Of course,' he said, indicating the flower petals, the candles, the lavishly hung bed, 'of course I *hoped* … Maisie and I, we've been getting rather close and I … well! Who wouldn't? But she … she—'

'She said "no".'

His head drooped. 'Yes, in the end, she did,' he admitted. 'But by then, she'd had too much wine.'

'There's no point discussing this now, Oliver. It's late—'

'It's only nine o'clock,' he objected, glancing at his watch.

Viola took a breath. 'What I mean is, it's *too* late, Oliver. This, whatever it was, has gone too far.' She kept her eyes upon him, watching her meaning sink in.

'Yes,' he mumbled, letting his eyes drop. 'I see that now.'

He turned and stumbled from the room. Moments later she heard him in the room below. The squeak and pop of a cork being drawn from a bottle set up in Viola a clamour of need so visceral that she thought she might implode. She launched into action, tearing round the room extinguishing candles, wrenching open the window to disperse the cloying scent of roses from the room. She extracted the coverlet from beneath Maisie and wrapped the shards of broken pottery in it, before straightening Maisie on the bed and putting her clothes to rights. The activity left Viola breathless but the chasm of temptation had been traversed.

Maisie slept on, peacefully oblivious, her face untroubled.

Viola fetched her bags from the hall and found her phone.

James answered on the second ring, his voice woolly with sleep.

'James,' said Viola, 'it's Viola Cutler. I'm sorry to bother you, but something's happened.'

She told her story as far as she was able. James listened without interrupting.

When she had finished he said, 'You sound different, Viola.'

She gave a harsh laugh. 'You mean, I'm not pissed. No. I'm sober. I have been for a month.'

'So …' She could hear him wiping a hand across his face, the faint rasp of his stubble, his mind computing possibilities.

She helped him out. 'I could call the police,' she said. 'I'm sure this is attempted rape, but then … I don't know … something about him … I'm not sure he *intended* to rape her.' She looked around the room at the extinguished tea lights and the scattered petals. 'This looks a lot more like a seduction scene than a rape scene.'

'Oliver will believe whatever he wants to believe,' said James. 'That's the thing about the Harringtons. They know what they want and, to them, that's enough to make it so. That others might want something else doesn't enter into their thought processes.' She heard him sigh. 'Right,' he said at last. 'I'd better come down, hadn't I? He's still in the house?'

'So far as I know. I haven't heard his car drive off.'

'Alright. I'm on my way. In the meantime, unless he gets nasty, don't call the police. I'll talk to him and … I'll deal with it.'

She waited for him to end the call. The silence stretched out between them. 'Okay,' she said. 'Thank you, James.'

Silence still. Then, 'Maisie … she's okay? He didn't … hurt her?'

'She'll be upset, when she wakes up. Such a breach of trust. But physically, she's unhurt.'

'Thank God,' said James, almost to himself. 'Thank God.'

Viola filled a glass with water and then she sat in vigil by the bed, as she had done so many times in the Southquay flat, waiting for her friend to wake.

Chapter Sixteen – Maisie & Viola

Maisie opens her eyes to a splitting headache and a vision of a woman in white—white hair, light as dandelion seeds, framing a face that is pale and thin and deeply lined. Is this apparition an angel? Or, given her hangover, a nurse? The otherworldly glow she remembers has been extinguished, and the heat has also dissipated. A draught of cool air brushes her skin. It must still be evening, or night. She raises her arm to check but her watch isn't there.

The woman leans over Maisie, entering a narrow field of vision, the perimeter of which is crazed and fractured, like looking through broken glass. Maisie recalls a broken glass, but dimly. She tries to speak but her mouth is as dry as bone and her lips feel bruised.

She manages to say, 'Water,' and soon a glass is pressed gently to her lips.

'There,' says the woman softly, and Maisie recognises the voice.

'Viola?'

Viola smiles. 'Yes, it's me, but not the me you know. I'm new. I've been through the fire.'

'So have I, I think,' says Maisie, struggling to sit up and fighting the nausea that rises to her throat.

Viola assists her with an arm that is surprisingly strong, considering its thinness. 'Not quite,' she says. 'I got here in time.'

Maisie's memory seeps back. She remembers the house, the pool, cocktails and wine—far too much of both—the omelettes, and Oliver, angry … the sense of that anger gives her a clutch of panic. Her memory is a whorl of inscrutable shadow.

'Where is Oliver?'

Viola shrugs. 'I don't know. Gone off with his tail between his legs. The important thing to know is that he didn't get it between *yours*. He'll have a headache too, if that's any consolation. I hit him with a vase.'

'You hit him with a vase? Oh Viola!'

'Oh! Don't worry. He's alright. I needed to stop him in his tracks, that's all.'

Maisie looks around her. She is in the blue brocade room. 'This isn't my room. I don't want to stay here.'

'Alright,' says Viola. 'I'll help you. Don't worry. James is coming, and everything will be alright.'

Maisie shuffles along the corridor and the galleried landing. She peers over the balustrade. There is no sign of Oliver, but she sees that, below, the lights have been switched off and the doors to the terrace are closed. The dizzying height makes her feel like her head will explode, her guts likewise. She makes a dash for the bathroom and gets there just in time.

Viola runs water into the basin. 'You've got the mother and father of hangovers. I know what that feels like.' She passes Maisie a damp flannel so that she can wipe her mouth. 'Better out than in,' she says.

Maisie allows herself to be tucked into the double bed she had earlier prepared for Frances. 'I've missed you, Viola,' she murmurs. 'Where have you been?'

'Shush,' says Viola, clicking off the bedside lamp. 'That's a story for another day. Sleep now, Maisie, and don't be afraid.'

Maisie is awakened by the soft click of a cup of tea being placed on her bedside table.

She has a feeling—but cannot be sure—that the air is torrid with fraught emotion, voices raised, accusation and denial. Something has happened but she doesn't know what; only that, in some way she cannot compute, she sits at the epicentre of the maelstrom.

She opens her eyes to find James Armstrong looking down at her. He looks exhausted, his chin shadowed with stubble, his eyes bruised with tiredness. His shirt is creased, as though slept in. His appearance confuses her. Hadn't it been Oliver, rather than James, who brought her here? She glances to the other side of the bed, but it is smooth, unslept in. This relieves her until she remembers Frances.

She struggles to sit up. 'Oh God,' she gasps. It feels as though a boulder is crushing her brain. 'My head is splitting,' she says. 'I'm sorry, I'm …' she rubs her eyes. 'Why are you here? I mean, it's lovely that you are, but …'

There is movement from across the room. Someone in a chair. White hair, a white towelling robe. 'There's a lot you won't remember, Maisie.'

James moves to the window and opens the curtains, flooding the room with light so bright that Maisie has to shield her eyes from it.

'Oh, sorry,' he says, adjusting the blind. 'Is that better?'

The woman in white has stood up, stretched, and taken the second cup James has delivered. They both look down on Maisie as she lies in the bed, feeling small and dazed.

'Viola?'

'Yes, it's me,' says Viola with a smile. 'We spoke briefly last night, but you probably won't remember.'

Maisie presses her thumbs to her eyes, searching her memory. 'I remember something,' she says. 'It's a bit of a blur.' She feels the mattress dip as Viola perches herself on it.

'Don't worry,' Viola says. 'Take your time.'

James paces uneasily before perching on the chair Viola has vacated, 'Tell us what you remember.'

Maisie sucks air into her lungs and casts her mind back. 'The journey here,' she says slowly. 'We stopped for afternoon tea. Then this house. Swimming in the pool …' She scans her memory banks. 'Oliver made supper … there were cocktails and wine … he was angry. It's a daze. I must have drunk too much.' An indefinable sense of dread washes over her in connection with Oliver. 'I expect he's furious with me, isn't he?'

'His feelings are rather beside the point,' says Viola. 'Oliver tried to rape you, Maisie. I'm sorry to be harsh. I know this is a shock.'

'Rape?' Maisie shakes her head. *I must be dreaming. If only I could think clearly.* Her mind does a quick assessment of her body. She does not feel bruised or sore but she does feel rather sick. *I know Oliver wanted to have sex with me, but would he really have gone so far as to rape me? The enormity of it is appalling.* She swallows back a sob and turns tear-blurred eyes to Viola. 'But he didn't?'

Viola shakes her head. 'No. I stopped him. You said no. I heard you clearly. He must have done too. But he wasn't going to stop.'

Maisie assimilates this. 'Where *is* Oliver?'

James jolts to his feet. 'He's downstairs. But don't worry, he won't be coming anywhere near you. Drink your tea, Maisie, if you can. It will make you feel better.' He picks it up and passes it to her.

'We ought to call the police,' says Viola briskly. 'He's guilty of attempted rape or, at the very least, common assault.'

'That's up to Maisie,' says James. 'She may not wish to press charges.'

'Oh no,' Maisie cries, appalled. 'I couldn't. Whatever happened, I don't want anyone to know about it. It's … so embarrassing … that I allowed myself to … and anyway, it's Frances's wedding. Nothing must spoil that.'

'But Maisie,' Viola cautions, 'he tried to rape you. I'm a witness.'

'*He* says,' James begins, 'that everything he planned for last night was the culmination of a long-term flirtation you two have been engaged in.' He throws Maisie a look that is loaded with wounded disappointment before turning abruptly away. 'He says you cannot have been in any doubt about what would occur,' he concludes bitterly.

Maisie tries to arrange her thoughts but they are muddled, and further muddied by the urge to cry. No wonder James is disappointed in me. He must think I've been stringing them both along.

'When I got here and saw this place, I suspected Oliver had some scheme in hand, but I didn't know what. He'd gone to such trouble, and such expense, and he was clearly so excited that I wondered …' she breaks off with a blush, 'well, for a while I wondered if he was going to propose! But before that … I was so mixed up. Perhaps I should have seen the writing on the wall. Other people hinted—but I was too naïve—you might think too stupid—to understand. I was confused about what was going on between us. Sometimes it seemed that nothing was! And then, at other times … well, yes, sometimes it was pretty clear.' She brings to mind—but does not describe—their combative encounter on the terrace behind *Old Farm Hall*. 'I'd asked him several times if we could talk, because I wanted to know … well … it's embarrassing, but I needed to know if he had *more* than just … sex on his mind.' She turns her gaze on James, but he will not meet it. He stands with his back to her, his hands in his pockets, looking down at the garden from her window. As terrible as the shock of Oliver's betrayal is, somehow, James's reaction feels worse. She wants to cry out to him, to reach out and touch him, but she is stuck in the bed under Viola's excoriating eye and hampered by the tea, cooling now, in its cup. 'He never mentioned the word "love",' she cries out brokenly. 'Not once.'

In a flash of humiliating illumination she realises that if he had—no matter how speciously, it probably would have been enough.

'And even if he had,' says Viola, 'even if you had declared undying devotion to each other, if you had driven to Gretna, instead of Oxford, and got married, at the last, your "no" should have stopped him.'

Maisie puts her tea, untasted, on the bedside table. 'I want to get up,' she says fiercely. 'I want to use the bathroom, have a shower, get dressed. I feel disadvantaged sitting here. I'm not a victim. I'm not ill. My family is coming. My daughter is getting married. *That's* what matters. That's what I'm going to focus on.'

She throws back the covers and gets up. The carpet is soft beneath her feet. Her legs tremble but she forces herself to stand firm.

'And what about Oliver?' says Viola, barely suppressing her outrage. 'Is he going to get away with it?'

'No,' says James heavily, turning back into the room. 'No, he won't get away with it. I'll see to that.'

Maisie's brief show of courage takes her into the bathroom and allows her to close the door behind her before her bravado evaporates and leaves her crouching on the immaculate tiles, stifling her sobs with one of the thick white towels.

Presently she crawls across to the toilet and sticks her fingers down her throat. The vomit is sour but there is not much of it. She recalls that she has already been sick. She gets into the shower and switches it on, allowing the hot water to scour her body while the steam enfolds her in a cloud of obscurity where it feels good to hide.

Even so, she can hear the sounds of argument that rise from the room below. Oliver's voice—strident and offended—rattles the bottles of Maisie's skincare regime on the glass shelf where she had placed them so carefully the day before. She hears herself described as "a stupid bitch" and "a frigid prick-tease." His rage is terrifying, curdled with affronted pride and pious indignation. Maisie feels his pain. In a way, he's right. Any normal woman-of-the-world would have recognised Oliver's behaviour for what it was: a slow, subtly choreographed road to seduction. And any normal woman would have been swept away by it. She almost had been, except that she had wanted more from him than just vague signs and gestures. She had wanted words, a promise. Only in this—perhaps old-fashioned—formality had he fallen short. No wonder he is so angry.

But then she remembers Viola's assertion that, though drunk, she had said a "no" that Oliver had ignored. James has often warned her of the Harringtons' arrogance, of their sense of entitlement. Oliver must have decided that, one way or another, he would have her.

An aura of betrayal rises with the steam, filling the bathroom. Viola is right. No matter what, 'no' is 'no.'

Interspersed with Oliver's yelling is the low rumble of James's voice, tightly controlled and yet resolute. He seems to counter all Oliver's sallies and to place an obstacle in the path of all Oliver's arguments. A chair scrawps on the Italian tiles of the kitchen floor, followed by a dull thud—a slamming door, perhaps—and then a thunder of footsteps explodes on the stairs and along the galleried landing.

Maisie switches off the shower and reaches for one of the white towelling robes hanging on the back of the door. She pulls it on and belts it securely.

Viola's voice rises just outside the door. 'No, Oliver. Absolutely not.' There's a rasp and slight press of Viola's body against the bathroom door.

James thunders, 'Pack your things and *leave*, Oliver. You can't possibly stay now. Think of Maisie, her family. Her daughter's wedding.'

'I *am* thinking of her,' Oliver roars. 'I think of nothing else, man. Why else would I—?'

'It doesn't matter what *you* think,' Viola says. 'It's what Maisie thinks that matters.'

Maisie hears James take a deep breath. 'Look Oliver,' James says gently, as though soothing a spooked horse. 'Listen to me. You're ill, mate. Like your mother and Louisa. A mental illness. I've spoken to a—'

'That's rubbish,' Oliver blusters. 'You just can't deal with the fact that I'm a better man than you. I always have been. My father was the same. He couldn't handle the competition, and neither can you. But if you think you're going to put *me* away, like you have Elspeth …'

Slowly, Maisie opens the door. The three of them are standing in her bedroom and turn to stare at her as she enters. Viola is just outside the bathroom door and has been serving as sentinel all the while Maisie was inside and probably heard all her retching and muffled weeping. Viola glances over her shoulder at Maisie before moving half a pace backwards, placing her body as a shield although she too wears only a bathrobe and, like

Maisie, is barefoot. Oliver stands at the foot of the bed, his expression dark, suffused with spleen, his normally gelled hair dishevelled; a lock of it falls across his forehead. He licks his lips with a dry tongue. Peripherally, Maisie sees her clothes and underwear laid on a chair, her personal requisites—hairbrush, makeup bag and jewellery box—arranged on the dresser. She feels—through her things—critically uncovered, naked. Such exposure to Oliver's view feels wanton. How far had he got before Viola interceded? But he himself looks more like a pouting child cheated out of a treat than a sexual predator and she feels a bit sorry for him. James stands in the doorway. The expression on his face moves Maisie the most. His eyes are fixed on her. Her hand moves to her face. No doubt she's a mess—eyes swollen and red from crying, hair wet and all anyhow—but his glance conveys a torrent of heart-rending affinity.

'Maisie,' Oliver barks out. 'Will you please tell these *idiots* that last night was just a mistake? I mis-timed things. I see that now. For God's sake, Maisie! Surely after all I've done for you, for your family … But there's no harm done, is there? I never laid a finger on you.' He tries a little smile, boyish and disarming. The dimple in his cheek flickers. He holds out a placatory hand. 'Maisie,' he says, slightly admonitory, 'don't you think you're over-reacting?'

Viola ejaculates a fierce, 'Ha! So this is all *Maisie's* fault, is it? Yes. It usually comes down to that.'

'I've told Oliver I think it's best if he leaves,' says James heavily.

'If he doesn't, I will,' Maisie says in a voice that is small but quite firm. 'I don't know what will happen about the wedding. Surely I can find a hotel room or something?' She glances at the bedside clock. 'If we call the others now, we can put them off. Frances will understand. She only invited them as a favour to me.'

Oliver's colour, already high, intensifies. 'You certainly can't stay here *without* me,' he snarls. 'I rented it. The contract is in my name.'

'But you didn't pay for it,' James puts in. '*I* did that.'

Maisie stiffens. 'You did? I thought everyone was contributing.'

'We are,' Viola mutters, 'eventually. But I think James stumped up in the first instance. Oliver couldn't afford it.'

This detail infuriates Oliver and causes a sudden shiftiness in his demeanour.

'And in any case,' Viola ploughs on, 'I think it belongs to friends of James's, so they'll be fine about it.'

'Friends of *James's*?' Maisie says slowly. She eyes Oliver. 'I thought you said they were *your* friends?'

His shoulders droop. 'I made all the arrangements. Several emails and then, as I told you, I called in. We *became* friends …'

Maisie nods. She suddenly feels calm and clear-headed. 'I see. Tell me, Oliver, is there anything about you that *is* true? Apart from the fact that you wanted to get me into bed?'

He summons a last hurrah. 'Lots of women would be happy to be in that position,' he flings out, burying his hands in his pockets.

'I suggest you give them a call,' says Viola, turning her back on him. She guides Maisie back into the bathroom and closes the door. In the privacy of its opulent interior, they enfold each other in an embrace. They remain that way for a long time, saying nothing, drawing comfort and reassurance from each other.

Presently there is a soft knock on the door. 'He's gone,' James says. 'I've made fresh tea.'

After some tea and toast and a couple of painkillers, Maisie goes back to bed and sleeps until noon. When she wakes she is alone in the room. She showers again and gets dressed. Her head is clear but her throat is clogged by a glutinous mat of shame at having allowed herself to be so entirely manipulated. The new confidence that has delighted her over the past months has shrivelled to nothing. She feels like the old Maisie: lost and afraid in a world that is too big for her. In her inner ear she can hear Clifford fulminating, 'What did you expect? What did I tell you?'

Downstairs, she finds James on his laptop at the breakfast bar. His hair is tousled, his chin still unshaven. He has various documents scattered about him and his mobile at his side.

'You should be in the office,' she says. 'I'm sorry I've caused so much trouble.'

He slips off his stool and comes towards her. She finds herself wary about whatever he is about to offer her. A hug, she thinks, would be nice, but she distrusts her instincts now. She is afraid of making the same mistake twice.

He holds out his hands very slowly and holds them palms up, the fingers very slightly curled, inviting her to take them but remaining a few paces away from her. If she wants to, if she feels comfortable with it, she must close the gap between them. She hesitates, but then puts her hands in his. He gives a gentle squeeze. 'It's me who should apologise,' he says from both their arms' length but looking her square in the eye. 'All this has been my fault. I've always known Oliver is … shall I say "unbalanced"? The entire Harrington family is off kilter one way or another and Oliver is a Harrington.'

'You have warned me, often enough,' says Maisie. 'You mentioned something upstairs. Some mental illness?' Their stance is becoming awkward, too redolent of a bride and groom at an altar. She wrinkles her nose. 'Is that coffee I can smell? I'd love a cup, if there's some spare.'

James drops her hands and reaches for a cafetière and a clean cup. 'There's a fancy milk frother thing,' he says, 'if you'd like a cappuccino. I'd recommend it. Viola made this and it's nuclear strength. She's in the pool, by the way.'

'Alright,' says Maisie, not because she especially wants a fancy coffee but because she feels he will appreciate the distraction of making it for her.

He sets about it. 'Yes,' he says, above the whir of the machine. 'Narcissistic Personality Disorder. I looked it up and this morning, I've spoken to the psychologist that Elspeth used to see. She says Oliver needs psychoanalytic therapy, but nothing will be effective if he refuses to recognise he has a problem. And of course, that's exactly the issue. To people like Oliver, it's other people who have the problem, not them.' He brings her the coffee and pulls out the stool next to the one he has been using. 'Anything to eat? I must say Oliver has provisioned us very well. There are croissants …'

She shakes her head. 'Tell me more about what the psychologist said.'

'Oh,' James waves his hand. 'She more or less described Oliver. People with the condition think they're special, or better, or more deserving than other people. They appear to have absolute confidence in themselves—failure, opposition, *any* alternative point of view is not an option. It doesn't even exist! But, beneath their bluster, their egos are quite fragile, so they need other people to recognise their worth and acknowledge it.'

'I've sensed that in him,' says Maisie, ' … a neediness.'

'And it's just the kind of thing that appeals to people with your nurturing instinct,' James goes on. 'I should have seen it, but rather than protecting you from it, I put you right in the lion's den.'

'No, James—'

'I *did*,' he insists. 'I told him to look out for you, to take a special interest in you, when I heard that Clifford had died.' James puts his head in his hands.

'That's why this is my fault. I was away at the time, if you remember. I'd taken Elspeth abroad, which did no good. Oliver was a life-saver then. He took over the whole shebang while I was away. Someone with his traits, you can imagine, in a business setting ... so I feel I owe him. I'm going to organise therapy for him, if he'll agree, in a residential centre. The psychologist is looking into it for me. And if Oliver doesn't agree ... well, he'll have to. I'll make it a condition of his continued employment,' he concludes.

'Look, James,' she says, reaching out and resting her hand on the arm revealed by his folded-back shirt sleeve. 'I do feel ... violated, although I know that nothing actually happened. I trusted Oliver and he abused that trust—there's no doubt in my mind about that. I feel hurt and disappointed. But I also feel ashamed of myself ... so green and trusting. Clifford was right all along and I think that's what riles me most! I'm at least partly responsible. I should have insisted on having things out with him.' She sighs. 'I don't know why I didn't. I tried ... but he wrong-footed me every time.'

James lifts his eyes to hers. His gaze is tortured with uncertainty. 'Did you think ...' he gets out brokenly. 'Were you in love with him?'

Maisie ponders, choosing her words. 'I liked him,' she says at last. 'I was flattered by his interest in me. But every time I thought about him I found I ...' She swallows, feeling like a fool. She has always felt her partiality for James, and there was, once, that kiss ... but I've got things so wrong with Oliver, how can I trust myself now?

James waits, his eyes steady and patient. He prompts, 'You found you ...?'

'Yes,' Maisie tries again, 'I found I compared him ... I compared him to ... someone else.' She falters to a stop again, her eyes fixed on his, trying to convey what she cannot bring her lips to articulate. Her hand still lies on his bare forearm. She gives it a gentle squeeze. Is this peculiar courage, or utter recklessness, trusting to a path that has proved so perilous?

But James invites her onward. 'Someone else?' Slowly, inexorably, he moves a reciprocal hand to cover hers, and curls his fingers around it. His gesture, and his quirked eyebrow, ask the question, 'Do you mean *me?*'

She nods. 'Yes. But …' Her voice is nothing more than breath. He leans closer and she whispers, 'But that's impossible, isn't it?'

Gently, oh so gently, James lifts her hand to his lips and places a kiss on her fingertip, the merest brush of a butterfly wing. 'For now,' he says.

That afternoon, Maisie and Viola tour the gardens of the house together. It is yet another perfect day, the flowers of the borders bright with colour, the sky an impossible blue, the air warm but lightened by a breeze that whiffles from the distant hills. Viola tells Maisie about her rehab.

'So you haven't been at Brian's?'

No,' she shakes her head. 'I'm the last person who would be wanted there. He's got a new partner, but it's complicated. She's also his step-mother.'

Maisie turns to look at her. 'What?'

'I know. You couldn't make it up. My first husband, Brian's father, married a much younger woman from Thailand about four years ago. He reverted to type and she ran away. Poor thing, she knew no one in the UK and, of course, he'd taken her passport and made sure she had no money. Brian was the only person she knew so she made her way to his flat. The rest, as they say, is history. I'm glad for them both, really. But having me there would be a bit like being haunted by the ghost of marriage past.'

'Your first husband was a bully, wasn't he?'

'Yes, an abuser. And I've worked with lots of survivors of domestic abuse since then. It's how I recognised what Oliver was up to. There was something about his tone of voice as he spoke to you on the terrace.'

'I don't remember very clearly,' says Maisie.

'Maybe that's just as well.'

They stroll along the herbaceous border, pointing out combinations of plants that work particularly well. 'Fleabane makes an excellent edging plant,' says Viola.

Maisie considers. 'It's so similar to the common daisy though.'

'Weeds are flowers, just like the cultivars. You've got to admire them, really. They're so tenacious, flourishing in the most unpromising soils and situations. You can drench them in weedkiller, tear them out, chop them up and throw them on the fire, but still, they survive. Like widows, really, when you think about it. Their world is hacked to pieces and yet, against all the odds, they survive. Singly, weeds are vulnerable—easy to identify and kill. Put them in a wildflower meadow though, and there's nothing prettier, is there? And it came to me, while I was in rehab, that I've wasted the opportunity I was given.'

'What do you mean?'

Viola stops walking and turns to Maisie. 'All these months,' she says, 'you, me and Minnie, we've all been going through the same hell. We've done it in different ways, but essentially we've been on the same path. We could have given each other such support. Well,' she allows, 'you have supported Minnie, I know. You've proved a wonderful friend to her. But I … I denied myself the friendship that was on offer, and I certainly didn't contribute any. I've been a parasite, instead of a friend. Like yellow rattle, which feeds off other plants, or knapweed, which leaks toxins into the soil …'

'Weeds—like people—need to be able to stand up for themselves.'

'I suppose so. But not against their allies.'

'Your rehab, *that* was a way of standing up for yourself.'

'Yes! Eventually, I recognised my real enemy. I'd been going off the rails for months, but something happened to throw me over the edge. I've been a terrible cow, I know. It's a wonder I have any friends. I can't promise to be nice, but I can promise not to be a drunk, so hopefully that will be an improvement.'

Maisie threads her arm through Viola's. 'I've always suspected you were nice, deep down.'

Viola laughs. 'Thanks for that! I hope you'll think I'm nice enough to be one of your housemates. Do you think Minnie will allow it? I've been *vile* to her. But I can't stay in my apartment. I need people. I know that now. Like a wildflower, I appear to better effect when I'm surrounded by others.'

'Oh Viola,' says Maisie, overcome. 'That would be so lovely. And to think, I'd have your help in the garden every day.'

'It's the garden that attracts me,' Viola admits.

'Oh, I know that,' Maisie says with a smile. 'I don't flatter myself *I'm* the attraction.'

But Viola turns serious eyes on her. 'Really, if Minnie can't stand me in the house, I'll live in the shed, Maisie, but I *must* have a garden, or I'll die.'

The sound of James's voice drifts across the lawn, through the open French doors.

'He's making phone calls, pulling in favours, reorganising his business empire so that, when you return to Millport, Oliver will be gone from it,' Viola says.

The news gives Maisie a secret thrill of pleasure. He'd go to all that trouble for *me?* 'Poor Oliver,' she says. 'He will be angry. He's to go to a residential therapy place.'

'He ought to be grateful not to be behind bars,' says Viola. 'He certainly needs therapy, although how you change the nature of a narcissist, I'm not sure.'

'The whole Harrington family seems bedevilled by mental illness,' says Maisie. She points to a glossy-leaved shrub in the border. 'That's lovely, isn't it? Verbena?'

'Viburnum. It's semi-evergreen so quite a useful shrub in a temperate climate.'

'Speaking of mental illness,' Maisie says tentatively, 'I didn't realise it until I had a talk with Michael, but I think my grief has manifested itself in a kind of madness. It's odd because most of the time, I haven't felt that I *am* grieving. I've felt … almost happy—and then terribly guilty about it. I've been so muddle-headed of late, and I haven't been sleeping well. To be truthful, I've hardly known myself. I've been angry, which isn't like me at all, and just … not able to think straight about *anything*. So I feel at least part of the misunderstanding between Oliver and me has been my fault.'

'Grief can rear its head in dozens of ways,' says Viola, 'but, if I'm honest, the symptoms you describe sound more like menopause to me. Have you seen a doctor?'

Maisie stops abruptly, open-mouthed. 'I hadn't considered that. But I'm still having periods.'

'Regularly?'

'Irregularly. I put it down to stress.'

'Mine stopped after Martin died, and never started again,' Viola says. 'I suppose somewhere in the midst of the alcoholic haze I've been inhabiting, menopause came and went. Stress can make you irregular, but with your other symptoms—'

Maisie clutches Viola's arm. 'Oh, my God,' she gasps out. 'Viola! You're a life saver, *again*. Really, I thought I was going mad, getting dementia—'

'You might be, for all I know,' says Viola matter-of-factly. 'I'm not a doctor.'

They saunter around the walled garden, with its pool and hot tub. Her memory of the hour she spent there with Oliver is vivid, curdled by the chill of hindsight.

'Gloria's going to love this,' says Viola, swirling her hand in the warm water of the hot tub. 'She loves a wallow.'

'The grandchildren would love the pool,' offers Maisie, 'but they're staying at a Premier Inn, and only for tonight. They have to go back straight after the wedding.'

'Why not invite them? There's plenty of room, after all—and Gareth too. I suppose he's on his way?'

'Oh yes,' Maisie checks her watch. 'His train gets in at three. I wanted him to come to the meal tonight with the Fothergills, but Frances says it should just be me. Do you think the others would mind if Dominic and Gareth muscle in? I don't mind paying their share.'

Viola says, 'No one will mind, Maisie. It's your family, your celebration. We're only here because of you. You should do exactly as you like.'

They turn at the sound of tyres on the gravelled drive and car doors slamming. Gloria's shrill, 'Yoo-hoo,' makes birds rise from the trees with a clamour.

'They're here,' says Maisie.

Viola threads her arm through Maisie's. They leave the walled garden and make their way across the lawn.

Chapter Seventeen – The Wedding

Mrs Fothergill is every bit as terrifying as Maisie has feared. A galleon of a woman, both broad and tall, she bears down on the table reserved for the small family party, sweeping aside other diners and waiters alike. Her loud 'Hallooo' brings all conversation to a shuddering halt and makes the glassware chime in a minor key. She removes her pashmina with a theatrical flourish and places it in the hands of a passer-by. Frances stands and goes to greet her prospective mother-in-law but she is swept aside as Mrs Fothergill makes a bee line for Maisie.

Maisie rises from the chair that Maxim has just settled her into, her fight or flight impulses warring, and allows herself to be crushed into Mrs Fothergill's bosomy embrace.

'Maisie, *darling*,' Mrs Fothergill booms. 'We meet at last. I've heard so much about you and all so perfectly delightful—'

'I don't know who from,' Frances says, with an attempt at levity. 'Not from *me*, certainly.'

Mrs Fothergill sinks regally into the chair next to Maisie, although Frances had been occupying it a moment before. 'From Maxim, of course,' she chides. 'He sings Maisie's praises from morning till night!' She leans her bulk conspiratorially over to Maisie, who has to shrink back to accommodate it. 'I'll be honest with you; I've been insanely jealous! But now I see what all the fuss is about. You're absolutely beautiful!'

'Oh,' says Maisie, frowning, 'no, I'm—'

'And so *young*,' Mrs Fothergill adds. 'You can't be a day over forty.'

'I'm forty-seven,' Maisie stammers. But it quickly becomes apparent that Mrs Fothergill requires little or no conversational input from other people. She monopolises the chat for the whole evening.

Frank Fothergill bobs in his wife's wake like a small tender attached to a super-yacht. He is a dapper little man, well-groomed, but as unremarkable as his wife is extraordinary. He slips unobtrusively into a seat on the other side of Maxim and it is not until at least ten minutes have passed and his wife is temporarily distracted by the menu that he is able to proffer a hand of welcome.

'Call me Frank,' he says, 'if you get an opportunity—however unlikely—to address a remark to me. I quite recognise its improbability. But let me say that I—'

'Frank!' his wife shrills. 'I don't see the terrine. We always have the terrine here. Will you enquire?'

Franks throws Maisie a resigned look, and signals to a waiter.

Conversation flows, or at least Mrs Fothergill's soliloquy does, as the terrine—naturally—is produced, followed by sole. The whole table finds they have ordered the same dishes; Mrs Fothergill's choices encompass them all and can by no means be opposed. She waxes so lyrically on Frances's charms and their utter delight in her that Maisie can hardly equate the convivial creature they describe with her intrinsically cross and surly daughter. Then, before Maisie can make any reciprocally complimentary remarks about Maxim, Mrs Fothergill moves on to arrangements for the wedding.

'Oh, what a tease she was, this naughty girl of yours.' Mrs Fothergill's corsets creak with mirth at the recollection. 'Pretending to want a quiet ceremony and no reception to speak of at all! A meal in a pub! Oh! So coy! But of course we couldn't hear of that, could we Maisie? So we summoned all our powers of persuasion.'

Maisie opens her mouth to say that no powers of persuasion she possesses have ever succeeded in moving Frances once her mind is fixed, but the first syllables are hardly formed on her tongue before Mrs Fothergill forges on. 'Frank knows the college vice-chancellor from their days at The Home Office, so it was the work of a moment to secure the chapel. Such delightful acoustics in there, and the altarpiece is a thing of such magnificence. You've seen it, of course?'

Again, Maisie's reply is swept away.

'The choir will sing Wagner's Bridal Chorus. I had it at my wedding, so there was no question of anything else. Frances didn't know what was traditional in your family.' Mrs Fothergill's eyebrows levitate a full five centimetres. 'She says you don't have old lace!'

There opens up, just briefly, an aperture where amazement and incredulity are permitted to manifest themselves in a balloon of Mrs Fothergill's astonishment before Frances pops it with a *sotto voce,* 'Old lace curtains, perhaps.'

'How curious. But never mind, she shall wear mine. Something old you know … Now, as to ushers … '

Mrs Fothergill's unrelenting diatribe takes them through dessert and coffee as she enumerates hymns, readings, the organ solo, the chaplain's address, the full quarter peal of bells, the order of the procession, alternative seating plans and the exact length of the speeches which are to be, she stipulates, no longer than four minutes each. Nobody else makes any attempt to interject and Maisie gives up on any conversational gambits of her own. At the conclusion of the meal she reaches into her handbag to pay the bill, but Maxim stays her hand.

'That's alright,' he says. 'Father will see to it.'

At last, she finds herself standing on the pavement outside the restaurant. Again she is clasped in Mrs Fothergill's whale-boned embrace. 'So delightful to get to know you,' Mrs Fothergill gushes. 'How we will miss our children when they go abroad. But we must be each other's comfort, mustn't we? I hope we shall see you frequently here, or in London, or in Poole. Do you sail? No? Oh that's a pity. Well, I shall bid you goodnight, and see you tomorrow. I shall be the woman in the enormous hat!'

Maisie and Frances climb into the waiting taxi and Maisie says, 'Well, I don't feel so aggrieved, now.'

'Aggrieved?'

'Yes. I'm afraid I've been very annoyed that Mrs Fothergill managed to persuade you to things you wouldn't countenance for me. But now I understand. There is no gainsaying her, is there?'

'None at all.'

'You poor thing. Now I can quite see how trying this has been for you. She really has imposed the whole nine yards, hasn't she? Every bell and whistle imaginable! I'd have been happy with just a flurry of confetti, but she … I'm amazed she hasn't flown the Archbishop of Canterbury in!'

'Oh, she tried.'

'Did she? How dreadful. No wonder you've been a little snappy.'

'*I'm* not snappy,' snaps Frances, but then her face softens. 'But I'll let you in on a little secret, if you like. Maxim and I were married on Wednesday, at the registry office, just as we wanted, and afterwards, we met our friends at the pub and had a quiet meal. So we've have the last laugh, haven't we?'

On the morning of the day that Frances and Maxim will appear to be married, Maisie wakes to the shrieks of the three grandchildren as they fling themselves into the pool. The bedside clock shows it is barely past seven. She wonders which grownups have been pestered out of bed to supervise.

Dominic, Pamela and the children came straight to the house from Nottingham, but by the time Maisie returned from her extraordinary meal with the Fothergills, all five of them had been tucked into bed in the attic bedroom and were fast asleep. Viola, Gwen, Amy and Michael were in the library playing bridge, while Gloria, Minnie and Val were turning prune-fleshed in the hot tub and halfway down their third bottle of Prosecco. James and Gareth were in deep and confidential conversation on the terrace. Maisie didn't know how Oliver's absence had been explained or what details of his treatment of her had been shared. And she didn't much care. The house had about it a subtle hum of contentment, overlaid by the occasional peal of laughter. People were happy, relaxed and enjoying one another's company. What more could she want?

Now, with Frances still slumbering in the double bed beside her, she stretches luxuriantly and anticipates the pleasures of the day.

Gloria has offered—and Frances has gracelessly agreed—to attempt the bridal hair and makeup. 'I can be quite subtle,' Gloria had coaxed. 'I promise you won't end up looking like an old slapper, like me.'

Before that, however, they are to convene for breakfast at nine—a family affair—after which they will disperse to shower and dress. I hope there will be enough hot water!

Maxim's sister is to be delivered at eleven, ready but for her dress, which Minnie will have on hand along with needle and thread in case any small alterations are required. At some point there is also to be a delivery of flowers. 'They are sure to set off my hay fever,' Frances has gloomily predicted.

There are to be cars—a stretch limousine to take the bulk of the party, followed by another for Maisie and the bridesmaids and a third for Frances and Dominic. 'Such a fuss,' Frances said, on learning of the arrangements. 'I hope they have blacked-out windows. I shan't want people gawping in at me, expecting to see a celebrity.'

Maisie gives a thought to the dismay that will greet the women on discovering their outfits are virtually the same colour, but she does not dwell on it. Her outfit is perfect and she can't wait to put it on. She pictures it in the wardrobe, its rich, ultramarine overlayer, the iridescent azure of its base, the perfect beaded handbag … Oh! It gives her a thrill of pleasure!

There will be a church service magnificent in its grandeur, perfumed by over-abundant flower arrangements, the whiff of incense and the heady air of Fothergill excess. She hopes the organ solos and the cacophony of bells will distract the congregation—and especially Mrs Fothergill—from the fact there is no registrar and that the ceremony is essentially a blessing as opposed to a proper marriage. They will drift from the chapel via a quadrangle filled with roses to the Great Hall, where more floral accessories and supernumerary accoutrements will contribute to the general extravagance. It makes her smile. But what pleases her most is the coterie of women who will accompany her.

Her reverie is disturbed by a knock at the door.

'Rise and shine,' says Pamela as she enters bearing a tray of tea.

Frances stirs. 'Oh,' she says. 'It's morning.'

'It certainly is.' Pamela puts the tray down and twitches open the curtain, then perches herself on the bed. 'And now I absolutely insist on knowing about your frock, Frances,' she says. 'I can't get a squeak out of either of the girls. Did you go for white?'

'Oh no,' says Frances, hauling herself into a sitting position and reaching for her cup. 'I'd look too insipid in white, and anyway,' with a cynical grin, 'I'm hardly a virgin.'

'Cream then?'

Frances yawns. 'Nope. Too bridal.'

'But you are a bride!'

'Oh I know, but it's too twee. I wanted a nice plain grey, but Minnie convinced me to go for something a bit more dramatic. The girls are to wear a pretty duck egg blue. Even Jessica didn't object when she saw the colour. Mine is a darker shade. It will be so useful for Embassy dinners and so on.'

Maisie's her cup is poised in front of her mouth. A terrible thought grips her.

'Frances,' she says, forming each word slowly, 'it isn't teal, is it?'

'Yes,' says Frances, 'sort of. A bit darker. It's bluey-green. It reminds me of the colour of peacock feathers.'

Maisie swallows. 'Oh dear,' she says faintly.

Your Review Matters

Thank you for reading this book. As a self-published author I don't have the support of a marketing department behind me to promote my books. I rely on you, the reader, to spread the word.

A short review provides great feedback and encouragement to the writer, and is a helpful way for others to know if they might enjoy the book. Please write a few words along with your star rating.

Afterword & Acknowledgements

It fascinates and rather frightens me that, as a writer, I can create worlds and people them with characters that feel so vital that, in real life, they remain in my consciousness. I think of them as people I know who simply inhabit a place at a distance. Long after the book is written, I wonder how they are getting on.

So it is not too surprising that Viola has continued to trouble me since I finished *The Widow's Mite*. In that book and its predecessor, *The Hoarder's Widow*, I made Viola into an appallingly vitriolic woman, a drunk, who was mean to Minnie and who soured the otherwise congenial sisterhood of friends. But nothing ever happens in a vacuum and it became more and more apparent to me that her story would have to be told. *Why* was she so bitter? I'd set myself an uphill task, because it felt necessary that even though I could not make my readers *like* Viola, I did have to offer a convincing rationale for her behaviour that might, perhaps, excuse it. I hope I have succeeded in that.

No small thing could have resulted in such misery; for that, I realised, is Viola's problem: she is desperately, abjectly unhappy. I had to plumb the depths of human suffering, to dredge up demons from my own life and from the lives of women I know. Very sadly, this wasn't very hard, as the #MeToo movement has made all too clear. We all know a Vanessa even though most of us don't realise it. What that movement perhaps ignores is that men can also be the victims of domestic abuse and coercive control. It's rare, but it's out there. I hope Martin's situation shines a little beam of light on it.

I am very grateful to Mary Joe Davis, a rehab counsellor who answered my call on a writers' forum, and who generously helped me get Viola's experience of rehab right. I am also indebted to Deirdre O'Grady (again) who brought her professional expertise as well as—bravely—her own experiences to bear in a beta-reading of the manuscript. Deirdre also advised on Narcissistic Personality Disorder and the best course of treatment for it. Alongside both of these women I would like to mention the great insight I was given when I one day stumbled upon the 2023 Reith Lecture on BBC

Radio 4. Author and musician Darren McGarvey was speaking on the subject of Freedom from Want, using his own experience of recovery from addiction to explain how accepting life as it is, is the first step to making life what we want it. I studied the transcript of his lecture and based Viola's recovery on its wisdom. In matters of law and police procedurals I am grateful to my friends Detective Constable Alastair Clarke and Chris Moss JP, both of whom responded to my several enquiries with great patience. Catherine Clarke, Senior Paramedic, helped me get the dreadful attack on Viola, and her treatment afterwards, right. Alastair Clarke drew the beautiful dandelion seedhead illustration for me. Thank you to Becky (writer B Fleetwood) and to Aimee (writer AE Walnofer) for their beta-reading of the book, and to my editor Sallianne (Quinn Editing) who deftly corrected my errors and encouraged me to delve into third person deep and free indirect discourse as a means of exploring the minds of my protagonists. She makes sure my very British books can be understood by my mostly American readers. Finally, and, as always, my grateful thanks and love to Tim, who encourages me to write, listens while I read the manuscript aloud and makes helpful suggestions. He also took the photograph of the wildflower meadow, on which the cover is based.

Questions for Reading Groups

1. Viola says that if she were to be cut in two the word 'gardener' would be found written through her. Is there any passion, role, relationship, value or belief that defines you in a similar way?

2. The novel is composed of two story threads and two time frames. Did you find this narrative technique easy to assimilate? What links and mirrored motifs did you see between Maisie's story and Viola's that made them two elements of one story as opposed to two parallel narratives? The two stories converge at the house in the Cotswolds. Did you anticipate how each woman would rescue the other?

3. Bereavement and grief are complex processes. What types of grief did the story explore? What did you think about the way the novel presents grief's various guises?

4. One of the novel's themes is women's friendship.

    a. Consider and describe the different members of the women's friendship group. Who do you like? Who *are* you like, if any?

    b. Do you think the women's friendships are a case of 'birds of a feather flock together' or 'any port in a storm'?

    c. How does the relationship between Gwen and Val change the dynamic of the group?

    d. Do you think Amy is right when she says the relationship between women can be as close, or closer, than a heterosexual relationship? Are there women that you have loved—as opposed to been in love with?

    e. On the other hand, women's friendships can be fraught with jealousy, gossip and spite. Why do you think this is?

    f. Why do you think older women rarely feature as central characters in fiction? The women in this novel are aged between their mid-forties and their eighties. What does their maturity add to the book? How would the book be different if the women were aged, say, in their twenties and thirties?

5. Attitudes about mental illness are different today than they were twenty or even ten years ago. Do you think it is legitimate to feature

mental illness in works of fiction? Nowadays, addiction, including alcoholism, is considered an illness. What did you think of the way alcoholism and Viola's rehabilitation were depicted in this novel? James says that Oliver's attitudes and actions are a result of Narcissistic Personality Disorder. Do you agree? Is he ill, a controlling bully, or simply a man confident of his own charms who made a mistake by pushing things too far?

6. Compare the characters of Oliver and James. How are they alike? How different? What did you think of the portrayal of the other men in the novel: Graham, Martin, Michael and Dominic?

7. Readers of *The Hoarder's Widow* and *The Widow's Mite* found Viola a difficult character to like. Do you think her story, fraught with hardship and tragedy as it is, excuses or at least explains her behaviour?

8. The abusive relationship between Vanessa and Clive is well known amongst their friends and yet no one but Viola offers to help. Martin and Susanne's abusive relationship, however, is unsuspected by anyone. How familiar are you with the signs that a relationship might be abusive? What do you think constitutes emotional abuse and coercive control? Can fiction raise awareness about issues like domestic abuse? Should it?

9. Frances and Maxim's wedding mushrooms from their initial plans for a quiet ceremony and a low-key celebration although, as Frances says, they have the last laugh. Why do you think there is so much pressure on couples to have large, expensive weddings? Which 'wedding day' do you think Frances and Maxim will look back on with the most pleasure?

10. How is the novel's title worked out in its content? Discuss the references to: Horticulture and gardening; Weeds that scratch and sting; Wildflowers; Weeds as a euphemism for clothing.

How on earth will Maisie solve the issue of her mother-of-the-bride outfit?

About the Author

Allie Cresswell was born in Stockport, UK and began writing fiction as soon as she could hold a pencil.

She did a BA in English Literature at Birmingham University and an MA at Queen Mary College, London.

She has been a print-buyer, a pub landlady, a book-keeper, run a B & B and a group of boutique holiday cottages. Nowadays Allie writes full time.

She has two grown-up children, two granddaughters, two grandsons and two cockapoos but just one husband – Tim. They live in Cumbria, NW England.

The Widow's Weeds is her fourteenth novel.

Find her on Facebook. Visit www.allie-cresswell.com. Follow her on Twitter @alliescribber or on Instagram @allienovelist.

Also by Allie Cresswell

Game Show

Relative Strangers

Crossings

Tiger in a Cage

The Cottage on Winter Moss

The Hoarder's Widow

The Widow's Mite

The House in the Hollow

The Lady in the Veil

Tall Chimneys

The Highbury Trilogy

www.ingramcontent.com/pod-product-compliance
Lightning Source LLC
Chambersburg PA
CBHW051313190726
48290CB00001B/139